KNIGHT AWOKEN

THE SHACKLED VERITIES
BOOK FOUR

TAMMY SALYER

KNIGHT AWOKEN

ALSO BY TAMMY SALYER

SPECTRAS ARISE SERIES

When all other options run out, never let go of your gun.

In a few hundred years, the Algol system becomes humanity's new home. The question is: Is it a better one?

THE SHACKLED VERITIES SERIES

In a Cosmos-wide war between celestials, humans are as expendable as pawns. Until Ulfric Aldinhuus, leader of the Knights Corporealis, uses the celestials' weapons to fight back.

OTHERWORLD OUTLAWS SERIES

A sawbones fae, a necromancer gnome, and a hoodoo priestess with a Sharps buffalo rifle—what could go wrong?

COLLECTIONS

A Scorpion's Heart: Four Twisted Tales of Love and Lust

SHORT STORIES

Artificial Fate * Creepers * No Suede Soles in Hell

Visit my website to see if anything new has been released since this publication.

www.tammysalyer.com

INTRODUCTION

Hello and thank you for being here! Should you enjoy the words on these pages (and I hope you do!), I encourage you to join my Book Club and visit me at:

www.tammysalyer.com

I occasionally send newsletters to my Book Club with new releases, special offers, and other bits of news. As a special thanks to new members, please enjoy a handful of novellas and short stories from my many and sundry universes FOR FREE.

CHAPTER ONE

Could anything make time move both slower, and quicker, than one's own children?

Isemay was turning seventeen today, or would be if Ulfric were reckoning time by Vinnr, but his daughter seemed to have forgotten all about the date in her excitement. To be honest, he had too, but Symvalline hadn't. She'd reminded him in the early morning hours, shortly before the last of Arc Rheunos's three moons had faded to ghosts in the sky and its sun rose over a land that was in every way renewed. Seventeen, and still when he looked at her, all he saw was his little girl. Verities eyes, Ulfric felt old. No, he felt *ancient*.

Despite his own mixed feelings about his daughter's celebration day, with the Equifulcrum bringing freedom to the Verity Mithlí and a reunification of Arc Rheunos's peoples, the realm was having a kind of birthday as well. Now that the long feud between the Minothians and the Zhallahs was over, the fear and deceptions that had divided the two peoples would soon be buried with that past. And before the sun reached midday, Isemay, his little Crumb, would become the first newly ordained Knight and protector of Mithlí the Everlight in nearly four centuries.

Archon, he reminded himself. *Here their Knights are called Archons.*

Ulfric's eyes, or rather Urgo's, flicked proudly toward Isemay, who sat side by side with the young Zhallah man Salukis in places of honor at a massive feast-laden table in Everlight Hall. Next to them was a shriveled old man named Widin, whom Isemay had insisted deserved a seat of honor. The old-timer had aided Symvalline in trying to rescue their daughter from the now dead and dishonored Archon Tuzhazu.

Wizened and gaunt, the elder's bruises were at least as much ghosts as the realm's moons now. When Ulfric had first seen him, he appeared to have been beaten and was barely able to walk on his own. But the Everlight had touched him, as she'd touched all the others who'd been wounded in the battle of two days prior, and he had straightened and smiled with a vigor that belonged to someone who hadn't lived long enough to accumulate half his wrinkles. That same vigor now seemed to flow through all those gathered at the feast. With their Verity freed and their realm now united, the people of Arc Rheunos could heal, not just from their physical wounds but from their centuries of suffering. Ulfric wanted to take some satisfaction in his small role in that, but he couldn't. Not yet.

A kind of internal doomsday clock still ticked in his mind. This realm may be free, but his own was moving inexorably toward complete domination and eventual ruin by Balavad the usurper. Yet looking into his daughter's smiling, nervous face, he tried to put this aside, just for the moment. Isemay deserved all his focus now, not only because he loved her and was filled with more pride than he could contain at her choice to join the Arc Rheunosian Archon Order, but because she, more than ever, was now caught up in the Cosmos-wide battle too.

The last living Archon, Deespora Raamuzi, entered the hall, though she was more than an Archon now. Deespora had become Mithli's vessel, and for the next three hundred turns, or years, as they were called in Arc Rheunos, she would be both.

Symvalline and Urgo, with Ulfric as passenger once more, stood against the wall behind Isemay. He saw Deespora's eyes flash briefly toward them as the rest of the assembly all swept to kneeling bows before her. In her glance was the woman he'd met upon coming to this realm. The Verity lay hidden in Deespora the way Ulfric himself was hidden in Urgo. Biding her time? Slowly, silently reacquainting herself with her creations? There was no way to know. A Verity's mind, if it could be called such, was as opaque and unknowable to him as ever. Perhaps more than ever. There'd been a time he believed he under-stand the Verities and his place in Vaka Aster's realm. But since Vaka Aster had all but abandoned Vinnr before Balavad had come to shackle her, since Ulfric had learned the fate of Himmingaze's own Verity, and since he'd become acquainted with the dark, plague-ridden history of Arc Rheunos, Ulfric no longer pretended he could understand even the simplest of the Verities' reasons or actions.

Flanked on either side by leaders of the reunified people, Isemay and Salukis had also taken a knee as Deespora approached. She carried the Arc Rheunos Scrylle with a Fenestros joined at the crest, creating an orb and scepter ensemble that reminded him of the one Arch Keeper Beatte carried in Vinnr, though hers was made of simple gold and gemstones. Deespora stopped in front of the two youths and said something too quietly for Ulfric to hear. Isemay and Salukis both looked up, and Isemay's wide eyes shined with wonder. This was it, his little girl's big moment.

Unexpectedly, Ulfric felt a burning, panicky sensation, as if his chest were being squeezed in a vise. Urgo must have felt it as well, as the bird ruffled his feathers and let out a low-pitched, uncomfortable churr. A few heads turned in their direction questioningly, but Ulfric hardly noticed.

Seventeen years old. *Only* seventeen years old. Had he ever known anyone to have joined the Knighthood at such a young age? No, the youngest had been a man of twenty-five, several hundred turns ago, Knight Peke of Magdaster, north of Asteryss. Isemay was too young, too inexperienced. He couldn't let her take this oath, pledge her life to a being that he could not deny would think almost nothing of it.

He almost gave in to the urge to push Urgo forward and grab his daughter with Urgo's beak, to yank her away before she could make this horrible mistake, when Symvalline's quiet whisper came to his ears.

"It's her choice, Ulfric. We can't, and have no right, to stop her now."

No right? He was her father! ... But he knew she was right. There was only a vanishingly small handful of things in the Cosmos he could control, and his daughter was no longer one of them. Hadn't really ever been, frankly.

One after the other, Isemay and Salukis swore the short, solemn oath of allegiance to Mithlí. When they finished, Deespora's colorless skin took on a subtle glow, like light at the edges of a crystal, and she said in a voice that resonated like singing crystal as well, "As you serve me in eternity, eternity is yours."

Then the ceremony was over. Ulfric was struck by how brief it was, just as it was in Vinnr. In each realm it appeared the charge of Knighthood was predicated on a sense of duty, not a desire for pomp. Even if the people of Arc Rheunos had once had more illustrious traditions for the ordination of a new Archon, no one was left who knew them besides Deespora. The last two—Tuzhazu and Deespora's sister Akeeva—had perished. Tuzhazu had murdered Akeeva, and he had been destroyed when the Cosmoculous exploded. Perhaps Deespora had decided a more traditional ceremony was unnecessary, or perhaps not quite right, when it came to ordaining a woman from another realm. Even Jaemus Bardgrim hadn't gotten this much.

Isemay rose to her feet and took a deep breath as she turned to face her parents. She smiled slightly, showing only a hint of teeth, and her eyebrows were cocked quizzically, as if to ask *That's it? I thought there'd be more.*

Oh, Crumb, Ulfric thought, *there will be. There will be.*

He projected himself as best he could through her memory keeper, now dangling around Symvalline's neck in order to keep from distracting Isemay at this important moment. He didn't know if she could see his reassuring smile—as reassuring as he could make it, anyway—at that distance, but she gave them both a tiny shrug and turned back to Salukis.

The young man had risen as well and smiled awkwardly at Isemay. Then he reached for her hand, and Ulfric could see how tightly she grabbed his. For a moment, he had the uncomfortable sensation that he was witnessing his daughter's wedding, not her ordination, and wasn't sure if that made him more or less panicky than before. Then Sym was striding forward and hugging their child.

"Congratulations, my darling daughter. You have no idea how proud of you we are. Ulfric and I both know you're going to be a great, no, a legendary Archon."

"Thanks, Mum," Isemay said self-consciously, and in some ways this reassured him. She was still young, still his little girl.

They parted, and Ulfric was able to speak to her as well, with the memory keeper no longer pressed between Sym and her. He realized he had no idea what to say. All that came to mind was, "Your courage and strength are already greater than your parents', and Mithlí is lucky to have you. I love you, Crumb."

Beaming now, Isemay responded, "I love you, too, Da." Her smile turned devious. "And that's *Archon* Crumb now."

THE FEAST and merriment lasted throughout the day. Hundreds more people were gathered in the courtyard and beyond outside, everyone who had recently been locked in battle in the vast Minothian valley now eating and drinking together in a timorous but hopeful peace. The fortress itself had been prepared for a feast already, Ulfric had learned. The Feast of Future's Hope, a celebration that was to have accompanied the Equifulcrum but had been stalled because of Tuzhazu's treachery. What a change this world had seen. Ulfric did his best to keep himself and Urgo still and patient, biding time until he could ask Deespora for what he most needed. A chance to peer into the Arc Rheunosian Scrylle, to search it for a way to free Vaka Aster and save Vinnr from Balavad.

Toward evening, the opportunity came.

Deespora sat aloof in an ornate throne built for the Minothian liege, watching Symvalline and Ulfric's approach. Urgo and Yggo had flown to a high gallery overlooking the feast chamber, but Ulfric remained visible in the crystal of the pendant around Sym's neck.

"I've been waiting for you to come speak to me," Deespora said, her voice slightly deeper, yet still recognizable.

"Our realm is troubled and we need to return," Symvalline said simply. She reached into a durable pouch at her side, one of the items of clothing she'd been provided by their Arc Rheunosian hosts, and pulled out two gleaming black fist-sized Fenestrii with tiny, almost imperceptible runes etched all over their surfaces. Balavad's celestial stones.

Deespora's eyes flashed as black as the stones briefly, then paled back to a blue so clear and light it was nearly invisible against the whites. The woman, as most vessels did, would likely harden to stone eventually. Ulfric had seen the stone edifices of former vessels lining Everlight Hall's feast chamber. It was one difference between here and Vinnr, where former vessels were rare, and those that remained received a ceremonial sending off in decorated ships to rejoin the realm at the bottom of the Verring Sea.

"But before you go, you would like to study our Scrylle." Deespora stated this as an acknowledged fact, though they hadn't yet discussed it.

"That is true," Ulfric averred. "Unless there's another Cosmoculous we can use to unshackle Vaka Aster as we did you."

"The Cosmoculous is of the Churss, and another shall eventually come into being. But it won't serve you in the way Akeeva learned until the next Equifulcrum, when Maiztos, Kahros, and Znopho are once more in alignment."

"In three hundred of your years," Symvalline said, her voice quiet. Deespora nodded, and Symvalline asked, "Then yes, may we search your Scrylle?"

"You don't wish to wait?" The curiosity in her tone was genuine, as if the passage of three hundred years was inconsequential enough to make their haste remarkable. It was just one more confirmation to Ulfric that Verities, despite their ability to emulate a human, were anything but.

"The people of Vinnr need our help now," he said, firmly but respectfully.

"Of course, then. But I am afraid it will disappoint you."

Those were not the words Ulfric wanted to hear. Deespora reached out to pass them the artifacts, and he noticed how smooth her hand had become. *Like marble,* he thought. Soon, all resemblance to the woman Deespora would fade, he knew. Many people who became their creator's vessel held on to themselves for a few thirty-nights, sometimes a few turns, but never for much longer. Was his body already hardening to stone? Would it be too late to return to himself, even if they found a way to unbind Vaka Aster?

Symvalline took the Scrylle and looked up at the gallery where the bruhawks waited. *We may need Urgo for this,* she sent to Ulfric.

Let's go outside where we won't be disturbed.

They started toward a stairway leading up to the bruhawks, but Isemay's voice stopped them.

"There you are," their daughter said. And in an attempt at sounding as if she were scolding them, she added, "I know what you're planning. Don't you think it's time I start to learn how to... how to read the archaneology of the Scrylle, too?"

Symvalline laid a gentle hand on her shoulder. "There will be time for you to learn everything you still don't know. And there is *much* you don't. But now isn't it. The situation is—"

"Dire," Isemay finished, her face a complex mix of fear and relief. "I know, and I understand." She glanced quickly toward Deespora's throne, then back to them. "Now that my, er, duty is here, just please promise you won't leave me without saying goodbye. I keep thinking of seeing Mylla at Aster Keep for the last time. And now she's gone, and I never got to... got to..."

Symvalline pulled her in a hug and held her for a moment. "We all miss her, Isemay." Through their Mentalios link, Ulfric heard the words Symvalline didn't say aloud. *And none of us will ever forget her sacrifice. The sacrifice all of us have sworn to make. Even you, my daughter.*

Isemay's shoulders shuddered once, then she relaxed, taking control of her emotions. She pulled back. "Sorry, Mum. I'm just—it has been a lot to take in these last few days."

Ulfric shared Sym's sadness and anxiety at seeing their child distraught. She was thinking the same thing he was. Isemay was too young, too inexperienced, too much of a child still to witness much less bear the burden of such turmoil and so many battles.

Yet, he reminded himself and Sym, Isemay had already saved one world from Balavad's treachery. Without her forethought and formidable courage, Tuzhazu would have spread Balavad's dominion indefinitely. *So like her mother. Stronger than the core of a mountain.*

So like her father, Symvalline sent. *More stubborn than a cheflbein shark tracking its prey.*

"This celebration is about you, Isemay. And Salukis," Symvalline said. "Would you like to come with Ulfric and I while we read the Scrylle or stay here and enjoy what you've earned?"

Isemay hesitated. "We *all* earned it. And neither of you are taking the time to enjoy it." With a sigh, she finished, "I'll come with you at least. I may not be ready to look in the Scrylle yet, but I might learn something if I pay attention. Right, Da?"

The maturity of her words struck Ulfric with more force than her vulnerability did. As she'd grown up, the time they'd spent together was a ceaseless litany of him telling her to *pay attention*, to *quit daydreaming*, to *focus, Isemay, for the love of the Verities!* His Crumb had finally, through the travails that he'd hoped would never mark her time, become an adult.

"Come then," Symvalline said, and the three of them trekked upward to meet the bruhawks.

Now looking through Urgo's eyes, which saw so much more than a person could, he watched Deespora's gaze follow them. Because of her warning, Ulfric already knew they would not find what he sought. He would leave Arc Rheunos just as empty-handed as he'd entered it. Still, there would be other rites and lore within the celestial artifact. Something in it could be useful against Balavad.

After reaching the hawks, they paced outside to the far end of the open balcony that overlooked the northern mountains rising behind the fortress. The overlook was secluded, with few sounds of the valley's revelry coming to them.

"This will do," Sym said and ran a finger along the edge of the memory keeper. "How will this work, Ulfric? You have so many ways now of *seeing*."

He thought about it a moment, then said through their link so both Sym and Urgo would hear him. *Urgo, up for it?*

The hawk consented, though he didn't speak in any human tongue, and Symvalline sat cross-legged before the birds, who lowered to their chests and settled. Isemay copied her, and Sym placed the Scrylle's flared base on the ground.

"Isemay, if you concentrate on seeing through the Fenestros the same way you concentrate when recalling memories through your pendant, you'll be able to look inside the Scrylle as well," she told their daughter.

"What's it like?"

"Like a flood, like your mind is at the mercy of a hurricane," Ulfric told her. "It takes training and practice to be able to focus and hold back the outpouring."

"And most suffer from a headache their first few times," Sym added.

Looking pensive, Isemay said, "I'll just watch you this time."

Sym gave her a reassuring smile, then sent to Ulfric and Urgo, *Ready?*

The woman and the hawk leaned toward the Scrylle and Fenestros. A moment later, thousands of years of Arc Rheunos's history and lore began to pummel Ulfric's mind. With long practice, he held back the tumult and started his search for any clue regarding the act of caging, and more importantly uncaging, a Verity.

There was a difference to his search this time, which he became aware of gradually. Despite Ulfric's own nearly two thousand turns of experience, his focus came more smoothly than he was used to. Every bit of knowledge came to him sharply, smoothly, clicking into place in his mind as if he'd always known the things he was only just learning. He barely had to concentrate before he could parse whatever his mind latched on to. Was it due to Urgo's assistance? Was this what it was like to have a predator's mind, and the singular focus of a bruhawk? Whatever it was, he reveled in it, though it wasn't long before this was subsumed by the truth he already knew—the Scrylle said nothing about his predicament. The way to unmake the cage wasn't here.

But many other things were. One in particular drew his mental gaze, the thing Vaka Aster and Balavad had discussed so heatedly just before battling in his warship: the Syzycki Elementum. Its lore blossomed within the Scrylle, and he heard Symvalline ask, *What does this mean?* at the same time he perceived a reference, like a prophecy, that read, *The final age of the Great Cosmos will turn on the Union of the Five, the Syzycki Elementum. It will bring the destruction of destruction and the remaking of the unmaking.*

Before Ulfric could try to answer Sym's question, though he had no idea what it meant either, his inner sight was filled with the sky at night. Like the sky over Vinnr, it was full of stars, near and far. Vinnr's was a sky he'd looked at for so long that it felt like an old friend, or a home he could sit in and comfortably relax, knowing its walls were sturdy and would keep him safe—until Balavad had arrived, that was. But the sky filling his inner eye now was more immense, more boundless than Vinnr's, which he'd never thought of as anything but infinite before. It was *not* a comfortable and familiar sky. It stretched into an infinitude that his and Urgo's minds combined were nowhere near able to apprehend. Just seeing it made him feel as if his mind was being forced to *stretch*. Its endless edges pulled at him perilously.

Blink, Urgo. Or look away. I can't... can't take it.

Everything went dark briefly, and when Urgo opened his eyes, the enormous and limitless skyscape had passed.

Symvalline? he asked.

She didn't answer right away. Just before he had Urgo look away from the Scrylle to check on her, she said, *I felt like I was lost in there for a moment. But I'm all right now. If that is the Great Cosmos, Ulfric, our home is less than a sparkle within it. We are infinitesimal, like smaller motes on dust, and I never realized it.*

I don't think it was the Great Cosmos that now exists, but the one that might be if the Syzycki Elementum happens.

The "destruction of destruction"? That doesn't sound promising, and that sky—it was so cold.

He agreed and knew he didn't need to say it. *Keep searching. We may yet find something useful.*

An unknown time later, filled with wonder but without any new tools for achieving their immediate goals, Ulfric finally had to relent. The buffeting by the Scrylle lore was exhausting. He told Symvalline he was going to return to awareness but wanted one last glimpse of that endless sky. He found it, gazed into it, hoping for some clue that could save Vaka Aster from their nemesis. As the cold void sucked at him, other words he'd read in the Scrylle slid through his head: *Where the Five Flames have burned, Fimm's final vessel will sing the Syzycki Elementum.*

Urgo gave a low catlike hiss and shook himself, and Ulfric was out of the Scrylle and back on the balcony of Everlight Hall.

Midevening had settled on the realm, and the mountains lay in total darkness. That final bit of lore washed through his thoughts again, giving him an internal shiver. Its meaning was lost to him, but he put considerations of it aside when he noticed Isemay standing at the banister with her back to him and Symvalline. At some point, she'd been joined by Salukis, and she and the Zhallah youth were speaking quietly, their faces close together in a show of intimacy.

Observing the wings growing from Salukis's back, Ulfric's thoughts wandered to the brief time he'd been sharing the young man's body and knew for himself what it was to fly under his own power—a yearning for adventure he shared with his daughter. And the tinkerer and inventor in him suddenly understood something that had long eluded him. *I've got it! I know how to make my wingsets work! Now all I have to do is live long enough, and get mine and Vaka Aster's freedom back, to try it!* He had a momentary pang of nostalgia for the simpler days of Knighthood before Balavad's coming, a feeling like a cold draft against his heart, but it quickly passed. He told himself they would defeat Balavad, and he'd get his chance to create wings for both himself and Isemay to fly like Salukis. He just had to keep his focus for this final challenge.

Isemay and Salukis hadn't noticed Ulfric's and Urgo's return to awareness, and he listened to them for a moment.

"If they ask you to go home with them, will you?" Salukis asked her.

Isemay's hand rose to the back of her neck as if to scratch an itch. Ulfric noticed for the first time that she had a mark there, something he'd never seen before. Despite the dim light, Urgo's eyes had no trouble making out the design. It was a pattern, about the size of a fist or a Fenestros. Several interlinked lines twining around each other. They looked like a simple labyrinth.

Urgo's eyes flicked toward Salukis and found the same mark. It was their Verity mark, given to them when they'd sworn their oaths to the Everlight, like the nine-pointed stars that marked the chin of each Knight Corporealis.

Isemay answered him, "I'll do whatever the Everlight orders. Maybe she would want me—maybe even want *us*—to aid my parents and the Vigil Star. If Balavad continues to attempt to control the realms, maybe that's what all the other Verities will want, too."

She said this as if hopeful she might be called into such service, and Ulfric had to fight the reflex to immediately disabuse her of the idea. After the battle against Tuzhazu, when Isemay had told him and Symvalline that she'd chosen to be ordained as an Archon of Mithlí, neither he nor Symvalline had taken it calmly, at first. They'd realized, though, at the same time, that it might be the best way, maybe the *only* way, to keep Isemay safe. She'd stay here, while they went back to Vinnr, and she'd be endowed with the resilience the Verities gave their sworn protectors. He and Sym would go back to Vinnr and resume their duty to Vaka Aster without the unbearable worry for their child's safety that had been consuming them both till now.

Thus, they had agreed to encourage Isemay, and he couldn't ignore the swelling of pride he had for her regardless of his own regrets about Knighthood. In the end, it wasn't as if she'd have changed her mind if they hadn't given their blessing. *Or maybe she would have,* he reminded himself. *She's grown up so much in the last few weeks.*

Beside Urgo, Sym took a deep breath, the sound drawing Isemay and Salukis to turn toward her. His heartmatch blinked a couple of times, then looked to Urgo, and her next words brought Ulfric out of his ruminations.

"Unless your luck was better than mine, Ulfric love, we have difficult plans to make. Vinnr cannot wait for us to unshackle Vaka Aster. The future of our realm now hinges on stopping Balavad on our own."

CHAPTER TWO

Aboard the warship *Primator*, a world-killer belonging to Balavad and filled with his army of Raveners of the Tooth, there had been pain, agony really, more than Mylla had ever known a person could experience and their heart continue to beat.

And then hers had stopped—hadn't it?

She didn't know for sure. She knew only that the pain was cut off abruptly, and then she was immersed in cold black stillness. Death, she assumed.

That was when the dreams began. Faces of people like her, their screams, fire in the night, terror...

It wasn't long before she realized they weren't dreams. These images had the crystal clearness of memories. The sights, the smells, the sensation of wind and heat on her skin—all things she knew she'd experienced, all now emerging from somewhere deep in her mind, memories of a past long buried that hadn't been probed since she'd been a child. An orphan taken in by the Prelates at the Resplendolent Conservatum, she'd given up trying to remember who she was soon after they found her. It was too painful to know her history, she'd learned, and much easier to form herself anew, like a sapling that pokes its first twigs from the scorched earth after a forest fire.

As her childhood came back to her in that cold darkness, she realized that if she was remembering things, then she couldn't be dead.

The first memory had slammed into her mind like a comet, sharp and painful as molten stone. In it, she was kneeling on a floor and watching a fireball blaze across the sky above her. She had been inside a round building with walls that seemed to be wood, but not cut wood. Trees grew from the packed earthen floor in tight bunches and entwined around and among each other more intricately than most tapestry weavers in Vinnr could match.

The walls rose overhead, but there was no roof. She could see there had been one, but it was obliterated. Pieces of it, wood and leaves, littered the floor around her. After the fireball was lost over the horizon, all that was left was a sky, black with both smoke and night. The dancing shadows of fires outside the building jumped and quivered against the roiling smoke, twisted dragørlike monstrosities that had made her small body shudder in fright.

A hand gripped her shoulder. "Come, Mylla, get up! We can't stay in here. They're destroying the city!"

It was a man's voice, one that strummed a familiar chord deep in her mind that should have brought her comfort. But instead, the urgency and despair in it only increased the terror the sight of the fireball burning across the ragged, smoke-blotted sky had ignited in her.

Outside, cries of fear and battle filled the night. She didn't move from her spot, too afraid of what would happen, too afraid of not knowing where the man, her father, wanted to take her. Then his face was before hers, his smooth full mouth tight with worry, his deep nearly black eyes, ordinarily so gentle but now slit with anxiety, staring into hers. The hand gripping her shoulder joined his other hand beneath her armpits, and he pulled her up and into his chest, holding her like an infant, though she must have been seven or eight turns. She immediately pressed her face into his neck, hiding in the heavy weight of his beard.

"Ayanna," he said, "forget going for the caravan. Leave everything but your weapons. It's too late to flee the city. I have… the Scrylle."

"The Scrylle?" a woman's voice, her mother's, said. "You can't stop the Ravener army with—"

"I know. I'm not going to stop them. There are too many. Come on."

Her father led them through the wooden house's doorway into the chaos of the city outside. Flames and people roared, fire and fighters and destruction sweeping toward them from the edges of the city. Mylla only opened her eyes for a split second, saw death everywhere, then returned to the safe darkness of her father's neck.

They ran. Ayanna, her mother, whispered between pants behind them, "Greven, if you don't go back to the fort, Fimm will punish you for abandoning the vessel, and for taking the Scrylle."

"No. No! I can't be blamed for trying to get you and Mylla away from Kaldrwoot." He stumbled, grasped Mylla tighter. "Besides, Fimm hasn't moved, hasn't done anything to stop the invaders. Damn our creator."

Mylla's young ears were shocked to hear her father curse the Verity —he'd made her chew soap for saying much less—but she kept her eyes shut, her throat tight against the cries that wanted to escape her.

Greven went on. "Let the rest of Wardens stand beside Fimm while the Verity just sits there, watching us get slaughtered. I have you and our daughter to keep safe. When you are, I'll come back."

The memory had trailed away there, but another soon replaced it.

A strange room of white stone. She was lying down, still a child. Was it days later? Weeks? She didn't think much time had passed, and then she saw her father's and mother's frightened faces peering down at her. Her father looked exactly as he had in the first memory, down to wearing the same clothes, his face unchanged by time—but then, he wouldn't age. He was a Warden Temporalis, timeless.

Another woman was in the room, and her appearance more than the strange furniture and unfamiliar stone walls jolted Mylla. The woman had no hair. Not just on her head, but even her eyebrows and lashes were missing. She was murmuring something as she handed a bowl barely larger than a cup to Mylla's mother. In the First Tongue, the woman told Ayanna to have Mylla drink it, adding, "We don't have a cure. Few live through the first week. But this will give her some relief."

And that's when Mylla realized the younger her was sick, very sick. A freezing sickness that made her stomach feel like ice, while her skin burned. Her mother put the cup to her lips and whispered, "This will help, my little one. Drink it all."

She tried, but the medicine was so strong and sweet that she gagged. The gag turned into a cough, and her lungs ached as she pulled herself into a ball, trying to stop their spasming.

"We call it the Great Waste. We've lost many already," the woman who'd given her the medicine said. "We don't know where it came from, and it's spreading so fast…"

The worst of the coughing stopped, and Mylla looked up to her parents again. Greven reached down and brushed her sweat-matted hair from her forehead, saying to Ayanna, "Vinnr. We'll take her there. She can recover there."

Ayanna said nothing, and Mylla's childhood self had stared at her, seeking the hope and the assurance in her mother's dark eyes that her illness would pass. She'd had brown-umber skin like Mylla, but instead of Mylla's raven-black hair, hers fell in loose braided ropes down her back just past her waist, red as dying embers, red as blood.

Her mother finally responded to Greven. "And what will we find in that realm? Not this plague, but maybe another? Maybe the forces of Battgjald? We ran from Ærd to save her, but this… this may be how we lose her."

From that memory and her mother's fearsick words, Mylla's adult mind finally understood—she finally knew where she came from and who her people were.

She was Ærden, a creation of Fimm the fifth Verity, not the child of Dyrrak exiles, as everyone had believed because of her umber skin and black hair. Not even from Vinnr at all. Now that she remembered her parents, she could see their resemblance to the southern people of Dyrrakium. But if her parents had brought her from Ærd to Vinnr, what had become of them? Why had they left her alone?

And with that moment of understanding, she was swept into her last new memory, the last trauma she'd experienced before being found as a child on the Great Province Byway in Vinnr by travelers on their way to Asteryss City. Why were all her memories of such devastating moments? Had she never experienced happiness before becoming an orphan, or had the terrible things she'd been through simply taken over and burned away the good memories?

In the final memory, she was well again. In fact, she felt more lively than ever in her young life of seven turns. Hand in hand with Ayanna and Greven, they walked a wide, well-maintained flagstone road. The Great Province Byway, though she didn't know it then. In the distance on the north side of the road and ahead of them, soaring snow-covered mountaintops tickled the sky. A warm sun beamed overhead, a mild yellow cloak of early summer. The kind of day she would spend outside at home in Ærd until twilight, playing with friends, exploring outside the walls of her home of Kaldrwoot's arboreal fortress while her parents followed their vocations, her mother a craftswoman, her father a servant of Fimm. The clothing the three wore was the same that they'd left Ærd in, but at least the smell of smoke had been washed from it sometime recently. How long had she been sick? It didn't matter, because she was well now.

To her father, her mother was saying, "It feels... wrong that Mylla was touched by Mithlí when none of the others in Arc Rheunos were. Greven, should we have told them that their creator healed her?"

Though mild, Mylla knew her mother's tone hid anxiety and uncertainty. She remembered them taking her to Mithlí the Everlight, creator of Arc Rheunos, her father begging the Verity to heal his daughter. He'd told the great winged man who served as Mithlí's vessel that they were travelers from Ærd, and when he'd said that, the Verity had finally taken notice of the ailing Mylla. He had made her parents promise to bring her to Vinnr and have her stand before Vaka Aster and... the memory was hazy about what the "and" was. Could it have been something about a song?

Not wanting the beauty and gaiety of the day to be spoiled, she tried in her childlike way to distract her mother. "Why did the winged

Verity soothe my sickness, Mumma?" her young self asked. "Was it because he liked the way I sing?"

Ayanna smiled at her, but it was not her old carefree smile. It was a weighted, harrowed, almost hunted smile that stole the joy Mylla was feeling. "Yes, my light, he did indeed. But who wouldn't like such a cheeky and smart little one?"

As a child does, she accepted that her mother may not have been feeling the gaiety she nevertheless forced into her voice, but Mylla's mood lightened nonetheless. "When I grow up, I want wings like his. Do they have them in this realm, too?"

"We'll find out when we finally meet someone," Ayanna said.

Her father's own worries made him immune to his family's attempts to find cheer. In a flat tone, he said, "If we'd told them what Mithlí did, they would have resented us, and if we'd stayed, they would have wondered how Mylla could have survived their sickness, when no others can. We couldn't leave her there." He looked at his mate. "We've talked about this, Ayanna."

"And we've talked about this too, Greven," Ayanna responded. "Once we've fulfilled the promise you made to Mithlí to take her to Vaka Aster—and Verities pray some greater cost is not exacted for the aid she was given—if we can't find somewhere she'll be safe in this realm, then we will take her home. You've run from your duty, but your duty won't let us rest. If we needed proof, we found it in Arc Rheunos. All the realms have their dangers. We were foolish to believe we could avoid it."

"Fools," her father mumbled, despair tinging his voice. Then more loudly: "I was a fool to ever become a Warden in the first place. And I've dragged you two into it with me." He laughed darkly. "If we'd stayed, we could have died quickly in the war Balavad of Battgjald waged against us, like everyone else surely has by now. We—"

Mylla's mother suddenly stopped walking. Her hand dropped Mylla's and grabbed her father's wrist. "Quiet," she demanded.

Greven stopped as well, forcing Mylla to a standstill beside him. He looked stricken. "I'm sorry, I shouldn't have said—"

"Quiet!" Ayanna repeated, more forcefully. She was looking into the thick woods that lined the north side of the roadway, her face a mask of focus and fear. "I heard…"

Mylla heard it too. Branches rubbing, brush moving. Then—

Several men emerged from the forest at the side of the road, pointing spears at her parents. She heard a strange *thwick* sound, then a thud, and her father was thrown backward. His hand still clutched Mylla's, and she was pulled to the ground on her back, hard, knocking the breath from her. Another *thwick* and her mother fell beside them. Mylla watched through tear-filled eyes as Ayanna rose tried to rise to one elbow and looked at her chest. A long stick of wood protruded from her breast, near her heart.

"Mumma!" Mylla cried.

"Mylla," Ayanna said, her eyes too filling with tears of both pain and fear.

The men came at them then. Mylla's father lunged to his feet, gripped her around the waist, yanked her into a side-arm carry, and sprinted away from the men, straight into the thick forest beside the road.

She could hear them yelling for a moment, then all she could hear were her own screams. "Mumma! Mumma!!!"

Her father clapped a hand over her mouth and carried on, running for all he was worth.

Slowly, their attackers fell behind.

When they could no longer be heard, her father let out a gasp of pain and stumbled to his knees, releasing Mylla. She jumped to her feet —and saw for the first time the shaft of an arrow through his shoulder. He remained on his knees, sucking in great panting breaths. With the hand he'd been carrying her with, he dug through a shoulder bag and pulled out a long metallic cylinder with a perfectly round crystalline orb in a setting at its crest.

He looked to her and said, "Come here, Mylla. We have to go… get you out of here."

She could barely see through the tears cascading from her eyes. Without thinking of the trouble it would bring her, she yelled, "No, we have to go back for Mumma!"

"Mylla, n—"

But, heedless of danger, she was already running back the way they'd come.

"Mylla!!!" she heard her father cry, then, as if the sun suddenly bloomed in the forest, a great scorching light exploded behind her. Her father didn't cry again.

She kept running, not thinking about the light or what it meant. She thought she was almost back to the road when she ran face-first into the wide, leather-clad chest of a man who stepped out from behind a tree.

"Gotcha now, I do." She hadn't known the language then, but she understood him now. He'd spoken in Ivoryssian.

The bandit had her around the throat and lifted her from her feet. She immediately began to choke, and kicked her legs, but as black dots erupted behind her eyes, her kicks became weaker.

"Thass good. Don't fight and I'll let you breathe."

Of course, she hadn't known what he'd said, but she'd stopped kicking anyway, the lack of air and her fear making her limp. He eased his grip but didn't let her go, and soon the bandit had returned to the rest of the men, still standing by her mother's body in the road.

Ayanna was dead, her eyes already glazed and fixed on some distant point in the sky. And the bandits had already begun rifling through her mother's garments and small bag of belongings.

"Where's the man?" another bandit asked her captor.

"Busy dyin'. He won't get much farther with that arrow in him. We'll find him tomorrow, if we feel like lookin'. I expect he'll be half-chewed by wolves by then."

"If the wolves get him, they might drag off anything worth a crimson."

"Look at them, idiot. Beggars, if that," said her captor. "The only thing they had worth crimsons is hanging right here." He shook Mylla a little, still holding her neck with one hand and the back of her shirt with the other.

"Dyrraks, you think?" a pale-haired bandit said as he threw her mumma's bag aside with a look of disgust.

The giant man holding her stepped toward Ayanna and squatted down. Mylla bucked and flailed her arms to get away. To her surprise, he released her, and she flew to her mother's side. Falling to the ground beside her, she took Ayanna's lifeless hands in hers. She couldn't sob, her lungs felt frozen. She just stared at her mother's glazed, unseeing eyes.

Her captor pointed at Ayanna's head. "I've never met a Dyrrak with hair that red before," he commented, then leaned forward and grabbed Mylla's shirt again, and she was buffeted by his unwashed odor. She cried out and lost hold of her mother when he yanked her up. Holding her in front of his face like a rare item found at the mercantile, he said with a sneer, "What do you think we'll get for you, little Dyrrak?"

Then, without warning, Mylla grew angry. She didn't know where it came from. Maybe it was because her father had abandoned her mother, and then her, taking a starpath well to escape instead of trying to save them—what else could the light have been? All of it was too much. It had used up all her fear and left her seven-turn-old body with nothing except a wild animal rage. She balled her fingers the way her older cousins in Kaldrwoot had taught her and threw her fist into the man's throat with all her strength.

He dropped her and grabbed his throat, gagging. She scrambled backward on her rear, knowing the fate that had just befallen her mother was coming for her too. She hoped her father would find out what had become of them, hoped he died from the shame. The other men around them began laughing and jeering at her captor, who quickly recovered.

With his eyes on hers, he reached to his side and withdrew a thin, curved knife from a sheath. Light from the midday sun danced along the blade, taunting her with false cheer. "Won't kill you, girl, and lose our payday." His voice guttered like water in a drain from his injured throat. "But they won't care if you're cut up a little."

He bent toward her, holding the knife in preparation to slash. She rolled onto her side, trying to scramble to her feet to run, but was caught short by another man's arm cuffing her hard across the cheek, sending stars shooting through her head. This time the stars were white instead of black. She collapsed against the cold flagstone of the road as heat from the slap roared across her cheek.

"Make it quick, Jarrel," the one who'd hit her said. "I've no taste for torturing children."

"Get kicked in the throat by one and your tastes will—"

He was cut off by another of the bandits crying, "What in the Vigil Star's eyes?!"

Even in her memory, what came next happened soundlessly. One moment the bandit was holding up his hands as if to ward something off, the next his body was shrouded in a blaze of fire so hot that his clothes turned to ash and his skin melted before what was left burned. Mylla's gaze froze on his face as it oozed from his bones, shrouded within a smokeless orange-red column of flame.

Then sound returned, men screaming so piercingly that their voices sounded like hawks' cries. "Dragør!" was the only intelligible word she heard, and within moments, she felt an inferno all around her, so hot her own skin felt as if it, too, burned. With one last look at her mother's bloodied and lifeless face, Mylla decided it didn't matter if she died as well. She closed her eyes and curled up on the ground by her mother, letting this terrifying world fall into blackness.

———

HER EYES OPENED, somewhere else, some*time* else. She felt herself again, Mylla the Knight Corporealis, servant of Vaka Aster, protector of the vessel of Vinnr's creator, three hundred seventy turns old. Which meant her parents were long dead. Her father's treachery no longer mattered. Her mother was at peace in the Great Cosmos, never gone, only diffused and scattered like dalla seed in the wind.

The first thing she saw through her hazy vision was a broken stone roof, steepled and rising high overhead. Familiar—she knew this chamber, a room she'd been in recently…

Mylla? Can you hear me?

The voice's owner came to her instantly. Safran, her sister Knight. As she began to piece what was happening together, heat flooded throughout Mylla's body, but not dragørfire, the searing heat that she'd witnessed melt flesh from bones and burn bones to dust. Rather, it was the heat of being healed, of her resilient, long-living body recovering.

Recovering…

She gasped as all that had happened came back to her. The warship, Balavad's malignant poison that had stabbed through her like a thousand venom-dipped blades.

"Safran," she tried to say, but her voice was broken. The last moments before she'd thought she was dead rushed through her mind. On the warship, she'd struck Ulfric with a Fenestros just before the monstrous Verity had wrapped her in the miasma that had crawled inside her, permeated her every fiber, seeped into her very heart. She had screamed her voice to splinters, blacked out, then awakened in time to warn the Glunt that Balavad's Ravener had her sword and was heading toward Ulfric. But not Ulfric—Vaka Aster.

You'll be all right now, Mylla. You're safe.

Safran, she said again, now using her Mentalios link, and was relieved to find she could still communicate that way. *What's happened?* She tried to sit up, got halfway, then felt strong arms stabilizing her from behind.

"Got you, novice. No need to be working yourself into a bother now, there's not."

Stave. His smoke-roughened voice was almost as much a balm as the Fenestros, still cradled in her hand, that Safran had used to rouse her. Mylla fleetingly wondered how many times the wysticism of the Verities would have to be used to turn her near-death back into life. And now, she knew, it had been at least once more, when the Everlight of Arc Rheunos had healed her as a child. Were all novice Knights as prone to so many near-death experiences?

Did we stop Balavad? she asked.

We will explain everything once you've had some time to recover. Mylla, the bigger question is, what happened to you?

The question confused her. She cleared her throat, tried to speak again, and this time managed it. "Balavad's poison—it almost killed me. But I'm fine now, since you've looked after me. How long was I out?

Was Balavad defeated?" she repeated. "I saw Vaka Aster. She came, she was—or Ulfric was the vessel, like the Glunt said. But Ulfric... where is he?"

Safran's eyes darted from hers to Stave's in an unreadable look, then she said, *Mylla, you weren't just* out. *You were* gone.

"What do you mean?"

Roibeard came and knelt down beside her. "Lost in the Himmingazian Sea. We all believed you'd been killed."

She blinked at his words. Nonetheless, looking in their faces—Safran, Stave, Roi—she was reassured. That made three of the Knights. The only one missing was Ulfric. Eisa, she assumed, was lost to them completely. Her mind whirled with questions.

She grasped Safran's empty hand, cleared her throat once more, and said, "Tell me everything."

CHAPTER THREE

In two dozen Glister cycles, Jaemus Bardgrim had gone from being a brilliant engineer en route to finding the secrets to saving the people of Himmingaze, to a reluctant participant and eventual ender of a battle between the peoples of worlds far removed from his, to this new predicament—a Knight Corporealis of Vaka Aster, Verity, a thing that had only been a rumor before this all began, which boiled down to being a soldier of sorts in wars being waged, apparently, across the entire Great Cosmos. Now, back in Himmingaze, looking into the face of a slangarook, he supposed one tiny shred of his original goal remained. He had managed to save if not all Himmingazians, at least those he was closest to: the crew of the *Bounding Skate*. Despite that, the only part of it all that he felt was worth celebrating at this particular moment was the fact that he was only being stared down by the slangarook and not consumed by it.

The moment the water dragør appeared in the doorway of the Creatress's temple and Knight Dondrin began speaking to it as if it were an old friend, Jaemus had assumed one of two things was true: either he'd gone completely muddleminded and was hallucinating, or he was witnessing a phenomenon so profoundly ominous that it must mean the end of days had truly come for Himmingaze.

Then the creature dropped the body of Knight Evernal from its jaws, and he decided there was a third option. Jaemus simply had to give up any and all of his expectations once and for all about the nature of reality and his assumptions about what constituted "good" and "bad," "right" and "wrong." The Great Cosmos simply didn't abide by his narrow understanding of how things should be, and he, therefore, would have to quit pretending he did understand it. From this point on, he decided he would call these moments of unreality Things I Have To Accept *Should* Kill Me But Might Not, and carry on as if it were just a normal day. Now that he was a Knight, perhaps it was.

Knight Glór was already sitting on her knees beside Evernal. *She's breathing! Knight Dondrin, quickly, give me the Fenestros.*

"Is she dead? Or maybe the question is: was she?" Jaemus asked Griggory. He'd never really be able to think of the old man as a Knight. He'd always been and would always be Griggory, the unusual vagabond his gramsirene had befriended.

"Is, was, could have been, likely will be again," the old man answered in his not-unexpectedly-confusing patter as he handed Safran the Fenestros taken from the Vinnr Scrylle.

Jaemus watched as Safran practiced the same action he'd seen Ulfric do over Evernal's body not so long ago. He wondered how many lives a Knight could redeem before they simply ran out.

Soon, in another example of the Cosmos being inside out, against every conceivable hope Evernal was once more alive, alert, and seemed no worse for wear than if she'd taken an overly long nap that left her in a bit of a fugue.

When she sat up, her eyes filled with the questions she naturally had—and he supposed there were many. But there was more in her gaze, something haunted. Perhaps a side effect of being—by most normal measures—dead.

As the three Knights were explaining all she'd missed over the last few cycles, or days in Vinnric terms, Jaemus listened with growing horror. Most of it was news to him as well, thanks to his having used the Scrylle to spirit the Himmingazian Glisternauts back to Isle Stonering before Dyrrakium was taken over. After Balavad had battled and beaten the Knights, he'd begun an all-out offensive against the people of the Dyrrakium Empire, and now he had Ulfric and Vaka Aster completely in his power. Jaemus wanted to kick himself for somehow leaving Ulfric behind. He'd thought he had a grip on the man…

As their discussion progressed, the Knights could only surmise that Balavad planned a full takeover of Vinnr, if not something worse. With Vaka Aster powerless, Balavad could wipe out the realm in a single stroke and reap vengeance for what Vaka Aster had done to Battgjald. In Himmingaze, the only way they'd know if it happened was by looking inside Vaka Aster's Scrylle. As long as it still maintained its archaneology, Vinnr still existed.

Griggory approached Jaemus as the Knights went over the situation, staring intently at his chest. Jaemus looked down and saw that his Vinnric robe was hanging loose and the Himmingazian Scrylle map, rolled into a tube, was sticking out.

Before he could react, Griggory had plucked the map from his pocket and unrolled it. His thick, blond-silver eyebrows scrunched together with his intense focus, then he looked up to Jaemus. "You've had this all along?"

He nodded, unwilling to implicate himself once again in its theft. He'd only just managed to convince himself that the Himmingazian artifacts were actually more his property than Griggory's in the first place.

But it wasn't accusation that blazed in Griggory's eyes as he gazed at Jaemus. It was… hope? Jaemus reached into another pocket and withdrew the two shards of the Fenestros he'd brought with him from Vinnr, one having belonged to Eisa, the other—Jaemus was still a bit squicked out by this—from the chest of the woman who'd been called the Speaker. "And these," he said simply.

Griggory's eyes widened. With close to reverence, he retrieved the third chunk of the Fenestros from a satchel and held it up next to Jaemus's hand, his two shards still in his palm. It was easy to see that the three would create a single orb if held together.

Griggory's lips tightened, then he said, "We have a task to get to now, Vreyja's grandling. At our fingertips lies the map to Himmingaze's future and we must follow it."

Jaemus started to ask what he meant, but stopped when Griggory knelt on the floor and spread the map out. Uncertainly, Jaemus mumbled, "Perhaps now isn't the best time."

The older man peered up at him with squinted eyes. "Time? How much time do you think Himmingaze has?"

As if to prove his point, an immense drawn-out roll of thunder boomed outside, shaking the temple hard enough to rattle a few pebbles loose from its walls. When the roar stopped, Jaemus had to knuckle his inner ear to dissipate the echo.

"If we don't act now, Bardgrim, the last of your people will be a memory. And only to those in this room. Your existence will be wiped from the Cosmos as if it never was." Griggory's eyes shifted meaningfully toward where the Glisternauts had amassed. "Is that what you want for them?"

Jaemus looked toward his companions, too. The drawn, vacant looks many of them held showed as clearly as a painting how close to overload they were. They'd seen so much, maybe too much, in the last few cycles, and none of it was easy for a people who'd barely even heard of a Verity before. Now they'd been immersed, like Jaemus, quite against their wills, in a Cosmos-wide battle for survival, and without the knowledge or tools they needed to win it. Among everyone in Himmingaze, only Jaemus grasped what was going on, and only barely at that.

He caught Cote's eyes and looked into them for some direction. Cote, knowing Jaemus better than Jaemus knew himself, gave him a tiny half grin, the wrinkles beside his mouth deepening in a way that Jaemus found irresistibly fetching. With a hard swallow, he hunkered down beside Griggory.

The unique parchment held only the most basic resemblance to the page he'd seen before being ordained by Vaka Aster. It had been plain off-white then, just a flawless flat rectangular sheet. Now, though, the white didn't seem so much like the color of a page, but rather a glowing light, pure and brilliant like a Glister Cloud speck. And the runic script written there was gone, replaced by ideas that seemed to flow from the map itself into his head. As he looked at it with Griggory, he realized he was looking at the realm of Himmingaze—the whole place at once. It was as if the world had been turned into a shrunken transparent orb that he now sat in the center of. He could look in any direction and make out every feature and shape he knew, as well as thousands he didn't. All he had to do was tell himself to focus on anything—the bottom of an undersea trench, plants and stones littering the seafloor, fish swimming in the water, and anything that lay atop the water too, such as his hovering home of Vann—he could see it perfectly, as if he stood next to it and could touch it. And he knew precisely where everything was.

"There," Griggory said. "All of them, near."

Jaemus knew what he meant. He could see them too. Only one of the Fenestrii had been aboard Balavad's warship—the one Cote had kept aboard the *Bounding Skate*—and Griggory had scattered the remaining three in the sea when he'd feared Balavad's coming. Now, all were visible in the Scrylle map. Yet, almost as if the Creatress's shrine were a magnet, none had been spread far from it. Each lay at different heights down the slopes of the undersea mountain that Isle Stonering now topped.

The quiet voice in the back of Jaemus's mind that was always right said, *It can't be this easy.*

Abruptly, Griggory released the edges of the map and rose, pacing hurriedly toward the shrine's entrance. After a moment, he turned back to Jaemus. "Come on, Bardgrim. We have the map, and soon we'll once more have the Scrylle, but we have no time to waste. Hither will take us to gather them."

Jaemus turned to the Glisternauts and raised a hand in a "hold on" gesture. "Don't worry, I'll be—" He cut himself off and turned toward Griggory. "Did you say *Hither* will take us?"

Griggory was facing the Knights, still gathered beside Mylla, and didn't answer him. Through the Mentalios, Jaemus could hear the whisper of a conversation as Griggory explained to them what he and

Jaemus were planning. Finally, the Knight turned back to him. "Can you swim better than a slangarook?"

Upon hearing this, the monster poked its head through the entrance again, its eyes resting on Jaemus's impatiently. *Impatiently?* his mind clamored. *What in the five realms would a monster have to be impatient about?*

Hither withdrew, and apparently tired of waiting for Jaemus to make up his mind, Griggory stepped out into the storm after the beast.

Jaemus's sense of urgency seemed to have withered with the spit in his mouth. With a hasty rationalization that was becoming his go-to mental tactic, he decided that riding a sea dragør through the Never Sea was just another thing he could now categorize as Things That *Should* Kill Me But Might Not.

THOUGH GRIGGORY WASN'T OFFERING Jaemus to the black-scaled 'rook for dinner, the idea of having to *ride* the thing was somehow worse. But after quickly explaining to the Glisternauts where he was going and persuading them to stay put until he returned—as if they had a choice—Jaemus clenched his jaw and forced his feet forward.

Griggory already sat atop the water dragør, beckoning to him. "Come, come. She's not one to be kept waiting."

She? Jaemus thought and had to stifle a maddened giggle. "*She's* obviously a very friendly beastie—"

"No," Griggory cut in. "She'd sooner use a Himmingazian as fleech bait than look at one. But this is Hither and her kind's world too. She would like us to preserve it since we were the ones to endanger it. Come now."

"Well, when you put it like that…"

The slangarook's eyes, as big as Jaemus's head, followed him as he got closer. He was mesmerized not only by their obvious message of *You look like a decent bite, little man, and I could pick my teeth with your thin bones,* but also by how much intelligence he saw in them. He'd never even considered how the other creatures of Himmingaze were being affected by the Glister Cloud's slow destructive force until now.

Another crack of lightning shattered the sky around him, as if the Cosmos itself were splitting in half, followed by another vibrating roll of thunder. His feet found a way to move faster, and Griggory took his arm and pulled him onto Hither's back with an ease that startled Jaemus. The man may only have the girth of a single strand of kelp, but he was easily as strong as Stave.

He straddled Hither behind Griggory, and with his hands gripping the Knight's waist, they launched smoothly into the sea. Under normal circumstances, Jaemus would have been delighted by the wystic klinkí stone bubble Griggory created around them that kept them dry. But nothing fit the definition of "normal" these days. The slangarook moved through the water as fluidly as any ship he'd ever designed, even more so really, swimming with a graceful effortlessness that Jaemus envied and had never been quite able to match in the Glisternaut fleet. There was no turbulence once they got a few dozen feet under the surface.

He soon lost track of time as they hunted. Too much strangeness had happened too quickly, and he found that the best he could do was hold on as the Never Sea flowed around him and the sea of his thoughts swamped him. Somehow, he was able to aid Griggory by reading, if that was the word, the Scrylle map, and the old man directed Hither to the celestial stones.

The deeper they dived down the mountainside, more and more ruins of ancient buildings and then villages dotted it, all almost untouched by time. They'd been built by Himmingazians with all the soundness of the temple that sat atop the mountain, meant to last. The currents of the Never Sea had done only hints of damage, and Jaemus could see that the temple abovewater was the worst for wear of all the structures they came across.

These were my people's homes thousands of cycles ago. My ancestors'. Himmingaze could be like this again, grounded, earth under our feet instead of waves. But what will the rest of the 'Gazians think of it? How will they react? He shrugged inwardly. *I guess we adapted once. We can do it again.*

Soon they came to the resting place of the last Fenestros. It lay exposed, a glowing pearl-white and gold orb on the flanks of the mountain. Griggory leaned forward and spoke softly to Hither. The beast swept up the celestial stone in her massive gob, presumably storing it somewhere in there with the others they'd gathered. Jaemus hoped very much the slangarook wasn't swallowing them, thus requiring him and Griggory to wait until they passed through her before they'd be able to collect them and reunite them with the broken one.

"Now for the final key to unlocking the realm's doom," Griggory said. "Hither, to the seafloor, if you will."

The water dragør swam farther, her great body moving through the water with such power and smoothness that it felt as if she were the water itself and Jaemus was just some cloddish, bobbing detritus being carried by a current. The sight of the seafloor, dimly lit by millions of tiny bioluminescent creatures, made Jaemus pause. They were surrounded by tall petrified pillars of a kind of flora he'd never seen in Himmingaze.

Those are trees, he reminded himself. He'd seen the seemingly infinite range of the Morn Mountains in Vinnr and now understood topography in a way no Himmingazian had in hundreds of decacycles. Old maps of his world still existed, of course, but no piece of preserved history of dead things that drowned in the Never Sea with everything else could truly convey the meaning of mountains, or forests, or even deserts like he'd seen in Dyrrakium. These were all things he now recognized as naturally as he recognized the sea itself. And he realized he'd been delighted by being introduced to them all in Vinnr, but he didn't remember feeling as if he were being introduced to anything terribly new.

Our bones must remember and pass that memory along. We may be adapted for water now, but Himmingazians will come to recognize and embrace the world of our past faster than we might think. Comforted by this, he brought his focus back to what Griggory was doing.

The old Knight had stepped onto the sea floor, still in his klinkí stone bubble, leaving Jaemus atop Hither alone. Being a Himmingazian, and being so wrapped up in his own wonders, Jaemus didn't notice immediately. But it wasn't an issue. Some adaptations had come easily to the 'Gazians, and they'd long since acquired the ability to swim to great depths without need for air. Buoyancy could have been in issue, but his feet were trapped against Hither's body by her fins, as if she'd known his mind was too occupied to notice Griggory's exit.

He pulled his feet free and joined Griggory. Nothing came too close to the slangarook, and Jaemus realized that he didn't feel the kind of fear he should have from so deep in the sea. He understood innately that nothing would come near the water dragør. Nothing that wanted to live, anyway.

The map floated at Griggory's feet, gently wafted by the sea current but held down on three corners by stones. He beckoned to Hither, who then disgorged from her mouth the four found Fenestrii. So she hadn't swallowed them. *One small thing to be thankful for.*

One by one, Griggory placed the Fenestrii around the parchment in a pentagram, laying the three broken pieces of the fifth orb at one of the points. Jaemus wondered if it would still be able to channel whatever wysticism it was meant to, being broken, but didn't ponder the thought long. Griggory was older than history, he'd heard, and he assumed the Knight knew what he was doing.

He stood outside the Knight's klinkí stone sphere and watched and listened as Griggory spoke a brief chant in Elder Veros, using the Mentalios link. The white and gold Fenestrii gleamed, and the shapes on the map bloomed up from the sea floor before Jaemus's eyes, like a model of Himmingaze itself. Or was it inside his mind? No, he decided, even the image seemed to wave slightly in the current.

Jaemus had barely oriented to their location before Griggory's finger poked through the floating image. "The Scrylle is there. Come."

With the celestial stones now joining the three broken pieces of Fenestros in Griggory's satchel, and the map back in Jaemus's pocket, they remounted Hither and were off, moving along the seafloor.

Little time had passed when Griggory spoke up, as if picking up a conversation they'd already begun. "They were all one Verity once, you know."

"… Come again?" Jaemus said.

"All the realms are so similar because the Verities began as one celestial, untold eons ago before the worlds were created, before even time was. And long before they began meddling with each other's creations. The Syzyckí Elementum, the One was called, before splitting into the Five."

Jaemus wasn't sure what to make of this, his specialty being engines and aerodynamics, not wysticism and celestial sprites with impulse control issues. *It's only a matter of time though,* he thought. *Eventually I'll be just another Knight of Vinnr, adopting and adapting to their ways more than my own. Like one big Syz-, Sizza-, Sizzling Element of sprite servants.*

"The Si-zee-kee Elementum," Griggory said, pronouncing each syllable slowly. Jaemus tensed a bit, realizing his thoughts must have passed to Griggory through the Mentalios.

Griggory went on. "The elemental union. And yes, the Mentalios lenses are a useful window into each other's thoughts. You'll need to get a bit more practice before you're able to pull the curtains on your mind so others can't see in when you don't want them to."

They quieted as Hither entered a petrified underwater forest, swimming as silently as a wraith among Himmingaze's ancient ghosts. According to the map, the Scrylle lay amid a litter of shells and rock that had been swept inside the decrepit hull of an antiquated seaborne ship near the center of the forest.

"Say more about the Syzyckí Elementum," Jaemus said. "Before, on the warship, Balavad told Ulfric, er, Vaka Aster rather, that he *was* this Elementum. Then there was an awkward discussion between them about who was what and what was who, and frankly, I was a little distracted by the fact that it looked like we were all about to die."

"Ah. Fascinating! Two Verities communing. I would have liked to have heard that."

"'Communing' isn't quite the word I'd pick, actually."

Griggory gave a snort. "Young Mystae, once you've lived long enough, you will be released from your fear. Fear comes from having limited time to live and not understanding that nothing ever ceases to exist. To *die* in the way we think of it. Everything is part of the Great

Cosmos, the Syzyckí Elementum. We are all in it, part of it, our bodies and our spirits, even if they've become separated. Without the shackles of time, you can appreciate the simple wonders of… everything."

Inwardly, Jaemus *simply wondered* if the man had lost whatever grasp on the rational he might once have had due to his incredibly long life. Fear of death? Wasn't that as natural to all living things as breathing?

"But you asked about the Elementum. Hmm… Nothing is done but not undone," Griggory continued. "All things move in cycles, whole to broken to whole again, renewed and anew, never the same but of the same parts. You see? Before there was time, the Syzyckí Elementum existed, always whole, always fixed. They chose, then, to become the Five in order to experience, in fact to *create*, change. Maybe it was the first change to ever be. From a fixed thing, they sundered themselves into many fluid things. But by becoming more, they also became less. They are each just a fragment, like a shard of a mirror, of their One self. And one day, they will see each other and be whole once again."

"You're saying the Verities are just a bunch of broken bits that will eventually be glued back together? If that's right, it kind of seems like Balavad wants to stop them. Er, it. The gluing part, I mean."

"We cannot know what the Verities seek to do. Sometimes I even question if they know."

But you seem to know quite a lot about them, Sir Knight. Who told you this much? The question was on the tip of Jaemus's tongue, but some creeping disquiet kept him from asking. According to what he'd put together from the other Knights, Griggory had always been a wanderer and had left Vinnr hundreds of deca-cycles ago, working in the shadows in Himmingaze, and mostly alone all that time. Who could say what else he'd been doing, or to whom he'd been talking? He was a strange one, no doubt about that.

"Like a broken mirror, or a broken lens," Griggory went on, "they no longer have clarity. Things are distorted, maybe even corrupted, among the Five. Perhaps this explains Balavad's desires. His vision of the Syzyckí Elementum is corrupted, so he seeks to prevent a return to it. He has lost sight of the One. Hmm…" He trailed off, musing. Then, after a moment, he turned to Jaemus. With a chuckle, the sound like a dull-edged saw cutting through metal, he said, "And there is one Verity who doesn't even know she is, or will be, a Verity."

Not sure what to say about a celestial being who suffered from something akin to foresighted amnesia, Jaemus muttered, "That must be very inconvenient for her creations."

"It is more inconvenient for those waiting for her to discover herself."

After threading through the ancient petrified trees briefly, Jaemus began to make out the ship's outline ahead in the dim water, thanks to the bioluminescent sea life flittering and flickering along with them.

The tub-shaped relic had been constructed from a type of metal that had long since been improved upon by Jaemus and the engineers who came before him, with portholes rising up its sides, now barely visible with the layers of sea life and sand that had partially submerged it. The Never Sea had not been calm enough for crafts to float on its surface in over a hundred anni-cycles, and Jaemus had only seen ships like this in historical records. Looking at it now, he was reminded of the boat they'd taken to Dyrrakium from Asteryss. It served to remind him that though much in Himmingaze was different from Vinnr, in many ways much was still similar.

Eyeing the sharp, ragged edges of a hole rent through the vessel's metal hide, Jaemus wondered if it would help to wrap his head in some of the discarded steel to keep Griggory, who seemed to be better at it than the other Knights, from peeking into his thoughts unbidden. He decided not to fret about it for now, though. Too many other things going on. What did it matter?

The gaping hole that had caught his attention was large enough for a man, but too small for a slangarook. When Griggory said simply, "We'll wait for you here," Jaemus almost looked over his shoulder to see who the Knight was addressing, then his eyes widened. Surely *he* wasn't meant to swim inside that dark wreckage.

"Nothing to worry about, nothing at all," Griggory said. "Anything that lives in there will be more afraid of you than you are of it."

"I very much doubt that, Sir Knight."

Griggory creaked around until he could face Jaemus. "Mystae Bardgrim, if it's the dark you're afraid of, you'd better get used to it quickly. Because darkness is coming. The darkest of days is still ahead." As Jaemus tried to take in these ominous words without visibly shuddering, Griggory's lips split into that toothy, unsettling grin. "But at least you'll live to see them, eh?"

Was that supposed to make him feel better? Shaking his head, he gave in and slid off Hither. As he passed her head, he suddenly felt a not entirely gentle blow on his back. He spun in time to see the Fenestros Griggory had tossed at him settling on the seafloor, giving off a mellow white glow.

"That will light your way, Mystae."

He shot Griggory one last incredulous yet resigned look and scooped up the stone.

The twisted metal of the ship's opening looked as welcoming as a doorway into an inferno. Holding the stone aloft, Jaemus channeled through it the words he used to illuminate his Mentalios, and was immediately blinded by the flare of light. As his eyes shut tightly, he heard the water-muffled, and more sinister because of it, sounds of disturbed sea life thrashing through the hull at the sudden bright disturbance. He quickly lowered the Fenestros and wrapped both hands around it to reduce its glow and opened his eyes, expecting to see a set of teeth or the sucking maw of a fleech about to swallow his face. But it was just empty gloom, no creatures visible that were big enough to fear. He started to relax.

Then he screeched out a torrent of bubbles when something shot by him, slapping him in the face with at least three of its who-knew-how-many tentacles as it went. He never got a good look at the thing before it had sped off into the undersea forest.

From behind him, Griggory's chuckling passed through the water in a distorted din. "Oh, Bardgrim, Bardgrim, your face. I haven't laughed like that in-in..."

He'd have retorted with something scathing and sarcastic if his heart weren't now filling his throat. Ignoring the old Knight, he reached out with the Fenestros and stepped forward.

The tentacled creature seemed to have been the hull's only remaining resident. That, or whatever else lived within was hidden, waiting for the right moment to strike.

Stop that! he chided himself. *Just get the Scrylle and don't think about how you might need a new set of clothes if something scares you like that again.*

The etheric glow of star-wrought metal soon caught his eye as he scanned the interior. It was partly buried in sand, which covered the entire floor of the wreckage, as if something had done a lackluster job of burying it. He supposed something would have had to bring it in here, and again wondered what things might be hidden amid the old and unidentifiable bumps and bulges filling the hull.

Quickly grabbing the Scrylle, he decided not to wait around to find out. He held the artifact up like a sword and backed out of the ship, then swam to Hither with just two quick kicks of his legs.

When he reached Griggory's wystic bubble, the Knight pulled him up and snatched the Scrylle from his hand. Before Jaemus could say another word, Griggory cawed, "That's that, then. Well done, Mystae Bardgrim. Now we go to die."

"We… what?" croaked Jaemus.

CHAPTER FOUR

The blue, white, and pale moons of Arc Rheunos painted the balcony as Ulfric said flatly, "You wish to cage Balavad."

Symvalline stared at him, unblinking. "Yes. If we're going to stop him, there is no other option. We've seen his power, and his ends. If we cannot, yet, unshackle Vaka Aster, then we shackle him until we can. Or longer."

Without waiting for him to respond, his heartmatch rose from her cross-legged seat, readying to begin their next mission. Red-hot blooms rose in her cheeks. Was it anger that made her flush? Ulfric knew better than to think it was fear. In their seven hundred turns together, she'd only ever shown fear of one thing: threats to their daughter. *Why would the simple matter of shackling one of the Cosmos's five creators unsettle her?* he thought darkly. *After all, it's been done before.*

Of course he'd had the same idea, to do to Balavad what he'd been tricked into doing to Vaka Aster. The irony was too bitter to swallow, and a laugh lodged in his ephemeral throat—funny how he could still feel sensations as if he had a body of his own.

Sym was staring at him in the memory keeper held in her hand. "You haven't forgotten how to do it, have you?"

The words nearly bled out of him: "I shall wither to dust before I forget the incantation that has turned me into this and caged the Vigil Star."

"Then what do we need to do?"

Now that the idea had been voiced, he truly contemplated it for the first time. Without a doubt, she was right. It was resolved. "We need five Fenestrii, four of his own and one belonging to another Verity. The celestial stones themselves are the cage, like a hall of mirrors that once the Verity has entered, they can't find their way out of."

"We have two of Balavad's Fenestrii here, and you said there are two in Vinnr with his forces. That leaves only a fifth. Vaka Aster's five must be in Vinnr as well."

"There's one more thing of import. Whoever speaks the words to make the cage must use a Fenestros belonging to their own creator. If you or I do it, we must use a Vinnric Fenestros."

She was about to say something, then thought for a moment. "You're suggesting the Fenestrii of another Verity might be used instead."

They both glanced at Isemay and Salukis. More, to be honest, at Salukis.

He's only a child, Symvalline cautioned, using the Mentalios. *He'd be no match for Balavad.*

I agree. Nevertheless, before we go home, I'll record the incantation in the Arc Rheunos Scrylle. Let's hope it isn't necessary, but someday, no matter what we do, it may be.

She gave a single nod. "Then you'll teach it to me as well. As far as we know, there's only one other Knight in existence who isn't Vinnric: the Himmingazian. What was his name?"

"Jaemus Bardgrim," Ulfric said, but his thoughts were spinning on a matter he'd hidden from both Symvalline and Isemay—the fate of one of Balavad's Fenestrii, now embedded in Eisa's chest. He hadn't been able to bring himself to speak of that mutilation, only telling Symvalline Eisa had sacrificed herself while opening the starpath to send him and the rest of the Knights to safety.

"There's not just one Knight who isn't Vinnric. There's also us, or

Salukis." Isemay had stepped up beside them and pulled Salukis with her.

"Isemay, you…" Ulfric started, then cut himself off once he took in the sight of her. The look on her face wasn't one of obstinance or haughtiness. Rather, she carried herself like an alert, poised bird. A sparrow, perhaps, or more precisely, a sparrow hawk.

"I what, Da?"

Symvalline stepped in. "We may need you soon in this great task that lies before us, my daughter. But do you think either of you is ready to match wills and wits with a Verity?"

To her credit, Isemay's natural defiance remained slumbering. "I'm sorry, I didn't mean… I just mean, Salukis and I are ordained. Deespora, what remains of her, is too. She'll guide us as Archons, and there are many others here who can teach us things. The Minothians to fight. The Zhallahs their wisdom and the secrets of the Churss. And eventually there will be more Archons. I'm just saying, don't forget what we are. And who *I* am."

She glanced between the two of them, letting them both see the sincerity in her eyes, then said, "I'm the daughter of two of the greatest Knights Corporealis who ever served."

Symvalline wrapped Isemay in a hug. When she stepped back to address them, there was only a slight quaver in her voice. "We must leave tomorrow, provided Deespora will open the starpath for us." She added tersely, the strain of their dependence on the foreign Verity showing in the tenseness of her shoulders, "I'm sure it's too much to ask we be lent the Arc Rheunos Scrylle."

Ulfric nodded, then realized Symvalline wasn't looking at the memory keeper and said, "We need to go to Himmingaze first. The others must be there, and if they're not, I believe Bardgrim may be. The last I knew, he had Vinnr's Scrylle. We need to regroup before we take on this task. And we need to know if they're even still alive."

Sym nodded. "To Himmingaze, then. But tonight, we celebrate the Cosmos's newest protectors." She beamed at Isemay, concealing well the note of trepidation that nevertheless thrummed just behind her eyes.

As EXPECTED, Deespora declined to lend them the Arc Rheunos Scrylle, but agreed to send them to Himmingaze. Or was it Mithlí who'd made the decision? There was no way to know which of the two was behind the eyes of the Archon, and Ulfric felt little need to probe.

Early the following morning, he, Symvalline, Isemay, Salukis, and Deespora traveled to Thallorn Valley before the sun rose. By mutual agreement, they'd decided not to open the starpath inside the Minothian city, not wanting to worry or frighten the people of Arc Rheunos with the wystic gateway. Those with wings flew those without to the valley, except Deespora, who was borne by a fleet-footed urzidae over the ruins of the labyrinth.

As the morning filled with a crisp pinkish light, the steeples of the Churss forest rose across the valley. The stones had already taken themselves back to the other side of the river and resettled on the opposite slopes, where they'd protected the Zhallah people for the last several hundred turns, or "years" as they were called in Arc Rheunos. The moving stone forest had done little damage to the grasses and bushes that spanned the distance between the mountain fortress of Aktoktos Gate and the opposite side of the valley, having moved in a long narrow train until it could reclaim its old space.

Ulfric and the rest of the group came to rest beside the river's dancing water, its mild burbling filling the air with soothing sound. From the memory keeper, Ulfric found himself the focus of Deespora's pointed stare. It was time to go, and more, it was time to say goodbye.

Symvalline caught Ulfric's thoughts and moved to stand before Isemay, taking her hands. Ulfric was the first to speak. It was one of the hardest conversations he'd ever been faced with, and he found it difficult to begin. "We'll be back here as soon as we can," he finally managed to gruff. "Until we are, stay close to Deespora during your every waking moment."

"Da," Isemay said, her tone gentle rather than bearing the impertinence of a half-ager, "she is hardly in need of our protection right now. The people of Arc Rheunos revere their Verity."

"True, Crumb. But it isn't her safety that concerns me. Until this thing is done…"

"I'll be fine."

"Here," he said, "I have another gift for you." He had Urgo step forward and lean down. "I'll need the memory keeper to speak with those who aren't Knights, but I want you to take my Mentalios."

Isemay drew the Mentalios chain over Urgo's head. She looked at it for a moment, and when she looked back up, Ulfric could see her eyes glistening. "I wish I could hug you," she said.

Feeling as if his own tears were coming, though he had no eyes of his own to cry with, he steeled his voice and said firmly, with conviction, "You will soon, Crumb."

"Love you, Da."

Through Urgo's eyes, he glanced at Symvalline and saw the reticence in her expression. He knew what she was about to say before she spoke. "Perhaps I should stay after all. They could use me here, and I'm not sure Isemay should be left alone."

Ulfric knew better than to make an argument for either case. This was her decision to make and hers alone. He'd stay himself if not for the fact that he'd never be whole again if he did.

At that moment, Urgo sensed a familiar prickling feeling that Ulfric picked up as well, like tiny bolts of lightning striking all over Urgo's skin. The bruhawk cocked its head at Deespora, and Ulfric was about to ask her to give them a few more moments before opening the starpath—

But she was standing still, the Scrylle scepter held at her side, staring into the sky expectantly. It wasn't she who was opening a starpath well.

Then who?

Urgo and Yggo ruffled their wings, preparing to take flight if needed. At that moment, the blazing pillar of impossibly blue light split the sky and flashed to the earth a few dozen feet away from them. Urgo's eyelids snapped shut at its brilliance. Almost as fast as it came, it dissipated, leaving the valley as still as it had been, as if nothing had changed.

But things had changed. Eyes wide, Ulfric and Urgo gazed in the direction of the starpath.

"Oh Verities tears…" Symvalline whispered. Her arms, once more adorned with her wrist-mounted miniature crossbows, rose as if to fire.

From beside them, Ulfric heard Isemay say uncertainly, "Knight Nazaria?"

It was the lost Knight, or the thing she had become. Adorned in a Dyrrak fighting uniform, she stood with her hallowed glaive Fate Forger in one hand and a short sword hanging in a baldric at her back. Her other hand was raised, and her nine klinkí stones hovered in a circle around it, glowing with a bloodred inner light instead of the blue they once were. At her back stood a cadre of ten Dyrrak Raveners, all armed and equally battle-ready. One had only to see a Ravener once to realize that Eisa was one of them now. Their pale, nearly translucent skin was made even more striking by the contrast to their traditional black- and red-dyed Dyrrak Phase scars, which now stood out in brutal relief. Their elongated teeth and gangly limbs would have been repulsive to anyone. The worst and most striking physical change was the blank gray void of their eyes. No pupils or irises, just a uniform emptiness.

Still, Ulfric knew the moment Eisa spotted them. Her colorless lips stretched and thinned in what might have been a smile. "Knight Lutair, you survived," she said, and her voice, though recognizable as Eisa's, now sounded stretched, becoming a reedy hiss.

Her leather jerkin was cut low. Above the neckline, the most hideous of her transformations stood out, now alight with a wavering, internal incandescence. The words "black fire" roiled in Ulfric's mind at the sight of the glowing ebony Fenestros embedded between her collarbones. The skin around it seemed to have adhered to the stone, as if melted.

"Your child as well," Eisa continued, her gray orbs moving toward Isemay.

"What happened to you, Eisa?" Symvalline asked through a constricted throat. "What in Vaka Aster's name?"

The ten Raveners flanking the aberrant Knight moved up behind her, tense and ready. Her free hand flicked backward, sending the klinkí stones a few inches away, commanding them to hold back.

"What in Balavad's name, you mean," she hissed cryptically.

Ulfric didn't say anything from the memory keeper, trying to hide that he was "present" as well. As far as he knew, Balavad thought Ulfric still remained trapped inside his body with Vaka Aster, and it was a potential advantage he intended to keep secret for as long as possible.

Eisa's eyes finally slid to Deespora. At one look, she mouthed the word *Mithlí* and immediately fell back a few paces. Her expression barely shifted, but Ulfric sensed her uncertainty, even fear. His mind ticked off options and questions in equal fervor. Was she a scout preceding an attack force? What should he and Symvalline do? What *could* they do? Abduct her, save her? Would Deespora help?

Save her. That was it. Eisa had been true to the Knights, in her way, for nearly as long as he had. He owed her his life many times over, and she'd have laid hers aside for him in days past. Standing up to Balavad and using the Scrylle now nested in her chest to extricate the Knights from Vinnr *had been* laying down her life for them. Because what she was now couldn't rightly be called living.

He was about to address Deespora and beg her to take Eisa under her power, but it was too late. Eisa was staring into the sky, and already the starpath's tingling celestial energy was washing over them.

Her eyes fell on them again. "We'll return for Balavad's Fenestrii better prepared," and the cerulean brilliance of the starpath engulfed her.

She and the Raveners were gone as quickly as they'd come.

The valley was hushed for a moment, then Ulfric, uncharacteristically shaken by the turn of events, grated at Deespora, "Why didn't you stop them!?"

Symvalline turned so the memory keeper around her neck was facing the Archon-turned-Verity, who looked at them steadily.

Her answer came in a tone that seemed a cross between the old Deespora's and a deeper resonant voice. "We Verities are divided. We do not meddle with the others' creations."

Ulfric, and it seemed Symvalline as well, was at a loss for words for a moment. He finally blustered, "But Balavad *is* meddling. He *has* meddled. His meddling is the reason you were trapped in a stone corpse for so long."

"Then he is breaking our pact," the Verity said simply. "You have my quin's Fenestrii. I've come with you today to send you wherever you wish, and you will take them with you. Now, you must go."

Infuriated, Ulfric wrestled with himself against responding. Before he could say something brash, Symvalline spoke for them both. "Yes, Mithlí. To Himmingaze, if you would." She looked to Isemay. "If all else fails, my daughter, hide in the Churss. You should, you *will* be safe there no matter what."

A breath later, Symvalline, Ulfric, and the bruhawks were whisking through the Great Cosmos.

CHAPTER FIVE

The Himmingazian named Bardgrim and Knight Dondrin slipped off quietly, Mylla barely even registering they'd been there. Her mind was a chaotic storm with all she'd learned. It wasn't possible. It simply was not. Ulfric and Vaka Aster irredeemably shackled and now at Balavad's mercy? Vinnr on the brink of war, waged by the Dyrraks? And, horridly, her companion Eisa was some kind of malevolent puppet wielded by the usurper Verity.

She was at a loss for words as she took in the news, her stomach swimming. She looked around at her fellow Knights, the few of them now the only ones left to swing the fate of the Great Cosmos away from Balavad's plans for dominion, servitude, and subjugation. The front she and her companions represented meant more now than it had before she'd nearly died. Because now she knew something more. Her own realm had faced a great war against the Battgjaldic Verity as well—her memories had made it plain to her what had become of Ærd and why it was now considered "lost." The attack there had been dire enough to force her parents to flee, taking her, their only child somewhere safe. Or so they'd hoped. She could have died in Ærd, almost four hundred turns ago, and Balavad's warmongering there would have remained unknown in Vinnr.

But she hadn't. More so, she now served a new Verity as a Knight Corporealis, and all this tragedy and horror had led to the day when she'd faced Balavad. *She* had faced the Verity of Battgjald, instead of her father, who was Warden before she was Knight. She wanted to laugh at the irony of it, but her mouth was too dry, her *spirit* was too dry, to conjure one. Would she have made her father proud? Did it matter after he'd abandoned her?

Her shock at what she'd learned of Vinnr and Ulfric was slowly being consumed by her bitterness at her own past, but she reined it in. Now wasn't the time for her to dwell on such an injustice, such a humiliation, even if it wasn't hers. And—there was something else... something tossing about within the detritus of so many newly loosed memories and thoughts bucking around in her mind. Ulfric had been tricked into caging Vaka Aster, and he'd hoped the Battgjald Scrylle held the secret to unmaking the cage, but it was empty.

Empty, yes, but it had not gone unread before it was purged. She had looked into Balavad's Scrylle, when Eisa had sent her to Himmingaze against her will. She'd found the Scrylle, and needing answers and a way to get home, she'd looked inside. Balavad had found her and nearly wrecked her mind, yet she'd been there awhile before he did. She'd seen something she hadn't understood and had immediately forgotten. But it wasn't forgotten, was it? A Knight's mind was more tenacious with holding memories than was typical. In Balavad's Scrylle, she'd seen the way to unmake the Verity cage.

Her companions were staring at her expectantly, as if waiting for an answer. She hadn't heard the question, but it didn't matter. She had more important news to share. "Safran, Stave, Roi—I think I know how to do it."

"It?" said Stave.

"Ulfric, the cage. I've seen inside Balavad's Scrylle—I was trying to open a starpath to return to Vinnr—and I think I read it. The way to unshackle Vaka Aster and the Stallari."

The three stared at her wordlessly for a moment, then Roi spoke up. "Do you remember it? Do you remember it perfectly?"

She blinked. Perfectly? How would she know?

"It's imperative that you do, Mylla, because this is not a thing that we can chance getting wrong."

"I would have to think it over," she finally said, frustrated at her own thoughts for being so helter-skelter at a time like this.

A moment later, Safran sent, *It might not matter anyway. Ulfric is... I'm not sure. Locked away? Absent?* "Only the maker can unmake the cage," he told us. *If Ulfric can't speak the incantation, even if Mylla remembers it flawlessly, neither she nor any of us can make use of it. Especially not now.*

"Then we have to get him back, we do. Get him back, and then *get him back*," Stave said.

Lightning flashed outside, suffusing the interior in a momentary blaze. Huddled on the far side of the temple, in a space that was mostly shielded from the pouring rain, sat the Himmingazian Glisternaut crew. The sight of them reminded Mylla of Bardgrim, and Himmingaze's own Verity troubles.

"The Glunt is a Knight now?" she asked.

"Aye, he is, and a natural, like you yourself were when Ulfric recruited you from the Conservatum," Stave acknowledged. "Though," he added, "a bit less handy with sword. But we'll fix that, we will."

Safran's sympathy-filled eyes watched her with friendly concern. The memory of Ayanna, Mylla's mother, came back to her. She'd had the same dark eyes as Safran's, same as Mylla's. How was she going to tell her Order, her friends, what she'd discovered about Ærd, about her past? All her childhood memories had just been released from the buried vault they'd been locked in almost her entire life, and all she could feel was… alone.

She shook her head and rose to her feet, wobbling a bit until Roi's firm hand gripped her elbow. With a deep breath, she straightened her shoulders and said, "So what are we going to do now?"

Thunder bellowed, the sky itself raging. The building seemed to shake in the reverberation, and several of the 'Gazians cried out at the roaring echoes that seemed to take minutes to fade. A purple-red crack of lightning directly above the temple followed. *So that's why the old Knight and Bardgrim were in such a hurry to find Himmingaze's artifacts. It truly does seem as if this world is about to end.*

Eyeing the remains of the ceiling with distrust, Safran sent, *We have no choice but to return to Vinnr at once. We have Vaka Aster's Scrylle. We have to rescue Ulfric.*

"We are at a marked disadvantage, Safran. Nothing has changed since Eisa sent us here, except that we no longer even have her with us. Balavad will be waiting for us." Roi's tone betrayed a simmering, sharp-edged anger that Mylla had never heard from him before.

"We're not leaving him in that boggin' slag's clutches," Stave protested.

"I'm not saying we should or will," Roi went on. "But without a plan or a means to stop the Verity, we may as well be returning with our hands already bound, and one of these"—he scooped up an unusual birdcage-sized metal container and hurled it furiously against a far wall—"already clamped on our heads."

The crash of the cage had the same effect on the 'Gazians as the thunder from a moment ago had. They tensed and eyed the Knights warily.

And what about them? Safran added after a moment. She didn't look toward the 'Gazians, but she didn't need to.

None could answer that. Himmingaze's doom seemed sealed and now rested on the shoulders of a long-absent Knight who, Mylla had to admit, had seemed not altogether clearheaded, and a young Himmingazian who had hardly heard of Verities less than a thirty-night ago. She questioned the odds of their realm's survival, bitterly realizing her own realm's gambit for survival might have already been lost.

Her own realm...

What realm *was* hers?

I am Ærden. Vaka Aster is not my creator, Vinnr not my true home. It never has been. It was a waystation my parents took me to so they could escape whatever cataclysm was happening in Ærd, and it's where my mother died, shot to death by bandits. Burned to char by a—dragør.

But how did I live? WHY did I live? Is there any meaning to any of it, or is the fate our Verities have created for us just as uncaring and fickle as they are?

She felt cold inside, and not from having been lying at the bottom of a sea for half a thirty-night. Cold and empty at the realization that no sacrifice she'd ever made, anyone had ever made, for a Verity had mattered. Not to the celestials. Vaka Aster hadn't even spared enough thought for Mylla to return her to Vinnr with the rest of the Knights when she'd destroyed Balavad's warship. Simply abandoned her to oblivion in the doomed world of Himmingaze.

That isn't true, she told herself. *Sacrifices do matter, because we don't make them for the Verities. We make them for those we call our friends, our family.* She looked at Safran's troubled face, at Stave and Roi, each brooding silently. *And that's what they are. My family, especially now that I know what happened to my real family, and I'd do anything for them, just like they would for me. I am not who my father was.*

A humming noise began to rise from somewhere outside. Not the storm, more like the sound of a flying dragørfly scout but several times louder. In moments, it had reached them and come to a stop overhead. Through the broken ceiling, distant flashes of lightning illuminated a ship of some sort.

The Knights automatically arranged themselves in a defensive semicircle, backs to the temple's wall, klinkí stones withdrawn. Mylla was dazedly surprised to find hers in her pocket still.

The 'Gazians reacted differently, however. The leader, a tall man with dark hair and gripping sea-green eyes, moved closer to the center of the floor, then said something to the others. They all watched, their expressions a mix of relief and surprise, as though this new ship belonged to someone they knew.

The ship, oblong and half the width of the temple, hovered overhead like the *Vigilance* once could. Warm yellow lights from its undercarriage flooded the temple's interior as a hatch opened at its base, similar, Mylla remembered, to how Jaemus's ship had been designed, and a ladder fell down into the building. Soon, half a dozen more Himmingazians had joined them.

The first was an elder woman with waist-length silver hair woven into a tight braid. Her face was lined, her eyes bright. When she planted her feet on the temple's floor directly in the center of Lífs's symbol and turned to look at the Knights, her back was straight, unbent by age. She regarded them levelly, and the Knights stared back.

Safran held out the Fenestros from Vaka Aster's Scrylle as if to speak to the strangers, when the leader of the Glisternaut crew stepped forward and said something to the older woman. To Mylla, it sounded like he said, "Varae Ya." A name?

It must have been. The woman turned around. Upon seeing the Glisternaut leader, she hurried to him and they embraced. Mylla relaxed a bit, as did her fellow Knights.

The other five new arrivals behaved with a bit more caution, backing toward the Glisternauts at the opposite side of the building while eyeing the Knights. One benefit to their arrival, Mylla noted, was the cover over the broken roof offered by the hovering ship. The constant heavy rain was reduced by half.

Safran sent, *That solves the problem of the Himmingazians, then. Whoever these new people are, they'll be able to take them back to their homes.*

However much longer they have them, Roi added.

Maybe they can help us? Mylla put in, but immediately thought it was a silly idea. The Himmingazians seemed like kind enough people, if not a bit meeker than the typical Vinnric. There was nothing wrong with this, of course, but meekness would not serve them against Balavad, if they ever had to face him.

Absurd, she thought with a jolt. *Even for us to think of facing a Verity. We must be crazy. No—desperate.*

As she thought this, the older woman and the leader of the Glisternauts approached the Knight. She stood before them, and to Mylla's surprise, she saluted them in the Vinnric way. Even more surprising, she addressed them in heavily accented Elder Veros.

"Hello, members of the Knights Corporealis of Vinnr. I'm Vreyja Bardgrim, friend of Knight Dondrin, and the grandsirene of your own newly..." She paused and glanced toward the Glisternaut leader and asked him a question. After he responded, evidently telling her the word she'd hesitated on, she continued. "Ordained Knight." At that, she stopped again and gave them a broad, proud smile. "My grandling, a Knight! It's beyond what even I might have imagined, though in

Himmingaze they are called Mystae. And we, loyal devotees of the Creatress, welcome you."

Roi took a step forward and returned the Vinnric salute. "Thank you, Vreyja Bardgrim. We are glad of your welcome," he said.

"So," she said matter-of-factly, "do you or don't you know how to stop this?" She waved toward the open sky, where a renewed deluge of lightning cracked.

"We're awaiting Griggory and Jaemus now," Roi said. "They are going to try."

Vreyja gave a curt nod. "That's what Cote tells me. We'll wait with you, then. There's going to be nowhere left to go soon anyway."

Mylla didn't have to think hard about what she meant. Much of the Cosmos seemed to be in a fight for its survival, and on the verge of losing.

Once more, she thought of her last memory of her native realm, the fires and destruction her parents had been running from. The battles they'd spoken of. And an idea bloomed at the edge of her thoughts.

CHAPTER SIX

Must have been water in his ears. Jaemus could have sworn Griggory said something about dying, which was ridiculous. Hadn't the old Knight just explained to him that nothing really dies?

They shot up from the seafloor so quickly Jaemus would have ended up swimming if he hadn't fetched up against Hither's back fin. By the time he'd regained his grip of Griggory's waist and convinced himself he'd misheard the Knight, they'd neared the surface enough that Jaemus could see the Glister Cloud. As they approached the surface, the water, so smooth in the deeps, started to beat and batter the slangarook, pushing her about as if she were a pebble inside a bottle being shaken by an angry toddler. It seemed that the Glister Cloud storm had grown worse in the few hours they'd been searching for the celestial artifacts.

When they reached Isle Stonering's shore, the Never Sea had escalated from its usual teeming swirl to heaving itself into great frothing waves that stacked nearly as high as some of Himmingaze's floating cities. Most of the waves broke before reaching the island, but Jaemus could see the incoming water lapping at the temple's steps. Ice-cold wind pushed through his Vinnric robes. They were not made for such malicious climes.

Griggory slipped off Hither's back and started toward the short stairs leading into the temple, leaving Jaemus to slide awkwardly from the beast on his own and hurry to catch up. Before the old Knight reached the door, Jaemus carefully placed a hand on his shoulder to stop him. Griggory spun around, standing nearly nose to nose with Jaemus. The old man had always seemed small and stooped to Jaemus before, but he realized how wrong that impression had been. Griggory stared him in the eyes, unflinching, the somber gold-flecked brown irises nearly mesmerizing in their intensity.

"Ahem," Jaemus began, "I'm sure it was just the water pressure in my ears, Sir Knight, but I definitely heard you wrong. You didn't say anything about dying, did you?"

Griggory remained stubbornly silent, and Jaemus did his best not to think of this change from his previous talkativeness as maudlin.

"See, I've tried the dying thing once," he went on, just as stubbornly, refusing to give in to what was turning out to be this most interesting —if by "interesting" one meant "deeply objectionable"—development. "It just didn't suit me and I'd rather avoid doing it again."

"Don't worry, you'll be fine. The time has come for me to make amends to Himmingaze and Lífs for what I let befall this realm so many turns ago."

"Amends? There are other ways to make amends. You could give to charity, for example. In all probability, whatever we're about to do with these celestial artifacts will open whole new avenues for amends-making." He paused, not enjoying the Knight's silence in the least. "It's all about just keeping a bit of the ole faith in the fight, right?" he finished blandly and, he thought later, dumbly.

Without another word, Griggory turned back to the building and headed up the steps to the entrance.

Sighing heavily, Jaemus was about to follow, but the Knight's words ate at him. *Make amends for what he let befall Himmingaze? How could he have been involved?*

Before he could ponder it further, other matters arose. The quiet hum of a Glisternaut ship's engines found its way to his ear, though muffled by the rain and nearly constant thunder. "A ship! Terrific!" he said, then thought more about it. "A ship... how in the Creatress's name am I going to explain... everything?"

Squinting, he did a slow spin around, trying to see where it was coming from, finally realizing it was already there and was hovering directly over the temple's dilapidated roof. It was a smallish hauling craft, one of the cargo ships used to sling goods between cities. Its landing apparatus would be useless on the island's steadily diminishing surface area, but the craft was Himmingaze-built, and like the world's cities, able to hover in stasis when needed.

As Jaemus stared, passengers dropped a ladder inside the structure and began to disembark. Upon realizing his jaw was agape, he closed it with a snap. It was a punishable offense to visit Isle Stonering. As far as he knew, no Himmingazian but he and the Glisternauts of the *Bounding Skate* who'd come to constrain him had set foot on it for anni-cycles, probably even deca-cycles. Who'd be coming here now, and why?

Griggory, now at the doorway, turned back. "Come on, Bardgrim," he called.

Jaemus tore his eyes from the cargo ship and walked with heavy feet up the steps.

At the top, Griggory eyed him curiously. "Something troubling you?"

"Now that you ask, yes. I'm not exactly in a hurry to embark on whatever you meant about dying, which you still have to explain. And we have guests, as you can see, and I can guarantee you, whoever's in there isn't going to be in the mood to hear about wystic artifacts and curses and banishments of celestial sprites. We'll be lucky if we're not constrained instantly."

Griggory stepped back and gripped Jaemus's tunic, pulling him up to the doorway without another word. Surprised at the sudden aggression, he let himself be hurried along, admitting that the newcomers weren't likely to change the course they were now hard-set on.

Everyone turned in surprise as he and Griggory stepped through the broken doors. The temple's dim interior was illuminated by lights from the hovering ship, and Jaemus was able to see the newcomers clearly.

"Grandsirene?" he said, his mouth once more gaping. "Is that you?"

Vreyja, a stately, indomitable woman, stood with the Knights, her shining hair tied in a rope spilling over her shoulder and down the front of her white Himmingazian tunic. Lightning from outside, which was constant now, flashed through the door and off the silver strands.

Jaemus ran toward his family matriarch, not quite able to believe whom he was seeing. "Grandsirene, what are you doing here?"

"Vreyja." Griggory said her name casually as he approached, as if her presence, and that of the others, was as expected and normal as meeting for tea.

The elderly woman's face was drawn with worry. Her eyes darted between Jaemus and Griggory for a moment, then settled on Jaemus. "Grandling, I am so, so happy to find you here—though I admit, after you took Griggory's artifacts, I should have expected it." She brushed his face affectionately, her fingers already cold from the pelting rain outside. "And you," she faced Griggory, "please tell me you know how to stop this. The cities are swamped, some may be beyond saving. Our homes are being drowned. We've been waiting a long time for a chance to make right with the Creatress what our ancestors did wrong. Tell us you can do it."

"Aha!" Jaemus exclaimed, feeling as if he'd just unearthed the final clue to solving a mystery. "So you *do* believe in the Verities. All that time when I was little, you said you were preserving our history, but this is... is..." He looked around at the other newly arrived Himmingazians, all older, all people he'd seen at one time or another with Vreyja. "Is this some kind of cult?"

It made utter sense. His grandsirene had never *just* been a dabbler in the Verity lore. She'd been its curator and, it seemed, a leader of spreading the old beliefs. And how many stalwart believers who would never give up their founding legends and myths had come before her? Jaemus's gaze lit on Griggory, and he knew: the old Knight had been here all this time, and had likely been responsible for keeping this tiny spark of belief alive.

His grandsirene gave him that look she'd had since he was a precocious child, the one that was equal parts exasperation and love. "Of course we believe in the Creatress, and all the others. Why wouldn't we? Besides, Griggory has been in Himmingaze for too many lifetimes for us to believe in anything else." She said this is if it were an obvious fact that a man who'd lived among the 'Gazian people for over seven hundred of his turns was proof of celestial beings. Jaemus thought it over for a moment, then shrugged. He guessed it kind of was.

"He's taught us and many generations before us the truth, even before the truth was forbidden. We knew we'd have to prepare for the Creatress's return someday, as long as our hope continued and outlasted the fears of those who gave up believing in her. Banning the mere mention of our creator's existence doesn't make her cease to exist, grandling. We believed she'd return, and when she does, someone has to be here to make atonement for our ancestors' wrongs."

He felt like more was being said than he understood, and it wasn't a good feeling. "Atonement? Making amends?" Looking to Griggory, he said, "I get the feeling you're expecting the Creatress to be a touch angry when we fix this. I'm no expert, but that seems like a not-so-good outcome. I'd love to hear how wrong my impression is."

He looked from Vreyja to Griggory and back. Neither met his eyes, and, grumbling, he took a step backward and began to run his hand through his hair, at a loss for any words that might resolve this new development. The rest of the Knights looked on inquisitively, listening but not understanding, he realized. He and Vreyja had reverted to speaking Himm.

Griggory said quietly, "You should not be here, Vreyja. None of you."

"Well, we're here anyway, and we'll do whatever we can to help. We are all prepared to give our lives if it means saving Himmingaze."

"Yes, yes, but it would be death for any Himmingazian to right this wrong. This is my task."

"All right, enough with the death-cult references," Jaemus cut in. "It's time you all let me in on the big secret. What exactly is going to happen once we start this rite or whatever it is?"

The two elders exchanged a heavy look, then Vreyja stepped over and embraced the Knight. "I've told you a hundred times, I know it wasn't your fault, and I know it isn't your sacrifice to make. But we are grateful, Griggory. More than you'll ever know."

He gave her a small grin, then to Jaemus said, "Come with me if you like. Outside, under the Glister Cloud. It's time."

As Griggory turned back toward the doorway, he stopped and gave Roibeard an intense stare. Jaemus had a distinct impression words were being exchanged, though not aloud. After a moment, Roibeard nodded somberly and said, "We too shall do what we can to help, when the time comes."

The other Knights nodded in agreement without hesitation. But what they were agreeing to remained a mystery to him. Before he could ask, *again*, they went with Griggory through the temple's doors. That, more than anything, got Jaemus moving. He wasn't going to be left out of this.

"Wait!" he heard Cote yell. "What's happening, Jaemus?"

What was happening? He had a cold feeling inside that had nothing to do with the unfavorable weather, but he didn't want to worry his lifemate. Cote came up and put a hand on his arm. He took it, pressed it into his cheek for a moment, and made himself smile. "We're just going to, you know, save the world," he said. "It shouldn't take long. Wait here and—no. Everyone." He raised his voice. "Everyone climb into Matron Bardgrim's ship. Be ready to head back to Vann when this is through. I don't know *exactly* what's going to happen, but it'll be better if you're…"

"What?" Cote asked softly.

After a pause, Jaemus shrugged. "Ready," was all he could say.

CHAPTER SEVEN

Back in the pouring rain.

Griggory was seated at the base of the temple's steps, the four intact Fenestrii surrounding him, the Scrylle held in his hands, and the three broken shards of the final celestial stone on the ground before him. Standing in a semicircle, the Knights observed from a short distance away. At the edge of the shoreline stood the slangarook, the water washing against her in increasingly violent spats and lifting and dropping her many trailing fins in contrastingly graceful undulations around her.

Going by Griggory's informal posture, so far, things looked simple enough. Jaemus walked down the steps and asked, "So what are you going to do?"

Griggory's eyes were closed as he spoke, as if he were concentrating. "It's not possible to explain how it works, but in simple terms, I am calling Lífs back through the Scrylle. It will be as if I and the stones are a lens through which all the celestial energy of the Cloud is conjured. When enough has gathered, the broken Fenestros will be made whole, and the Glister Cloud will once more resolve into the vessel it was. I don't expect to survive it."

Jaemus heard a weak squeaking hiss in his ears and realized it was coming from him.

"Bardgrim?" Knight Evernal said.

He coughed, putting a stop to the sudden leak he'd sprung. "That is, er, somewhat unfortunate. I hadn't really prepared for that kind of outcome, Griggory. Maybe we could look into some alternatives?"

"There are no alternatives," the elder Knight said.

Still, Jaemus wasn't ready to watch anyone die today. He was going to fight it till—well, till the expected outcome changed or someone shut him up. A new argument occurred to him. "Eisa seemed to feel somewhat strongly about the matter. Perhaps we could see if she has some ideas on other ways to go about this."

It was then that he realized he hadn't yet learned what had become of the ill-humored Dyrrak Knight. But when he caught sight of Roibeard's face, chiseled with resigned sorrow, he decided now wasn't the time to ask, if there ever would be a time.

Roibeard, however, caught his glance and said, "Eisa is lost to us."

This got Griggory's attention, and he leveled a resigned gaze on Roibeard. "Lost?"

"Taken by Balavad. Turned into an abomination. She gave her life to get us here."

Nodding gravely, staring at the artifacts scattered around him, Griggory whispered, barely audibly, "Then she has atoned." Setting the base of the Scrylle on the stony ground, he picked up the three shards of the broken Fenestros and configured them into the orb they should have been, then placed that into the Scrylle's setting. His eyes flicked to Roibeard. "Remember this, old friend. Don't let the future Knights make the mistakes of the past."

Realizing he was about to start the... whatever, Jaemus gave it one more try. "Don't do this, Griggory. At least let us try to help. We're all companions here, all Knights and the various terms meaning the same. Can't we somehow do this together? Isn't there some saying about two heads being better than one or something? We have six here. We shouldn't have any problem handling the summoning of a mere creator of all the Great Cosmos."

As if to chide him for belittling the power of a Verity, the sky above them suddenly lit up as bright as Halla. Each of them tilted their head back in wonder, and fear. As they watched, the brightness coalesced into a flaming orange-white ball, easily the size of a small star and high on the horizon. It grew larger and larger, and Jaemus realized it was shooting through the sky, closing on Isle Stonering. It moved so fast that he'd no more than realized it before it was nearly on top of them.

Without thinking, he fell to the drenched ground, his hands covering his head, and his eyes squeezing shut. *This is it, this is the end of Himmingaze. We're too late.*

The air above and around them began to crackle, like the sound of water thrown on a hot rock. A rumbling noise began to crest, nearly deafening him, and drowned out the pelting drops of rain hitting next to his ears, the crash of waves on rock, even the near-constant thunder. His senses tapered to nothing but boiling heat and roaring sound that crescendoed rapidly overhead—

—then began to retreat.

He cracked his eyelids and saw the blazing ball crash into the sea a few miles distant. It had shot right above them.

Shakily, he pulled himself to his feet. "Everyone okay?" he asked. "Looks like we were lucky."

He caught Griggory's eyes. What he saw made him realize his comment about luck might have been hasty.

The man's features were squeezed into a puckered frown, his gaze still on the horizon. Aside from the sparkling bodies and swirls of gases that always spun inside the Glister Cloud, the sky dimmed to purple-black again. Yet, distantly, the lightning reflected off a rising wall of mist where the meteor had struck. Mist and... something else.

"What in the names of all the celestial sky sprites is that?" Jaemus breathed.

In a moment, he had it. It was a wall of water, a monstrous wave easily tall enough to submerge the last bit of the island and the temple in the middle of it. And it was moving, inexplicably, toward them.

It rolled forward slowly, like a behemoth, but inevitably nearer, soon swallowing up the entire horizon. Jaemus could see things like ribbons emerging all along the wave's surface. Emerging, then diving back inside, as if they were alive. He watched, horror-stricken, unwilling to believe what his eyes were seeing.

"Fleeches," he moaned. "That water is filled with them. They're coming."

Griggory bowed his head and stared into the broken Fenestros, and Jaemus realized he was diving into the Scrylle lore. He let hope bloom in him. In moments, Himmingaze would again be what it once was thanks to Griggory. And Griggory, his gramsirene's oldest friend and the catalyst for Jaemus becoming who he'd become, would be dead.

It was wrong. Jaemus couldn't put aside that fact. This was Himmingaze, *his* home. Wasn't saving it supposed to have been *his* destiny? He'd talked about doing it for so long. And here was his chance. Was he ready to let an old man, someone who wasn't even from this realm, do it for him? Giving Himmingaze a future had always been his goal. And now, it was his *duty*.

His throat tightened as the cracked orb atop the Scrylle glowed dimly. He looked out at the stormy Never Sea. The slangarook Hither was still there, crouched in the water and staring at the looming tsunami. The sky's bursting radiance bounced almost festively off her scales, and her great eyes flicked to Jaemus a little too keenly for comfort.

His eyes on Hither but speaking more to himself, he said, "It was never going to be easy to be the glint engineer who saves the world, was it?"

Hither cocked her head as if to say, *Why would you have thought differently, silly meatstick?*

He sighed and put a hand on Griggory's shoulder, giving it a tiny shake. "Stop," he said.

Griggory's eyes shot open, blazing with an inner wystic light that startled Jaemus into taking a step back. "Agh!" Griggory swore. "We have no time for arguing. None!"

Despite the Knight's anger, Jaemus's response was calm. Not numb, precisely, but distanced. He felt... ready. "I know. But this isn't your task, Griggory. It's mine. I'll be the lens or conduit or whatever you called it." He sat down cross-legged beside the Knight and pulled the Scrylle between them. "You read the Scrylle with me and show me what I'm looking for, then you get out. I'll reverse the Creatress's banishment, fussless and mussless, and you can finally go back to Vinnr. You've done enough for Himmingaze. But this is a thing that should be done by... well, by a Himmingazian."

Griggory's eyes cleared and widened. Was it admiration, Jaemus saw? Whatever it was, for a moment it made him think his decision was worth it. But only a moment.

Stave stepped closer. "You sure about this, novice? It's, mmm..." Completely uncharacteristically, the Knight fell silent, his misshapen eyebrows knitted with concern.

Jaemus tamped down a waver of unresolve, then cleared his throat. "Yes. I mean, if I was given this 'gift,' it must have been for a reason, right? And I hope Cote appreciates the fact that I'll never steal his pillow again. Someone better tell him what I did." They didn't say anything, but he felt their acknowledgment. "Just make sure they name something after me, something big. Bardgrim's Expanse has a nice ring. Or maybe the Empire of Jaemus."

With one final glance at the encroaching wall of water, he closed his hands around the Scrylle and focused on the fractured orb. The words to help him focus played through his mind. *Cycle of light, balanced by dark, focus my sight, into my heart...*

Like last time he suddenly felt as if he were yanked into a tempest, first his feet, then the rest of his body losing touch with any physical sensation of being in the world. He tensed internally, preparing for the firebolt of light to spear his mind, followed by a Cosmos-sized Never Sea crushing him with all the lore of the realm at once. And that shock to his mental senses came, but unlike last time, he didn't feel his mind splintering and being whipped asunder by the onslaught. And he knew instantly that he wasn't alone.

With me, Bardgrim? Griggory said.

If that's what you call it, he managed.

Good. Follow me.

Follow? he thought. But there was... then he saw the outline, or rather the void of darker space illuminated all around by streaks of lore, like stars whipping past it, leaving long trailing lines of knowledge, wisdom of ages that were transformed into pure lights of all colors. The void was vaguely human-shaped, and Jaemus positioned his ephemeral self behind it, out of the path of those streaking lights, where it was calm. *Neat trick,* he thought, and moved forward.

They pushed through the storm for an eternity. Jaemus knew time wasn't passing in reality the way he felt it here, but before long, floating behind the dark form of Griggory, it began to seem as if he'd never been anywhere but here, as if inside this celestial stream of ages, all of time existed in a single instant, and that instant was his entire life.

Ahead of him, Griggory stopped moving. The empty space in the shape of his arm rose, cutting through the stream of light, and he pointed to his side. *There it is.*

Jaemus looked where he was pointing and saw, of all things, what appeared to be a looking glass. More precisely, a perfectly oval looking glass with several cracks running through it. As soon as his wystic sight fell on it, the light streams of Himmingaze's lore shifted and began to stream toward the mirror. All of it was channeled around the floating oval, making it look like a circle of smooth calm moving at thousands of miles an hour through the stars.

When you look through, Lífs will be drawn to look through too, Griggory's somewhat ethereal voice said.

And what will she see—besides me, obviously? he asked, hesitating.

She'll see through you, he said as if it were as obvious as that.

And that's when I'll, er, cease to be, as it were... he mused, accepting that this was not going to be something he could include in his new category of Things That Should Kill Me But Might Not.

Griggory, tellingly, didn't answer.

Bardgrim's Expanse, he thought. *That's the one I hope they pick, because if I'm never reminded of the Empire of Dyrrakium again, I'll... well, I guess I won't, will I?*

With a deep internal breath, he took a step toward the mirror.

And felt something, some*one* beside him. *Griggory?*

No, a different voice said. *It's me, Mylla. I remember what you did for Vaka Aster and Ulfric. Let me, let* us, *do the same for you.*

At that moment, he felt the others, too. Stave, Safran, Roibeard, even Griggory had moved up to him. He was surrounded by more silhouettes, amorphous and without detail, but he could still make out their individual shapes.

Are—are you all going to help me?

Of course we are. Did you think we were going to let the novicest of all novices have all the glory to himself? said Stave.

Roibeard cut in. *You're a Knight, Bardgrim. It's going to take all of us to stop Balavad, so we'll face this test with you, as we should all tests. As one.*

Giving a nod he wasn't sure if anyone could see, he said, *As one,* and stepped up to the looking glass.

The way the light streaked to either side, he half expected to see it converging into a distant point inside the celestial oval—a portal, he realized—but that was the only expectation he had. He simply couldn't guess what he might see. And when he did see it, he still didn't know how to describe it, and knew he never would. The only words he could find were, *It is the entire Cosmos, infinity multiplied by infinity...*

Then, as if a great being the size of mountains suddenly became aware of them, he sensed himself being discovered, scrutinized. At the same moment, he began to feel... the word "full" didn't quite fit. Ballooned, as if he were being inflated, and the infinity on the other side of the portal began to move.

For a moment, vertigo overpowered him. From his side of the portal, at the periphery of his vision, the light streaked toward it. But from inside, the infinitude was moving the opposite way, toward him, and increasing in speed. He wanted to say something but found himself immobile, frozen. The others around him were equally still. He had the sense he was in a speeding Glisternaut ship hurtling into a tunnel, while at the same time the tunnel was hurtling itself at him, *into* him.

The sense of internal pressure increased, and he knew without a doubt he was simply going to fill to the point of exploding. He distantly thought of the mess it would make on Isle Stonering when he and the rest of the Knights did. Nothing was going to stop it. The pressure grew and grew, the light on the sides of the mirror blazed brighter and brighter, and if he could have screamed, he would have screamed louder and louder.

At the moment he thought the end would come, as the fibers of his ephemeral spirit seemed about to tear apart with fantastic force, a voice passed through his mind like the gentlest brush of cloud.

Another Mystae to welcome me back to my creation. One last sojourn before the Syzycki Elementum.

JAEMUS OPENED his eyes and quickly closed them again, expecting Himmingaze's heavy rain to thump his eyeballs, and realized a moment later the rain had stopped.

Everything was silent. *I'm dead? Odd to feel stones beneath my bum if I'm dead.* Then he realized it wasn't silent. He could hear water gently lapping against the shore. His eyes opened again.

For his thirty-seven anni-cycles, every time Jaemus had looked into Himmingaze's sky, he'd seen the swirling glints and swirls of the Glister Cloud, a beautiful yet threatening cloak wrapping his world in a turbid and impenetrable shell. He'd believed before Ulfric came that he and his fellow Himmingazians would have to break through that shell to see the rest of the Cosmos and find a world that wasn't slowly devolving into chaos. And after Ulfric, he'd learned there simply was no Cosmos outside the shell, that his realm, his reality, had been cut neatly away from it and was doomed to cease existing entirely because of the curse of the Mystae who'd banished the Creatress from her creation.

He had to admit he couldn't entirely fathom what all that meant, but at this moment, staring into the sky over Himmingaze, he didn't care. Because for the first time in his life, there *was* a sky. The Glister Cloud, the broken vessel of Lífs according to Griggory, had been made whole again. Who knew who or what it had become? But that wasn't a concern to dwell on at the moment, because, like the illimitable night sky of Vinnr, the vision above him was open, edgeless, infinite, and filled with stars that expanded ever outward far, far beyond the limits of his sight.

They had done it, they'd broken the banishment and returned Lífs to her realm, and thereby returned Himmingaze to the Great Cosmos. What had been sundered had been remade.

And he was pretty sure he hadn't died doing it.

Sitting up, Jaemus caught sight of the rest of the Knights on all sides of him, including Griggory. They were moving around, all breathing, staring about themselves as surprised as he was. Also, marvel of many marvels, not dead.

Aside from a residual prickling sensation in the roots of his hair and at his fingertips and even his toes, not unpleasant but noticeable, he decided he was no worse for wear. He leaned toward Knight Evernal and reached for her shoulder to gently nudge her awake but caught something in the corner of his eye near the shoreline. Hither still stood there, still half immersed in the water, and the beast's eyes were fixed on him. Her eyes were... swirling. Like Ulfric's, a celestial dance of silver-blue and golden light filling them.

Their gazes locked. Finally Jaemus whispered, "Creatress?"

Hither's long body slid backward into the water, and with serpentine grace, she turned into the next riffle and was gone an instant later. He watched her, or rather the water she disappeared beneath, a moment longer. So. The Glister Cloud was gone, and a new vessel had been chosen.

He mentally poked around the edges of the idea that a slangarook, large and, according to tales, ferocious enough to consume the populations of whole cities, was now the physical embodiment of their creator. But he quickly decided this was a consideration best left for another time. As he began picking himself up, a voice unlike any human's he'd heard—but the same as the voice he'd heard inside the Scrylle—spoke inside his mind. *Mystae Bardgrim. I will remember you.*

He jolted a little, then said aloud in a somewhat shaky voice, "I hope she meant that in a 'Don't worry, I won't forget your birthday' kind of way, and not a 'I never forget the face of someone I may eat someday' kind of way."

"You've got something on your head, you do."

He blinked and realized Stave was staring at something between Jaemus's eyes. He lifted his hand and touched his forehead, feeling that prickle in his fingers turn into a shock when he made contact. "Am I bleeding?" he asked, unsure what was causing the sensation.

Movement next to him alerted him that Griggory had risen as well. When Jaemus looked at him, Griggory blinked, then gave him a slow, toothy grin that showed his large teeth too plainly. "By the Verities, you've been twice ordained!"

"Twice... huh?"

Safran, Roibeard, and Knight Evernal had finally stirred. All began to rise, and Stave grabbed Jaemus's hand and pulled him to his feet.

"You've done it, haven't you, Jaemus?" Evernal asked after taking in the calm water and sky. "You've saved Himmingaze."

He blinked. Hearing it said made it feel real all of sudden. "I suppose, I, I mean *we*, did. All in a day's work for a Knight, right?" His humility wasn't feigned. It was simply that no experience in his life compared to what had just occurred, and he found he didn't yet know how to react. What did one do when they pulled a world from the very precipice of annihilation? Take a bow? Sing, buy their friends a round of drinks? With no answer coming to him, he looked back at Griggory and said again, "Twice what now?"

"You bear Lífs's mark, that line like a lightning bolt on your brow, to match the star on your chin. The spark of two Verities, Jaemus. You're both a Mystae and a Kn—"

Griggory shut his mouth abruptly and looked toward the sky just as Jaemus felt it too. The tingling of a starpath about to strike. His gaze shot to the Himmingazian ship over the temple, where the starpath tended to open, but found it missing. Where had it gone? Before the answer came, the brilliant blue pillar of starlight speared through the broken roof and vanished a moment later.

The six Knights stood motionless, those with klinkí stones now wielding them, and Safran and Griggory holding the Scrylles of Lífs and Vaka Aster. They waited.

Jaemus found his heartbeat was slow, much slower than it should have been for someone who half expected to see an army of malformed soldiers belonging to a Verity bent on enslaving the Cosmos come through the temple doors. He counted six beats until whoever had arrived appeared.

It was not even close to who he expected. A woman, shortish, older than him and pale-skinned like Griggory, emerged, flanked on either side by two quite familiar birds the size of a human. She stopped at the top of the steps and gazed down.

But it was even more surprising to hear Ulfric's voice, apparently channeled through a pendant she wore around her neck. "Hello, Knights. What did we miss?"

CHAPTER EIGHT

Statues could not have stood more still than the six Knights on the shore of Isle Stonering when Symvalline walked out of the shrine. The moment only lasted a breath, then nearly everyone spoke at once.

"Sym, is it truly you?" Safran cried, using a Fenestros.

"Verities eyes, I don't believe it," Roibeard whispered.

"Hah!" Stave shouted. "I knew no scabby Verity slag could stop you, Symvalline."

But Mylla remained quiet, circumspect, before asking, "… Isemay?"

Symvalline rushed down the stairs and was quickly wrapped in Safran's embrace. From over the Knight's shoulder, Symvalline said, "Safe. She's in Arc Rheunos." She pulled away. "And you all are safe too, yes?" Her eyes caught the eldest of the Knights, who'd also remained quiet, but his thin lips were stretched in a grin. "Griggory?" she said softly. "Are my eyes deceiving me?"

"It's been some ages, Knight Lutair, and you're still as fair as the glint of Halla on Lake Cuffdeach in springtime."

"We're safe as kórb seeds, we are," Stave said, looking around. "But I heard Ulfric speakin'. Where's the old man at, then?"

Symvalline took Roibeard's hand and squeezed it, then did the same with Stave's. Mylla had remained a few steps back, wrestling with the guilt she'd been carrying at believing she'd been partly to blame for Symvalline's and Isemay's deaths back on Mount Omina. That her friend and mentor had survived, when they'd all accepted that she was dead, hadn't quite gotten through yet.

"Mylla," said Symvalline, her voice and the smile she sent Mylla soft and knowing, and telling Mylla the guilt she'd carried was utterly unnecessary. Then the Yorish Knight looked around at everyone and reached for the pendant she wore. Mylla recognized the memory keeper. She'd seen it a couple of times when Ulfric had been carving the stone into a dragørfly shape as a gift for their daughter.

With the pendant now held aloft, they could all see something so fantastical that none of them could quite believe it for a moment. Ulfric's face in the center crystal, only the size of a thumb, but his face nonetheless.

"Knights, we have much to discuss," he said gravely.

"THE ONE THING we know with any certainty is that if Balavad were planning to destroy Vinnr, he would have done so by now," Roi stated. A hint of dawn light began to brighten the sky to their east.

"You don't think enslaving the whole realm and all its people is akin to destroy it?" Stave asked grumpily. His scowl had turned into a trench in his forehead that a ship could have been lost in as Ulfric and Symvalline had unfolded the harrowing yet captivating tale of defeating Balavad's plot in Arc Rheunos, and the freeing of the realm's Verity from a cage like the one that Ulfric and Vaka Aster now shared.

As fantastic and improbable as their story had been, even Ulfric had lost the ability for speech when Mylla had told him she thought she knew the way to unmake the cage. Strangely, after he'd seemed to accept this, he quickly moved the conversation to confronting Balavad rather than freeing Vaka Aster.

"My meaning was clear, Stave," Roi said. "We are now at an advantage, if you can call anything about this an advantage. With Balavad focused on a war, rather than on revenge for what Vaka Aster did to

Battgjald, we may have a chance to retrieve…" His voice trailed away for a brief moment as he gazed at Ulfric's pendant. As they all were, he was still trying to understand what had become of their leader, his disembodiment and unusual partnership with Urgo. "A chance to retrieve Ulfric. His body anyway." The first rays of sunlight lit his pale hair and made his topaz eyes glitter. Their brightness contrasted the deep crow's-feet grooved beside his eyes, lines deeper than his age would suggest, and Mylla remembered that Roi had been a seafarer before he'd been a Knight. The weathering of his features had always made him look just as sober and grave as he behaved. A truth supported by his next statement. "War, if nothing else, makes an unequaled distraction."

"You're suggesting we may be able to slip into Dyrrakium and spirit him away," Safran said.

"Aye. We have two Scrylles and seven Knights now. Nine counting Urgo and Yggo."

"Nine and half if you count Ulfric, even though he's taking up a lot less space than he used to," Jaemus commented distractedly. His gaze was focused on the east, where the outline of a sun began to crest the endless waves of the Never Sea.

Like he's never seen a sunrise before, Mylla thought, then realized he hadn't, not in Himmingaze at least. She had to give the man immense credit for how well he seemed to be handling it. It couldn't have fully sunk in yet that he'd just saved his world from extinction.

In fact, upon Ulfric's and Symvalline's explanation of all that was happening, they'd all needed a handful of moments before they'd gotten their bearings back. In that time, the Himmingazian ship returned, having moved from the island when the comet first struck to assess any danger. The ship now floated in waters so strangely placid that it almost seemed they hadn't saved Himmingaze so much as had been transported somewhere completely new. Jaemus had gone to check on the Himmingazians, and finding his friends unharmed, he then joined them in their conversation. Mylla supposed a person could get used to an awful lot rather quickly if not just their life but their world, and many others, depended on it.

"It is true, it is," Stave said. "Our numbers are strong, stronger than most armies."

"Let's not get carried away in assessing our own strength," Roi said, adding, "But we'll be stronger yet if we can purge Eisa of Balavad's influence."

Eisa... Mylla shivered again at the description Ulfric gave them of what had become of her. Yet, she felt oddly detached about the Knight and her fate. Neither sympathy nor compassion had found their way into her heart for the woman. Until today, she'd thought Eisa had betrayed them all, and it was she who had sent Lock into the war-torn, Ravener-infested city of Asteryss to retrieve the final Fenestros without a shred of care whether he lived or died. Yet in the end, Eisa had saved the Knights, and had even saved Mylla, if Ulfric's full story was to believed, at the expense of her own freedom and probably her life. Mylla didn't know *how* to feel about Eisa, besides conflicted.

She noted how Symvalline looked at Roi with pity as she said, "Eisa will need to be dealt with. And now she'll be more than she was. She'll be a force."

"Dealt with" didn't ring the same note as what Mylla would have expected her to say. "Saved" seemed more in line with the plans she'd imagine they'd want to start drawing.

Ulfric jumped in. "Because, despite knowing how to unmake the cage thanks to Mylla, we can't go back to Vinnr with only that plan in mind. We have to do more than free Vaka Aster. We have to aim our sights on stopping Balavad. Permanently."

This got everyone to focus sharply on him. After a few weighty moments, Stave said, "Stop, you say. Stop Balavad. A Verity with the power of the Cosmos at his fingertips." He glanced around at the others. "This sounds like the kind of war even the Knights couldn't win. I'd ask if you've been hit in the head one too many times, Ulfric, except that you no longer have one."

"Ulfric's right," Symvalline said. "Balavad will be more driven than ever to get his revenge, especially if we did somehow manage to free Vaka Aster first."

"Well, then, at that point, won't Vaka Aster simply give him the boot if he starts stirring up trouble in Vinnr?" asked Jaemus. He looked at Griggory. "And what about Himmingaze? Will the Creatress protect us from him?"

It was Ulfric who answered. "As we've learned from the Arc Rheunosians, there is more than one way for a Verity with ill intent to poison a world. Balavad's Raveners assaulted Ivoryss in an out-and-out attack. But before that, he brought Yor under his thumb through quiet deceit. And who knows how long he worked his subtlety? Yet Vaka Aster never even stirred from her ages-long repose. Another thing we know with certainty is that despite the Verities' great powers, they also have great weaknesses, chief among them the inability to see each other from afar. Vinnr is our world, as much as our maker's. Maybe more, as we have the most to lose if it's taken from us. And it's the same for you here now, Jaemus."

"And therefore, it is up to us to save it, as Jaemus did Himmingaze, as you did Arc Rheunos," Safran said.

"Cage Balavad," Roi mused. "And you retained the knowledge of how this can be done, Stallari?"

"Five Fenestrii are needed. Four of his own, one belonging to the maker of the cage. Symvalline and I have two Battgjaldic Fenestrii, we know two more are in Vinnr. Eisa… has one. One of Balavad's servants was left behind in Vinnr and has been taken as his new vessel, so now we know that even though his realm was destroyed, he may have other Battgjaldics lying in wait, maybe spying, maybe ready to be taken over by Balavad and used as his vessel. In Vinnr, in other worlds. The fifth Battgjaldic stone may be with one of them, and finding them should be another of our missions, once we've achieved this one," Ulfric confirmed.

That was an optimistic statement, Mylla thought, her own doubts echoing the other Knights'. Cage a Verity who was not only present in a way Vaka Aster had not been in ages but who also knew the rite they could use to shackle him? She'd been ready to face whatever challenges Knighthood could throw at her when she'd joined the Order, or so she'd thought. But this was beyond a challenge. This bordered on pure madness. Yet it was clear why Ulfric and Symvalline suggested it. What peace could there be if Balavad wasn't, as Symvalline had said of Eisa, "dealt with" once and for all?

"Say more about the Fenestrii belonging to the cage maker," Jaemus said. "You mean that if, say, I were to call up the cage, the final Fenestros would have to be from Himmingaze?"

"That's exactly right," Ulfric said. "Which means all of you will have to learn the incantation, and we'll have to go to Vinnr armed with multiple options for who will be able to perform the rite when it comes to it. Namely you, Bardgrim."

The green-skinned 'Gazian gave a polite laugh, as if to acknowledge a joke he hardly found funny, saying, "I've just finished freeing one Verity from her constraints, in a manner of speaking. Wouldn't it be a little, er, presumptuous for me to turn around and do the opposite to another?"

Mylla could see Ulfric was about to speak, but Safran jumped in, "That's fair, Jaemus. You're not of Vinnr, and you've done more in the last few weeks for our people than, I think I'm right in saying, any Knight has ever done before. If you wanted to sit this fight out, none of us here could blame you or find fault. You've your own realm to look to now."

This argument didn't settle well with Jaemus. His mouth puckered and his brow wrinkled in an expression that spoke of inner turmoil. Mylla sensed that Ulfric wanted to argue, but he didn't, and no one else disagreed with Safran.

Finally Ulfric added, "But you should learn the cage anyway. Just in case. And Mylla will have to teach us all the unmaking spell as well." His eyes fell on her, that stern gaze just as weighty from within the memory keeper as it had been in his full presence. It didn't help that Urgo was also eyeing her. Was it true Ulfric could see through the bruhawk's eyes? What must that be like?

She shook off the curiosity, as a subject of even graver consideration needed airing. "If we had the Fenestrii of the other realms," she began cautiously, "our chances of both rescuing you, and thus Vaka Aster, and caging Balavad increase, correct?"

"As we've seen," Symvalline said, giving Mylla a considering look.

"Are you thinking we ought to try persuading the new Archon from Arc Rheunos to collaborate with us?"

"That's a thought, yes," Mylla acknowledged. "But I had a different realm's celestial stones in mind. You see"—she took a deep breath, finding it harder to reveal her true heritage than she'd anticipated—"the rite to unmake the cage wasn't the only memory that came to me while I was lying at the bottom of the Never Sea."

CHAPTER NINE

For the next hour, Mylla spun a wondrously ominous and shocking tale. Shocked at her revelation, Ulfric frowned. Of course. Of course she was not from Vinnr! He couldn't believe he'd missed it. She had been brought to the Conservatum as an orphan when he'd already been fourteen hundred turns old and thought he'd seen it all. Even by that point, he might have called himself "worldly," but "jaded" would have fit just as well. If nothing else could have confirmed it, his simple inability to see the obvious showed him he had been a Knight too long. What if the Ærdens had been hostile to the Vinnrics, and Mylla had been sent as a spy? He'd suspected nothing, not once. Fortunately for them all, she'd been a mere lost and orphaned traveler, and had grown to become as faithful to the Knights as any he'd ever served with. Yet, as he'd already accepted when this war with Balavad had begun, he knew he needed to move on. He was far beyond ready.

The shock was broken by Stave. Wearing a bemused grin, he turned to Jaemus and clapped him on the back. "Well, isn't that the goat that drank its own milk, novice? Here you thought you were the first Knight from another world to be adopted and ordained by an outside Verity, but all this time it was our Mylla after all! Heh!"

Jaemus, looking confused, merely said, "That's fine with me. It's not like I can pee lightning now or anything."

Stave couldn't resist. "You sure about that? You are still the first—that we know of—to be... what did you call it, Griggory? Twice ordained? Maybe you should give it a shot, huh?"

"Mylla," Safran said, bringing the conversation back to heavier subjects, "are you sure? These memories weren't a sort of fanciful vision that was brought on by being lost in the Never Sea? Or by Balavad?"

Mylla looked to the ground and toed a loose rock, like a child struggling to accept a rule she wasn't sure she liked. But then, to Ulfric, she'd always be a child. He and Symvalline had both been fond of her when she'd come to the orphan homes in the Conservatum, so young, so shy, clearly traumatized but unable to recall her past. A Yorish merchant caravan had found her cowering by the roadside along the Great Province Byway, tattered and malnourished. Mylla hadn't spoken to the Yorish, and it took her months to speak to the acolytes who'd cared for her in Asteryss. But when she did begin to speak, to the astonishment of most, she'd used Elder Veros steeped in a strange accent. That, along with her dark eyes and hair, had led all to assume she was a Dyrrak. Even after she began to talk, the only thing she'd seemed to recollect was her own name: Mylla Evernal. It was not one of the Six Noble Lines of Dyrrakium, but that was no reason to believe she was anything but a commoner of the empire.

Ulfric recalled now how she'd seemed so simple to the acolytes because she'd reacted to everything, from the foods to the people and buildings to the sky itself, as if it was all a wonder she'd never seen before. For her first year at the Conservatum, they'd believed she was feebleminded and had been preparing a future for her that would have fit her abilities. But the fact that she could read the Elder Veros runes perfectly and learned every new concept almost instantly belied a soft mind, and before two years passed, everyone could see she was, in fact, quite gifted, mentally and physically. As gifted as any chosen for Knighthood, Ulfric had thought then, which had planted the seed in his mind early that he might one day ask her to serve in the Order. It had been the reason he'd paid such close attention during her forma-tive years, and from his removed station, he'd quietly influenced and nudged her in that direction during her acolyte tutelage. That and her strict self-discipline and quickness to adhere to new rules and customs were so pronounced that it had reinforced the belief she must have been from Dyrrakium to all who knew their strict and rigid customs.

Maybe he had sensed something was different about her then, but he would not for the life of him have guessed it was her true background.

Ærden all this time. I've served beside a member of the Lost Realm and had no idea. It was such a wonder that Ulfric wasn't sure if he was more awed at the uniqueness or bothered by his own short-sightedness.

A more recent memory whispered through his mind then, unset-tling him. The last thing he'd read in the Arc Rheunos Scrylle, like the words of a prophecy. *Where the Five Flames have burned, Fimm's final vessel will sing the Syzycki Elementum.*

Mylla glanced around. "I know it's a shock. Believe me, none of you are more surprised than me. But, please... don't stare at me like that. I'm still me, Mylla, Knight Corporealis of Vinnr."

"I'm sorry, Mylla, we didn't mean to. It's just..." Safran said.

"We are all the more inspired and buoyed with even greater hope by your truth," Symvalline said matter-of-factly, though still with warmth. "You're our sister and companion, and all of us are indebted to you for many reasons. Nothing has changed."

Mylla smiled gratefully, then glanced at Ulfric. He knew why. She was seeking his affirmation, as she always had, like a daughter more than a pupil. He fit a smile to his memory keeper visage, which took a moment to feel natural.

"As Symvalline said, this changes nothing. I would embrace you if I could, Mylla," he said.

She took a deep breath. "But you see the door this opens for us, don't you? If I got to Ærd, perhaps I could—"

"Go to Ærd?" he cut in. "The memory you mention, the battle you were in, there is a great deal of danger in going to the Lost Realm. We know almost nothing about it. The Vinnr Scrylle mentions it only once."

"I'll go with her," Griggory said, surprising them all.

Mylla's eyes darted to the eldest Knight uncertainly. At that moment, the Glisternaut Captain Cote Illago approached. The Himmingazians had been waiting patiently for Jaemus since Ulfric and Symvalline arrived. They had very little understanding about what was going on—the newly risen sun, for example, something that had been missing from this realm for over seven hundred turns—and Jaemus was the most likely of any of them to be able to explain things.

Cote said something quietly to Jaemus, who then turned to the rest of them. "Excuse me a moment," he said and returned to the Glisternaut ship with Cote.

Mylla picked up where Ulfric had left off. "We know Balavad was there, or his Raveners were. We know a war like what is about to occur in Vinnr already happened there. If I go, I may find answers to questions we don't even know to ask yet."

She was gathering momentum in her argument, pushing harder to go the more she spoke "And the Ærden artifacts would cement our advantages. Could even a Verity break through a shield if we built it from the celestial stones of a third realm, possibly even a fourth, if we were to get the Arc Rheunosians to help too? We might be able to face Balavad head on with that much strength in our hands."

"But we don't know, Mylla. That's not something we can know without attempting it, and if we failed, we would doom the Cosmos," Ulfric argued.

"And we'd be splitting up, further weakening our advantage," Mallich pointed out.

Safran was circumspect, her concern for Mylla clear in her face. Ulfric could see her wrestling against words she wasn't sure she wanted to say until she did. "And if you went, Mylla, how would you get back? We could use Vaka Aster's Scrylle to open the starpath to Ærd, but we keep it with us. You'd be trapped."

"Then… then I'll be stuck there—unless I do find the Ærd artifacts. And if I don't, you'll have to come get me when… whenever you can."

Despite the hesitancy in Mylla's voice, Ulfric could see the determination in her eyes. She'd already made this decision. And did he really want to dissuade her? That prophetic line from the Arc Rheunos Scrylle chewed at him. *Fimm's final vessel... the Syzycki Elementum.* What did it mean?

Symvalline spoke to him, using the Mentalios. *Ulfric, I can feel you're troubled, and it is more than just concern for Mylla's safety. What is it?*

He wondered if it was worth bringing up. None of them knew what the Syzycki Elementum truly was. Why worry them with another unresolved and potentially unresolvable quandary? *We can talk about it later, Sym,* he said. Then aloud: "Mylla—"

"I'm going," she cut in. "You can't understand, but I *have* to know where I came from."

"And I agree," he said kindly. "We have no right to stop you."

Her eyes flashed surprise, followed by gratitude.

"When will you go?" Symvalline asked.

Mylla dropped her head slightly and held out her hands. She flexed her fists, once, twice, as if assessing her own strength. Then she looked up. "I can't think of any reason to wait." Looking in Griggory's direction, she asked, "What are your thoughts, Knight Dondrin?"

In answer, he nodded, tightened his ratty robe, and said seriously, "I believe Himmingaze has seen all it needs of me."

Mylla took a long breath, then reached toward Symvalline. "Let me see Vaka Aster's Scrylle. I'll record what I learned from Balavad's Scrylle about how to unmake the cage inside it, as well as I can remember it. You'll all have it then."

Symvalline retrieved the Scrylle from inside her satchel. It fell to her to carry it, naturally, as one of the older Knights and as an acting surrogate for Ulfric. She passed it and the Fenestros to Mylla.

She took the artifacts and joined them to each other, closed her eyes, then opened them and peered into the scepter. In a few moments, she blinked, snorted a sigh through her nose, and removed the celestial stone. "It's there. I-I think it's right," she said, then passed the artifacts back to Symvalline.

Ulfric said, "If you find the Ærd Scrylle and can open a starpath, meet us in Vinnr. Sooner, rather than later, we'll have to return there and finish this."

"We only just got you back, Mylla," Safran said and stepped up to hug her.

"And you too, Griggory," Mallich added.

The eldest Knight, in his casually strange way, said, "But there's more time now. Half a cycle ago, there was none, but now there is some." At Mallich's confused look, he added, "We won't be gone long," as if that was something over which he had control.

"And we'll drink many a draft of Yorish wine when you return. It's been far, far too long, old friend," Mallich said and gave him a Yorish gesture of companionship.

Stave had stepped up to Safran and wrapped an arm around her waist. To Mylla, he said, "This time, try not to be gone for half a thirty-night, eh? We haven't told you the stories about our new novice yet, and trust me, they are worth telling." He gave her a smile and a wink that on his twisted and scarred eyebrows looked like a caterpillar hunching its back. "And one more thing. When you get back to Vinnr, take a look beneath the dais where the vessel used to stand inside the sanctuary on Omina. I left a little something for you, I did."

Mylla smiled back, though it was strained, and thought about asking what he was talking about, then decided to leave it. She stepped closer to Griggory and nodded at Symvalline to show she was ready. As Symvalline prepared the starpath and the tingle of it began dancing on all their skin, Mylla said, "Tell Bardgrim I'm glad he got his world back. Maybe now I'll get mine. We'll be back as soon as we can."

CHAPTER TEN

Jaemus returned to the group in a bit of a daze. The starpath well had opened once again, but as unbelievable as it was, he had started getting used to such occurrences. As they had been discussing when he left with Cote, old Griggory and Mylla Evernal had gone.

As he stepped up, the remaining Knights looked toward him. "To quote our unusually ghostlike leader, what did I miss?" he asked.

As the Knights briefly filled him in on Mylla's plans, the Glisternaut ship engines began rumbling. Moments later, the ship whisked off.

Stave gave Jaemus a surprised look. "Your ride's leaving without you, novice."

With his gaze lingering on Cote's departure into the miraculously bright horizon, Jaemus said simply, "I decided, or well, I was *told* that I can do more good with you than by staying here. In Himmingaze. My home, in case that wasn't clear." He brought his attention back to the suddenly quiet group. "After all, what good is being turned into a lightning-peer if I don't find a use for my newly begotten gifts? Perhaps Balavad isn't fond of lightning. Or pee."

Their laughter should have lightened his mood—at least they seemed to finally be understanding his quirks of humor—but it didn't.

While Mylla was sharing her surprising revelations with the group, Cote had asked him to come speak to the rest of the crew, including Vreyja and her ilk, to help them more fully understand what he'd just done—and more to the point, to help them figure out what *they* were supposed to do now that Himmingaze was transformed. They could all see how it had changed, but more than that, it was a *feeling*, a sense of safety when for their whole lives they'd constantly felt under threat. Maybe it was a sense of hope, or liberation.

Whatever it was, the group was ready to go home, so he put the facts to them as straightforwardly and swiftly as he was capable.

Long ago, their realm had been doomed to destruction by the self-serving actions of the ancient Mystae, protectors of the vessel of their Verity Lífs, aka the Creatress. "Yes," he'd said, speaking to just the Glisternauts, "I know that most of you assumed the Creatress cult was mere superstition and myth, but as you've all seen in the last few Glister cycles, it isn't. The Verities are as real as we are. They are, in reality, ur-real, the original reality." Their confused and crumpled brows warned him that he shouldn't delve too deeply into theory, and he got back on track. "And thanks to the intervention of our friends from Vinnr, Himmingaze has been restored and the Glister Cloud will threaten us no longer." (Looking back, Jaemus realized he hadn't given himself credit for saving the world. Of the many changes he'd undergone lately, or that had been foisted on him, *that* had to be the biggest.)

The obvious questions for the Himmingazian citizens were then: So what do we do now, and what do we tell the rest of the 'Gazians, given their long, long history of denying there was any such thing as the Creatress?

And they expected him to know the answer to that?

Apparently. So, he'd done his best. "I suppose the first thing we need to do is speak to the Council of Nine Crests. Aside from the truth—that the Creatress and all the old lore associated with her are real—what other reason could there be for us all to now be able to look into infinite heavens that were simply not there yesterday? What else would explain the disappearance of the rain and lightning?" (Again, looking back, he wondered if he'd jinxed himself by giving voice to this question, because, as it turned out, imaginative Council members could come up with many other reasons for the wonders that had befallen the world. And they weren't complimentary to Jaemus at all.)

Aside from a long-ingrained stubbornness against anything Creatress-related, the Himmingazians were a marvelously practical people. Telling the Council the truth, especially with it as obvious as it was, would undoubtedly be the best approach.

Even as he'd been considering how exactly he would explain it all, as it seemed the task should fall to him as the man who most clearly understood what had happened, Vreyja had been eyeing him with skepticism. "We'll tell them, grandling. While you join the Knights Corporealis and finish the quest that's begun."

"Finish the… quest?"

She gave him the same look she had since he was a child. *Listen and be quiet.* "I overheard enough from the Vinnrics, and know enough from our own history along with what Griggory has shared, to know this isn't over. Hardly. It has, in fact, only begun. Now, you are something special. I've known it since you were too short to bite my knee, and because of that you've been chosen for something even more important than you ever imagined. You're not a Himmingazian anymore, grandling. Or not merely one. Now you're a part of the Great Cosmos, and if you want those you love"—she gave Cote a pointed look—"to live the lives they deserve, you'll do what's necessary to ensure they have that chance."

Few people had ever been able to persuasively argue a point against his gramsirene. Jaemus was not one of them.

Cote had stepped to his side then. "I'll be here waiting, Jae. We'll let the Council know what you've done, and we'll be ready for you when you return. And you know what else? You're a hero now. Don't forget it, because I never will."

After a more emotional goodbye than Jaemus was going to admit, he'd returned to the Knights on Stonering's shore.

Now, Stave stepped up and whacked his shoulder good-naturedly. Despite the fact that the much shorter man had to reach up to do it, he never failed to make Jaemus wobble a bit with his physical chumminess.

"Glad to have you with us, Knight Bardgrim. Or is it Mystae now?" Stave asked.

Jaemus gave him a thin smile. "Jae will do."

"Knight it is, then," said Stave and returned his focus to the group. "Now, what's our first step going to be?"

Sighing inwardly, Jaemus turned his focus to the future as well. *Heading back to Vinnr, obviously,* he thought. *Then... well, Jaemus, if nothing else, Vigil Tower had a lot of inventions you didn't get to explore yet. Maybe you'll get a chance to help Ulfric perfect those wing sets you never got a chance to test. You may be the least sword-savvy Knight... Mystae... whatever, who ever lived, but you can still show them a thing or two about contriving ways to flee certain death.*

CHAPTER ELEVEN

Urgo was hungry, and Ulfric realized the bruhawk probably wasn't the only one. He'd been so caught up in the urgency of defeating Balavad that he'd forgotten that his lack of physical form didn't mean the rest of his Knights didn't still have normal human needs. As the old saying went, an army, like a serpent, travels on its belly. The Knights may have been few in number, but in the coming days, and indeed in days gone by, they were no less an army.

Soon, friend, we'll find something for you to eat, he told Urgo via their mindlink.

"If I were planning to control Vinnr, the first place I'd fortify with an armed horde of those ugly creatures would be the starpath well, I would," Stave was saying.

"You have an excellent point, Stave," Symvalline responded. "It's only been a short while since Ulfric, the hawks, and I saw Eisa in Arc Rheunos. She had a force of at least a dozen Dyrrak Raveners with her, and for all we know, they've taken over Mount Omina since returning. Our first challenge is going to simply be entering Vinnr."

They all nodded thoughtfully.

"If she is there, that'll make the next part of the plan that much easier, it will," Stave continued. "She's got Balavad's Scrylle and a Fenestros—though 'got' is a strange way of putting it, it is. In any case, we'd be able to take them, regardless of how many of those gangly bastirts she's leading."

Ulfric caught the look Mallich threw Stave. It wasn't quite hostility, but it was close. Mallich and Eisa had lived side by side for centuries. They were closer than most brothers and sisters, and he often wondered how far Mallich's affection for Eisa went, or rather, where it stopped. The Yorish Knight had never taken a lover or a heartmatch in all his hundreds of turns, but his loyalty to Eisa had been constant, as unwavering as everything else about him.

Darkly, though, he suspected Stave was right. Eisa may have increased power and resilience from Balavad's affliction, but he was sure they could defeat her with their greater numbers and the aid of both Vaka Aster's and Lífs's artifacts. His eyes strayed to Jaemus. That was, if the Himmingazian Knight consented to their use of them.

"None of us should doubt that facing Eisa, or what she's become, will be difficult if we encounter her at Mount Omina," he said through the memory keeper. "And that's an important point we must all bear in mind, as hard as it might be. We don't know if she is still Eisa, deep inside. We simply have no way of judging how deeply hollowed out Balavad may have—"

"I'm stopping you there, Ulfric," Mallich cut in. "We've all seen with our own eyes that every transformed Ivoryssian and Yorish Vaka Aster brought back from Balavad's warship retained who they were after she withdrew Balavad's poison. Eisa is Eisa, and we still owe her the same loyalty we owe each other. None of us should forget it."

He was right, and Ulfric was ashamed for a moment about what he'd said. But it was Stave who pointed out: "That may be, Roi, but whether she's herself or no, we can't let her go about killin' all those too weak to kill her first. She's one of us, she is, and that means it's not just our duty but our responsibility as her friends and companions to stop her if she tries to do something we all know she would never do if she could help it."

The two Knights stared each other down, Stave having to look up to meet Mallich's eyes. Neither would budge if pushed, and Ulfric forged ahead, trusting neither would hesitate to do what had to be done when the situation was at hand.

"And if she isn't there," he said, "we'll still have to face her eventually. But we'll get to that later. First, obviously, we must get home, then we'll go straight to Asteryss and Vigil Tower."

Vigil Tower? Safran asked. *Not directly to Dyrrakium?*

"No. Even if the Dyrrak forces haven't gained control of the starpath, they'll know better than to leave the interrealm well in Dyrrakium unguarded. And there is a task for us in Asteryss first. We're assuming Balavad will use the Dyrrak people as his new army for spreading his dominion. Truth be told, given how prepared the Dyrraks were to aggress against Ivoryss before Balavad had even gained the foothold he now has, we already know our assumptions are correct. So..." He paused, turning the idea over in his mind once more, then continued, "We need to meet with Arch Keeper Beatte, and the Yorish Keeper as well if he's still there, and persuade them to surrender to Balavad when he comes."

Stave let out a mocking bray, then clammed up quickly, realizing Ulfric was serious. "The Dragør Marines surrender to those painted zealots? Ulfric, Ivoryss may have taken a beating by Balavad's first assault, but those people aren't going to just lie down for another one."

"I know it won't be easy. But what's better? Either they swallow their pride and save their remaining people from slaughter while we try to salvage the future of the Great Cosmos—or they die in waves the likes of which haven't died since the War of Rivening two thousand turns ago, where death would be their *best* outcome."

Stave bowed his head and stared at his boots, chagrined, as Mallich spoke. "You know I don't relish the thought of a war, but as we've already discussed, Vinnr at war would make a useful distraction for Balavad and his Raveners. It may be the only real advantage we have, the one we need to get back to the Dyrrakium citadel and get you and Vaka Aster out."

"Agreed," Ulfric said. "But the Dyrraks, the Raveners that is, will still come for Ivoryss, whether the Ivoryssians stand down or not. Some will fight back, even if Beatte commands them not to, but they will be overcome. Likely sooner than later. And when they are, the Dyrrak Raveners will have to leave an occupation force there to control them. Which means Balavad's army will be busy for a time. May be enough time for us to do what needs to be done."

"What that really means is that we'll have to work as fast as possible," Symvalline said. "Our duty is to Vaka Aster first, but that doesn't mean we can face this task without accepting that the lives of all Vinnrics depend on us too."

Ulfric looked around at their faces and saw no dissent. Their resoluteness was as reliable as time, and a wave of pride and gratitude to have such fine friends and companions washed through him. Then he caught Jaemus's expression.

In other circumstances, the Himmingazian's tightly pinched face might have been comical. It looked as though he thought himself surrounded by lunatics proposing a plan that seemed to him to be the pinnacle of madness, but about which he completely agreed. It was a dyspeptic, almost apologetic expression.

"Bardgrim," Ulfric said. "What are your thoughts?"

Jaemus opened his mouth, closed it abruptly, then cleared his throat. Finally, he said, "I think, erm, the Fenestrii can be used to help us speak to each other over farther distances than our own Mentalios lenses, correct?"

Surprised at where this was leading, Ulfric nodded.

"In that case, along with us learning the way to unmake the Verity cage, we should split the Fenestrii up among us. It could help if we were to get separated." His mouth remained open for a moment as he considered what else to say, then he shrugged and went quiet.

Stave immediately jumped in. "Spoken like a true strategist, that was, novice. Being twice ordained seems to have given you a boost in the brains, huh?"

"My brains have never needed a boost, actually," Jaemus came back.

Not in the least rebuffed, Stave went on. "It's true, it's true. But don't make me feel useless just yet. I'm still going to turn you into a battle-axe-brandishing beast yet, I am. Speaking of which, where might Himmingaze stash all its weapons? The kind that can smash a Verity?

They'll come in handy against the Raveners, and that worm-slurper's vessel if needs be."

Of the many things Stave had just said that might have put Jaemus on his back foot, the last was the only one that did. "Weapons? Himmingazians aren't, ehm, warfare focused. As far as I know, the most dangerous weapons we have are shelksies and shullets, and those only put you to sleep for a time."

Stave eyed Jaemus expectantly for a moment, as if patiently awaiting the end of the joke. When it didn't come, he said thoughtfully, "I suppose that makes sense, seeing how easily Eisa was able to tromp the old Mystae that started Himmingaze's troubles to begin with."

Ulfric raised his eyebrows at Stave's statement. Eisa had only confessed her indiscretion to him, when they'd been alone aboard the ships heading to Dyrrakium. How had Stave known?

Stave caught his glance. "I may not be as gray-haired as you, Ulfric, but I'm not exactly a novice like Jaemus here either. Eisa never told me the story, but it ate at her, it did. Made her Mentalios discipline when you and her were talking a touch flimsy. We all know what happened here, and what she did."

"We do?" Jaemus said. "All but one, you mean."

"Two, actually," Symvalline added.

Stave eyed Ulfric, waiting for him to stand aside or confess in Eisa's stead. Ulfric wanted to do neither. Eisa had confessed her mistake to him, and though it had been nearly literally world-ending, her wrong had been righted and she had redeemed herself. What good did it do to disparage her now, after she'd given so much of herself to duty for so long? Had, in fact, given everything, in the end.

Stave must have sensed his quandary and mumbled an explanation to the others. "She—she put down the Mystae who needed putting down." With a scowl, he finished, "And so here we are."

Ulfric? Symvalline said. *Is there more I need to know?*

No, Sym. That will do. Eisa is not blameless, but she has paid the price for deeds that are now buried under so much history that they no longer need to be remembered.

She gave the inward sigh that meant she accepted his words, and he moved on to gauge Jaemus's reaction. The 'Gazian seemed steady enough, accepting too without needing the details. Ulfric wondered briefly what his experience of Eisa had been, and what impression he'd had. Something told him it wouldn't have been wholly convivial. But then, only a handful of people in the worlds had had any kind of bond with the second-eldest Knight—now third, given that Griggory was still alive. *Can she still be considered a Knight, though?* he wondered. *After what she's become, is there any of the true Eisa left in her? If there is, how are we to reach her?*

He shook off his dark musings and addressed his companions. "All right then. First, you all need to know how to create the cage that will hold Balavad for eternity, and then how to unmake it. Then we'll be ready to face the tyrant and get revenge for the many lives he's cost. In all the realms."

Even as he said the words, Ulfric marveled at them. *I've become a man of the people instead of protector of the vessel. If I ever confront Vaka Aster again, it will be interesting to see what her judgment will be.*

CHAPTER TWELVE

A blast of power, a fragmented sense of reality, a *whoosh* that easily outsped a shooting star, and the next moment, the six Knights and two bruhawks were dropped onto the rocky flank of Mount Omina.

Each of them who stood on two legs, save Jaemus and Symvalline, were on their feet and brandishing their klinkí stones almost instantly. Symvalline was up just as fast, but though her klinkí stones had been destroyed, she had been reunited with her forearm crossbows. The bruhawks were able to find currents of air to settle slowly before their talons touched the earth. Urgo alighted next to Jaemus, who was holding his head as if he'd slept in a vat of ale and had just now regained consciousness.

One benefit of age, I suppose, thought Ulfric, *I'm better accustomed to being harrowed by wystic and celestial forces than a novice like Jaemus. But he's gaining experience faster than most. He'll be nearly as proficient a Knight as our Mylla soon enough.*

"I'm never going to get good at this," Jaemus proclaimed loudly. "It's like having your body shoved through a grater, then mushed back together and shocked by a pond of eels."

"Hush!" Mallich warned. "We're in the open." The Yorish Knight yanked Jaemus to his feet and shoved him behind a large boulder with char marks covering one side. Jaemus gave a grunt but managed to hold his tongue.

Instilling a common-sense understanding of danger in him is going to be one of the bigger challenges, Ulfric thought. *Or maybe just some common sense.*

Urgo perched atop the same boulder and scanned the surroundings, giving Ulfric a long view of Mount Omina's western flank.

The starpath had delivered them near the ruined cave they'd used as a sanctuary and hideout for so long. Its gaping entryway was visible only a few hundred feet away, the wooden lintel beams that had buttressed it for ages now sagging and splintering. Something would need to be done to brace them before long, or the Knights would lose access to the interrealm well hub completely.

Ulfric had developed the interrealm wells through trial and error and the application of every wystic power he could access nearly a thousand turns ago now. There were five other portals in Vinnr, and each of those would lead directly here, to Mount Omina: one in the Citadel Suprima of Dyrrakium; one beneath Aster Keep in Ivoryss; another in Vigil Tower; another in the Knight's Temple in Umborough, the capital of Yor; and the last in Magdaster in the extreme north of Ivoryss. Of course, only Knights who had a Mentalios lens and knew the proper incantation could trigger them, but they could bring along passengers.

Over the turns, they had been crucial in untold conflicts and predicaments, allowing the Knights to share information over vast distances almost instantly compared to typical modes of transportation, and allowing them to be prepared for anything they needed to be long before commoners possibly could.

They had less vital advantages as well, Ulfric acknowledged, remembering when Symvalline had come home to Vigil Tower unexpectedly from a jaunt in Yor on a crisp winter evening a little over seventeen turns ago. She'd found Ulfric tinkering in one of his crafteries, and the moment she'd stepped in the doorway he'd seen how rosy her cheeks were and the unique shine to her eyes, and he'd known.

They were going to be parents, and she'd come to share the joyful news.

He shook himself from the memory, feeling nearly dizzy with being overwhelmed and overjoyed at the same time. He'd just spent weeks thinking he'd lost Symvalline and Isemay. He'd wanted to kill the monster who'd taken them, and now he wasn't even sure if he thought the monster was Vaka Aster or Balavad.

In the last few days, he kept having to remind himself that they were safe, not dead. He'd believed so strongly they weren't. Looking through Urgo's eyes toward Symvalline, that dizziness surged. No, not dizziness, a relief so great that he might have wept if he'd had eyes.

But a moment later he gritted his mental teeth against a sour roil in his core. Yes, they were alive and, at least for now, safe. But what of him? He could neither weep nor embrace his wife and daughter. Before he'd found them, he would have gladly died ten thousand times if it meant they'd be saved, but somehow knowing they had been, and that he was denied even the simple pleasure of touching them, was a cruel irony.

I'm seeing no one, Safran sent. While Ulfric had been stewing in self-indulgent bitterness, she and the others had been searching the area for signs of Eisa and her squad of Raveners. *The area is clear.*

Mallich appeared from the cave opening. "Clear inside, too. Come on."

"Wait!"

The sound of a young man's voice from a cluster of boulders some distance away made them all spin. Yggo gave a shrill squawk and dived for the rocks. Ulfric caught the sheen of Halla light bouncing off a helmeted head just before the man ducked from Yggo's talons. She fluttered over the rock and began dipping and diving, her claws seeking the person still in hiding.

They heard a breathless cry, then the voice yelled, "Call it off, please! It's me, Havelock Rekkr!"

Havelock? It boded well to find a Dragør Marine here. Ulfric asked Urgo to draw Yggo back, then he shouted through the memory keeper still worn by Symvalline.

"Wing Rekkr, come out. You're safe with us."

The man who stepped out from the boulders looked as if he'd aged by fifty turns since last Ulfric had seen him. As he approached the Knights, who now formed a wide semicircle, his eyes were wide with disbelief. Ulfric was himself a bit surprised at the serendipity of finding a Dragør Wing Marine here whom he knew. But then, that was only because there weren't many left.

"I'm glad to find a familiar face at the starpath, Wing. I assume you're here to stand watch?" Ulfric asked.

Havelock seemed to have gathered himself, but when he heard Ulfric's voice yet couldn't see him, his head tilted quizzically. "Yes, Stallari, that's correct. And I can't tell you how relieved I am that it's the Knights Corporealis who came through this time, and not the band of Raveners. But where are you?"

"He is here," Symvalline said, and held the pendant up. "It's a complicated story, but Ulfric now joins us through wystic rather than physical means."

The Wing blinked at Symvalline, then gave her a deep nod. "I am most happy to see you're back, Knight Lutair. Mylla and I feared the worst. "And what of—" His mouth snapped closed against his next question.

Sym guessed it anyway. "Thank you, Wing Rekkr. Our daughter is also safe."

"I couldn't be more happy to hear it. But I don't understand. Stallari, you were Vaka Aster's newly chosen vessel, were you not? If you're now here, then..."

The Knights looked at each other, none having considered yet what they'd tell any Vinnric they encountered who knew Ulfric as the vessel. Finally, Ulfric decided that the truth should be shared, at least to this particular soldier, known to them all as both reliable and prudent. But not yet.

"We'll explain, but first there are more pressing matters to discuss, Wing," he said. "When did you last see this band of Raveners, and what's become of them?"

IT DIDN'T TAKE the Dragør Wing Marine long to explain that Eisa and her squad had passed through two days prior, as Ulfric and the Knights had expected. As sentry, Havelock had been wise enough only to observe under stealth and not engage. Eisa's band had gone immediately to the interrealm well hub inside the cave and been whisked away. He couldn't know where to, but it seemed fairly safe to assume it would be back to Dyrrakium to report to Balavad what had occurred in Arc Rheunos.

"And what is the situation in Ivoryss?" Ulfric asked as Havelock concluded his tale.

"We're rebuilding as quickly as we can, just the same as before you left for Dyrrakium. But the Arch Keeper has begun requisitioning materials and raising taxes in order to reoutfit the Marines first. We all saw the size of the Dyrrak forces."

So Beatte wasn't entirely without wisdom. The people of Ivoryss were doing everything in their power to bolster their defenses now, exactly as they should. Even assuming they didn't know what was becoming of the Empire of Dyrrakium.

Safran, speaking through a Fenestros she'd borrowed from Symvalline, beat Ulfric to his next question. "So the Arch Keeper's court and people of Ivoryss haven't heard yet?"

"Heard…?" asked Havelock.

"Of Balavad's return," she said solemnly. "The Verity has control of Dyrrakium, and his mind is bent on spreading his dominion throughout Vinnr."

Havelock's face fell in somber contemplation. After a moment he said, almost to himself, "I assumed something of the sort when I saw what has become of Knight Nazaria. But I didn't want to think it was that bad."

"So no one in Ivoryss knows," Ulfric pressed, and Havelock shook his head. "Then we'll be the first to warn them. When is your relief coming?"

"First—and I know you have no duty to explain—I would like to better understand what's become of the vessel. If Balavad controls Dyrrakium, what does that mean? Where is Vaka Aster's vessel?"

"This may be difficult for you to understand," Ulfric began with a sigh.

The Wing's hands had clenched into tight fists by the time Ulfric was done explaining. He studied the ground for a few moments, and Ulfric let him think it over in silence. If learning of Balavad's return was the worst he'd imagined before, the shock of hearing not only that Vaka Aster had been shackled but that the man who'd done it had been her leading protector *and* that her cage was under the power of Vinnr's greatest enemy would have sent a less hardy man to his knees.

A few ponderous breaths later, Havelock looked back to Ulfric. "It seems you're saying that now the only thing standing between Ivoryss and the Dyrrak army are you six and the few dozen working Wing fighters and couple of hundred men and women who can still fight."

What could Ulfric say to reassure him? "We're doing everything we can to prevent it going that far." It seemed a trite response.

It hardly mattered. Havelock barely even seemed to have heard him, and responded to his earlier question. "The next watch comes in a week."

"Good. Stand fast until then, and stay out of sight. You're a good soldier, Wing Rekkr, and you've been a good friend to the Knights. I know Mylla will be happy to see you when she returns, and that may even be before you're relieved."

He watched Havelock's face move through a complicated sequence of emotions before landing on something that might be hope. "Mylla? She's—I was told she is dead." His tone made it clear he feared Ulfric was making a cruel joke.

Safran jumped in. "We all did, Havelock, but we were wrong. She lives still and is currently on an ancillary mission. We hope to have her rejoin us soon."

Ever the diplomat, Safran was cautious about what to tell him, and Ulfric approved. He'd been dubious about the relationship between the soldier and his youngest Knight, but he was a practical man. You couldn't demand someone not love the person they were meant to. It would lead to resentment, and a strong unit didn't function well when its members resented each other. It was inevitable that Mylla's heart would break when she lived on and her lover didn't, but Ulfric didn't know many Knights who hadn't learned that lesson the hard way at some point. It was just one of the prices one paid in service to their creator.

"Stay safe and out of sight. Those who've been changed into Raveners are stronger than normal, so avoid a fight with more than one or two if you can," he told the Wing as he used the Mentalios link to direct the Knights to retreat to the interrealm well.

"Wait," Havelock said. "You can't go to Asteryss. Arch Keeper Beatte has…"

"Has what?"

"She's proclaimed the Knights to be traitors. She's commanded the whole of the kingdom to kill you on sight."

"Well that escalated quickly," Jaemus commented.

Ulfric wanted to kick something, hard. The foolish woman! Why couldn't Balavad have at least done them the favor of ending her life before he'd chased Ulfric down in Himmingaze?

And what options did that leave them?

Before he could decide, Havelock went on. "Commander Brun"—he cleared his throat—"she's still your ally. If you can speak with Brun, together you might find a way to get the news to Beatte and prepare for the Dyrraks to invade from there. You must avoid Beatte learning you're in Ivoryss."

"Brun," Ulfric said aloud, though his mind was racing at the options that still lay open to them. "How can we find her?"

"In that," the Wing said, "luck may be with you."

CHAPTER THIRTEEN

A frozen Ærden wind pushed hard against Mylla, straight into her bones, even as the whisper of needle-sharp pinpricks from traveling through the starpath well diminished.

She began to shiver almost before her eyes could focus on the landscape spreading before them. The cold that had reached to her very heart from the Never Sea had only just finally dissolved, but she could tell it wouldn't take nearly as long this time for her body to drop into that polar chill. She wished she'd thought to bring a cloak or a blanket. For now, the warm shield of her klinkí stones would have to do, even if they drained her of energy. If she'd been thinking rightly, she'd already have them out in case a defense was needed. She was slipping.

The wind blustered over her again, nearly pushing her a step back before she retrieved her stones and set them aloft. In their light, combined with a dim, misty sky, she looked around. Beside her, Griggory stood rigidly, his face wondering and his neck swiveling around as if he were searching for something. But beyond that he showed no sign of sharing her discomfort. He hadn't bothered with his own klinkí stones, and she didn't know whether to take his lack of concern for his safety as wisdom or foolishness.

The world they'd arrived in was bleak, all browns and grays. Behind them spread a wide, flat plain with patches of frost-hardened earth on either side of a wide flagstone road leading off into the distance. The shifting mist diffused the light and made it hard to see the end of the plain and where the road led. Was it morning here, or evening?

They stood upon a flat circle of masoned stone inset into the earth. The round platform was wide enough to land a ship the size of the *Vigilance* on, and inlaid with a design or pattern, but it was too broad to tell what it was. Her instincts told her it had been constructed for this precise purpose: to welcome travelers of the starpath well. The flagstone road intersected it in a straight line. In the opposite direction, the direction the wind blew from, it led into a forest.

But it was not like any forest Mylla had seen. Twisted trees rose from the hard ground and bent nearly halfway over thanks to the relentless wind. She could taste the sea in the gusts, but it was bitter and left a chalky flavor in her mouth like ash. The trees terminated in a straight, unnatural line that extended to the left and right of the road to the edge of her sight, as if they were sentinels guarding what lay beyond from any travelers. Or, perhaps, guarding any travelers from what lay beyond.

They grew too thick to easily pass through, except for where they overlapped in a dense tunnel over the road. It was dark in that tunnel, and the wind roared down it like a bellowing dragør. She thought for a moment about what to do—follow the road through the tunnel or follow it back toward whatever was in the other direction. But it wasn't really a question. It seemed obvious, as if there were voices whispering underneath the wind, telling her to follow the path through the woods toward the unseen sea.

"Come on, Knight Dondrin," she said, and began walking.

They'd not gone far when the sky's light abruptly dimmed and night fell thickly, like a shovelful of dirt into a grave. It seemed prudent to find shelter from the coldness of the wind and any unseen things that might be lurking in the thick, heavy woods. With a bit of searching for anything that might shield them from night creatures' eyes, aided by the mute light of a single glowing klinkí stone, they soon found a modest hollow between the roots of a hoary old tree. It lay within sight of the road, for which she was most grateful. If they got lost in this place, it seemed unlikely they'd ever find their way again.

Fortunately, the night passed quietly, if sleeplessly. Too quietly for her comfort in fact, the constant wind the only sound to break the stillness. They started out early, nibbling on the small bit of food Griggory had with him. Mylla found the unidentifiable foodstuffs revolting and ate little, but the old Knight noshed away contentedly as if it were a delicacy. Knowing that keeping their strength was important, she forced herself to down several bites, chewing only enough so that she wouldn't choke, then asked him to pack away her remaining share for later, hoping fervently that "later" would find them back in Vinnr, where food tasted like food.

As the morning progressed, Mylla lost all track of time. The night had seemed interminable, and she soon found the day shared the quality. The sky's light barely fluctuated. The change was so minute, however, that she wasn't sure if she was imagining it. How could the sun, wherever it might be hidden in the dull grayness above, not move?

They paced slowly onward, on the lookout for any movement, any life whatsoever. She grew weary, but at a certain point her weariness leveled off and didn't worsen, her celestial spark sustaining her. But how long would she need it to? Did the road simply go on forever?

Obviously, she needed something more than counting her steps or the stunted, gnarled trees they passed to occupy her mind. It occurred to her that she knew almost nothing about her present company. Only that Griggory was older than even the Stallari, making him likely one of the oldest beings to ever walk the Cosmos. Outside of dragørs, of course. And though he walked purposefully and seemed no more (or less) fragile than she, she found she couldn't help but think of him as an old man. Furtively, she extended her klinkí stone barrier around him to protect him from the bite of the wind as well. He looked over and gave her slight nod of gratitude. Old, yes, but still just a person who felt the cold and discomfort nonetheless.

A sharp crack underfoot brought her focus back to the here and now. Nothing but a thin layer of ice as their boots stepped along the rock road, yet she felt jumpy. Was nothing left alive in this realm? Were she and Griggory the only ones who were? Ærd, the so-called Lost Realm because it was mentioned no more than once in the Vinnr Scrylle. As far as she knew, no one had ever visited Vinnr from here, and no Vinnric had ever had call or cause to come here. She glanced at Griggory. Or had they?

When she'd told the Knights her origins, their expressions had been what she'd expected: the wideness of Safran's and Roibeard's eyes, the blinking of Symvalline's, the predatory, focused stare of the bruhawks, and the squinting scrutiny of Stave. She remembered looking closely at Ulfric's face in the pendant. His expression had been… unexpected. Not surprise. Had it been worry? Something deeper. Fear, maybe?

And Griggory, he'd looked at her in an odd way too. His gaze was expectant, as if she'd merely begun telling them a fable and he waited on tenterhooks for the end.

"Griggory," she asked suddenly, her voice sounding much too loud in the emptiness. She pitched it lower. "Why did you want to come with me? What do you know about Ærd?"

"Ah, good question, good, yes. Ærd, the land of the lost, the land where time still walks. It's because of those I met before that I wanted to return, of course. I'm a bit surprised not to see them now, to tell you the truth. They should have been expecting us."

These words jolted her. "Who should be expecting us?" she asked, wondering if he meant the Wardens Temporalis, or perhaps the Verity called Fimm.

"The time walkers. The walkers who were time but are now bound by finitude."

This was not so much said as lectured to her, like a teacher to a student. And she listened as closely as a student would, though it had been a while since she'd been one, unless you considered Eisa a tutor. The Dyrrak Knight had never let up on Mylla, training and testing her till she was nearly catatonic with exhaustion. *All those turns I looked up to her, despite her callousness toward me, hoping for her approval because she was the only Dyrrak I knew. All my wishful thinking that she would accept me and let me feel as if I had a people of my own—how pointless it all was.*

Despite her putting Eisa on pedestal, the older Knight had never approved of Mylla. She knew Eisa thought her unworthy because everyone believed her parents had deserted Dyrrakium. Though Eisa had never come out and said she thought Mylla was as tainted as her dishonored parents, Mylla had always known. *No use letting it bother me now. After what happened to her, it's unlikely she and I will ever cross paths again. ... And I'll never get to tear her off a strip for all the slag she threw at me for all these years.*

A mild sense of guilt trickled through her at her uncharitable thoughts, but it quickly dissipated, leaving her with little more than a cold and distant bitterness. Whether it was *for* Eisa or *toward* her, she couldn't say, and didn't really care.

But Griggory now, he was a new puzzle she hadn't been prepared to have to put together today, or any day. His cryptic statements about —what did he say, time walkers? What did that mean? And what in all the worlds was "bound by finitude"? She suspected his helter-skelter jumble of thoughts was what happened to the mind of one who had lived for so long. Still, she wondered if he really was a lunatic or if his mind simply worked at such an elevated and advanced level that she couldn't comprehend him. How was she even to tell the difference?

"When were you here, then?" she asked, deciding to go for questions that should have more obvious answers.

He looked around at the stunted trees on his right, then his left, as if looking for a calendar. "When? Hmm... when the sky was still blue and the earth was still warm," he finally answered.

Fair enough. I don't know if it would be easy to pinpoint a date when you've lived as long as him.

"So, does that mean you don't know why it's so... well, so harsh now?"

"You said there was a war. I assume it's this way now because Balavad won," he said matter-of-factly.

She had no response for that and could only surmise he was right.

They trudged on. And very shortly, proof of just how dark and destructive the war had been confronted them.

Within the confines of the tree tunnel, it would have been too dim to see more than a few feet if not for Mylla's glowing wystic stones.

When she realized that more solid light was coming from the opposite direction, which meant the tunnel was nearing its end, her first reaction was relief, until she saw what had been hung from the trees along the tunnel wall.

Corpses, dozens of them, strung from branches by their necks with chains. Though many of the bodies were mildly rotten, the cold, dry wind that blew endlessly down the path had preserved them to a greater-than-usual degree, making their features and clothing obvious. Chillingly so.

They were Raveners. Though their unsettling gray eyeballs were long gone, their lips had shriveled away from elongated, glassy teeth. If that hadn't been enough to show her what they were, their uniforms, thin, gangly bodies, and clawlike hands made it unmistakable.

Mylla stopped at one of the bodies and approached it for a closer look. The corpse was hung high enough that her face was level with its torso. The Ravener's clothes were strings and rags, barely enough left to flap in the constant gusts. She scanned it quickly from boot tips to head. His, or perhaps her—the corpse was desiccated enough that its gender was indeterminable—eye sockets had something sticking out of them. The spindly objects rustled, and she nearly jumped back in fright and disgust, thinking it was an insect or reptile. But she looked closer and realized small, stiff vines had grown up into its skull and out through the eyes. She looked quickly away, finding it too grotesque and unnerving to view for long.

The tunnel of death showed clearly that the Ærdens had fought and won a few battles at least and then displayed their enemies' corpses as threats of what would happen to others who stood against them. It was grisly.

Avoiding the eyes, she examined the rest of the corpse, wondering if they'd died in battle and been hung afterward, or if hanging itself was the cause of death. Either would be gruesome, but which it was would tell her a bit more about the Ærdens. Had their actions been purely malice-based, or were they simply being pragmatic? Just how much suffering were her forbearers willing to inflict on others? Mylla had learned early in her soldier training that a people's actions and methods of conducting warfare gave the clearest insight into their true hearts. Cruelty or torture, even if it was hoped it would lead to some good, denoted not pragmatism but something dark. Cruelty was a monster that lived in the hearts of some and demanded its tribute, regardless of the supposed good its application might evoke. The words *And once you feed cruelty, it only grows hungrier* whispered through her head. Her eyes flicked back to the chain around the corpse's neck. Had it been Eisa who'd told her that?

She was reminded of Commander Brun of Ivoryss, and the Ravener she'd had chained up similarly in the catacombs under Asteryss City. The leader of the Dragør Marines had never struck Mylla as particularly monstrous, despite being unerringly stubborn and suspicious of the Knights. But if the adage was true that being cruel was a sign of an inner darkness, then Brun was herself a brute, like the prisoner she held. But then, maybe Mylla was just being naive. Maybe the truth was that it took a monster to slay a monster, and if not for people with the constitution and willingness to do whatever was necessary to stop darkness from spreading, people like Brun, maybe they would all be forced to live in that darkness. Perhaps most grisly of all was that Mylla could see no major wounds on the corpse. This Ravener, and the others, had died from suffocation. She was descended from the people who'd done this, a dark-hearted people.

The body still wore a thick belt at its waist, with a heavy buckle that looked to be made of medal. A black stone was embedded in the center near the bottom, and a familiar pattern of three chevrons peaked over it. The mark of a Flesh Caster, Balavad's order of protectors. Heeding a strange impulse, she reached out to run her finger over it. Through the blue light haze of her klinkí stones, she misjudged the space between her hand and the buckle and nudged it harder than she'd meant to.

The corpse was pushed backward into the tree, its mass barely the weight of a feather. Upon striking the trunk, the whole figure and much of its remaining clothing disintegrated into fine dust and was instantly dispersed through the trees by another blast of wind.

Mylla stepped back, aghast. A jangling sound came from above her.

The chain that had been hanging around the Ravener's neck swaying in the gust.

That wasn't the only thing left of the creature. The belt buckle had fallen to Mylla's feet. The last vestige of the Battgjaldic soldier. She almost stooped to pick it up, a dreadful souvenir, but didn't. Why would she want such a thing?

Griggory had witnessed her actions silently, but he now said, "Come, My Evernal. To the end we shall go."

Grateful to be pulled from her gory fascination, she followed, keeping her eyes on the light they approached as it grew brighter, trying to ignore the dead faces hanging on each side that seemed to be staring down at them.

My Evernal? she thought. *What an odd thing to call me. As odd as everything else about him, I suppose.*

Another night was settling around them when they at last emerged in a wide field. In the dimness several hundred paces before them rose a titanic fortress. Between where they stood and the fortress, the remaining trees thinned gradually until they were gone completely. The open space ensured no one could approach the construction without being spotted from a distance.

It rivaled Vigil Tower's footprint in size, spanning as wide as a city block, but that was the only similarity. The outer walls rose so high that a low bank of gray clouds covered the top, and she couldn't tell how far up it went. The road led on to its main gate and ended. From this distance, she could see the fortress was built at the edge of a cliff, though it wasn't possible to tell how high it was, and the sound of waves crashing on rock somewhere below joined the constant howl of wind.

Like the plain behind the starpath platform they'd arrived at, the bare field between them and the fortress was devoid of signs of life. But it didn't matter that they could be seen from the fortress when they crossed the open space. She wasn't here to be sneaky. She was here for answers. Yet, even as the darkness thickened, no lights came from windows that might have dotted the walls of the fortress—it was already too dim to make out the finer details of the structure—and she feared that the inside could be even blacker than the night outside.

"Do you think we have anything to fear?" she asked Griggory as they paused, still among the trees.

He scratched his chin as if pondering a depth to the question she hadn't realized it could have. "There is always something to fear, don't you think? What you know, what you don't know—all can be fraught. It's how you face the fears, and *if* you do, that's important, yes?"

She groaned to herself. *Never a straight answer with him, is there?* "I mean, do you think we should wait for light before..." She jerked her head to indicate the fortress.

"All I can say with certainty is that time will pass whether we stay or go, now or later. But I cannot say how much time will pass."

What did that mean? Was he saying he thought they shouldn't tarry because the others might need them back to face Balavad soon? Or was he saying that biding their time might be better in order to give them a chance to better observe what they might be facing? She couldn't guess from his expression, which was as placid and featureless as a calm lake's surface. She did know that Ærd set her teeth on edge. Yes, she feared things here, what she might find, and what she might not. And nightfall's secrets only worsened those fears. The image of the desiccated Ravener bodies rose in her mind, and she had to hold back a shiver at the thought of coming across more of them inside the sprawling citadel, where she might accidentally brush up against one in the dark and feel their dead, dry flesh on her own before she saw it.

"We'll wait for morning," she decided aloud. "Better to see what awaits us." *And what might come for us.*

They settled in, and Mylla knew that she would not sleep.

As THEY APPROACHED the fortress walls at first light, she couldn't quite make out what material they were constructed from. Either it was unique, or she was having trouble focusing. When at last they stood beneath the walls, she found that what she'd thought was bad eyesight turned out to be the most astonishing thing. The walls were not built of stone and mortar, but wood. And not hewn wood, but growing, interwoven trees—just like the buildings in her memories. She'd assumed those, at least, were fanciful inventions of her childhood mind. But it appeared that was not the case. People in Ærd dwelled in living buildings.

Or they had. The tree-walls of this fortress had long since withered and died. They were stripped to gray-white like the skin of the Ravener's corpse now, but grew so thickly that she still couldn't see through them. She began to suspect the world was dead everywhere. Is that what Balavad had wanted? Dominion over nothing but the dead?

Staring up at the tree-wall, which seemed to rise to the height of the horizon itself, her wonder turned to astonishment. There were faces in the wood, or face-like visages, and they were massive. She blinked and looked again. No, not faces, but the sheer volume of twining and twisting branches and vines that comprised the wall seemed to be moving. Each time she shut her eyes and reopened them, the pattern seemed different.

She quit looking, suspecting that her mind was becoming a bit too overwhelmed. She needed to block out her reactions and keep her focus honed.

The only nonorganic component of the tree-wall was the gate itself, a giant iron-barred portcullis that had been left down. From the maze-like twisting of the tree-wall, she couldn't tell how it worked, or whether there was a winch or hinges. It wasn't important, though, as time had done enough damage to the wall itself to have left a gap next to the gate large enough for her and Griggory to fit through. Mylla considered calling out to ask to be received, but letting her voice break this condemned silence seemed a bad idea.

"Have you been here before?" she asked Griggory in a whisper.

He shrugged. "I was not allowed inside. The time walkers disapproved."

She swallowed around the tightness in her throat. "Well, the time walkers, whoever they were, don't seem to be here to stop us now. Inside it is, I guess."

He gave her a curious look and then, without hesitating, slipped through the crevice.

Mylla, however, did hesitate, dreading the thought of moving through the bramble that may or may not contain some kind of living creatures with faces that stared at her and disappeared before she could be sure she was seeing them. *Just quit this, Mylla. Griggory is older than you by the age of the Cosmos, relatively, and thus wiser by default. If he isn't scared, why should you be?*

She chuckled sardonically to herself, then followed, moving as quickly as she could until she was right on his heels.

The thicket, if it had been filled with leaves, would have been impassable. But barren as it was, they were able to squeeze and climb through to the interior, getting poked and gouged by sharp branches on occasion. On the other side, they came out into a titanic open keep. What she'd thought were walls surrounding a courtyard were in fact the walls of a single structure, and only by craning her head back all the way could she finally see the ceiling. It was in the shape of a massive dome high overhead, also woven from the thicket of trees and vines.

For a moment, she had a vision of the space filled with light and many-colored vines writhing up the tree branches, flowers blossoming from floor to roof, with small animals and birds living tranquilly among the immense growth. It was glorious and vibrant, a menagerie of abundance and life and warmth. For a heartbeat, she was moved by a sense of joy. Then the vision vanished, leaving her surrounded by skeletal trees and bleak death again. *That's what it used to be like here,* she thought. And on the heels of that came: *Could it be again?*

Beside her, Griggory was taking in the sight as well. She heard him mumbling to himself, but his words were too faint to make out.

With only trifling swatches of the outside light breaking through the roof, she could make out very little past where they stood. Again she thought about calling aloud. What did it matter if she did? She sensed the inevitable. No one was here. She wouldn't be heard.

But they did need more light, that was a fact. She'd had to put away her klinkí stones inside the bramble and use both hands to climb through. As she reached for them now, she felt something poke her in the back, like a thin branch. But she wasn't moving, and the thicket was behind her—

Suddenly something gripped her around the shoulders, the waist, all the way to the top of her knees. Something sharp and boney, and it squeezed, vise-like, then yanked her from the ground so fast her chin hit her chest. No, not her chest, something hard, like bark on a thick tree stump.

"Rook's balls! What—" she started to shout, but her body was whipped sideways and spun halfway around, twisting her neck painfully again.

She blinked away black dots from the whiplash and finally saw what had grabbed her. She very well might have screamed, if not for the enormous pressure squeezing her lungs shut.

CHAPTER FOURTEEN

The first thing Mylla's mind tried to tell her was that it was going to be all right, she was having a momentary lapse of reason thanks to the many strange phenomena she'd been party to over the last thirty-night or so. It would pass. It *had* to pass.

Because there was no way she could be staring into a face of an extraordinarily tall bark-skinned… man? Rather, a manlike creature. No, a… a…

A moment later, even the survival instincts of her mind couldn't pretend there was anything remotely human about the thing that had grabbed her.

A tree then, her mind gibbered. *A tree with the sentience and visage of a person. Deep breath, Mylla. This is just your mind playing tricks.*

But she knew that wasn't true. She felt no different from her normal self. Then even her assessment of the thing as a tree was pushed aside. Though she knew all of this was real, there was simply nothing in her language to account for what she was seeing.

It became apparent to her as soon as she looked down and saw how high up she dangled that the thing glaring at her from depressions that reminded her of eye sockets, which were easily the size of her head, was over a story tall. *Things*, rather, as from the corners of her eyes, she could see two more flanking the monster that had her.

It wasn't comparable to anything she knew. It appeared to be composed of the same vine and tree amalgamation that the building was, except also… not. Its whole form seemed to writhe and twist as if it were a bundle of impossibly long snakes, but inside all that movement, blue, red, and green lights twinkled here and there. *Like the Glister Cloud in a way,* her mind yammered. The only reason she assumed she was being glared at, or that it even had eye sockets, was due to a mass of little lights filling the two hollow spaces she was being held up before. The lights in these glinting hollows seemed focused and unmoving, as if examining her.

The proxy eyes, however, were where all resemblance to a human form stopped. It had no arms, unless the dozens of branch-like appendages of various sizes springing from around the central trunk of the creature and jutting off into the air around them could be considered arms. Three or four of these were wrapped around her body, and her closer vantage of these showed their color to be a grayish brown. Their roughened surfaces, again reminding her of bark, were peeling and crusted, a bit like stained and weather-beaten shagbark hickory.

Also un-humanlike: the thing didn't have legs. A bundle of sapling-like cords coalesced around a central point and thickened as they got closer to the ground, like a tree trunk. If her eyes weren't deceiving her, these "trunks" didn't stop at ground level but extended into the earth like roots.

The thing held her in front of its eye-lights long enough that the loudest of the buzzing panic in Mylla's mind began to subside. Her next thought was, *These things were the faces I thought I saw in the wall. These things* are *the wall, or part of it. Why did I think they looked like faces?* she wondered, because now that she was close, nothing but the hollows filled with eye-lights was face-like. *And how can something so large move so silently?*

Her next thought was for Griggory. She didn't want to move or wriggle, didn't want to give the thing a reason to squeeze her harder, but she had to know if the old Knight had been harmed.

She craned her neck to look over one side of the... branches? holding her, then the other side. Griggory, amazingly, stood right where she'd left him, feet on the ground, staring up at the creatures mildly. And possibly... delightedly?

"Griggory," she wheezed, unable to yell with the pressure squeezing her torso. "Are you safe?"

He didn't respond to her, didn't even act like he'd heard her. His eyes moved from one to the other of the creatures. She counted three total.

"Knight Dondrin!" she yelled louder, finding some bravery in the fact that these things didn't seem to be concerned with him. So far. "Can you hear me?"

This time he looked to her and frowned. "Shhh, My Evernal. This is a sacred place, and still. A place of stillness does not favor mortals' demands."

She stared at him incredulously. Was he chiding her? Now, when there were monsters present? What in the five realms of the Great Cosmos was going on?

She decided to try a different tactic. Looking directly into the thing's light-filled hollows, she spoke in Elder Veros with as much strength as her restricted lungs could summon. "I mean you and your kind no harm, creature of Ærd. But I do ask that you put me back down on the ground."

All the twinkling pinpoints of light in the creature's long body suddenly froze and dimmed, and she got the distinct impression that the creature was fading from existence. But that couldn't be, because she still felt its grip around her. She heard what she could best describe as the sound dry leaves made when they began to burn, a quiet crackling. First, there was only one crackling whisper on the air, but it was quickly joined by a separate whisper, then another until the crackling whispers grew to a gale, filled with the snaps and pops one might hear in a forest fire. In moments, it sounded as if the interior of the fortress itself were becoming an inferno, and the lights in all the beings blazed and pulsed strongly again.

She writhed, wanting her hands free to cover her ears before her eardrums burst. Abruptly, a forceful gust overrode the others, and all the noise cut off. After only a moment of relief, the first whisper came again, leaves burning in a breeze.

"Stop," she said aloud. "What do you want from me?" But then she heard it, actually *heard* it. Words, spoken in Elder Veros, somehow forming within the clattering wind.

"We have been waiting for you, Mylla Evernal, last of the Ærdens. The time has come to mend time."

It took her a moment to make sense of the words. "You can speak?" This was all she got out before she had to take a breath, her lungs only able to fill halfway. "H-how do you know me?" she added, and more questions overtook her thoughts—*What does it mean, last of the Ærdens? Could that be true? Where is this thing from? Are these Balavad's servants?*—one after the other, too fast for her to keep up.

Stop. Get control, she ordered herself, putting her raging thoughts in line. What the thing had said about time struck her. *Time to mend time.* And Griggory's cryptic statements from earlier made sense. "You're the time walkers, aren't you?"

The breeze-like noise died down, and something in the thing's eye-lights shifted. She got the distinct impression it was displeased by what she'd said, but she likewise didn't think the displeasure was aimed at her. She heard Griggory rustling around below as the thing addressed him.

"We are not time walkers anymore, Knight of Vinnr," it wisped.

"No," Griggory answered. "Of course, your roots are more bound than ever. I know the timepaths are broken. But I'm a believer in speaking the truth that will be as much as the truth that was."

What struck Mylla the most was the fact that Griggory *knew* these creatures. How many more impossible secrets did the old Knight hide?

She picked her next question, maybe not the most important, given what was happening, but certainly the most curious. "How do you know my name?" she repeated. Then quickly added, "And could you set me back down"—*try politeness, it works among some sentient creatures*—"please?"

The branches wrapping around her clicked open in an almost mechanical motion. She dropped instantly and braced to hit the hard-packed floor. But just as quickly, another branch snatched her and dropped her, then another until she'd reached the ground in a not-entirely-gentle landing.

Pulling herself to her feet, she assessed that nothing was too badly bruised. "Thank you," she said, adding to herself, *I guess.*

Her freedom did not necessarily translate to a sense of safety. Now that she was on the ground and looking up at the thing's, the time walker's, eye-lights, she appreciated just how dwarfed by it she was. Any one of the three beings could squash her and Griggory without noticing it, if not for the fact that she'd been right about their trunks. They were, to borrow Griggory's analogy, rootbound and sunk into the ground. But if that were the case, how did it move, and how had they gotten from outside the wall to inside?

Before she could press them and Griggory for an explanation of what was happening, an image flashed in her mind. A new memory. They seemed to be coming more frequently and clearly.

"Pay close attention, my little evening star."

My little evening star, she thought. *That's what my mother used to call me.*

Her mother sits on a stool across from Mylla, who can't be more than five or six. Mylla holds a contraption Ayanna has just given her that contains dials and arms and gears, something that looks both fragile and durable, depending on how it's handled. The general shape of it is round, though not uniform because of the pieces that jut from it, and it's made from a rich mahogany wood. She is wonderstruck at receiving such a gift and treasures it immediately.

Her mother begins showing her how the gears and arms move as she tells Mylla about time.

"The timepaths once connected everything. In the same way the Cosmos has only one sky, it also once shared a single past and future. Everything lived

and died in the same history. This can show you the time, the true time, everywhere. But only when the timepaths are whole again."

Mylla watches her mother closely, then asks, as she so often asks, "What do you mean?" She understands there's a mystery here that isn't going to be explained simply, and she wants to know more.

"The timepaths show the sun and moon when to rise and set, and this is true in all the five realms. When you bring this little box into their light, even if their light is dimmed, and turn the dials to any of the other of the four realms, you can see their time too."

As Ayanna speaks, she shows Mylla one of the spinning arms on the side of the device and moves it with a finger. The point of the arm can be aimed at five smaller crystal circles, their colors ranging from bright yellow to glistening black. "Right now," she continues, "it only works in Ærd. But someday, if the realms are reunited, it will work in them all."

Her young mind is amazed. See time? It's magic! Then a new thought occurs to her. "But, Mumma, what broke the timepaths?"

"The same thing that broke everything. The fracturing of the One Verity into the Five. The timepaths are now fractured too, but they start here, in Ærd. If they are ever allowed to branch again, it will start in our home, our realm." Her mother gives her a beaming smile, sharing the delight of being part of a world with a unique and special trait. A world, it seems, that contains the magic of time.

Despite Mylla's fascination, something about this unsettles her, but she is too young to understand what. She turns the contraption over in her hand, examining every edge and carved notch. "What is it called?" she asks.

"It's a tesselock, after the timepaths, which we call—"

She snapped out of the memory. "Tessalopes," she whispered to herself. Then more loudly: "That's what you are, the tessalopes. You're the creatures who create the timepaths that once joined the Cosmos together." Her thoughts whispered with the memory of her father's voice, from another time, explaining this to her. *"When the timepaths were whole, they were like trees, every branch and root connected to a part of the Cosmos. It's why the tessalopes look like trees to some people now. When the timepaths were broken, they became trapped in Ærd, and now we call them the 'time walkers.'"*

The thing's eye-lights blazed for a moment, then resumed a slow flicker. "You are remembering your past, last of the Ærdens. Memory exists in the timepaths as well."

It was a lot to take in—again—and she recalled not understanding, but at least accepting it, with much greater ease as a child. Now that she'd lived so many more turns, she gleaned a new insight into what her mother might have been saying, and it was simple: Ærd contained the time walkers, who created the timepaths, or more precisely, *controlled* the timepaths. *Could whatever controls time control the Cosmos? Is that why Balavad's Raveners were here? To enslave the tessalopes?*

The tumult in her mind kicked up again with more questions. Did this mean the Ærdens had the key to stopping, possibly even reversing time? Could this be a secret way to stop Balavad from taking over the Cosmos? Could the time walkers help them? Which begged the question once more, and she asked it aloud, "What did you mean by me being the last of the Ærdens? How can there be no others? My father, he was a Warden of Time, a Temporalis. He could still be alive. He could still—"

The tessalopes' whispering sounds picked up again, and she realized this was the way they spoke with each other. She clapped her hands over her ears, letting them speak without interrupting them.

Using her Mentalios, she addressed Griggory. *Do you know what they're talking about?* And because she had too many questions to limit herself to one at a time, she added, *What else do you know about these creatures?*

Seeming unbothered by the tremendous noise, Griggory watched the tessalopes but answered, *I wandered many worlds in my time. I wandered them all, I think. Ærd was greener then.*

He said no more, and Mylla waited, thinking he was having trouble calling up the memory. It was quite some time ago, after all, and he was, despite his outward appearance, a very old man. When after a few moments no further explanation seemed forthcoming, she opened her mouth to prompt him, but the tessalopes' gale-whispers subsided.

She dropped her hands and stared at them expectantly. Several tendrils broke from the lower trunk of the tessalope who'd grabbed her and snaked toward her again. Fighting the urge to back away, she watched them closely, wishing she had her sword Star Spark.

"We shall have it now, last of the Ærdens."

"Have… what?" She blinked. "I, that is, we, haven't brought anything. In fact that's why we're—" The gale-whispering cut her off, raucous in its obvious agitation.

Shortly, the lead tessalope spoke again. "Come with us."

This constant lack of clarification had finally pulled the last thread of her patience, like an errant thread on a sweater, to the point of unraveling it completely. "Look, Knight Dondrin and I are going no further until you—"

The trunks of the gargantuan shapes were sliding through the earthen floor like mist, and the leader was bearing down on her. Mylla threw herself aside before it flattened her and felt a peculiar cold sensation, as if ice had not been thrown on her but forced into the very pores of her skin. She sensed she had not avoided the tessalope, not completely, and the creature had simply dissolved as it moved through her.

She rolled to her back and followed the creatures' passage with her eyes. They still looked as solid as the branches of the one holding her had. "What in all the worlds are these things?" she whispered to herself. Then more loudly: "That's fine then. We'll come with you if you promise to help us!"

Empty, pointless words. If anyone with any power was left in this world, it wasn't her. Starting to regret the mistake of leaving the Knights so she could pursue this fool's errand, Mylla picked herself up and looked toward Griggory. He'd stayed in the same spot, and she knew the tessalope must have gone right through him, but his expression and posture hadn't changed an iota. Griggory was *enjoying* this, and Mylla was just going to have to follow both his and the time walkers' commands like a lackey until, somehow, she got what she'd come for.

CHAPTER FIFTEEN

Mylla and Griggory were led deeper into the expansive building until even the minimal light coming from the gap in the wall they'd entered through had disappeared. Yet it wasn't completely dark. The flickering lights that pulsed through the tessalopes gave Mylla plenty of illumination, as long as she didn't want to see beyond a few paces.

Nothing to fear here, she kept telling herself. In her head, she believed it, but the way her skin prickled at every little sound, real or imagined, showed that her body had other ideas. She was a mere speck next to these giants, and if they turned on her, well… she'd already felt her ribs nearly crack when the first had held her.

Still, for being so mighty and seemingly solid, it was a wonder how they moved. She hadn't been imagining it when she'd thought their trunks were like mist. They did indeed pierce the earthen floor of the structure, *like roots,* she thought again, but they shifted forward with no more solidity than the air coming from her lungs. It was such an odd thing to see that she started to wonder if any of this was actually real or if she was perhaps still in a black fugue at the bottom of the Never Sea in Himmingaze, dreaming it all.

It's ridiculous to think I'm dreaming, but at least it makes sense how they could have come up behind Griggory and I so quietly. It's like they are both real and unreal at the same time.

The tessalopes' ephemeral forms made no noise as they crossed the chamber. And because Griggory had already scolded her for yelling, not to mention that neither he nor the time walkers had yet answered any of her questions, she held her silence for now as well.

Eventually, she sensed the structure's far wall looming before them. She couldn't judge how close it was, but the blackness *thickened*, or at least that was how she articulated it to herself. Where were the tessalopes leading them? What was this place?

The three time walkers stopped suddenly and spread out in a semicircle. Mylla stopped behind them, but Griggory seemed drawn to whatever lay ahead and kept going.

"Griggory!" she whisper-shouted. "Wait!"

He paid her no mind, and since she wasn't here to babysit, she said nothing more. Let the old Knight worry about himself.

The tessalopes crackled to each other again, then the one who'd picked her up—at least she thought it was the one; in the dark and with the way they'd moved, she couldn't be sure anymore—raised several tendrils. The differently sized branches whipped around slowly in the air for a moment, like an eel that's been picked up by its tail, then converged into a single arm-like appendage. It was pointing ahead toward where Griggory was walking.

Follow him, I guess, she thought, and did so. But not before warning the creatures in a tone she carefully modulated to sound nothing like a threat, "Whatever you want me to see, it's too dark in here for me. I'm going to have to pull out a set of wystic tools that I carry for… light. Just know that I intend no harm."

She had her klinkí stones in her palm, but before she withdrew them from her pocket, the three tessalopes began to glow. Her breath caught at the sheer beauty of what was happening. The small lights moving up and down inside their tendrils sharpened and expanded, their many colors—reds, purples, greens, blues, oranges, and all hues in between—getting stronger and deeper. Each light point began to extend as well, not in a rounded shape like stars, but in length, until they flooded the creatures from top to bottom, like a vertical rainbow. The light ropes curved and spun around the things' inner tendrils, curling up and down them like fire consuming a tree from its center.

After a moment, she had to look away, their brightness too much for her eyes. She took a few more paces forward, and when the creatures were to her back, she opened her eyes.

For all the fiery likeness of the tessalopes' grand show, what she saw next chilled her blood.

She stood before another tessalope. This one was so massive and wide, it made the others look like saplings standing next to a thousand-turn-old oak. Its size, though, wasn't due particularly to height and width alone. This creature was spreading out, expanding along the fortress like ivy on a garden wall. Instead of being inside the structure, it appeared to *be* the structure. Its eye cavities were where she expected to see them, even higher up than those on the time walkers she'd already met, but the rest of its branch-like tendrils extended from a central trunk and spread around the structure's walls like a net, not weaving into the walls and ceiling but comprising them. She suddenly had the feeling that she'd been swallowed by a forest made of a singular tree.

Whatever made this tessalope like this, one thing seemed certain. Unlike the rest, this one was stuck fast. If it was indeed part of the fortress, and not the structure itself, it appeared the whole thing would collapse if the tessalope tried to free itself, if it even *could* free itself.

A moment later, it became clear what made this one different. Griggory stopped a few feet from Mylla, knelt on one knee, dropped his head, and said reverently, "Fimm, creator of Ærd, I have waited lifetimes to meet you."

At Griggory's statement, the Verity's eye-lights blazed like a kiln's heart. Mylla fell back a step at the ferocity, shielding her own eyes with a hand. This time, there was heat as well, tightening the skin of her face and back of her hand. Then came that dry, crackling sound like fire on wind but in words she could understand.

"Bring me the Scrylle, Mylla Evernal, daughter of Warden Temporalis Greven Evernal."

The eye-lights dimmed enough for her to face the creature. Unlike the rest, the Verity's, or vessel's, lights were a solid blazing cavity of fire. As she looked, she had the discomfiting sensation that they were tunnels that led into infinity, and if she stared too long, she would fall in and burn forever.

She blinked when something tugged her pant leg. Griggory was beside her, pulling at her, and she abruptly joined him in kneeling.

Fimm. Verity of her home realm. The one creature who would surely give her the answers she sought. But now that she was confronted with her chance to ask her questions, all she felt was confusion. The Scrylle?

"Fimm, my maker, I'm—" *What? Pleased to meet you?* No, she couldn't say something so droll. Best to just get to the point, as it seemed no Verity cared about ceremony as much as humans did. "I don't have the Ærden Scrylle. My father took it when I was a child so we could travel the starpaths. He left me in Vinnr and came back to Ærd. So now I've come to retrieve it. Vinnr is under attack, you see, from another of your kind, Balavad of Battgjald, and if we could *borrow* the Scrylle, we might be able to stop him."

Even as she spoke, she felt her hope sinking. If the Scrylle wasn't here, where had her father taken it? A coward twice over. Not only had he abandoned her but he'd never even returned to Ærd to face the consequences of what he'd done. He'd stolen their greatest advantage against Balavad, if her memories were correct, and never brought it back.

The Verity confirmed this a moment later. "Warden Evernal has not been seen in Ærd since before its ruin."

Mylla's hopes hit the bottom of her spirit and dissolved into nothing, like the last drops of rain on the desert floor. "So it's gone then, the Scrylle. And Balavad was victorious in Ærd, so there's no one here who can help us or Vinnr." She looked beside her to the older Knight. "I'm sorry for dragging you into this, Griggory. But it looks like we're stuck here."

"Come closer, Mylla Evernal," the vessel said, the tone of its crackling voice stinging like sparks against Mylla's eardrums.

She couldn't very well refuse, though she had no idea what the Verity wanted from her. For some reason, she grasped her pocketful of klinkí stones, as if they would help her, then stepped forward until she had to crane her head back to see Fimm's eye-lights.

"What do you hope to find in the Scrylle?"

"A way to stop Balavad and save Vinnr from becoming slaves to his will," she said simply. "Maybe other realms as well."

"You wish to stop a Verity." The Verity's tone was hard to read, but Mylla couldn't imagine it was anything but affronted. Did Verity's feel insulted? Did they even feel? She had no idea. Vaka Aster had gone into a state of stillness almost immediately after ordaining Mylla, and few of the Knights ever spoke of their exchanges between them and the Verity before Vaka Aster went silent completely.

"I wish to do whatever I can to stop my adopted home from falling to ruin like Ærd. Maybe the Scrylle can't *stop* Balavad, but it can be used to—"

Stop! Griggory yelled through the Mentalios so loudly that Mylla nearly put her hands to her ears. Shocked at his outburst, she turned and discovered he'd come up beside her. *Do you think it's wise to tell one of the Five that you mean to put another of them in a cage?* he asked, his tone as dry as the time walkers'.

He was right, of course. She was being incredibly foolish. She cleared her throat, but before she tried to walk back what she'd been about to say, several tendrils shot out from up and down the core of the Verity and wrapped her like a spider wraps a fly.

Mylla's mouth flew open to protest, or beg, whatever it would take to keep herself from being torn to pieces by an angry Verity. Cringing inside, she expected to feel that dreadful cold agony that had seeped into her when Balavad had immersed her in his toxic miasma. "Forgive me, I…"

Her voice trailed away as a strange sensation beat through her, something like Balavad's poison in that it came from the Verity, but nothing like it in that it wasn't, thank the moon and stars, painful. Something flared inside her, like a stoked ember, then it was gone. She felt nothing more besides the grip of Fimm's hard fibrous tendrils. A moment later, they released her and she dropped back to the ground only a foot or two below. She landed comfortably on her feet but nearly toppled anyway, half expecting to have been rendered infirm. Yet she felt… fine.

Fimm spoke again, voice unchanged. "The Scrylle will show you what you seek."

She was caught flat-footed again. Suddenly the Verity was being helpful? She wanted to chide herself for being suspicious. "It can tell us how to save Vinnr?"

"It can put an end to Balavad's deeds." At these words, Mylla's mouth fell open. "Find the Ærden Scrylle, Warden Evernal, and bring it back to me, if this is truly what you want."

"F-find it?" How was she supposed to do that? Her father could have taken it anywhere, and she didn't have a Scrylle of her own to travel the starpaths. "I want to, My Creator, more than anything. I would gladly do as you require, but I have no idea where to look. My father, Greven, was a traitor to you, even to his family, and it's been centuries. He could be anywhere in the Cosmos. Is there another way, anything I can do besides that? If you can help me save Vinnr, why do you need the Scrylle?"

The inferno eye-lights of the vessel blazed on, but the chamber settled into a charged quiet. Mylla waited, hoping Fimm was simply considering her words and would at any moment give her another option, any option. But the vessel didn't stir.

That rage Mylla remembered she'd had even as a little child suddenly reared. "Your own realm is all but dead because of Balavad. Don't you care? Don't you want to—to get even? *I'm* the one who lost everything! You can remake this world or a new one anytime you like, but you just sit there. Why should I do anything for you when you've done almost nothing for us?"

As her fire burned itself out, she took several deep breaths. From the corner of her eye, she could see Griggory shaking his head like a disappointed schoolteacher. She was still too enraged to care. And, damn the Verities, she was right to be angry. "What does it matter anyway? I can't even leave Ærd now without a way to open the starpath."

"Mylla Evernal," a tessalope wisped from behind her, and she turned to face it. "Greven Evernal never left Vinnr. He died—"

The creature suddenly did a most peculiar thing. All the lights along its tendrils shot toward its peak and burst from it, flying up toward the ceiling and dispersing like flickering fireflies, or like Vaka Aster's dragørflies. They spread out in every direction, then winked from existence. As they did, the tessalope's form grew harder to see, and then, like the lights, it disappeared too.

"What just happened..." Mylla whispered. Her eyes caught on something gleaming on the floor where the creature had stood. She took a step forward.

A crystalline sphere, filled with swirling fire. It looked like—no, it undoubtedly was—a Fenestros.

Needing confirmation that her eyes weren't playing tricks on her, she turned back to Griggory to see his reaction. He looked... glum, like he'd bid farewell to a friend. "Griggory, is it... dead?"

"It walks no more," he confirmed.

"Why? What caused it?" Nothing was making sense. Her father was dead? The tessalope was dead? Was everything coming to an end before her eyes?

Griggory didn't answer before the Verity spoke again. "Now you know where to look, Warden Evernal. Return with the Scrylle and you will see an end to Vinnr's trials."

A pinprick-sharp tingling began dancing along the skin of Mylla's arms and neck, a familiar sensation. A starpath was forming. "Fimm, wait!" she cried. "I have more questions!"

She realized she needn't have bothered asking the Verity for any favors, as her body began to change, to diffuse. She lunged for the Fenestros, wanting to take at least something of her one-time home with her, then she was space dust shifting ephemerally through the Cosmos once again.

CHAPTER SIXTEEN

"Shite on all this!" Mylla yelled, kicking a rock hard enough to bruise her right toes. So she kicked another one, using her left foot, and cursed again when it hurt as badly.

She spun on Griggory, who was gazing around the flanks of Mount Omina as if he'd never seen it, or any mountain, in his life. *I'm home,* she thought. Well, at least the Verity had done them *that* favor. They could have just as easily ended up somewhere else, given what little help they'd gotten in Ærd.

Immediately, she realized the season had changed. But of course it had. She'd been floating like a corpse in the depths of Himmingaze's Never Sea for something like a thirty-night while Vinnr had slid closer to early summer. The mountaintop air was still crisp, though, and piles of snow still lay in the shadows. But the real question was, how long had they been in Ærd? It only felt like a couple of days, but those days, spent first trudging under the gloomy, changeless sky, then within the unfathomably vast cavern of a once-living fortress, felt different. The time felt different, incalculable. Had they been gone just two Vinnric days, or more? Certainly not fewer. Having lost her bearings on time only added to her frustration.

Glancing at her traveling companion, she said, "So, we're back in Vinnr." She sighed. "Lucky us."

She'd hoped she would find a receptive audience for her frustrations with him, but it didn't take knowing him more than the short time she had to see he was anything but. The man lived in his own world. Unsurprising, she supposed, given how many worlds he'd seen. Then it occurred to her: *Might only be one more than you at this point.* She chuckled wearily at that thought. It didn't make a difference how many worlds she'd been to, how many she'd seen, if she only ended up back in Vinnr with no more answers but many more questions than when she'd left.

Considering their next move, she said aloud, but mostly to herself, "If I never cross paths with another Verity or wystic creature full of riddles, it will be too soon."

Something about that statement seemed to catch the old Knight's attention. "Wystic creature? How do you define that, hmm?"

He was peering at her as if expecting a deeply thought-out, possibly academic, answer. All she had was, "I don't know. Anything besides a human who's working in cahoots with a damned Verity."

He nodded thoughtfully. "A dragør, for instance." His eyebrows were raised, giving her the impression this was some kind of trick question.

No idea where this is going and don't care. "Yeah, sure, whatever. Look, we need to get out of here and find the rest of the Knights. We don't have time for any more of this trogghopping rubbish, and quite frankly, I'm sorry we even went to Ærd in the first place. Especially when all we have to show for it some more cryptic Verity nonsense and an impossible task that hardly seems worth the bother."

He looked pointedly at her hand, which still held the fiery Fenestros.

"All right, yes, and this. But what good will it do us?" Her toes throbbed, and her companion made her head throb right along with them, and she was utterly sick to death of these games.

"You don't believe Fimm spoke the truth, then?"

"What, about stopping Balavad if we bring the Scrylle back to… it? I know you're more of an expert on the topic of Verities than I'm likely to ever be, but what does it matter if Fimm spoke the truth or not? Something strange is going on there, no doubt, and I'm sure Fimm would like to have its trinkets back. But I'm not a messenger for a Verity. Not anymore. And I don't trust them either. Not after what I've seen." She thought of Balavad's toxic miasma. "And felt."

Griggory had caught sight of the half-ruined cave where the Knights had taken refuge for hundreds of turns and was staring at it wistfully. Without looking at her, he said, "So you're renouncing your oath, are you? The one to serve Vaka Aster."

When he put it like that, she felt more than slightly seditious. *Was that what she was doing?* "I… I mean, renouncing it is a bit extreme. I'm simply… what I'm doing is deciding exactly what the parameters of that oath are as I go along."

"Well, it's good then that your ordination by the other came as a matter of course. One cannot break an oath one has not taken." He stepped over to her and, for some odd reason, tapped her meaningfully right in the center of her throat.

She took a step back. "What are you—"

A memory flashed. Her father standing before a mirror with a razor in his hand. He'd been shaving, his chin tilted upward as he brought a straight razor over the bottom of his jaw. She'd been watching from near the hearth and saw the red circle in the center of his throat, right over the top of his prominent Adam's apple, with five jagged red lines radiating from it. The mark of the Wardens Temporalis. Fimm's mark.

Her hand flew to her throat. The skin felt normal, no different, but then, so did the skin on her chin where her indigo nine-pointed star was. When Fimm had wrapped her in its tendrils—that was when it happened. Now she realized why the Verity had called her Warden Evernal. "You're joking," she groaned.

"It's been many turns since I made a joke. It took me so long to understand humor, you know, the formula and the timing, but then it hardly took any time at all to forget. Funny. But not funny like a joke," he said.

She stared at him disbelievingly, mouth slightly open. Was Griggory incapable of normal reactions to anything?

"But now you'll have something unique to discuss with your new companion, Jaemus, won't you? You're now the closest in rank, even higher-ranked than the rest of us. Though, I'm not sure if rank has anything to do with anything." He looked toward the sky thoughtfully. "Except for Ulfric, of course. Being a vessel, he still has seniority. The *seniorest* seniority."

That was that, then. She was ordained now not only by Vaka Aster but by her true maker. "Twice ordained," she mused, unsure of her own feelings about it, and Griggory gave her his odd smile.

"I do so hope we learn what you're now capable of," he said. "Unlike Bardgrim, I don't believe you'll have the power of lightning at your... power." With a blink that seemed more flummoxed than embarrassed, he looked back toward the sanctuary.

She gave short derisive grunt of laughter. "Well, you're right about one thing. I didn't ask for this and didn't consent to it. And sure as a gimgree sloth smells like it's been thirty nights dead, I didn't take an oath to Fimm. Which means I owe the Verity nothing, and I have *no* obligation to find that Scrylle—as if it would even be possible. How big is the Weald anyway? And my father could have gone anywhere in Vinnr in the last three hundred odd turns. No, forget it. We're done with that quest, now with so much else at stake."

"Hmm," was all he said. "Night's falling. Let's get inside and rest awhile, shall we? Halla light often brings clarity to more than the land."

She replayed her words to herself as they walked toward the sanctuary, wrestling with her own impetuousness. She knew she *should* find that Scrylle. Not only because it could still aid them in their war against Balavad but now for more personal reasons. Knowing what happened to it might help her learn what had happened to Greven. And, though she felt justified in her disdain for him, she now had questions that weren't so easily answered by a simple "because he was a coward." The tessalope had said he'd died. Here in Vinnr. Which made her wonder, how had he died? *When* had he died? The last she'd seen of him, she'd been running away to try to get back to her mother, and there had been a bright light behind her. She'd assumed it was the starpath and he'd simply jumped away, leaving her behind. But what if it was something else?

What if she was wrong about him?

And now, because the possibility had been raised, and because she didn't want to feel this dread that her past was a maelstrom of shame and betrayal, she knew she would not rest peacefully until she knew Greven's fate, which was tied to the Scrylle's.

They passed through the splintering supports of the sanctuary's doorway. The interior was nearly full dark as Halla set outside. Mylla walked to the far wall where the keyhole to the interrealm well was. Restored, as her companions had assured her it would be. She reached out to run a finger over the fresh ruins carved there, preparing to discuss the options of where to go with Griggory.

At that moment, out of nowhere, a wave of exhaustion slammed into her. So much had happened so quickly. Not least of which was returning from the near-dead, followed by realm-hopping, and all her memories resurfacing. How could she be anything but tired? Turning, she put her back to the wall and slid down to a seat, not realizing she sat in the exact spot Eisa had just a few weeks prior.

"Griggory, before we figure out our next step, I just need a short nap. Can you take first watch?"

Before he answered, her eyes had shut and her haggard thoughts had given way to silence.

WHEN SHE OPENED her eyes again, Griggory had built a small fire and was now sitting at it, poking it lazily with a stick. The billions of lights of Vinnr's sky blazed through the rent in the cave's ceiling, and only a few hours had passed. She watched his gaunt face before saying anything, wondering what was going on behind his light-brown eyes. The little gold flecks in them picked up the firelight and glittered brightly, as if his eyes had stars of their own. The flickering reminded her a little of the time walkers, how the lights danced along their forms. He *knew* them, she thought. When had he even been in Ærd, if he'd been in Himmingaze for over seven hundred turns? His years serving as a Knight went on even longer than the Stallari's, something like two millennia. A man with so much history, so much knowledge. Yet he knew little of Vinnr anymore, he'd been gone from his own realm for so long…

As if hearing her thoughts, he spoke. "Seven hundred turns, and yet it hardly seems a day has passed since I last saw home."

She cleared her throat and sat up straighter, pulling her light tunic tighter. The cold that had seeped into her bones from Himmingaze's sea had been resummoned by the chill of Mount Omina. "You must be anxious to see everything, and see what's changed," she said.

"No, I'm not." He paused, deep in thought. "Though there is one whom I'd like to meet again."

"A Knight?" There wouldn't be anyone else left that had been alive in his time. The last few Knights, besides her present companions, had left the Order not long before she'd joined. She realized he must be speaking of Eisa.

"Of a sort," he said and circled a coal with his stick.

Mylla rose and moved closer to the fire, warming her hands over it. "Griggory, when the tessalope told me that my father had died and never left Vinnr, what happened to the creature? I know you know. I saw your face."

He tilted his head up and smiled at her, his big teeth glistening. "Timepaths, yes?"

"Are—are you asking me?" She didn't know what else to say except to agree with him and hope he fumbled into clarity somewhere along the way. "Um, yes?"

He nodded, as if that was the right answer. "Time walkers? Um-hmm," he answered for her. "And… time seers. You understand?"

No, she did not.

"They see time, My Evernal. They *are* time, therefore they know everything. The past, the future. The now."

She dropped her eyes to the coals, giving herself a moment to take in what he was saying. "So you're telling me they know the fate of everything and everyone?"

"They see, yes. But not everything and everyone. They only see the fate of those in their own time, in Ærd's time, because they are bound to Ærd until the timepaths between all the realms are remade."

She thought back to the memory of her father explaining the time walkers to her. "Like trees, they should be able to branch to all the realms."

He nodded again, vigorously. "Yes, yes. Like trees. When the realms were first created, the timepaths spanned among them all. Once, there was a time when every realm was connected, not by starpaths, which only leave a realm and enter a new one, but by time."

She didn't quite understand. "But it seems as if time flows the same in all the realms, even if they're not connected. Wouldn't that mean the timepaths aren't broken? Maybe they still exist somehow?"

"Ah, good question. Time still flows within realms because it's never been stopped."

"Are you saying time can be stopped?"

"If one knows how. But if one did stop time, then the realms' time would discontinue being in sync until the timepaths were reconnected. Did you notice how differently time passed in Ærd?"

She nodded.

"That is because a time walker is missing, the one your father took away. Time now moves slower there than here."

Intrigued despite the press of their own concerns, she asked, "Do you know how to stop time?"

He looked at her so keenly that she worried for a moment she'd insulted him. But it was a valid question, wasn't it? Finally, he sighed and went on. "If I did, My Evernal, seven hundred turns would not have passed in Himmingaze, with so much lost before it could be restored."

He appeared to be so dejected about Himmingaze that she felt bad for asking the question.

Soon he went on, seeming to have gathered himself. "But the time walkers do. That is why the Wardens Temporalis were called such, you know. They always focused more on learning the secrets of time than they did on tending to Fimm. But then, Fimm was different before Ærd was lost, and didn't need protectors. If only I'd been able to persuade them to tell me their secrets. I tried, I did, but they were resolute about hiding them. We are a destructive creature, you know. If just anyone could control time…"

After a moment where they both pondered this, Mylla turned the subject somewhat. "So then, what broke the timepaths?" It was the same question she'd had for her mother, though she didn't remember ever getting the answer.

He looked at her, his eyebrows raised. "When a thing that was flawless in its completeness is fractured, inevitably the pieces that compose it are also flawed. One might say, corrupted. That is the corruption that now runs through all things created by the Five, who were once the flawless One. The corruption that runs through Balavad. "

Of course it was Balavad's doing. Isn't everything?

"Do you know what the Fenestrii are, My Evernal?"

"Please, just call me Mylla. But, yes. They're celestial stones gifted to the people of the five realms to help them protect the vessels."

"That's true, but also untrue." He rummaged through the deep pockets in the heavy, tattered robe he wore over his strange Himmingazian costume and pulled out the Ærd Fenestros.

"Hey!" she said.

"You were sleeping," he said simply. "What were you going to do with it while you were sleeping?"

Pursing her lips, she deferred. "Go on. What am I missing about the Fenestrii?"

"These"—he held the orb up to catch the firelight—"are the means to restore the timepaths. They are the… the seeds of time. Yes, that quite works. The seeds. If they grow again, they will create new timepaths from wherever they are, and then they will all connect again. The Ærden tessalopes will, how did you put it? Branch, yes. And then time will once more run unbroken through the fates of *all*."

Funnily enough, this made an odd sort of sense. "Wait, tell me this.

The tessalopes in Ærd knew my father's fate because he is, was, Ærden. That means they know my fate, right?"

He blinked at her, eyebrows raised, saying nothing.

She went on, assuming she was on the right track. "So that means the tessalopes know if, and where, I'll find the Scrylle. Wouldn't it have just been easier to tell me that? And secondly, the one that started to change into a Fenestros before it could. Why did that happen to it?" Thinking about it anew infuriated her all over again.

"Ah, I suppose I should not be surprised that you know so little. You were young, weren't you, when your parents took you from Ærd? And you are still young, so young." Staring into the fire, he seemed to go off into his head for a bit the way he often did, and though she was getting used to it, her patience couldn't stand for it this time.

"And?"

Without taking his eyes from the fire, he stirred the largest coals, then went on when he was ready. "When the Verities made time, including the future, they chose not to give their creations control of it, or the power to see into it. This is one of their laws, a natural order of things that none but the Verities may affect. When the timepaths were severed, the tessalopes came into being and were trapped in Ærd. Though they can still see what we simple mortals call fate, they must yet adhere to the Verity laws. That one who spoke to you of your father broke this constriction, and so fulfilled its own fate."

"Its fate was to be reduced to a Fenestros?"

"Its fate was its fate. All the Fenestrii are merely timepaths waiting to sprout."

"You know, Griggory," she scoffed, "the more I learn about Verities and their ways, the less I like them."

"Hmm, and how do you feel about stars?"

"What?"

"The stars. Do you like them much?"

"What… I don't know, I don't have any feelings about stars. They're just shining rocks in the sky."

"And Verities are just Verities. How we feel about them does not influence or change what they are. They aren't people, Mylla.

Remember that. They will never feel things the way you and I do. You waste your time when you love or hate them. And now you've seen that time is precious."

She wanted to disagree with him, tell him his opinion was flirting with futility, but didn't bother. He'd finally spoken to her about things she needed to know and that actually made sense. Mostly. She let the conversation lag for a bit as she thought it over.

The time walker told me Greven was still here, and it... was stopped. Which means telling me that was in some way influencing my future, or fate. Does that mean that it's my fate to find him, or at least find out what happened to my father, then? And why?

Why indeed.

One thing was clear, she needed to learn what had become of her father and the Ærden artifacts. Yet she was beginning to think it had to do with more than merely stopping Balavad. She just didn't know what.

CHAPTER SEVENTEEN

Griggory slept for less time than Mylla had, and Halla's rays were slanting through the broken ceiling when Mylla rose, stretched, and blew some heat into her hands. She was about to awaken Griggory when her eyes snagged on the broken platform where Vaka Aster's vessel had stood.

"Stave's surprise," she mumbled. "I almost forgot."

The flat top of the dais was a thin sheet of stone and slid away easily. A hardy wood plank beneath it covered a hidden storage compartment. When she looked inside, her joy bubbled over.

"Star Spark!" She reached in and retrieved both sword and scabbard. They'd been with her nearly her entire Knighthood, and she hadn't realized till that moment how naked she'd felt without the hallowed weapon.

"The smithy who made that sword could juggle ten knives while singing you sixty verses of the Song of Figments and Fables without missing a word or a throw," Griggory said behind her, apparently awoken by her uncontained cry of delight. "His voice, though, Verities tears, it was like listening to a frog with the croup being squished in a vise. Even a deaf man would wish he was deafer at the sound. But Gudmund Øster could forge a sword like no other."

She stared at him, nearly unbelieving. Star Spark was at least as old as Ulfric. It had never occurred to her anyone alive would still know its pedigree, or its maker. By now, though, she was getting used to Griggory's many surprises.

"It had a sister sword, too. Lovely steel with a blue tinge. The way light glinted from it when you swung it, it looked like an icicle hanging from a glacier. What was its name… ?" He trailed off. "That was it, Winter's Bite."

"Yes," she said, nodding. "That sword still lies in the vaults in Vigil Tower."

As Griggory gathered himself, she rummaged through the storage container, finding a waterskin, several packets of nuts and seeds stored for emergencies by the Knights, a hallowed dagger called Dragørglint and its belt and sheath, which she offered Griggory, and various items of clothing. Gratefully, she found a jacket, shrugged it over her thin shirt, and tied some heavier cloths to her shins using leather ties she found inside as well. They'd likely need to come off once they were out of the mountains, but for now she relished anything that would warm her permanently chilled bones.

When she was done, she said to the eldest Knight, "Well, it's either to Vigil Tower through the interrealm well, or we have a long walk through the Howling Weald before us."

Griggory was tethering his ragged robe closed. At her comment, he spun toward her with a look of surprise. "A walk? Through the Weald?"

She nodded. "Well, I'm pretty certain Ærd Scrylle's not in Ivoryss, or else the Knights would have known about it. Which means it's probably still in the forest. If my father never left Vinnr, he must have died in the Weald, and with my memories coming back, I may be able to find where it happened. If his bones rest there, maybe the Scrylle does too."

"When was the last time you saw him?"

That was the question, wasn't it? She'd thought he'd left her for dead and taken the starpath well, but what if, in fact, she was the one who'd left him? "Shortly after we got here," she said. "We came from Arc Rheunos and were walking along the Great Province Byway.

Bandits attacked and killed my mother, and Greven grabbed me and ran. When we stopped, we'd gone deeper into the forest. I saw him readying the Scrylle to open a starpath, but I ran off before he did. I wanted..."

She paused for a moment, finding that along with her memories of that horrid day, her emotions were coming back too. That panic, that sheer anguish of seeing Ayanna fall by the roadside, was right now making her words feel thick and heavy. In a moment, she went on. "I wanted to get back to her. I think I knew even then that she was dead, but... so when my father set me down, I ran toward the road. I felt, or saw—I'm not sure—a flash like an emberflare cannon's behind me. I thought he was leaving me, taking the starpath and leaving my mother and me both. But now I think it might have been something else."

"A dragør."

She shouldn't have been surprised he guessed it. "Yes, a dragør. When I got back to the road, one of the beasts showed up and inciner-ated the bandits, along with my mother's body. I don't remember seeing it, but there's nothing else it could have been. That's where it all stops, my memories. I think I must have been found not long after." *I'll probably never know why the dragør spared me,* she thought. *Or why Vaka Aster left me in Himmingaze after the fight on Balavad's warship, for that matter. I seem to be perpetually forgotten or ignored.*

"If the dragørs have the Scrylle, that would explain much," Griggory said as he tightened down his dagger belt and started for the entryway, raring to go.

His statement was curious. The dragørs might have the Scrylle? It made some sense, she supposed. They'd been around, as far as humans were concerned, forever, and had been Vaka Aster's first protectors. They'd know the value of a Scrylle as much as anyone. "You're all right walking into the Weald to look for the artifact, knowing how dangerous it is?" she asked.

"It's a long walk. Shall we?"

His note of impatience did not go unnoticed. Shrugging, she followed him out.

The chilled high-mountain air outside the cave was enough to wipe away any last residue of fatigue she felt, and it propelled them quickly down the mountain. The west side of Mount Omina had the most direct paths to the Great Province Byway, and in the process would put them on the Ivoryss side of the Morn Mountains and closer to the capital, Asteryss. Most importantly, these were the paths her parents had traveled all those turns ago. Perhaps they would jog more of her memories.

Mylla didn't savor having to traverse the avalanche-strewn slopes and blackened forest along the mountain's flank, where she'd thought they'd lost Symvalline and Isemay, but knowing the two of them had survived gave her a boost of resolve. To help matters along, it was clear that other travelers had come this way and already found the easiest path down since Mylla had last set foot on the mountain. *Must have been the Ivoryssians Vaka Aster brought back from Himmingaze. Whatever the reasons Verities do, or don't, aid their own creations, I'm grateful she decided to rescue so many from Balavad.*

But not me...

She and Griggory picked plants and berries to eat with their preserved nuts on the way, even such meager sustenance enough to revive them. The rough going of their descent found them at the mountain's base by late evening, and they spent the night short of reaching the Great Province Byway.

The byway was an ancient road that had been there even when Griggory was still young. Though its maintenance grew shoddier and shoddier the farther one got from Asteryss, there was no way to miss the wide flagstone passage, and their pace quickened when they reached it early the next morning.

Once, they heard a speeding skimmer coming toward them from Ivoryss. Deciding to err on the side of caution, they hid in the thick brush beside the road. Mylla's guess was the travelers were heading to Yor to warn of danger and possibly seek aid. By now, the realm must be teeming with news of the Dyrraks and their potential aggressions, and it seemed best to simply let them be on their way. The Knights had their own plans, and once Mylla found what she was seeking, she hoped to rejoin them.

By late evening, she was beginning to recognize landmarks from her memories. The moss growing on the stones edging the roadside was thicker, some of the trees younger, and many older, but the shapes of mountains never changed no matter how long one lived. She now knew the highest peaks to the north as Dryft and Tarmvred, and in the distance almost too far to see was the Wilt, where the bruhawk aeries were hidden. *I wish Yggo or Urgo was with us now. They might be able to aid us if we do encounter a—*

That thought was cut off abruptly as she spotted something familiar. "There, that crooked rowan. I remember that."

As a child, she'd noticed it immediately when Ayanna had warned her father to stop speaking. Their eyes had all shot to the side of the road where the brush was moving near the old rowan's trunk. It was at least twice as wide as her arms could reach around and had been split midway sometime long past. But these Weald trees did not die easily. One branch of the split had continued upward, still growing strong, but the other had bowed into a half-rainbow shape with time. It was still sprouting green leaves, and its lower branches dipped down toward the earth like a willow. It was striking in its resilience, and it had remained lodged in her memories.

Griggory was looking around him as if lost, and she continued. "This spot is where we were standing when... when the bandits struck."

That panicky feeling resurged, tightening her throat. She scanned the road around them. She didn't know why. It wasn't as if she'd see the bodies or the char left by the dragør, not after this long. But then, she did. Or the mark at least of where they'd been, for several large flagstones had been laid down that were clearly newer than those around them. *Those are replacing the ones burned by dragørfire. Is it actually hot enough to burn, or even melt, stone?* The bandit's skin had melted from his bones, so she knew it was at least that hot.

"We need to backtrack a bit. My father carried me back toward Omina when we were attacked. It shouldn't be far."

They'd paced barely twenty yards when she saw what she now expected. Two more rowans with a set of branches that reached for each other and entwined in a natural arch. She'd passed under those in her father's arms.

The sky to the west was beginning to darken. "We probably shouldn't stay on the road tonight. There may be more travelers, and there's no reason to interfere with them. Ready for a night in the Weald, Griggory?" She looked to her left, where she thought he was, but he was gone. "Griggory?" She just caught sight of him as he disappeared beneath the arching branches. "I guess that's yes."

Mylla might have known one relatively calm and peaceful night was all she should expect, for it was certainly all she was going to get.

She and Griggory had set up a bare-bones camp by a massive, hoary downed tree beside the road just as Halla set. As expected Mylla's leg coverings had become unnecessary, and they'd used the thin leather straps that had secured them to her shins in hare snares, catching two for their dinner. Without even considering why she thought he knew, she'd asked Griggory if he thought a fire to roast them was safe. Griggory, it was obvious by now, had spent more time in the Weald than probably any human living, and she assumed he'd know what risks they might safely take before arousing the attentions of predators, such as a dragør.

His concerns, if he'd had any, apparently hadn't been worth remarking on, and the fire cooked the hares to perfection. In fact, they were unaccountably delicious. Mylla supposed their good flavor was due to her having eaten little in the weeks prior, given that she'd been seabound and near dead.

As they chewed the savory rabbits, she asked, "How did you know to look for me? I mean, after you saw the warship explode."

"Oh," he remarked. "I didn't. The slangarooks know a marked one, though. They saw you there, sunken and waterlogged, and word got back to me."

Her brow wrinkled. "Slangarooks? You mean those water dragør creatures?"

He nodded, snapped a small bone, and sucked the marrow out. She guessed he didn't even realize the low, pleased sound he was making in the back of his throat.

"Good rabbit?"

"Good? Mylla, good is warm water splashed over your face, the feel of a velvet scarf around your neck, maybe the sound of a lullaby when you're a child. This"—he raised the stick his dinner was skewered on—"this is the taste of divinity. I had quite forgotten how good creatures of Vinnr, creatures that live on land, could taste."

His innocent joy at a simple spitted rabbit made her smile. After chewing a few more bites, she pressed, "These slangarooks, then. Are they able to speak like myths say dragørs can?"

Instead of answering, he set his carcass, now just bones, down, and gave her what she had come to recognize as his school's-in-session stare. "Have you ever wondered why the creatures of every realm are so similar? Maybe not in color and shape, but in all ways that matter? We can breathe each other's air, recognize each other's seasons, eat foreign foodstuffs. Hmm?"

"I, um, I hadn't ever thought about it, I guess."

His head was bowed toward the fire, but he peered up at her crabbily beneath thick brows. "What can they be teaching at the Conservatum anymore? Well, I'll spell it out, I suppose, since you don't seem to be learning it elsewhere. We all come from the same Five, yes?" Before she could answer, he went on. And she was grateful he did, because her own grumpiness had been triggered. "The Five were the One, as you know. At least, you know *now*. So we all come from the One. Are you following?"

"I think so."

"That is why the realms are similar. The One. And that is why the answer to your question is yes. The slangarooks, the dragørs, all cousins, they all… communicate. They all know the First Tongue, though you wouldn't say they *speak*."

"… They communicate, but they don't speak. That right?"

"It's what I said, yes."

Overcoming the urge for a sarcastic response, she opted for a diplomatic one: "It's clear I have a great deal more to learn." Deciding she wasn't in the mood for his pedantry after all, she rose and stepped outside the firelight to bury her own bare rabbit carcass before he could continue lecturing and kick her patience to death.

Once finished, she moved back to the fire and said, "We should sleep while we can. I'll take—"

But she was speaking to no one besides the rabbit bones Griggory had carelessly dropped.

Looking around, she called quietly, "Griggory? Hey—Knight Dondrin?" Even as she spoke, she slowly backed away from the fire until she was just another shadow among the forest's many. He might simply be taking a moment to pass water or look for more fallen twigs to burn. Whatever he was doing, though, he should have known better than to just disappear without a word to her.

Her fingers already clenched her klinkí stones, now held at her side. From behind a wide tree trunk a dozen paces from the fire, she kept a silent vigil, waiting for his return.

Minutes passed as she watched and listened. To her straining ears, it seemed that the forest grew quieter rather than familiar. She didn't call for him again. Her guts were telling her he was… gone.

And soon, they told her something else. Griggory might not be present, but she wasn't alone.

CHAPTER EIGHTEEN

Jaemus recognized Havelock Rekkr from his brief glimpse of him at Vigil Tower, when Safran had told him that Mylla had died. He'd forgotten about that until now. The mix of emotions that danced over the man's face at learning his love still lived moved Jaemus, but it also made him realize how complicated his situation with his own lifemate had gotten. Cote was just a man, after all. *He'd be so much better at this role than I am, though*, Jaemus thought and knew *that* conversation was in their future. Their *near* future, he hoped. If Jaemus was going to live forever, or some approximate length of time that might as well be, he damn well wasn't going to do it without Cote.

He pulled himself out of his thoughts and refocused on the conversation.

Havelock was telling the Knights: "Brun has turned Vigil Tower into a garrison. Between its walls and Aster Keep's, and potentially some of the catacombs if we can barricade them well enough, the whole city should be able to take refuge if we're attacked again. And the towers offer unequaled defenses."

"Thanks to the armory Roi and I've been hammering out for that last few centuries," Stave grumbled. The Knight's inner blacksmith had never been idle, and Jaemus knew many rooms in Vigil Tower were positively bursting with all the weapons he'd crafted over his many years.

"Yes, and we should be thankful the fruits of your calling won't have gone to waste," Symvalline said to Stave. "And Brun has always seemed a competent commander." She looked at Havelock. "Am I right in guessing she's kept Vigil Tower from being too badly… I don't want to use the word 'looted,' but Ulfric has told me that the city folk and Beatte were"—she cracked a cynical smile—"*disgruntled* at the circumstances of the Knights' leaving."

"Which is Beatte's own fault, it is," Stave proclaimed.

Havelock was nodding. "As far as I know, Commander Brun is protecting it as much as occupying it. You had an herb garden in the western tower, didn't you, Knight Lutair? I wouldn't be surprised if the commander has laid a pallet down among your plants and guards them with her life."

"Brun is a gardener?" Symvalline asked.

"She's a fair hand at growing anything, but she's especially skilled at hops and rye."

Jaemus saw Stave's unshapely eyebrows rise in surprised appreciation, though he couldn't guess why these particular plants called hops and rye would elicit that reaction.

"Wing Rekkr," Ulfric cut in. "It's a favor I wouldn't ask otherwise, but there is too much at stake not to. Would you precede us at the Vigil Tower and prepare Brun for our arrival? I know I'm asking you to leave your post, but—"

"Say no more, Stallari. I know what's at stake. It will take me till nightfall to reach Asteryss."

"No, Wing. You're going the fast way," Ulfric said.

Havelock's eyes widened. "Through the interrealm well?"

"Safran, will you accompany him?"

She nodded.

"Then you go ahead and speak to Brun. We'll follow in two hours' time. Let's get to the well."

"First, I should show you where I've left my Wing fighter. You may need it."

He walked the Knights to a stand of trees about six hundred paces down the flank of the mountain. Several of the trees seemed to have been chopped in half by a tremendous ax. The top half of about a dozen of them had splintered and fallen over, coming to rest in the branches of the still-whole ones, creating a chaotic jumble. As they approached, Jaemus could see a small flying craft situated as far back in the copse as it could go, camouflaged with broken-off branches. It could only be spotted from close.

His engineer's curiosity was immediately aroused. It was smaller than any craft he'd flown or built in Himmingaze, and sleek, like an insect of some sort. He wanted—*now, be honest with yourself, Jae*—he *had* to know more about it.

Turning to the group, he said, "While we're waiting, Wing Rekkr, would you mind if I took a peek at your, er, did you call it a 'fighter'?"

"I FIGURED you'd be back one way or another, Stallari."

A dark-skinned, sharp-chinned woman wearing heavy-looking armor stood before the Knights as they stepped into the Verity chamber at the top of Vigil Tower. Her eyes were a light gray, and when her sharp gaze fell on Jaemus, he felt for a moment he was being stared at by the slangarook again. When she blinked, her eyelids moved slowly, as if her penetrating gaze was all-seeing all the time, immediately putting Jaemus ill at ease. So he did what came naturally.

"Ah, hello, madam. Commander Brun, is it? We haven't yet met. I'm Jaemus Bardgrim, Knight Corporealis—newly minted Knight, actually —and a pilot and glint engineer by way of Himmingaze. Not to mention a Mystae of the Creatress. It's a pleas—"

Ulfric saved them all from his further babbling. "This is our newest member, Commander. He's Himmingazian, hence his unique features, but ordained by Vaka Aster."

"As I was saying," Jaemus couldn't help but add, then stopped himself from saying more.

"Given what Wing Rekkr and Knight Glór have said, you'll need all the Knights you can get." The commander dismissed Jaemus and turned to another soldier standing near the room's doorway. "Wing Owers, wait outside and close the door. Tell the company that I don't want to hear a knock until I'm done here unless a Verity itself is asking to speak to me. Clear?"

The soldier, unarmored and wearing a light tunic like Wing Rekkr's, nodded and paced outside.

Brun then addressed Ulfric in the memory keeper. Safran had apparently prepared her ahead of time for the oddity. "Let me just tell you right now, Stallari Aldinhuus, your best intentions have sunk us all in not just a pot of hot water, but an ocean of it. I know you thought you were helping when you called on Vaka Aster, and maybe you were. But thanks to that little party you and the Dyrraks threw in Aster Keep, and how badly you humiliated Beatte, where you're standing at this moment is as close as you're going to get to the Arch Keeper. This war you say is coming will start the moment she knows you're here."

Even in miniature, Ulfric's scowl was obvious to everyone in the room. "I was afraid of that. Commander, your level head is the only thing that's going to ensure Ivoryss prevails against the Dyrraks serving Balavad. We need your help in handling the Arch Keeper."

The commander snorted. "Her confidence in me has waned somewhat." Brun began pacing back and forth before the heavy, ornate seat on which Vaka Aster had once sat. "Beatte trusts me to fight our enemies, but she now only listens to a handful of advisors, and I've been reporting to them of late. So from Vigil Tower, I'm doing my job to protect this city, while being somewhat less conversant with the Arch Keeper. What I know is, we've had scouts watching the shipways from Dyrrak since you left, and they are coming. A small forward force of thirty ships has amassed at Udunum Island in the Verring Sea."

"That's a half day's sail from Asteryss, isn't it?" Mallich asked.

"A full day on an Ivoryssian ship, but I'm sure I don't have to tell you how fast our enemies' are." She paused from her pacing long enough to pass a censorious eye over the Knights, then resumed. "They've stayed put for the last three days. We assume they're waiting for further orders, but of our own fleet, what wasn't damaged or outright sunk in Balavad's first attack was all but finished off by the Dyrraks when they, and when you, left. We can't do anything about them on Udunum, so we're fortifying our sea walls with heavy armaments and have emptied both Aster Keep's and Vigil Tower's armories." She looked to Stave. "Which are *very* impressive."

"I know," Stave said.

"And what of Yor? Has Beatte secured their allegiance against Dyrrakium?" Ulfric asked.

Brun snorted. "Fergus and his entourage were gone before the dock fires were out upon your departure. I don't think he has confidence in Beatte to handle what's coming."

The Knights exchanged worried glances, and Jaemus began to wonder if he'd made the wrong choice in coming the Vinnr.

"As far as Balavad goes," the commander went on, "I only know what Wing Rekkr has told us. The Battgjald Verity is back, according to you, and he's taken over the Dyrraks." Stopping to speak face-to-face with Ulfric, she said, "If Balavad was going to take over an army, why couldn't he have gone after the Yorish? We would have had a chance against them. But the Dyrraks? However over-keen I might find their adherence to their ancient traditions, there's no denying their strength and discipline are going to make them nearly impossible to beat—and that's if we were at full strength. So you tell me, Stallari, what are we going to be up against? Because it was obvious to me before you and your Order even left with them that they'd be back." She added coldly, "The only way to stop fanaticism is to slaughter it."

At this point, Jaemus felt so out of his element that he was considering whether or not he could sneak away and be unnoticed. He glanced toward Ulfric, who was staring fixedly at him, as if he'd read Jaemus's mind—which, he hated to admit, wouldn't be the first time. With a "who me?" smile, he forced himself to stop glancing toward the door and listen as Ulfric provided Brun with what explanation he could.

The commander's face grew hard as Ulfric outlined in brief but discouraging detail what they'd seen of the Dyrrak forces: several dozen squadrons of aerial combat craft, ten to each squadron; a fleet of at least three hundred troop-carrying oceanic ships; and an empire's worth of warriors who'd trained to fight since they were children. Lastly, many if not all these Dyrrak warriors would be celestially cursed to increase their resilience so much that one of them would have the strength of five Ivoryssian soldiers. To Jaemus, the whole situation sounded as unnerving as it did unwinnable. He couldn't imagine living in a world where it was not only normal that your neighbor or your kingdom's neighbor might attack you at any moment, but it was also so common that people had written entire libraries of books on strategy for counteracting (or performing) such actions and built entire war-waging machines for just that possibility.

"In short, Commander," Ulfric concluded. "There's only one way Ivoryss will endure their attack. When they come, you must surrender."

Brun's pacing had resumed as she'd listened to Ulfric. At his last statement, she came to an abrupt stop, the metal of her armor clicking distinctly.

Then she began laughing, but there was no humor in it.

"Stallari, if you think Ivoryss would give up without a fight, you've been out of touch with your own people for far too long." She wiped her mouth with the back of a hand, and the last of her grin turned into a thin-lipped frown. "A statement like that might even make me wonder if you're working for our enemy."

It was Ulfric's turn for a humorless chuckle. "You know better than that, Brun," he said flatly.

She held her stiff pose silently, her eyebrow cocked in a challenge. "Do I?"

"Do you have a choice?"

CHAPTER NINETEEN

Ulfric and Brun stared at each other long enough that Ulfric began to strongly suspect they would have to disarm her and her entire garrison and lock them up until they could figure out another way to persuade the Ivoryssians that fighting was suicide. That, or simply let them meet their slaughter head on. Then the Knights would be free to slink ignominiously into Dyrrakium and retrieve his body and Vaka Aster's vessel while the Dyrraks were wading in Ivoryssian blood.

Shortly, though, her good sense saved her, and maybe Ivoryss as well. She broke eye contact, glanced at each of the other Knights, and said, "I've never been a gambler, but the only way I can see to survive as a realm is by putting all our efforts behind whatever you Knights plan to do." She looked pointedly at Ulfric. "Please tell me you have a plan."

Careful to hide both his relief and his sudden dread, he held back the truth. The fact was, they didn't have a plan, not really. Except for the one that had started to form as he'd explained things.

His companions weren't going to like it, and it cut him a little inside too, he had to admit. But it was time to tell not only Brun but the rest of his companions what he'd decided the next step would be. "For now, I need—"

His voice was drowned out by a clanking and clattering coming from the stairwell, and the sound of several sets of boots. They weren't coming in a calm, measured manner, but quickly. Everyone turned to the doorway, still closed after Wing Owers was set on watch.

"Mallich, bar the door," Ulfric ordered.

A moment after the Yorish Knight had lowered the stout beams, someone began hammering against the heavy wood, followed by a voice: "Commander Tannir Brun and Knights Corporealis, open this door immediately or we will break it down."

"Owers, that bastard," Brun growled. "He turned you in."

"Jimp wouldn't do that—" Wing Rekkr began, but Brun held up a hand sharply to silence him.

She stepped toward the door and squared up to it as if she'd fight first it, then anyone who dared come through it. "By whose authority, Marine? Or did you forget I'm the commander of this military?"

There seemed to be a hesitation, but it was short. "Arch Keeper Beatte's authority, Commander Brun, and you don't command the Keeper's Guard. Now open the door and face your fate for the crime of harboring and aiding the traitors."

Brun turned away from the door, grumbling about her disdain for someone named Jarmand, presumably the leader of the Keeper's Guard. "Always had more ambition than honor." She spat, then looked at Ulfric in the memory keeper. "Take the interrealm well back to Mount Omina and just go. I'll face this on my own. I'm not going to open that door to a fight I know those guards can't win. Your wystic stones will shred them before they'll even know what hit them. Some of those soldiers aren't sensible enough to see how foolish and delusional Beatte is, but that doesn't mean they deserve to die."

"What about you, Brun?" asked Safran, using a Fenestros to be heard.

"I'll... do whatever's necessary."

"Magdaster," Havelock suddenly blurted, and the thunk of something heavy and thick slamming into the chamber's door punctuated him.

"What?" Brun said.

"The Knights should go to Magdaster." As an afterthought, he added, "And so should you and I. Commander Nennus has the city battened down as tight as a drum. It's walled, it's fortified for a long siege, and their heavy cannons have been able to hold off dragørs for a thousand turns. They should be able to hold off the Dyrraks for at least as long." He looked to the Knights. "If you go to Magdaster, Nennus can be persuaded to help in whatever plans you have for facing Balavad."

The door was battered again and the hinges rattled. Bits of stone dust fell where the iron of the hinges was embedded in the thick stone walls as the apparatus was jolted. The door would hold back a dragør itself, but the hinges might not for much longer.

Brun considered this and asked the Wing, "Your father and family are still there, right?"

Havelock nodded.

"What do you think?" she asked the Knights as another strike hit the door.

"If Asteryss falls to the Dyrraks, Magdaster will be the last defensible city in Ivoryss, it will," Stave said. "It'll be a good place to hold out and let Balavad come to us. Fight him on our own soil in the arena we choose, a solid advantage. And we know that worm-slurper will come, eventually. He'll not want to miss the sweet moment of victory, but we'll have a few surprises that make that sweet turn rancid, we will."

Ulfric immediately recognized the strength of this argument. Balavad had already shown by his mere presence how much he relished the feat of conquering other Verities' creations in the flesh. "Magdaster it is. Brun, you'll come too."

Brun looked so offended at that, it was as if Ulfric had said something disgusting about her mother. "I'm not a coward. I won't abandon my city."

THUNK.

"Is it more cowardly to be killed because of stubbornness and lose the fight, or to do what you must to live long enough to beat your enemy?" Ulfric said flatly. He understood Brun's knee-jerk reaction. Her kind, and he'd known hundreds over the centuries, had so much honor they sometimes almost choked on it. If given enough time, he hoped her sense of reason would break through her misguided ideas of what was right.

THUNK. The bottom hinge popped free of the wall. He just hoped it didn't take more than the next few seconds.

"Nennus will need your insight into the Dyrraks," Mallich offered in his infinitely calm manner. "His command is only as strong as the knowledgeable and skillful troops at his side. You have more of both than most. And you've faced both the Raveners and the Dyrraks already. You can help him fight wisely."

Brun appeared unconvinced.

Ulfric gave it one last try. "Commander, I know it was wrong to ask you to tell your soldiers to surrender to Balavad. They are noble and decent fighters, to the last. And when we prevail"—*THUNK*—"the people of Asteryss and the Dragør Marines will need to be able to look back at this war and know that they kept their honor and their spirit and never backed down.

"But the only way they'll ever have that chance is if we *beat* Balavad. And to do that, everyone must sacrifice, and everyone must play the part they are best suited for. Asteryss can't hold out for long. Magdaster can, and if you help keep their garrison standing for long enough, I swear to you on my Knighthood"—*THUNK*. Another hinge popped—"you'll get vengeance for your troops who've already fallen and who may yet fall."

Brun turned partially away from them, her head lowered. She sighed. "When did turning traitor become my duty?"

None answered her—what was there to say?

Finally, she faced Symvalline and the memory keeper, wearing a mask of fury. "I'll come, but you have to swear one of you will help me get the rest of my troops that I'm being forced to walk away from out of here and to safety."

Ulfric's oath to Vaka Aster, taken so long ago, sprinted through his mind. His duty was to Ivoryss, not to any commoner, no matter how noble.

But inside his heart, he'd forsaken that duty a hundred times already. It wasn't hard for him to respond, and he only hoped he responded for all the Knights. "You have our word."

Not one to dally, Mallich turned to Havelock. "No time for us to send you in advance. You and I will go first. Sym, Ulfric, you and the bruhawks follow me. Then Safran and Brun, Stave and Jaemus."

Everyone crowded around the hub to the interrealm portal. As Mallich placed his Mentalios in the keyhole, Ulfric knew it was time to tell them his alternate plan.

He said simply, "Try to draw Balavad to you in Magdaster and hold the Dyrrak forces off as long as you can. I'm not coming with you. I have to go Udunum Island."

CHAPTER TWENTY

To his utter lack of surprise, Ulfric was right, they didn't like his plan. But with only one hinge remaining before the door fell, there'd been no time to argue.

They'd tried anyway.

"Vaka Aster's eyes, Ulfric, don't be crazy!" Stave had shouted. "You infiltrate the Dyrraks alone and you may as well walk up to Balavad and hand him the rope to hang you with—not that you can walk… or be hung, actually. But you know I'm right!"

Ulfric couldn't have missed the shock in their faces if he'd been blind, but it was to Sym he spoke next. "Hold the memory keeper where I can see you, my love."

She raised the pendant. "Ulfric, I can't let you do this. It's not just your life you're risking—it's everything and everyone."

"My love, I know it seems that way. But we don't have a ship that can carry the lot of us, and even if we did, Stave's right. Going as a group to the island, or Dyrrakium itself, may as well be purposely jumping into Balavad's trap. We can't take on their entire army. Balavad has to know Eisa was able to help Mallich, Safran, and Stave escape before she succumbed. And Eisa knows you're alive now, too,

Sym. They'll be waiting for all of you. But they won't be waiting for me. And you're all forgetting something."

"Forgetting when it was you lost your damn mind," Stave grumbled. "Was it before or after you turned into Vaka Aster herself and blew that bastirt Balavad's whole realm into extinction?"

Ulfric, grasping his patience like a drowning man grasps a log, went on as calmly as he could. "No one will even know I'm there. I have some *unique* abilities when it comes to stealth." *Don't I, old friend?* he said to Urgo.

The bruhawk startled everyone with a blunt screech and ruffled his wings.

They each looked toward the bird, the realization of what Ulfric was talking about dawning quickly. A moment passed, then Brun helped force the decision along. "Figure out your plans, Knights, because if we don't leave now, some of us may not leave at all."

That had done it. At Ulfric's direction, Symvalline had draped the memory keeper onto Urgo's neck. Jaemus also passed Yggo one of the Himmingazian Fenestrii in a small pouch that hung around her neck. It would aid long-distance communication and give Ulfric a few extra wystic options.

With a final explanation of, "I'll figure out what needs to be done, then I'll meet you in Magdaster. Don't worry, Knights, I'll see you all soon. Help them hold their walls until I return. And keep your faith in this fight, because it is far from over."

He'd wanted to say more, much more, but he knew if he'd told Symvalline what he'd been thinking—*When you see our daughter again, tell her how much I love her and always will*—she'd have interpreted it the way he half-feared she should—as a goodbye, his final words before he disappeared from their lives for eternity. And he wasn't going to entertain the idea that he, that any of them, was going to die. Not yet.

As the Knights made for the interrealm well, Yggo had launched from one of the chamber's high-arched windows immediately. But he'd had Urgo wait on the ledge, watching as the Knights whisked through the well. Symvalline had gone last. She'd said nothing, but he'd known what she was feeling. He'd been feeling it too. They'd only just been reunited, and now had to take separate paths again. Being a Knight Corporealis had never been easy, but it had also never been this cruel.

As soon as she was gone, the chamber's door shuddered and fell inward. Ten armored soldiers pushed through and had been comically stunned to find no one there to fight. Their leader spotted Urgo just before the bruhawk alighted, and of course he recognized the enormous, regal bird. There were only two in Ivoryss, known to all the commoners as companions of the Knights. Urgo hissed at the Keeper Guard, then they were soaring through the air above the city, making for the sea and Udunum Island. The bruhawks, being descended from dragørs, and these two in particular being ordained by Vaka Aster, flew at speeds that easily matched the fastest Ivoryss ship. It only took them a few hours.

Despite the anchored Dyrrak force, which was large enough to break through Asteryss's remaining sea-facing defenses, the island was relatively easy for the bruhawks to reach. Ulfric needed information, and if he and Urgo were very crafty, he'd be able to get it without even needing to land. The hawk simply had to drop the memory keeper close enough to a Dyrrak to draw their attention, and once they picked it up, Ulfric could slip inside their mind like a thief.

The hawks flew high enough to remain unseen by those on the island, and upon arrival, they circled like vultures, their great silvery eyes and unparalleled vision observing the force below. The lighthouse on Udunum had been unattended for several decades, thanks to undying illuminate orbs providing light to seagoing vessels. Only on occasion did work crews come out to ensure the ancient tower itself was maintained and to check the condition of the light. Otherwise, it was a small, barren rock alone amid the waves of the Verring Sea.

He counted exactly thirty ships present, anchored all around the island. One was the *Gildr*, the ship he and the Knights had so recently sailed in to Dyrrakium. Seeing it jolted that spark of hope in his chest —if the fleet's leading ship was here, it was possible, perhaps likely, the force was being led by the Domine Ecclesium.

The thought of seeing the turncoat sent a wave of eager wrath through Ulfric that spilled over into Urgo, who emitted a piercing, ferocious trill like the last sound heard by the bruhawk's prey before it was ripped apart in his knife-edged talons. *This disembodiment would be made worth it just for the chance to serve justice to that traitor myself—using the old ways, before civility made torture unseemly,* he mused.

They timed their arrival for dusk. As Halla fell below the western horizon, the bruhawks fished the waves for a hearty dinner, and as night fell, they found the perfect place to perch and wait for a likely victim where they'd never be seen: at the peak of the lighthouse's roof. Anyone who looked directly toward it would be blinded by the massive illuminate orb that had spent all day absorbing Halla's rays.

There they waited, needing only one isolated Dyrrak for Urgo to sweep in on stealthy wings and drop the pendant near. Before the night had progressed far, their prey came to them.

A shore party of five Dyrraks arrived in a dinghy with a variety of tools and equipment under tarps and in boxes piled in the boat's center. As they alighted and began to unload, the bruhawks kept a close watch for any who strayed far enough from the others to give them their chance. Two sets of two carried boxes toward the light-house entry, leaving one alone at the boat.

With the memory keeper held in his talons, Urgo dove like a comet and dropped the pendant with expert precision around the lone Dyrrak's neck. Ulfric was already whispering the now intimately familiar chant: *With thine eyes, these eyes too see.* And in as little time as it took to draw a breath, he could feel himself shift from Urgo and slide into the man's thoughts.

But they were not the kind of thoughts he'd been expecting. They felt as cold as a snake's belly, and thick, almost soupy. The Dyrrak was a Ravener, and whatever his mind may once have been, it was now an inhuman thing under the sway of its master.

Loathing overcame Ulfric at once, and it was all he could do to refrain from calling Urgo back immediately. The Ravener felt the pendant drop around his neck, and his hands shot up to rip it free. Ulfric was only just able to stop him. Forcing his control of the man's arms was easier than it had been of Salukis's wings, which he supposed he should be grateful for, yet that feeling of his own mind brushing against the creature's remote and *wrong* thoughts made it hard to concentrate.

Just my luck, he thought as the remaining Dyrraks took their equipment inside. *I hadn't thought about what it would be like to inhabit something so foreign and so... cursed.*

"Venerate," a woman's voice called from ahead in the darkness. "What are you waiting for? Get over here and hold the door."

Ulfric froze. He wasn't sure if the man was expected to answer, and if so, how?

"Hurry it up, Venerate… or whatever you are," the speaker finished, her last statement mumbled to herself.

If he didn't want to arouse any suspicion, he had to do something. Forcing the Ravener to hide the pendant inside his leather overtunic, he hurried the man to the lighthouse entrance. The creature didn't resist, but he'd become somewhat enervated and hard to motivate. This was almost worse than having to fight the man's own will to make him do what Ulfric wanted, and his bonelessness forced Ulfric to divide his focus between forward momentum that looked at least somewhat natural, and keeping him upright in the first place.

The resulting first step was little better than a shambling lurch, and Ulfric's worry surged at how obvious the difference in the man's behavior would be. But that wasn't even the worst problem. He'd lost the ability to see.

At first he'd thought he was simply getting used to his new senses in the night's darkness, but that assumption was quickly squashed. Ulfric had become used to his sharpened vision as Vaka Aster, and then as Urgo, and being suddenly visually incapacitated was somehow worse for that fact. He'd never felt so vulnerable.

Of course they're sightless, fool, he told himself. *You've seen their eyes. But they're not bumbling and useless—they're trained and effective fighters. Which means they see, somehow. Now keep moving and... figure it out!*

He put the man's next foot forward, reaching out with his mind and grasping every sensory element he could for guidance on where to lay the foot down. Sensations reached him, almost as if he had summoned them: the damp mist, swirled by a slight easterly breeze; the ebbing smell of brine as the breeze passed him; the lapping of water inside a hollow between the shore's rocks and against the dinghy; the scrape of one of the oars in its oarlock; the warmth of the pendant—now that was surprising, he hadn't known the memory keeper emitted warmth. He realized he could use it to see from, but if it were pulled from the Ravener's tunic, it would become visible to the others.

Moments ticked by as he shambled, feeling like an eternity. Yet he was already feeling more "at home" in his new skin than he would have thought possible and simply gave up the idea of trying to use the creature's eyes. The instant he did, a moving image formed in his mind, a gray and black contrasting sight that precisely distilled every sensory clue he'd just taken in. He was "seeing" what he'd only intuited from the sounds, smells, and feelings of the world around him, and the image was as sharp within a few feet of him in every direction as if his eyes worked. The farther from his borrowed body things were, the fuzzier they appeared, but he knew immediately what was happening. The Ravener brain was somehow able to understand the physical world around it through every sense except sight, and miraculously, the result was every bit as precise and serviceable as sight was to Ulfric.

Even as he let go of vision and let the Ravener's senses work in the way they were designed, the rest of the man's natural instincts began to come back. Soon he was walking without resembling an animated corpse. Still, Ulfric was grateful for the darkness that hid the man's awkwardness.

He didn't turn the man's head to look at the four Dyrraks waiting to deliver their boxes inside as he passed them. When he reached the door, the smell of recently gouged metal and a few brushes of his hands against the lock told him it had been forced open sometime earlier. It was beyond miraculous to him that he could "see" the door so perfectly just from the way the noise moved around it and scents came from it.

"About time, Venerate," the leader of the group said. "Her Holiness Balavad didn't do you any favors by bringing you into his fold, did she?"

Without a word, he made the man push the door open all the way to the interior wall and stand with his back to it, trying to conceal himself in the interior's shadows as much as possible.

It struck Ulfric then that of the five Dyrraks, the leader was the only one not changed into a Ravener, and the sudden curiosity of this made him turn the man's head to better sense her as she came inside. She caught his dead glance and immediately looked away, the expression on her face betraying an immediate distaste, perhaps even fear.

After a beat, she looked back and said, almost as if speaking to someone behind him rather than *to* him, "Not that anything Her Holiness would do is imperfect, of course. It is a great gift to be consecrated, one that I too hope to earn soon."

She snapped her mouth closed and hurried toward the center of the interior chamber, almost pulling the other footman carrying the box inside.

She is frightened of Balavad. And she should be. But why isn't she consecrated?

On the heels of that, a wild unease pushed its way to the front of his thoughts. *Balavad can see into their minds and control them, and she knows this. Will the Verity sense that I'm here, too? Will he, or rather she now, even know to look?*

Ulfric had no idea by what mechanism or wysticism Balavad was able to use other's senses of perception, and if Ulfric's presence was found, there was no telling what kind of power Balavad would have over him. He may be disembodied in one sense, but in another, he was now re-embodied. Would Balavad be able to take control of him the way he controlled this once-Dyrrak?

He had to get out of this body soon. But at the moment, the only way he could see doing it was by killing all but the woman in the lighthouse and using her as his new host.

Like the warrior he was, he began laying out his strategy.

CHAPTER TWENTY-ONE

Ulfric's host, a First Phase Dyrrak Ravener, the lowest ranked in the Dyrrak legion, didn't have a single weapon on him besides a short dagger that was more suited for work tasks like cutting rope than for murder—which would have been suitable enough for Ulfric's needs under normal circumstances. But being a passenger in someone else's flesh was anything but normal, and he wasn't certain such a small close-combat weapon against four others who were equally if not better trained and who didn't have the handicap of walking in a foreigner's skin would do.

Then there was the other issue: he didn't want to murder these Dyrraks. He doubted they had been given the choice to become Raveners and therefore Balavad's puppets. Even if they did have a choice, how could they have possibly refused when a Verity with the powers of the Cosmos and a truly sanguinary level of cruelty was the one offering that "choice"?

But he needed out of this man's body, and there was only one other suitable person he could swap for. Of course, however, if he slew the four Raveners and only the untainted Dyrrak was left standing, the rest of the fleet would have questions about why she'd killed them, for who else would it be?

He supposed he could simply make his host cast off the pendant when no one was looking and have Urgo retrieve it, but then Ulfric would be moving backward and getting nowhere. Or he could put their bodies in the dinghy and throw them overboard, then have his new host tell the fleet the boat had been hit by a rogue wave and the rest lost to sea. But that was back to the murder part. His sense of justice had been overly stoked of late, and he found he was unwilling to sacrifice any more people to the Verities' games than were absolutely necessary. Balavad had already cost too many lives. Every new one surrendered in an effort to stop him would diminish any victory they hoped to take. And he knew these Dyrraks lost to Balavad's consecration could be restored. He'd seen Vaka Aster do it before.

The more of them you kill, the easier it will be to save the other Vinnrics from Balavad's poison. Yes, that was true. But the Dyrraks were Vinnrics as well, for Verities' sakes, and besides, that was taking the burden a step too far. Having to decide which lives were more valuable? No, he refused to be the judge, jury, and executioner. He had to stay focused…

From somewhere in his brain's depth, a new idea sparked. Instead of killing the members of this advance force of Dyrraks, what about sabotaging them? Hobble or sink enough of their ships, and they would be rendered impotent for at least a while.

It was an excellent idea, but one he had to push to the back of his mind to consider later. First on his list was to shift to a new host.

In the end, the resolution turned out to be something he hadn't even considered. He was clearly losing his touch.

"What is that, Venerate?" The lead Dyrrak was staring pointedly at Ulfric's host's neck. "You know the uniform code doesn't allow personal accessories or"—she reached out and pulled the pendant from the Ravener's tunic and looked into the crystal in the center of the dragørfly carving—"… What in Vaka Aster's eyes?" she said, her tone more curious than angry. "I'm taking this, and your infraction will be discussed with Chancellor Aoggvír." The leader pulled the pendant's copper chain over the Ravener's head.

At the same time, Ulfric jumped into hers.

The Dyrrak captain wavered on her feet a fraction at his intrusion, but Ulfric had some practice with this now, and he tucked himself into a tight mental huddle in the recesses of her brain, quiet as a flittercat stalking its prey. The woman brushed the back of her hand against her forehead and blinked a few times, then stood tall again.

"Finish unpacking these," she ordered. "We have three more loads to bring ashore tonight."

With an inward sigh, Ulfric let himself relax the tiniest bit. He was undiscovered, at least for the moment. Now the task was to steal through her mind and find what he needed to know.

"Where did it come from, Venerate Egsil?"

Seldeg Aoggvír, Heir of the Third Line, Chancellor of the Dyrrak Phalanx—Ulfric would never forget the title, or the woman—stared into the face of Ulfric's new host. The chancellor's lucent gray eyes seemed to look through a person to their spirit, then cut it, just to test their mettle. Like most Dyrraks, her hair was cut severely short along her temples, leaving a thick strip in the middle that grew long down her back and was braided and wrapped in a leather sleeve. Hers was blacker than oil smoke, except for a pure white streak starting at her forehead and drawn back in the braid. She was easily Ulfric's own height, and her muscled arms, unsleeved in the Dyrrak fashion, were fairly black with the Dyrrak Phase tattoos that denoted her rank and achievements. Of all the Dyrraks he'd met, she was one he would first have to consider whether the odds of a one-on-one fight would be in his favor or not.

"From First Phase Venerate Ozlaus," the Dyrrak soldier said, her tone flustered, but not because of Ulfric's presence.

"You said that, Venerate, but my question is *where* did it come from? The First Phase wasn't wearing it when you left, so did he find it in the lighthouse?" The chancellor's Elder Veros was clipped and steady, but even Ulfric knew she would not ask the question again.

"He must have, Chancellor," the underling said. "You know how difficult it is to get a clear answer from the… newly consecrated."

Aoggvír held the pendant up to the illuminate orb in her cabin. They were on the main deck of the lead ship, the *Gildr*, in the same cabin the Domine Ecclesium had used when they'd traveled to Dyrrakium. Ulfric's new host Egsil had brought the pendant directly to the chancellor while her crew of four Raveners loaded their second stack of cargo to take to the lighthouse. Because of the accommodations, Ulfric surmised it was the chancellor who was leading this advance force. And she, too, had not been turned by Balavad, like the Domine Ecclesium and like this Third Phase Venerate Egsil.

This he found surprising. While the chancellor was the second in command of Dyrrakium, in his brief time in the Citadel Suprima, he hadn't gotten the sense from her that she craved power the way the Ecclesium so clearly did. All the Dyrraks were devoted to a fault to their ideas of how best to prove their worthiness to Vaka Aster, but devotion, even zealous devotion, wasn't something that always led to the domination and forced subjugation of others, as was the Ecclesium's plan. Ulfric didn't see how he could refrain from passing judgment about Aoggvír's moral core, if she had one, for she was, after all, leading a mission to destroy Ivoryss. Yet he still found himself doing it. He wasn't Beatte, who assumed all Dyrraks were hopeless warmongers. He'd known many fine ones in his life.

None finer than Eisa, for all her faults. This thought tugged at him painfully. He'd have better chances of besting Balavad hand-to-hand than he did of putting the loss of his friend behind him.

He stayed tucked deep within Egsil's head, listening. Her mental barriers so far were tougher to crack than he'd expected, though he fortunately hadn't been discovered. Every time he thought he was about to break in and glean information about the Dyrraks' plans, Balavad's whereabouts, and Vaka Aster's current status, she would stop whatever she was doing and rub her temples, as if a headache was coming on. He'd been forced to retreat each time and wait for another opportunity. He needed her to be distracted, as she was now.

"Seems an unlikely trinket for someone to forget or leave behind in such an isolated place," Aoggvír commented as she held the pendant up to her face for a better look.

Ulfric was tempted to jump into her at that moment, but stopped himself. The lines around Aoggvír's eyes and mouth showed her life had not only been harsh but considerably longer than Egsil's. If Egsil was hard to crack, the chancellor with her much-advanced mental discipline might well be impossible. Likewise, given her status, there was more than a fleeting possibility she would at some point meet with Balavad, and Ulfric wasn't convinced the Verity wouldn't see directly through her mirror-like eyes and find Ulfric lurking there. No, he needed his anonymity for now.

Aoggvír carried the necklace to an open-topped box sitting on a writing desk built into the cabin's interior wall. "For now, I'll keep it. You've done well to bring it to me. Return to your duties, but first, go to the command berth and tell Fifth Phase Venerate Sveinungr I've sent for him."

"It is done, Chancellor." With a bow of her head, Egsil retreated.

It was approaching Hallumbrum, which meant there was little activity on the upper decks as Egsil paced toward the ship's bow. Anchored about two hundred yards from the island, the ship barely rocked in the slivered moonlight's ebony waves brushing against it. The Verring Sea was calm and easy, seemingly oblivious to the chaos that would soon speed through these waters toward the Ivoryssian coast.

The dread of this happening reminded Ulfric of his thoughts about scuttling the Dyrrak fleet. If only he'd not been so confined to his own cabin on the journey to Dyrrakium—for his and Vaka Aster's safety—yet another curse to add to the many that came with being the vessel of a shackled Verity. If he hadn't, he'd have a better idea how he might bollix enough of the ship here and there to effectively disable it.

Venerate Egsil came to an abrupt halt on deck. "Who said that?" Her eyes darted left and right. "Who's speaking of scuttling the fleet?"

Her voice was commanding and angry, but he heard an underlying tone of anxiety. *Rook's balls. Did she hear me?*

"Yes. Now come out and face me." She spun around in a complete circle. "Who's dares speak of sabotage?"

"That is a good question, Venerate."

Egsil stopped spinning and focused on a shadowy alcove between several barrels and the base of a sail. As she stared, a figure emerged, a tall Dyrrak man with a face nearly covered in Phase markings, which made his eyes glitter in the moonlight even brighter in contrast. A heavy-handled glaive rose over his shoulder, hanging from its holster on his back, much like Eisa's did.

Egsil's eyes fell to his hands. In one, he carried a ball of what appeared to be twine, in the other a knife. Some unknown black powder stained his fingers.

"Fifth Phase Venerate Sveinungr," Egsil said and dipped her head, though her eyes stayed on his hands, "Chancellor Aoggvír sent me for you."

Sveinungr stood before her now and peered into her face as if searching for treasure. Or treason. "To whom were you speaking, Venerate Egsil?"

"I can't say, Venerate. I thought I heard someone speaking from the darkness." Egsil, to her credit, remained composed, but Ulfric could feel doubt whispering at the edges of her mind. "Fifth Phase, what exactly were you doing among the rigging?"

As a leader himself, Ulfric sensed the higher-ranking Dyrrak's surprise. Was his underling being impertinent? Would she dare?

This wasn't a situation Ulfric wanted to escalate. He needed Egsil docile, and more than that, he needed her to be trusted and therefore invisible to her chain of command. If she was naturally inclined toward disrespectfulness, she would stand out, and therefore, he would too. But what could he do to stop her?

As before, the answer came much too easily.

"Come, I shall show you, Venerate." The higher-ranking Dyrrak moved back into the dark. "Come now."

Though his voice didn't change, the steel in it brooked no dispute from Egsil. She took two steps forward, her mind now blaring a caution that some more-obedient part of her seemed unable to heed. From the dark came a whisper of movement, a bludgeoning pain exploded in the venerate's chin, and she fell.

Ulfric was alone in the dark in the woman's form, trapped like a snared animal.

CHAPTER TWENTY-TWO

A lot of things could have gone wrong when the Knights, Commander Brun, and Havelock Rekkr arrived in the inter-realm well chamber in the depths of Magdaster's Gusting Hall. Jaemus just didn't realize this until later, and by then the danger had shifted from their being arrested and dropped into a dark, damp hole for some transgression the Knights had committed against the Magdastervians sometime in the recent past, to merely the run-of-the-mill danger he was already used to. Namely, the advancing war-intent fleet of Dyrraks who were no longer exactly human but quite monstrous in both their resilience and their intentions. Jaemus figured he'd get used to the constant threat to life and limb eventually. People could get used to anything, right?

He became aware of the Magdastervians' quarrel with the Knights during a discussion with the swarthy late-middle-aged Commander Nennus and a group of equally stout locals regarding the coming fight. It was something about the Knights having arrived aboard a cloaked airship and concealed their intentions from Nennus after Balavad's first attack, then hurrying off without a word of explanation, leaving the city with more questions and fewer answers than before they'd shown up. Commander Brun had quickly smoothed over this "misunderstanding," settling the Magdastervians and Knights into milder terms.

Afterward, they'd pivoted to planning for the Dyrrak invasion agilely, leaving Jaemus constantly rushing to keep track and keep up. Their easy transition to war planning showed him that yes, indeed, getting used to the idea of war could become as natural as breathing if one practiced enough. He found himself not at all comforted.

They all drank heavy mugs of some warm, sweet liquid at a table in Gusting Hall as Nennus reassured the assemblage. "Those Dyrraks cannae get their attack ships within a mile of our walls. Not with our cannons. There's one every seventeen yards from the seaward wall to the Weald wall. Fields of fire cross like a spider's web over the city. Anything trying to get through will be blasted into small enough chunks to scrape up with a spoon."

"It may be," Mallich said, "but it's not the Dyrraks' ships we have to worry about. It's their weaponry. We know they based their fighter designs on ours, so we can assume they have the same weapons: emberspark guns. They'll be able to fire from too far off for the full strength of an emberflare to reach. Their impact will be less, but less doesn't mean none. We'll still need shields for the city. What will serve?"

Nennus got a funny look on his lined face—funny in a different way from how he'd first looked at Jaemus, who'd gotten used to the Vinnrics' reactions to his distinct coloring by this point. "Shields? Knight Roibeard, did you forget where we are? We've been building shields against dragørs since before your..." He trailed off, evidently realizing his statement comparing the longevity of something to a Knight's life wasn't quite what it would normally be. "That is ta say, we have mobile shield-walls that can hold off dragørfire for a bit. They should do against whatever the Dyrraks can conjure."

"Can they withstand both heat and impact?" Safran asked, amplified by a Fenestros.

"Nothing hits hotter nor harder than dragørfire," he reassured them all. "If we can guard against that, we can guard against anything."

"Then our other concern is their numbers," she calculated.

"We have five thousand fighters," Nennus said confidently. "And over a thousand cannons. We can fire every single one of them at least sixty times before we'll be out of juice."

"Five thousand *ground* fighters. Is that correct?" Mallich clarified.

"That's right, and—ah, I see your point. Airships in Magdaster are as useful as a toothless shark. Dragørs would just turn them into falling slag. Our navy isnae much to speak of either. Never expected to have to fight on the sea. Dyrraks are too far off, and the Yorish would have to sail nearly around the world to get to our shores. They'd be half-starved and full-crazed if they ever tried."

"Then who is your ground army for?" Jaemus asked out of curiosity.

Nennus peered at him through brows so heavy, they were practically a stole worn across his forehead and made Stave's look tame in comparison. After a moment, he pursed his lips and said, "Being from so far away, I'm guessing you aren't too familiar with the map of Vinnr. Magdaster sits at the narrowest point of the Howling Weald between Ivoryss and Yor. Our North Byway—the only road through the Weald into and out of Magdaster—links to the Great Province Byway down south. Once were the days when the two kingdoms were less friendly than we are now, and Magdaster has the best metal in the realm. We make steel so hardy you could break more steel with it. Time was when the Yorish thought they'd march over and take some, along with the north of Vinnr, for themselves. We showed them how mistaken their plans were."

Jaemus squinted in a look he hoped conveyed his deep, though utterly feigned, wisdom regarding such matters. "And that was not long ago, then?"

Nennus looked toward the ceiling, calculating. "Before my time," he said, as if that narrowed it down.

"My grandad fought in that skirmish, he did. The Battle of the Byways," Stave put in. "Before he was hanged, that is."

Jaemus's eyes flicked from Stave to Nennus and back. The volume of violence described in their brief exchange—starving navies, battles, and hanged men, etc.—was enough to make him dizzy, but this was held off by his puzzlement over something else. "Stave, haven't you been a Knight for over six hundred, ah, turns?"

"Thereabouts," he answered amiably.

"So you've kept a standing army active in Magdaster since a battle that took place around ten lifetimes ago?" he said to Nennus.

"The moment you stop being prepared, you start being a target," Nennus gruffed, as if this nugget of knowledge was so obvious even a child would know it. It became clear to Jaemus where Stave's many aphorisms came from, him being a Magdastervian originally. He cleared his throat and said quietly, "Just curious. Continue."

They did, and he was happy enough to let them. This wasn't his area of expertise, and he'd come to terms with it.

Yet, for all that, an idea had been sparked in his mind, and now it was pushing itself to the forefront little by little. They'd discussed shields strong enough to withstand the Dyrrak ships' weapons, at least for a while. And Nennus had talked about how much ammunition they had. What would become of the Magdastervians when they ran out? More to the point, with the Dyrraks so heavily reliant on their air fleet, what would they do when their own firepower ran out?

Mallich was saying something about naval options, but Jaemus cut in. "How do the weapons carried by the Dyrraks work? Embersparks, you called them?"

Mallich eyed him tolerantly, then explained, "Halla, to put it briefly. The light is captured and focused through lenses into the emberspark barrel reservoirs. Triggers release a fine grain of powder made from flint stone, or more likely from puurite in the Dyrraks' version—it's more combustible—into the barrels, which are then ignited and channeled via the weapon's mechanism."

Jaemus was nodding but still quizzical. "Light and powder, got it. But how is that damaging?"

"What comes out of those barrels is like a bomb made of fire that turns whatever it touches to, as Nennus put it, chunks of slag," Stave said matter-of-factly.

"Ah, all right. Slag, that's not good."

"Are you going somewhere with this, Jaemus?" Safran asked.

"What happens when they run out of this catalytic powder?"

"I'm sure they're bringing a good supply aboard their water fleet," Mallich said, but his tone had an edge as if he had begun to guess what Jaemus was getting at. "The air fleet would simply return to those on the water to resupply. It would take some time before they used all their reserves."

"Yes, but if their attack craft run out, for instance in flight or during a skirmish?"

Stave answered, "Then their ships will be useless for battle, they will—unless they want to turn themselves into bludgeons and die right along with whatever they target."

Unconsciously, Jaemus began to pace like Brun. "So if we draw their fire long enough, their airships will use up their weapons and be defenseless. If they're kept defenseless, the advantage will be ours—" He reached the near wall and spun back. Something golden and hazy, moving fast, caught his eye just before a fur-covered creature about the size of his head landed on one of his shoulders. He flinched and let out a yelp. When he reached up to brush the thing off, it was no longer there. Just a flash of something sliding beneath the table, but he couldn't make out any details. "Sorry, did you all know that you have… flashy, jumpy *things* in here. Did anyone else see it?"

Everyone looked at him curiously. Nennus spoke up first. "By 'things,' Knight Bardgrim, I assume you mean the flittercat that just used you as a launch pad. His name is Scintilla."

"Scintilla? The flittercat? So… not dangerous, then?"

Nennus laughed at him with genuine humor. "They'll eat your guts out if you intrude in their territory. But they only kill people they don't like." One of his eyes squinted in a look of intense sincerity. "So stay on his good side, would be my advice."

Jaemus had not resumed pacing. He couldn't seem to pull his gaze from Nennus, waiting for the grizzled commander to admit he was joking. Nennus stared back, unblinking and unbudging.

"Ahem, I'll, um, do my best," he affirmed and forced himself to look back at the group instead of searching the floor for the gut-munching creature. "What I was saying is, if we can sink the Dyrraks' supply of puurite or disable their ability to access it while their ships are weaponless, they will have to resort to ground fighting, just like Magdaster."

"And be as weak as a spider with no venom," Nennus enthused. "No one's getting through Magdaster's walls. Even dragørs have to put in a bit of effort to take them down."

"Exactly," Jaemus nearly crowed, having unearthed an unexpected pride at his blooming strategy skills.

Brun spoke up for the first time in a while. "You make many valid points. Except we don't want to draw their fire inside the city. Even with shield-walls, the damage would be too great. And we'll never get near their water fleet to cut off their resupply. Magdaster's navy is ill-prepared to handle a battle, and we don't have any flying craft at all. I thought we'd covered that."

Jaemus wanted to smile but thought better of it. "What if we did?" No one spoke, all waiting for some kind of plausible reason to be discussing folly. "I happen to know where to find a fleet of airships that I'm pretty sure can be made perfectly capable of achieving exactly what we need."

Symvalline, the Knight who knew him least well, was clearly trying to be diplomatic when she said, "Knight Bardgrim, I'm not sure if this is a taste of Himmingazian humor. If it is, I apologize for being short with you, but we haven't the time—"

But he was on a roll now. "I'm actually quite funny, once you get to know me," he assured her, "but that's not what this is about. I'm talking about the Glisternaut fleet!" He held out his hands in a "there it is!" gesture, as if he'd just explained a great mystery.

They all stared at him as if he'd begun sprouting another head, complete with Himmingazian green skin.

"I see…" How to explain what he meant in as few words as possible? "Listen. The Glisternaut fleet comprises some two hundred ships. Most are much bigger than the Dyrrak fighters, though not quite as nimble, true. But that's the beauty of it. They were built to fly through lightning and storms the likes of which, if you don't mind my guess, Vinnr has never seen. In just a few cycles"—he reverted to the

Himmingazian term in his excitement—"we could rig the Glisternaut ships with some of your own weaponry and fight back against the Dyrrak forces. It would be like hawks against a swarm of gnats. Their embersparks would barely scratch the surface of a Himmingazian-built ship. They're already reinforced with a shield of my own design, let me add. And, again I'm guessing here, we could very likely get close enough to the Dyrrak water fleet to put a stop to, well, the whole attack."

Stave, looking like he'd been poleaxed, said, "But they're in Himmingaze."

"I'll simply go and get them," he said. "I think after what they've been through and seen lately, it won't be hard to convince them that they're needed here in Vinnr. The Council of Nine Crests are well-reasoned and wise, and they'll agree quickly that they, to put it bluntly, *owe* it to Vinnr for everything you've done for Himmingaze. And my lifemate is the fleet commander, after all."

Mallich was nodding, coming around to the idea more quickly than the others. "The world is different in Himmingaze, though, Jaemus. The *skies* are different. I know from my own days as a sailor that a ship built to float a lake differs substantially from one built for the sea. Would your other-world ships even be capable of flying in this realm?"

Jaemus was ready for this question. "Most definitely. It's not so much a matter of aerials as it is power that differentiates ours from Vinnr's ships. On Mount Omina, I took a close look at Wing Rekkr's fighter and learned some useful things. Vinnric ships are powered by Halla but use other mechanisms that aren't so different from a Glisternaut ship. Ours, though, are powered by water and lightning. If I can get to the Glisternaut fleet and their crack mechanics—I trained most of them, naturally—I know exactly what modifications it will take to shift their power systems to Vinnr-compatible ones. With enough help, we could have them all modified inside a few Vinnric cycles, er, days."

He smiled again broadly. But the smile dropped from his face the instant he felt that soft, warm sensation of something rubbing against his cheek again, and the not-so-soft sensation of what seemed to be tiny daggers stuck in his chest. His gaze shot downward to his chest, where Scintilla clung like a barnacle. The creature's hideously large eyes, golden like its fur though darker and parted transversely by moon-shaped pupils, gleamed up at him. "Ah! Why does it keep doing that? And why is it stabbing me!?"

A moment later, the eyes, along with the tiny daggers, were gone again. He looked around but saw nothing. "And one last question, how in the Creatress's celestial balls of power does it disappear like that?"

"Flittercats can bend light. If they want to be seen, they will be. If not…" Nennus trailed off with a meaningful, if amused, look.

"So you're telling me that if he decides he wants to nibble on my innards, I'll never see him coming?" Jaemus asked. "If he's going to keep jumping onto me like that, I suppose I'm going to need detailed advice on how to stay on his good side."

"Later, Jaemus," Mallich said. "Let's talk more about the Himmingaze fleet. Tell us exactly what you'd need to make them viable in Vinnr and who's going to fly them."

Crossing his arms low enough to protect his belly, he said, "It'll only take a short bit for me to list the parts we'll need. As for pilots—leave that to me."

CHAPTER TWENTY-THREE

Staring into the maw of a shelksie was not the first thing Jaemus expected to be doing immediately upon arriving back in Himmingaze.

The starpath delivered him to the Creatress temple, and he was just picking himself up off the floor and counting himself lucky he hadn't broken anything when he heard the timid not-quite-command, "Hold still and remain quiet. You are hereby being constrained by order of the Council of Nine Crests. If you don't behave as commanded, you'll be constrained bodily."

Which to Jaemus meant if he didn't do as told, he'd find himself struck by a disabling, and not totally painless, shelksie projectile. With a glance toward the voice, he froze.

A Glisternaut, one he didn't know, stood in the shadow of one of the shrine's large interior pillars, pointing the aforementioned wrist-mounted shelksie. It was a simple weapon that fired shullets, pebble-sized gas pellets that would explode upon impact and put their target to sleep almost instantly. The sleeping part wasn't uncomfortable, but Jaemus had learned, thanks to Ulfric, that being struck by a shullet was like being hit with a thrown stone, if the stone were thrown by someone whose arm was powered by a Glisternaut ship's thrusters.

There was no lasting damage beyond a deep sleep and a memorable bruise—but that was all beside the point. Was this any way to treat the man who'd just saved the realm from dissolving into Cosmos dust?

"It's me, Spark. Glint Engineer Jaemus Bardgrim. I'm sure the *Bounding Skate* crew has had time to inform the Council that"—what was the best way of putting it, exactly? That he'd saved the world? That their celestial maker the Creatress was not only real but was now embodied by the fiercest creature ever to swim the Never Sea, a slangarook who happened to have the uncanny name of Hither? He wasn't sure which, if either, of those options would most succinctly and directly convey the message he wanted to get across, so he finished with: "I mean surely you've seen what's happening outside. No more Glister Cloud! *That* is what the Council should know by now."

The spark engineer, his young face a cartoon of inexperience and confusion, merely glanced toward the shrine's broken door, then shrugged.

Jaemus couldn't contain his incredulity. "… You're telling me you don't know that Himmingaze has been—I mean, I don't like to brag— but *saved* would not be too strong a word."

"The Council is…"

The Glisternaut stopped speaking, as if unsure what he wanted to say, so Jaemus prompted him. "Is?"

"Is… not officially sure what's become of the Glister Cloud. So they've stationed me here to bring anyone who, um, shows up back to Vann to be questioned."

Jaemus was beginning to guess what might be going on, but he had to ask, "Do you even know who I am?"

"Glint Engineer Bardgrim, of course." It was the first thing the young man appeared to feel confident about, and not just because Jaemus had already said his name aloud. He supposed he should take some pleasure in his celebrity, but he was getting the sinking feeling that, for some inextricable reason, while he'd been gone it had changed more to notoriety.

"And what have you, personally, heard about what's happened in Himmingaze and my involvement in it?"

The spark engineer glanced outside again, his round eyes not able to conceal his wonder at the newly transformed world. "They say you brought back the old ways, the Creatress… They say Himmingaze has been returned to the Great Cosmos, that it had been cut off and—" He caught himself. "What they say isn't what matters. What Captain Illago and the crew of the *Bounding Skate* have testified to is that you, disgraced Glint Engineer Bardgrim, were found here at this forbidden shrine, and when they came to constrain you, you created some kind of mind trick that led to a mass illusion and made them think they saw and heard things that they could never have seen or heard. The Council forgave them all and released them, and now the fleet's orders are to constrain you the moment you come back from… come back. You're in serious trouble Glint Bardgrim, and I recommend you come with me without adding more." On seemingly realizing how presumptuous it sounded for a mere spark engineer to be giving orders to a glint, he added, "Please?"

Jaemus had stopped paying much attention to him right after the part where he'd said the Glisternauts claimed he'd brainwashed them, and was busily thinking about all the times Cote had played a practical joke on him—because what else could this be but a gag? Unfortunately, the number was in the low zeros, the absolute nevers. Cote just wasn't the joking kind. His relationship habits tended more toward thoughtful romantic gestures and sincere, meaningful conversations— or sincere, meaningful imputations if Jaemus was acting on one of his more impracticable whims.

But there was no way, *no way* Cote would have turned on him. And even more farfetched was the idea that he would somehow come to disbelieve everything that had happened. No conjurer or trickster, no matter how skilled, could have pulled off a deception as intricate and amazing as everything the Glisternauts had been through since Balavad came to Himmingaze. On his own, Jaemus himself couldn't even have imagined half of the wild things he'd lately seen and done.

So, evidently things had taken the most unfortunate turn they possibly could have. The Council had for too long been wedded to the idea that the old lore of the Creatress was a dangerous superstition and hadn't been able to bring themselves around to believing the evidence right in front of their eyes, even after Cote and his crew had explained it. He imagined how things had gone. The Glisternauts and Vreyja and her companions had gone to the Council and explained exactly what had happened here at the Creatress's old temple, and the Nine Crests had decreed them muddleminded, or worse, heretics, and likely would have locked them up had they not changed their story. All the while, the Council members would have been eagerly spinning tales and superstitions of their own to account for the fact that Himmingaze once more had a horizon and, beyond it, millions of distant stars that no living Himmingazian had ever seen before.

The more he thought about it, the more Jaemus realized he couldn't blame the Glisternauts for scapegoating him. It wasn't as if he'd been there to stick up for himself anyway, but he was definitely going to give Cote a peace of his mind—a large and forceful piece—when next they crossed paths.

What now, though? Gramsirene Vreyja had always been considered eccentric, but if Cote *and* his entire crew had been unable to make the Council believe the Creatress had returned and Himmingaze was restored, Jaemus had no chance at all. He had, after all, been constrained once already for coming to the forbidden Isle Stonering against Himmingazian law. And now he apparently had a "new talent" of controlling people's minds, and for some strange reason got his kicks from making people believe they'd traveled to distant worlds and fought monstrous marauders whose minds were controlled in much the same way by a mythical Verity.

Old Jaemus would not have known what to do in this situation, other than comply meekly with the spark engineer and been flown off to face the Council's inquiry. But he was not old Jaemus. He was Knight Bardgrim, now. No, he was *Mystae* Bardgrim, and it was his duty to protect his Verity's creations. Even if they didn't want it, approve of it, or appreciate it.

The Glisternaut was showing signs of addled impatience, uncertain what to do about his distracted not-yet-prisoner.

Jaemus asked, "That's the way it'll be then, you wish for me to come with you?" He slipped a hand into his Vinnric robe pocket. "Of course, as you please. But what about my partner there?" With his other hand, he waved toward the doorway.

The spark engineer, exactly as Jaemus had anticipated, started and turned toward the door, shelksie still raised. Jaemus pulled his one klinkí stone from the pocket and targeted the man's weapon hand.

The spark engineer yelped at the impact and fired his shullet into the wall. The shelksie was now empty until reloaded. His eyes widened again, this time in fright, as Jaemus pulled the wystic stone back a foot or two, then held it up to hover menacingly before the young man's chest.

Not quite believing his own actions, Jaemus did what came naturally next. "Gah! I am so, so sorry, Spark. Are you okay?" The klinkí stone, now just as devoid of malice as Jaemus himself, dropped to the ground.

The younger man was staring at him in utter disbelief. "You, you hit me with a rock!"

"Technically, it's a klinkí stone, but I would never, that is to say, I *won't* ever do that again, I promise. Unless you force me to like just now, but I don't *want* to. So if you don't mind, could you just put the shelksie down and, um, I guess have a seat by the wall while I wait for the rest of my supplies to arrive?"

The Glisternaut blinked several times and seemed unconvinced the danger had passed as he quickly stripped off the shelksie and dropped it. It landed beside Jaemus's barely glowing wystic stone. They both looked at the two objects as if they'd never seen anything quite so strange, quite so hostile and harmful, and it just wasn't sinking it what any of it meant.

When the man looked back at him, Jaemus pointed to the wall, an apologetic lift to his eyebrows. Finally, his "prisoner"—which wasn't the word Jaemus wanted to use, but his mind was too rattled to think of a more appropriate one—paced near where his shullet had struck and turned with his back to the wall.

"What are you going to do?" he asked simply.

Jaemus thought a moment, then waved his stone back to him and pocketed it, not liking the slight pressure of it against his leg. He'd been so intrigued by the things when he'd first seen Ulfric use them, but a single one was next to useless for any purpose other than the violent kind. He decided it would remain in his pocket until he forgot about it or he had more of them, enough to put to uses that didn't require someone else getting hurt.

Stepping to the spark engineer, he said, "Let's go and see your ship."

CHAPTER TWENTY-FOUR

Jaemus locked the spark engineer inside the cargo closet of his small Glisternaut ship, no bigger than his own *Octopod* had been, and took a seat at the ship's controls. Now, staring vacantly out into the wide, newly incandescent world, he tried to think. If Cote and the other star-jumping Glisternauts had truly turned on him, it would be his lone venture to, not to put too fine a point on it, *steal* their ships and jump them into the fray in Vinnr. There, he'd have to put the Magdastervians to work re-rigging the ships' power systems, rather than have the well-trained Glisternauts here to do it. Every Glisternaut was an engineer on some level (from Wick, to Spark, to Glint—his own rank), which would have made the retrofit easy if they were doing the work. The Magdastervians were no doubt diligent builders and designers of their own devices, but it was going to be one of his life's greatest challenges to teach them the mechanics of Glisternaut ships and simultaneously run a crew of them efficiently. And it wasn't as if he had a great deal of time to do it, either.

He sighed at the daunting task that lay ahead and tried to ignore the distraction that had become Himmingaze, now spread across the horizon outside the ship's windows. This was his home as he'd never seen, as he'd hardly even imagined it. Everything shone so brightly his eyes hurt. There was a sun somewhere above, but he sensed it would be a while before his eyes were conditioned enough to the horizon's effulgence to seek it out. He'd forgotten the star's old name—if he'd ever known it. It had hardly seemed important to a world that was locked inside an impenetrable Glister Cloud of dust and gas. Once all this was done, he promised himself he'd dedicate himself once more to both advancing his home world and to finding out what lay beyond it.

No time to linger, he finally told himself. Safran and Stave had taken the lead in organizing the parts he'd requested to modify the Glisternaut ships. They would begin delivering them before night fell in Vinnr, he expected. If he jumped back there now to tell them not to bring the parts here, he'd just be wasting time. His plan was to lure the Glisternaut fleet to Isle Stonering, then jump the whole lot of them back to Vinnr at once. Picking up the delivered parts on the way would be easy enough.

"Let's see what we have here," he said to himself as he perused the little ship's operations controls. "Ah. Power—thrusters—lift. Up we go!" As he spoke, he brought all the little ship's systems online, and a moment later, they jolted upward and out over the Never Sea. He had them cruising toward Vann, his home city and the fleet's main port, in no time.

Before Isle Stonering had disappeared behind them, a shape began materializing on the horizon ahead, a dark spot in the prevailing whiteness. At first, he thought it was an afterimage from all the blinking he was doing at the unusually bright sky, but instead of fading as he focused, the shape was growing increasingly sharper.

He sat up straight in the pilot's seat. No, it was not an effect of light. That was a Glisternaut ship, and it was coming straight toward him.

Over his shoulder, he called, "Were you expecting some company you forgot to mention, Spark?"

"I didn't forget to mention them. I just didn't."

Jaemus grumbled.

The craft he was flying was a basic transit hop for getting from one hovering Himmingazian city to another. Nothing flashy or, of more immediate note, speedy about it. Jaemus's piloting expertise might get him launched from Isle Stonering with no problems, but he'd never outrun the approaching ship.

"By the way, they already know you're here. I called Commander Illago right after your, er, arrival," the spark called.

Slag it! he thought, finding Stave's crude reactionary language to be perfectly suited to the moment. Then he realized what the spark had said. "That's Cote's ship?"

"I contacted the commander himself. Maybe you should let me out of the closet now, before they add 'menacing and harassment of a Glisternaut crew member' to the list of charges you're already facing."

But Jaemus had stopped listening to him. Swinging the pilot's seat toward the wave-speaker, he hailed the incoming ship. "This is Jae—rather, this is the Glisternaut ship *Council's Crest* coming from Isle Stonering. I see you ahead. Please have Captain Illago come to the wave-speaker right away."

"Sorry, *Council's Crest*, this is Flight Leader Drustim, captain of the *Deep Sea Gem*. We intercepted your transmission to Captain Illago and the *Glistering Horizon* a short time ago. We're in closer range than the captain, so we came immediately." The flight leader paused, then came back on and said conspiratorially, "Is it true? You captured the renegade heretic?"

Jaemus's shoulders drooped. No thank you. This wasn't what he was planning at all. He did not want an entourage as he approached Vann. He simply needed time to sneak into the docks, slip aboard the nearest cosmocruiser unnoticed (fancying that his newly acquired celestial gifts conferred an automatic excellence at the finer covert crafts he would be able to draw from), and abscond with it and as many others as he could remote pilot to the island. And if that failed, he'd simply send them from Vann to Vinnr via starpath. No fuss, no muss—at least not until he had to explain to any who might have been aboard when they were sent across the stars how they happened to be in a very new, very unfamiliar world. But that was an issue he was willing, no, *happy* to ignore for the time being.

Enabling a few settings on the control console, he readied the ship to give its all in an attempt to outfly the *Deep Sea Gem* and this Flight

Leader Drustim. Hopefully, they would be too stunned by his sudden rush away to muster a rapid pursuit. He'd lose them over the open water, then circle back to Vann.

From the hold's closet came: "Glint Engineer! What are you—"

"Shush!" he said. "I'm getting us out of here and don't need any distractions at the moment. I'll get back to you when I'm done."

"But—"

"Silence! I command you!" he cried, feeling foolish for his faked authority, but he had to get going and didn't have time for pleasantness. It seemed to work for now.

The Glisternaut's question, apparently a popular one, was repeated via wave-speaker. "Spark Engineer Saxton, what are you doing?"

Jaemus turned down the volume and accelerated, enjoying the smooth ride of the ship in a way he hadn't realized he'd missed. He was a man born to water and air, not the hard earth of Vinnr, and they would always feel right to him.

"Glint Engineer!" said his captive. "If you go much further, we'll be stranded!"

Saxton's voice sounded more concerned than angry, and the unexpected tone pushed itself to Jaemus's ear. Stranded? As in stopped cold and stuck in the Never Sea? That was impossible. Glisternaut ships could fly forever as long as they were amply fueled with—

"Water and lightning," he cursed. "How could I be so stupid? No Glister Cloud storm, no lightning—no power reserves!" Glisternaut ships were designed to run on the two most common resources in the realm: seawater and storm lightning. Without both, the ships were just metal bubbles of air, with unfortunate Himmingazians stuck inside.

As if to confirm what he only just realized, the craft's control panel sent him a friendly, quiet little message. *Ping.* In his mind, it sounded like, *Hey dimwit, you realize you're running on fumes. Shoot me with some Glister juice now, or I'm going down and taking you with me.*

Overhead, the craft pursuing them shot by, but not before Jaemus saw it begin to slow. They'd spotted him.

As the *Council's Crest* settled into the mild waves, staying afloat for now, the spark called out again. "Are we out of power?"

"That seems to be the case."

"You should have listened to me!"

His unwilling passenger was silent after that. As Jaemus pondered what to do next, the shadow of their pursuer returned.

The *Deep Sea Gem* was much larger, equal to a couple dozen of the spark's small transport craft. It came to a hover overhead, and Jaemus rose to collect the only onboard weapons: a shelksie. He didn't want to use it, but he had already grown so averse to using his klinkí stone that the stun weapon was his default choice of tool in case he had to act forcefully. They'd send down a rescue soon to fish him and the spark from the water. And from there, he'd simply have to hijack the bigger ship. "Simply" being the word he was not yet sure how to define.

That was when the *Crest* began to sink. *Double slag it!* he thought. *What else could go wrong?*

More concerned about what might be drawn to the disturbance in the water outside than being stuck in a sinking craft, Jaemus dithered momentarily. His plans of surprising the *Gem* crew who came to get them had relied on them not knowing he was currently free and actually in charge of the ship. But a floundering man that has been forced to abandon ship was hardly in a position to surprise anyone, much less gain the upper hand. He would just be a sitting duck, waiting to get constrained once he and the spark engineer left the craft and waved for a rescue.

Nothing is easy when there are rules to break and worlds to save, is it? he thought grumpily, and released his captive from the storage closet. To Saxton, he said, "As you can tell, we're sinking. It's going to be a long swim to the surface, but look on the bright side: you've caught the most wanted heretic of Himmingaze's history."

The spark engineer looked unimpressed. "And lost my ship."

"Yes, I do apologize for that. I failed to foresee the current power issue. You would understand my lapse if you knew the kinds of things I've been dealing with lately. We should probably go." He pointed toward the hatch.

Saxton's face betrayed his growing frustration with the day as he grabbed the hatch release and gave it a firm pull. He grunted when it refused to budge, then pulled harder. Then harder still until the light green of his features began to darken with effort.

"Let me help," Jaemus said, wondering if he might be able to muster some celestial-powered might he didn't know about. Taking a grip beside the spark's hands, he helped pull, the two giving it everything in them. To no avail.

"Jammed," Jaemus grumbled just as the quietest whisper of what could only be water leaking into the hull sounded from somewhere. "This really isn't how I saw this day going at all."

"They're not going to be able to retrieve us if we sink too far," the spark said with an unmissable hint of accusation in his tone.

Jaemus stepped away from the hull and thought a moment. He'd seen Ulfric once use a klinkí stone to melt through a cell-door lock. On reflection, though, he didn't think that would do them any good. He'd simply create one more hole for water to splash in, and they'd still be stuck inside.

However, the windows would crack to pieces if he put enough holes in them. "Come with me," he told Saxton. "But wait by the cockpit door. I don't want you to be harmed."

Jaemus entered the pilot's space, leaving Saxton behind him, and pulled the stone from his pocket. He wasn't worried the spark would try to overpower him or something else as heroic. Once Saxton's eyes caught the stone, he seemed most content to wait where Jaemus suggested, thoroughly distrusting of the wystic object's abilities.

With one arm raised to cover his face should the front window do more than crack, Jaemus focused on the klinkí stone and drove it with the full weight of his thoughts into the transparent glass-like material.

He'd misjudged just how forceful he could be. The stone shot through the window and kept going into the thoroughly dark waters outside. They'd descended so far that no more light pierced through.

"Oops," he said, trying to maintain a modicum of calm. He hadn't attempted to use the stone without having it in his sight before. Now, the real test was whether he'd be able to retrieve it. With eyes closed, as water rapidly filled the small cabin, he called to the stone with his most commanding mental voice.

There was a sharp crack, and he opened his eyes. The stone had responded. Another hole, barely larger than his thumb, had joined the first about two feet away, and between them branched a deep and still-growing crack.

"Brace yourself," he called to the spark and rushed from the cabin. The window was going to give any moment.

He was right. With an unexpectedly subdued *hssshhhh* sound, the window broke apart and the sea rushed in. The next instant, they felt the ship thump gently on the Never Sea's floor.

Jaemus took hold of the spark's arms and nodded toward the opening to freedom. He wasn't exactly urging Saxton to go first, but he was certainly hesitating himself. It was a long swim to the surface, and this was the Never Sea, home to many things with teeth and mouths and the urge to make meals of Himmingazians. Last time he'd gone for a swim—was that only two days ago?—he'd had the protection of Griggory's wystic stone shield and a slangarook to scare off everything else. Now it was just him, his single stone, and an innocent Glisternaut to protect. He didn't know how to use the Fenestros or the Scrylle he carried to aid them, unless he wanted to swing it around like a club, which seemed not only unlikely to be of much good but also uncouth.

Maybe learning to use Winter's Bite would have had its uses, he thought as the two men exited the cabin and began kicking toward the surface with all the strength they had.

He could have used his Mentalios lens to illuminate the darkness, but he didn't want to waste the energy—and he really didn't think he'd want to see the great maw of any fleech that came toward him anyway. That was one bit of ugly, horrific fauna he'd seen quite his fill of. They moved nearly as fast as lightning and struck as hard as a lead hammer. He'd know if one had ahold of him without needing to see it, yes indeed.

And then something did strike him.

"Strike" wasn't the right word. Something tickled one of his feet, and in a single beat of his heart, he knew he was simply dead. No dying, no white light, just dead. Because the fear he felt was far too humongous not to send him into instantaneous heart failure.

Silence your thoughts, Bardgrim, a voice rumbled in his head. *You make more noise than a school of tunafish.*

Before he could pull himself together, the sensation in his foot spread to his other, then he was being buoyed upward through the water on something solid, hard, and once his fingers brushed it, surprisingly rough. Not a fleech—it felt more like…

At this new voice in his mind, Jaemus's panic momentarily stilled. *Hello?* he sent after a moment. When no response came, he added: *Hither? Is that you?*

Shhh! Your speck voices are like grains of sand rubbing against our eardrums.

Jaemus took a breath, mentally whispered for light from his Mentalios, and took in the sight of the great beast below him, the great beast that had inexplicably arrived and decided to… give him a ride? He didn't need the Mentalios, however, as they were approaching the surface rapidly. A moment later, he could see both the beast he now sat atop and the body of Saxton held in one of its great claws clearly. The slangarook's scales were a sheen of blueish-purple that bordered on black, and the many fins along its flanks and the ridging its long undulating tail were the same gossamer thinness of Hither's. But since this was not Hither, the question of why it was helping them came to mind.

You can—can you speak? This was the first time he'd realized the creatures were not only sentient but conversant, and all of Griggory's seemingly one-sided conversations with the slangarook that'd become the Creatress's vessel fell into place.

Better than you can think, speck.

Hey, he sent, settling into the mental link. *That sounds suspiciously like an insult.*

Shall I shake you off and let you discuss with the sea worms how sorely I've rubbed your feelings?

Um, no. That is to say, no thank you. And also I suppose another kind of thank-you is in order. Why exactly are you helping me?

Lifs sent us. Now shh! The slangarook shoal is about to dine, and I've heard enough of your noise to last my next eons. Hold on.

Hold—? Before he could finish his statement, the creature surfaced so rapidly that his whole body cleared the sea. Jaemus barely had time to grip one of the creature's great back-swept horns, then they settled and floated atop the water. He rubbed the water from his eyes and immediately came to understand what the creature's statement regarding the slangarook shoal being about to have dinner meant. In the near distance, the sea was being thrashed to foam by an untold number of creatures embroiled in battle. Occasional slangarook fins broached the choppy waves, and worse, the occasional arch of a fleech's back could be seen. So the *Council's Crest* had created enough disturbance to inspire the fleeches to come searching for a meal. If the 'rooks hadn't arrived, Jaemus was sure he'd have ended his day as a digestif.

Spark Saxton's body rose languidly to the surface, face upward, eyes closed. He looked asleep, and Jaemus's fears renewed. "Is he dead?" he gulped.

That depends. Do specks die of fear?

Er, I've never actually seen it happen, but—

He was spared further distress when the spark's eyes opened suddenly, wide enough to be mistaken for saucers, and he sputtered. The moment he spotted the slangarook, he let out a screech and dove. He got nowhere, though, as the slangarook gave a sudden whip of its long tail and plucked Saxton from his attempted escape in its claw once more. *Specks are grossly predictable.*

"Please—ah—help!" the spark cried.

Sure his assurances would fall on deaf ears, Jaemus tried breaking through the man's panic anyway. "Saxton, Saxton, listen to me! You're not in any danger. The slangarook is a—friend?" He knew better than to believe that was the specific truth, but perhaps of all words it would be one that would calm the spark.

"I don't want to die!"

Or not.

If you do not find a way to silence him, speck, I will, came the slangarook's ominous warning.

"Er, well"—a blast of a wind caught his back, and Jaemus turned to see a much larger Glisternaut ship than the one they'd just encountered settling to the surface—"just let him go, I suppose. It looks like our rescuers—that is, our Glisternaut rescuers, are here."

The creature did as asked, and Saxton, having seen the ship as well, began to kick his way toward it with a haste that would almost have given a fleech a run for its money.

The slangarook did a slow spin in the water to face the newly arrived craft. It was at that moment that Jaemus realized he no longer held the shelksie. A side hatch of the cosmocruiser—for he could see now that it was the same type of command ship as the *Bounding Skate*—had begun to open, readying to send crew out to retrieve him and the spark, who was already nearly close enough to touch its hull.

As the cruiser's staff aided the frantic Saxton inside, the slangarook sent: *In as few words as you can possibly manage, tell me what other aid the shoal can provide you. We know the danger the rogue Verity poses for Himmingaze and shan't be idle until the one called Balavad has been dealt with.*

Sighing, Jaemus sent, *I don't suppose you could convince the rest of the Himmingazians that the Creatress is real, could you?* He thought a moment. *No, I imagine the only reason I can hear you is because of the Mentalios. If you spoke to the Council of Nine Crests, or anyone 'Gazian, they would probably think your roars were the opening notes to a dinner fugue.*

You really are a simple species if you believe your minds are that impenetrable to us. Lifs shall do what needs to be done for Himmingaze. Now, if you don't mind, go and rejoin your own. Call us when our aid is needed again, Mystae Bardgrim. But only if our aid is needed. Spare us your insipient speck prattling...

With that, Jaemus found himself floundering alone in the sea once more, the slangarook having swum off so fluidly that he barely noticed its leaving. The danger to the Himmingazians seemed to be gone. That was, if you didn't count a giant sea dragør capable of swallowing a human whole dangerous. He supposed he no longer did.

CHAPTER TWENTY-FIVE

Jaemus paddled to the cosmocruiser, somewhat desultorily if he were to admit it. If the slangarooks really could bring the whole of Himmingaze around to a better understanding of their new lease on the Cosmos, the question of "what next?" still remained. Would his world accept the truth of things, given how much more persuasive a giant, potentially man-eating beast could probably be than a few literally starstruck Glisternauts? And it struck him—was he more worried about that, or was this dispiritedness about his no longer feeling that he, personally, had much purpose anymore? His purpose had finally been achieved, after all, and the thanks he'd gotten for it was not thanks at all.

He nearly sighed again but caught himself. There had been quite enough of that. If he was incongruously sad about having nothing left to do after saving his own world, he could at least take cheer in now helping to save another. But really, was that anything to be cheerful about? He caught a glimpse of the preposterousness of his own whirling, bizarre thoughts and sympathized with the slangarook that had saved him for a moment. He really did burble a lot, didn't he?

Upon reaching the cruiser, he steeled himself for the rough

handling he expected to be in for and looked up toward the hatch. A ladder had been lowered, and a Glisternaut he recognized, Spark Engineer Bannus, was at the top, waving him up. And… smiling?

"What kept you, Glint Bardgrim? We came as soon as we could. Captain Illago will be so pleased you're back," the Glisternaut called down.

Pleased?

Once aboard, he still fully expected to have his hands bound. Instead, the crew member handed him a towel and asked after his health.

"… I'm well?" he half asked, half stated.

"Good, come with me. To the bridge."

As they began the lengthy traverse through the cruiser's passages, a handful of other crew members, all of whom he recognized from the *Bounding Skate* and subsequent trip to Vinnr, welcomed him back. He tried to ask what in the worlds was happening, but his escort merely said that Captain Illago would explain it all.

The bridge was expansive and well-lit, with Cote seated at the helm, where he belonged. As Jaemus entered through the main doorway, Cote spun around and stood up.

Jaemus lingered in place a few breaths—and realized he had no idea what to say.

A heartbeat later, Cote's arms were wrapped around him. "I'm so glad you're safe, Jae. I know I said you were a hero, but for all our annicycles together, I'd always thought that was supposed to be my job."

For maybe the first time in his life, Jaemus was speechless. Finally, words returned. "But… Spark Saxton said you told the Council I wystified all your brains and tried to turn you into heretics."

Cote gave him one more hard squeeze, then stepped back, his hands still clasping Jaemus's elbows. "Of course we did."

"Of… course. You did? I understand your words, but I have no idea what you're saying, Cote. And I'm supposed to be the smart one."

"Sorry, sorry, let me back up. I was just too excited to see you. I forgot you don't know."

"Don't know…" Jaemus was starting to feel self-conscious at his new habit of trailing off, but nothing in his life had fully, or even slightly, prepared him for this new and worrisome sort of intrigue.

"The Council didn't believe us, Jae. Not a word. They insisted that we *must* be muddleminded, that nothing like what we were describing was possible. They would rather have confined us all to a home for the incapacitated for the rest of our lives than believe the Creatress was real or celestial powers had brought Himmingaze out of the Cloud. So we had to think fast, and I knew the only way we would be able to stay out of lockup and be here to help you if you and the Knights needed us was to say what they wanted to hear."

"… That's good then, I guess. If I have it right, I'm actually the only heretic in Himmingaze, at least *officially*, then."

"Well, you and Vreyja and the rest of her group of Creatress followers."

"Oh, water and lightning! Tell me they haven't tossed my gram-sirene in a cell."

"No, no. Don't worry. She's as wily as you are brilliant, Jae. She never stepped foot in Vann. The moment the Glisternauts were off their ship, she and the others just… disappeared. No one has seen them since." He winked then, and Jaemus realized Cote knew exactly where Vreyja was but would be keeping that secret from anyone that couldn't be trusted with it.

Jaemus took a step back and leaned heavily against the wall. He looked around the bridge and took in the smiling but guarded faces of his old crew. They were on his side, still on his side. The relief he felt was almost staggering, and a sense of fatigue suddenly hit him. Saving the world was indeed a memorable achievement, but he'd never realized it would be so tiring.

"Cote, I can honestly say I've never felt less like a hero. If we could just go home right now, drink every last drop of chuffee in the house, and sleep for forty Glister cycles—although, I guess we're not going to be calling them Glister cycles much longer—I'd be willing. More than willing."

"I know, Jae. Me too. But since you're here now, does that mean… ?"

He shook his head. "No, things in Vinnr aren't going as we'd hoped."

Cote's sea-green eyes sharpened, his gaze and posture shifting from mere man to commander of the Glisternaut fleet. "So since you're here, that means—what is it they need from us?"

"Nothing big really. Just, well, Vinnr needs the fleet."

CHAPTER TWENTY-SIX

"You were supposed to have been done laying charges at the mainsail hours ago, Sveinungr, not getting yourself caught out by a Third Phase. I don't think I need to remind you what's in store for us if we're found out."

With slowly dawning awareness, Ulfric recognized first that his hearing was returning, and then that the voice belonged to the chancellor. His senses of the outside world had been badly muffled by his host's Egsil's unconsciousness, but he could hear Aoggvír clearly now. Egsil must be coming to. He was thrilled on one hand, on the other, Egsil's own blooming alarm colored the awakening.

When her eyes opened, he caught a grainy, out-of-focus glimpse of a wooden floor through her vision. This suggested an indoor setting, and he guessed from the vantage that they were seated. Egsil gave her head a brief shake, sending a shooting pain through it that started at her jaw where the blow from Venerate Sveinungr had struck her.

"Hmmph!" she tried, and she and Ulfric realized at the same moment her mouth was gagged. "Hrrrmph!" The next moment, they discovered her arms and feet were lashed tightly to her chair. Her head was the only part of her that moved.

A sour taste exploded in the venerate's mouth, like rancid lemon juice. Her sight came back sharply, only minor tatters clouding the periphery of her vision now.

"Stay still, Venerate." Aoggvír moved closer. "For your own good." She gave Sveinungr a meaningful look that Ulfric couldn't read, and judging by Egsil's confusion, neither could she.

The Fifth Phase venerate stepped closer too, staring into Egsil's wide-open eyes. Ulfric's host seemed to have little idea what was happening, but he was beginning to put it together.

"We can use her, perhaps," Sveinungr said. "Should anything go wrong when we launch our first assault, if the charges I've laid are discovered, we can blame this one."

"It would mean her death," said Aoggvír.

Sveinungr nodded. "True, and by our own hands. We couldn't let Balavad have her. She already knows too much, and we've both seen the way he's able to get… inside. There are no secrets from the foreign Verity."

At this, everyone in the room grew still.

The chancellor came and stood over his host. "I would like to release you, Egsil, I would. You stumbled into something you shouldn't have." Aoggvír's tone sounded truly regretful. It did little to ease the venerate, however. Looking back at Sveinungr, Aoggvír continued. "You'll need to make it look like she died accidentally while setting a charge. Take her down by the keel. Her body won't be easily found, yet it would be the obvious place for someone intent on sabotage."

Egsil's breathing picked up, drawn frantically through her nostrils, and Ulfric couldn't help but pity the woman. Overhearing the terms of one's own death being discussed would probably be more unsettling than the manner in which one died.

Sveinungr nodded. "And what if the Ivoryssians never attack? What should we do with her? The dishonor would taint her Line for a century."

While the two Dyrraks discussed the woman's fate, Ulfric made his own calculations. He was shocked to learn that that the chancellor and her cohort Sveinungr had plans of their own to disable if not outright destroy some or all of the advance fleet. The reasons why—greed, self-preservation, treachery—would be easy to guess if they were anyone but Dyrraks. Yet he couldn't quite believe any of these would be the chancellor's intentions. Dyrraks thought of themselves as one thing: incorruptible servants of Vaka Aster. Nothing mattered to them but showing their worth. Even the Domine Ecclesium had not totally subverted this norm. He'd done exactly as Balavad had commanded him, arguably to *prove* his worthiness, even if it were to another Verity.

So what, then? Treachery was the only option with any teeth, but he couldn't imagine the chancellor would be attempting to aid the Ivoryssians. The Dyrraks' disdain for them was as fundamentally Dyrrak as breathing was.

To find out, he'd have to ask. And to do that, he'd have to reveal himself.

"Get her up," Aoggvír said.

Egsil was panicking, her body shaking uncontrollably at the knowledge she was about to be murdered. Ulfric had to face the reality that he had gotten the woman killed, and potentially disastrously, he had no idea what would happen to him.

"Wait!" he shouted, projecting himself through the memory keeper still on the chancellor's desk. "I propose we discuss other options."

Weapons materialized in the two Dyrraks' hands immediately, conjured as if from nothing. The surprise on their faces as their eyes darted around the room exceeded any expression he'd ever seen on a Dyrrak, including those who'd recently worshipped him.

"Don't be alarmed, Chancellor. You most likely remember me. Here, I'm speaking from the pendant Venerate Egsil brought earlier."

Everyone looked toward the open-topped box containing the pendant. From Egsil's eyes, Ulfric could see the glow within, the crystal now illuminated with his presence. With a dart of her chin, Aoggvír gestured to Sveinungr to retrieve it. The Fifth Phase approached and stared down at it, and his face blanched. He dropped to a knee before the desk, speaking two words.

"Vaka Aster."

After throwing Egsil an unreadable glance, Aoggvír crossed the room. When she saw Ulfric's face in the crystal, her eyebrows drew together sternly, even angrily. Ulfric hadn't expected the Dyrraks to think he was still Vaka Aster and was spinning through the ways he might be able to use this to his advantage. This brief encouragement, however, quickly deflated.

"No, I don't think so," the chancellor said. "Stallari Aldinhuus, I'll admit that your many tricks and illusions are intriguing, but the time for such games ended when the Domine Ecclesium stained Dyrrakium eternally with his infidelity to the true Vaka Aster. Explain yourself now, starting with two things: tell us where you are, and tell us why the Knights Corporealis betrayed our maker." She stepped closer and picked up not the pendant, to Ulfric's frustration, but the box it was in. "If you don't, this pendant goes into the Verring Sea to spend eternity in its depths. And you, I hope, with it."

She knew. She *knew*. Maybe Ulfric yet had an ally in Dyrrakium who could help him turn the tides of war away from Ivoryss.

He'd never needed to be more convincing in his long life, even when he'd worn the guise of Vaka Aster herself.

"The Knights Corporealis never betrayed Vaka Aster. I did." Good start, he told himself as he watched Aoggvír's scowl turn into something frightening in its severity. "And that, even that, was because of Balavad. Let me explain."

<hr>

By the time he'd wrapped up the story, leaving out most of the events of Arc Rheunos, he had no assurance they believed him. The Dyrraks' enduring impassivity was every bit as remarkable as their devotion to their maker. Finally, Aoggvír set the box back on the desk and broke the silence, but she wasn't speaking to Ulfric.

"You see, I was right," she said to Sveinungr. "The Ecclesium lost his faith and has tainted all of Dyrrakium because of it." In a fluid, unexpected swing, she buried her dagger angrily in the desktop beside the pendant. "When I'm finished carving him up, his bones will be used as serving ware, and I'll crush his eyes to jelly on Penitence Rock while all the empire watches."

Ulfric let the image of that pass unexamined through his thoughts, knowing she meant each word literally, then said, "So you'll help me?"

"From what you've told us, Aldinhuus, you're as effective in stopping Balavad as a fly. What good can come from helping a fly?"

Ulfric clenched his ephemeral jaw. She was acting exactly like he'd come to expect—like a Dyrrak, to be precise. "You think you can stop a Verity on your own? He obviously has no concerns he won't be able to control you, and hasn't even seen a need to make you into one of his puppets."

He thought he detected the skin around her eyes tighten at the insult, but her self-control was infallible.

"I truly want to know, Chancellor, why scuttle the fleet under your own command? What are your plans from here, knowing that the Domine Ecclesium has all but handed the realm to a foreign Verity and broken every vow to Vaka Aster the Dyrraks hold as dear as the honor of their own Lines?"

She studied him, then looked at Sveinungr, saying nothing aloud but much through her eyes. The Fifth Phase venerate appeared to consider her unspoken words and tilted his chin a fraction in agreement.

"We need to draw the might of the full Dyrrak Phalanx away from Dyrrakium," she finally said. "It's the only way we'll be able to attain Vaka Aster's vessel and steal it away from Her Holiness Balavad—and from Dyrrakium if we have to."

Her? Ulfric thought, then remembered the Knights' explanation. Balavad's new vessel, a spy left behind in Vinnr, was a Battgjaldic woman. With Battgjald destroyed, the spy was just one of who knew how many remaining. Balavad had had the foresight to seed the Cosmos with many other potential vessels in his quest to control it all. Though the Battgjaldics didn't blend in well among the Vinnrics, there was no saying how many still existed in other realms, saved from Battgjald's destruction by their absence.

Putting that aside, Ulfric said, "You're trying to protect Vaka Aster's vessel."

"Since you failed to, yes."

That one stung. But the truth of it was right there, undeniable.

The chancellor continued. "Despite it being certain death, we're sure the Ivoryssians will launch whatever paltry attack they can at some point, and when they do, Sveinungr, I, and several others will damage our own ships enough to make it seem as if the Ivoryssian forces have more strength and weapons than they do. We'll be able to force our crews to withdraw and reassess, and buy our allies in Dyrrakium more time. If the Ivoryssians have any sense, those who can will flee and save their lives."

"Your allies in Dyrrakium. You mean other Dyrraks?"

"Yes, those whose loyalty to Vaka Aster is untainted. Believe me, it only took one look into the eyes of one of our transformed kin to know theirs is a death without dying that I want no part of." She yanked her dagger from the desktop and seated it in a sheath in the small of her back. "And despite what you may think of the Dyrraks, Aldinhuus, this choice to attack Ivoryss and then Yor, it's not a true choice. Most of my people are being used, as you said, like puppets. The quarrels we had with the lesser kingdoms are ancient. An age has passed, and it's time to let our hatreds pass too. Perhaps if we already had, the three kingdoms would not have been so blind and would have seen Balavad's true intentions sooner."

At that moment, Ulfric would have given half the glory and knowledge he'd gained in his life if Seldeg Aoggvír had been the Domine Ecclesium instead of Starkas Nazaria. "Why have you and others not been turned? Doesn't Balavad seek to control everyone?"

"The foreign Verity needs us, leaders and those with particular talents. It seems to be harder to control the Raveners the farther away they are, so she has left some who've proved their loyalty as we are, unchanged."

The way Aoggvír's eyes hardened again at her last statement made Ulfric decide not to question exactly how they were made to prove their loyalty. "Chancellor," he said, "I need to reach your allies in Dyrrakium. I know how to free Vaka Aster, and I'm the only one who can do it."

She scoffed. "You're nothing but a voice in a rock. What can you do as you are?"

"The Knights retained Vaka Aster's Scrylle. With it—"

"Then where are they? Why aren't they here?" Her tone had an edge, part from anger, but, Ulfric suspected, part from desperation. "You've failed Vinnr and you've failed Vaka Aster too many times to be trusted further with this task, Stallari of the dishonored Knights Corporealis or not."

"Don't be stupid, Aoggvír. The realm doesn't have time for it."

He could see the words struck her like a slap, but they needed to be said. Even with her flowery talk of putting hatreds aside, she was still as fallible as the next person. Being filled with Dyrrak pride didn't shield her from fear, and fear, if left unchecked, eventually made anyone's sense of reason questionable.

"He speaks the truth, Chancellor." Sveinungr's comment drew the ice of her stare, but he continued undeterred, albeit with carefully lowered and visible hands. "The Knights Corporealis may be all that stands between the rest of us becoming Balavad's slaves. And"—he glanced at Ulfric—"who else can stand against the Nazarian, now?"

At the mention of Eisa, Ulfric asked, "What's become of Knight Nazaria?"

Looking troubled, the chancellor said briefly, "She's gone to the south. No one knows why, only that she was sent by Balavad."

The south? Dyrrakium's Anzuru Desert took up the continent's southern half, a hostile landscape. No humans lived there, only dragørs, and even those had long since retreated to their towering aeries, rarely seen by people. There was nothing there for her to do but become a dragør's lunch.

Yet, this could be a boon. If Ulfric could free Vaka Aster before Eisa returned to Elezaran, Vaka Aster could undo the desecration Balavad had wrought on his fellow Knight. If Ulfric could press Vaka Aster to save her, he would beg on his knees if it came to that. He owed Eisa that and more.

Ulfric charged ahead. "You want to know what I can do, Chancellor?"

He smiled. "I can *be* anyone who touches the pendant." They all looked at him, even Egsil, with puzzled expressions. "When Venerate Egsil said she heard voices on the deck, she did. Mine, from within her own mind."

"That's…" Aoggvír trailed off, her expression doubtful. Egsil, on the other hand, was nodding her head vigorously, as if learning the answer to a question that had stumped her.

"Hold the pendant, Chancellor. I can show you," Ulfric said.

"Don't be stupid, Aldinhuus. I don't have time for it," Aoggvír rejoined his earlier barb testily. "Sveinungr, remove Egsil's gag. Venerate, don't shout or draw attention. If you cooperate, your sacrifice for Vaka Aster may not be needed in the end."

Egsil nodded and Sveinungr did as told.

"Now prove what you've told us, Aldinhuus," Aoggvír commanded.

Ulfric took his focus from the pendant and settled back into Egsil's mind. *Do you hear me, Venerate?*

She flinched, the action visible to everyone in the room. "Yes."

Tell me something about yourself that I couldn't know, but they would.

"I—"

No, not aloud.

Grasping his meaning, she withdrew into her thoughts with him. Her mental voice started out hesitant, but quickly grew equal parts confounded and infuriated. *You can hear my thoughts?*

Yes.

How—why are you in my head? Get out!

I wish to, but first you must help me. Let me do what's necessary to convince the chancellor, and I will do everything in my power to see you are spared. You have my word. Now, what's something they'd know but I wouldn't about you?

She thought briefly, then said, *In my Third Phase fight, I was stabbed in the liver. My opponent slipped in my blood, and I used the advantage to slash a tendon in her left knee. I won the fight.*

The ferocity of this altercation took Ulfric a moment to contemplate, as did the apparent genius of the Dyrrak healers who could save a woman from having her liver pierced by a dagger.

Tell them! she demanded, not appreciating her nonconsensual relationship with him in the least.

He relayed the story through the pendant, watching the chancellor's face closely to gauge her reaction.

"Who was the opponent?" she asked.

"Gara Aoggvír," he passed on, wondering at the relationship to the chancellor.

Aoggvír's eyes flicked between the pendant and Egsil for several beats. Eventually, she said, "My niece still limps, Venerate, but you impressed many with your skills that day."

Cautious relief flooded Ulfric's host. "Thank you, Chancellor," she said. "I—"

Aoggvír's raised hand stopped whatever she'd been about to say. The chancellor beckoned to Sveinungr, who stepped up close enough that she could speak into his ear. Ulfric wished he were still benefiting from the heightened senses of the bruhawks, and a moment later, Sveinungr looked down at the pendant and cautiously lifted the box it lay in.

"Say nothing," he told Ulfric, then stepped out of the cabin. On the other side of the cabin door, he said quietly, "Ask the venerate to stomp her feet. Twice with the left, followed by twice with the right."

Clever, Ulfric thought, then passed on the instructions to Egsil.

The door was opened a moment later and Aoggvír stood there. "Most impressive, Aldinhuus. Perhaps you will be useful to us."

CHAPTER TWENTY-SEVEN

Nothing in Ulfric's last few weeks had been predictable, even in his remotest imaginings, but perhaps the least predictable was this moment—being ensconced within the mind of a high-ranking Dyrrak warrior and flying aboard one of their fighter crafts into the heart of Dyrrakium to steal back his body and his Verity.

Once Aoggvír believed Ulfric could do what he said he could, it hadn't taken less time to convince her that he was more of an asset than anything else she and her cohorts had at their disposal and persuade her to work with him. She'd seen the wisdom in sending Ulfric to Elezaran and the Citadel Suprima at once, and had even considered allowing him to take residence in her own mind. In the end, though, she couldn't abdicate her responsibility to the advance fleet without arousing suspicion. Sveinungr, however, had more flexibility and had insisted he become Ulfric's host. Once Ulfric joined him, he found it unsurprising how alike he and the Dyrrak man thought, at least tactically, and their partnership had so far been nearly seamless.

If nothing else came of it, Ulfric was relieved that he had managed to save Egsil's life. He'd sworn he'd help her if he could, and he'd not yet let go of his need to stand by his promises. More simply, he didn't want to live with the knowledge that she'd died needlessly simply for doing her job, even if her job had been to attack the Ivoryssians when her commanders ordered it. Unbending loyalty and strict adherence to discipline were instilled in every Dyrrak from birth, and Ulfric couldn't blame her for being who she was. In his own younger years, he'd followed orders more than once without looking deeper at their provenance and knew the power of unquestioned allegiance.

In the end, both he and Aoggvír had asked the Third Phase whether, after all she'd overheard, she could be trusted to remain loyal to Vaka Aster and conceal Aoggvír and her cohorts' plans—or not. Naturally, she'd insisted she was trustworthy, a dedicated devotee to their maker with faith eternal. Ulfric had probed as deeply into her thoughts, even those she tried to guard, as he could, using his substantial mental strength to drill into and assess the veracity of her promise, and he'd been convinced she would do as she'd said. She, too, hated what Balavad was doing to her fellow Dyrraks, and it didn't require much imagination to see that being a Ravener wasn't a savory existence. Convincing Aoggvír of Egsil's obedience had taken some doing, but because it was obvious Ulfric's special abilities gave him a kind of access to a person's innermost mind that had no equal, she'd agreed to let Egsil live, though her every move, every breath, would be watched by those loyal to Aoggvír.

We shall be there by High Halls tomorrow, Sveinungr sent, cutting into Ulfric's own musings so easily it was as if he'd been doing it his whole life. *I have known Venerate Egsil's family since I was a child, and she will do as she promised.*

My apologies, Venerate Sveinungr, I didn't realize my thoughts were being intrusive, Ulfric said.

It's fine. I feel it's... better, for both of us, if we hide as little as possible from each other. And it's Gusun. Just call me Gusun.

I shall. Thank you.

It will save time.

Ulfric repressed a mental chuckle. The man's pragmatism shouldn't have surprised him.

Gusun flew the small craft, virtually identical to the dragørfly scouts the Knights had built, expertly. They were flying southeast, leaving the night behind them, and would see the rising sun before Ivoryss did. Ulfric thought back to the hundreds of ships like this one he'd seen in the Dyrrak airfield from the top of the citadel, knowing that all of them were now once more on their way to Ivoryss. Instead of lining the airfield, they lined the decks of the Dyrrak fleet, saving energy to be used only for battle. This time there would be no turning the Dyrrak fleet back if Balavad ordered them to go to war. According to Havelock Rekkr, Ivoryss had fewer than three dozen of their own Wing fighters left. The Dyrraks could wipe them out in a breath.

Ulfric had wanted Gusun to bring him to Magdaster, where he could retrieve Vaka Aster's Scrylle. With it in Dyrrakium, he could perform the uncaging rite and release his Verity the instant he gained access to her. But that proved impracticable once he learned that the rest of the Dyrrak fleet was expected to join Aoggvír's within two days. He and Gusun would lose those two days flying to Magdaster for the Scrylle, then another three at least getting to Dyrrakium. By that time, the Ivoryssian capital of Asteryss could be decimated, and the Dyrraks would be moving up the coast for Magdaster. He didn't want to be caught there, and he had to trust the Knights and Nennus to hold them off.

In fact, he'd pressed the chancellor to abandon her orders and surrender to the Knights. She'd flatly refused—not that Ulfric had expected differently. Her precise words were "If you fail—again—to free Vaka Aster, you'll leave me no choice but to fight. Ivoryss will come for Vaka Aster's vessel, if they have any honor in them. My people have no reason to think they'll be any more merciful toward us than fate would force us to be toward them. I'd rather have my skin ripped from my bones and flown as a flag than betray Dyrrakium and its people or taint our worthiness."

It was just like speaking with Eisa. Leaving only one course remaining to him. He had to reclaim his body, and Vaka Aster, as soon as possible. Caging Balavad to put an end to the Verity's assaults for good was still the ultimate goal, but taking the option for Balavad to simply wipe Vinnr out by destroying Vaka Aster's vessel was the more prudent and potentially more achievable step now, given Aoggvír's accomplices in Dyrrakium.

He'd considered sending Urgo and Yggo to Magdaster with a message for the Knights about the evolving plan, with instructions to wait for him there. The Knights needed to be ready. Once he had Vaka Aster back, he would bring the vessel to them. That, however, would have left him completely at the Dyrraks' mercy, and he had to admit, he didn't trust them fully, no matter how much it was in his interest to do so. The Knights were capable, smart, and knew the stakes. And Aoggvír had sworn she would hold off the fleet for as long as she could, until she had word from Dyrrakium regarding Ulfric's success or failure. Thus it was decided that the bruhawks would stay with Ulfric. Their dragør lineage and Verity sparks gave them the strength and speed to reach Dyrrakium alongside Gusun's fighter.

Gusun's thoughts began to lose their sharpness, and when he yawned, Ulfric realized the Dyrrak was growing tired. They'd been aloft for quite some time, and was approaching Hallumbrum a full day after their middle-of-the-night departure.

Get some sleep, Gusun, Ulfric said. *I can fly us the rest of the way.*

What?

Trust me. You aren't the first person I've done this with. If you close your eyes, I can see from the memory keeper. I don't need to sleep, but you'll be responsible for a much greater task than landing this craft come tomorrow. We both need you fresh.

Though the man's doubts came through to Ulfric, he nevertheless let his posture relax and his head rest on the back of the pilot seat. With Ulfric's steady, smooth flying, it didn't take long for his eyes to shut and his breathing to deepen.

As calm as any Knight, Ulfric mused. *It's time, past time in fact, for the Dyrraks to rejoin the rest of Vinnr. As Aoggvír said, we're far too hindered by our disunity, and the price we've paid has been much too high.*

Gusun awoke at Ulfric's summoning just before reaching Elezaran and landed the fighter smoothly in the airfield near the city. Immediately, a squad of Dyrrak Raveners and a singular unchanged Dyrrak surrounded the craft with weapons drawn. Gusun wasn't exactly taken into custody like a criminal, but they hadn't expected him and he was therefore not trusted to walk freely.

A Fourth Phase venerate, the only non-Ravener, took charge as Sveinungr dismounted. "Fifth Phase, your arrival was not planned. I've been instructed to bring you to the Domine Ecclesium at once."

Inwardly, Gusun warned Ulfric, *This soldier is not among my and Aoggvír's friends. Don't do or say anything. I'll handle this.*

Ulfric was content to watch and wait, as they had planned for this. The Domine Ecclesium would be their first trial, and their cover story had already been prepared. After Gusun was allowed to return to the Phalanx, they'd meet the rest of Vaka Aster's loyalists and move forward with their plan to acquire Ulfric's body.

Gusun reached for his glaive, a move Ulfric flinched at. Would this squad see this as a threat and react accordingly? His worry proved unnecessary. A Dyrrak's weapon was as much a part of their uniform as their Phase markings, and the squad ignored the movement. Besides, what did a squad of ten against one have to be concerned about?

As they made their way up the Citadel Suprima's rampart toward the gallery leading inside, Ulfric steeled himself against the fresh memories of the horrors he'd witnessed on these stairs—Eisa's mutilation, the Knights hanging from grotesque cages by their heads, and worst, Balavad's reemergence in Vinnr—as well as against the sinister pall of quiet that lay over the city and the citadel. There'd only been about a hundred fighters remaining in the airfield, and the amphitheater of seats surrounding the citadel's courtyard was completely empty. He didn't even hear sounds coming over the walls from the enormous city outside. Dyrrakium had mobilized for war, and now the majority of them were either fortifying their homes or were aboard the fleet of hundreds of ships that was headed for Ivoryss.

Was Balavad among that fleet, or was the Verity here? According to

Gusun, when Her Holiness was in Elezaran, she spoke to few besides the Ecclesium, and it was unlikely they'd face her. Ulfric, only partly confident he would not be visible to the Verity's eyes through Gusun's own, hoped he was right.

They found the Ecclesium in a planning room off the main hall.

Their Fourth Phase escort saw herself into the chamber, whose door was ajar. "Domine Ecclesium, I have Fifth Phase Venerate Svein-ungr with me. He just now arrived."

The Ecclesium looked up from the table he sat at, which was covered with scrolls, pens, ink, and books. Looking into Starkas Nazaria's face, Ulfric's loathing pulsed through his ephemeral self as strongly as any hurricane had ever crashed against a beachhead. Despite being very tired of seeing so much death of late, his dedication to justice had not diminished. And death was the only justice that could serve a man who'd betrayed not only his adversaries but also his own people.

"Alone?" the Ecclesium asked mildly.

"Yes, Domine Ecclesium."

The Ecclesium rose from his chair and beckoned to the venerate. "Bring him in."

Gusun stepped in front of their escort and dipped his head respect-fully. "Domine Ecclesium, I've brought an urgent dispatch from Chan-cellor Aoggvír."

The Dyrrak Ravener squad had followed Gusun inside and arrayed themselves beside and behind him, but the Ecclesium's eyes remained fixed unflinchingly on Gusun. They were unreadable, but Ulfric would never think of them as mild. As sharp as a bruhawk's, and as shrewd. As Gusun faced the Dyrrak leader, Ulfric noted something interesting, however. The man's hair, previously black and only lightly streaked with gray, was now uniformly steel colored. It seemed being the turncoat that led to the downfall of one's own empire was taking its toll on the man.

"What is it, Venerate Sveinungr?"

"Our spies from the Ivoryssian capital have not reported in since the advance fleet arrived. We don't know if this means they've been caught or if they've simply been unable to meet us as planned without drawing the unworthies' suspicion. Either way, the chancellor sent me to convey her concerns. She wished it to be known that we no longer have timely information about the Ivoryssians, and we may wish to seek alternative means of assessing their strength before the fleet launches a full attack."

The Ecclesium stared at him a moment before turning back to the table and running his long fingers absently across the spine of a book. With a smirk, he looked back. "Does the chancellor really think the Ivoryssians have anything we don't already know about that could cause our forces to so much as blink? I know Seldeg isn't losing her nerve."

Flatly, Gusun said, "I can only deliver the message I was told to."

"And why you?"

This question caught Gusun off guard. "The chancellor is my commander and has ordered me forth. I don't question the reasons of my commander, Domine Ecclesium."

The Ecclesium paced back to Gusun and fastened him once more with his cold gray eyes. "Yet she specifically requested you be her second on the *Gildr*." In a smooth, clipped motion, he raised both hands and beckoned to the Raveners beside Gusun. "Seize him."

The mildness of his tone was undercut by the hardness of his words, and a heartbeat later, the squad of Raveners had both Gusun's arms locked in their grasps, another had an arm encircling his throat, and his glaive had been stripped from the holster at his back.

Gusun only struggled for a moment, relinquishing to the futility of it quickly.

"Search his belongings."

This was where Ulfric began to panic. *The Fenestros,* he said to Gusun. *Verity's curses, we shouldn't have brought it.*

But it was too late for should-haves. Before launching from the *Gildr*, Ulfric had summoned Yggo and retrieved the Himmingazian Fenestros, counting on it as a source of backup aid if needed. Bringing the celestial stone to Dyrrakium was a gamble, but Ulfric had truly believed the Domine Ecclesium wouldn't question Gusun's presence. How could they have underestimated the man so badly?

The Raveners found the Fenestros in Gusun's belt pouch quickly. The memory keeper hung around his neck, the chain hidden by the high collar of his leather shirt, and the strap of his glaive holster crossed over the outline of the pendant on his chest, concealing it. For now.

One of the Raveners carried the Fenestros to the Ecclesium, who held it in his cupped palm. He stared at it for a moment, and for once, his expression changed. When he looked back at Gusun, he said wonderingly, "A Fenestros, but from which realm?" He moved close enough that he could hold the stone before Gusun's face, almost touching his chin. "You know what I'll do to you if you lie to me any more, Venerate, but you have no idea what Her Holiness will, and you should be grateful for that. Now speak the truth, where did you get this and what are you planning?"

Tell him nothing, Gusun, Ulfric said hastily. *Stall until I can figure out how to—*

Gusun cut him off. *Be ready.*

With a show of strength Ulfric could hardly believe, the Dyrrak yanked both his arms at once, pulling the Raveners holding them off balance. At the same time, his head slammed back into the face of the Ravener who held his throat from behind, and with one arm now freed, he tore the arm of the rearward Ravener from his neck. Then he lunged for the Ecclesium.

Who had withdrawn a dagger. It slid between Gusun's ribs, nearly into his heart, like water sliding over a rock.

NOOO! Ulfric yelled. The man would surely die, and then what would become of Ulfric?

The Ecclesium pulled his dagger free, slowly, as if savoring the motion, and stepped backward. A splash of Gusun's blood arced across the floor, then began rushing from the wound in a pulsing stream. Gusun sank to his knees. Around him, the Raveners closed in but seemed unconcerned he had any more fight to offer. The dying man reached for his neck, and Ulfric could feel how difficult lifting his own arm's weight was, like lifting a tombstone with a single finger. But he managed to hook his thumb beneath the memory keeper's chain and draw it from his shirt.

"Your false faith… has… stained Dyrrakium to its core… Ecclesium. But… soon it will be wiped clean."

Gusun fell face-first onto the floor, and Ulfric's cries for him to fight, not to give up, elicited no response.

Through his wide, staring eyes, darkness began to tear away Gusun's vision, but not before he saw the Ecclesium lean down.

In a low, curious voice, the Dyrrak leader said, "And what is this?"

CHAPTER TWENTY-EIGHT

Stripped of all sense, sight, sound, and feeling, Ulfric did the only thing he could: he pushed himself through the memory keeper into whoever may be close enough to host him.

It was either the best or the worst decision he'd ever made.

The Domine Ecclesium staggered to one side as he straightened up, the memory keeper held in his grip. His hand flew to his forehead as if it were pierced with pain. Ulfric, disoriented, felt the man's hand on his own skin, felt the dryness of the air through his nostrils, took in the scent of red dust that permeated all of Dyrrakium, and finally, saw through the Ecclesium's eyes. It was not Ulfric's plan to inhabit this traitorous Dyrrak, but there was no doubt it had been Gusun's. Now Ulfric was going to have to struggle to make it work. He had no other choice.

"Ecclesium, are you well?" asked the lone non-Ravener Dyrrak who'd escorted Gusun to the planning chamber.

"Yes," the Ecclesium answered shortly, though Ulfric could feel the confusion in his mind, the way he was at the same instant trolling his own interior for an answer to what had struck him. The man sensed him in a way none of the others had, his own deep cunning like that of a rat that had outlived every attempt to catch it triggered by the change.

Ulfric was darkly amused at the comparison to a rat, for that was exactly what the Ecclesium had become. But his amusement quickly dried up when he heard a thought—directed at him.

I feel you, whoever, whatever you are. I know you're here with me. Aloud, the Ecclesium ordered, "Throw the venerate's body to the yorvics. He has betrayed his Line and Dyrrakium and will not lie in the tombs of his family."

"What shall I tell his family?"

The Ecclesium's brow wrinkled thoughtfully. "Has he any who've not been consecrated?"

"I… I'm not sure, Domine Ecclesium. I'll seek them out."

"It can wait, Fourth Phase. He is merely the first casualty in this war. There are sure to be more, and the dead rolls can be spoken when the final tally is made. Or when it becomes necessary to better motivate anyone who may need it. Dismissed."

When the soldiers and Gusun's corpse were gone, the Ecclesium casually pushed the door of the chamber closed and took a seat at the broad table.

Calmly, he placed the memory keeper before him and looked into its crystal pointedly. Only then did he speak. "Now, stranger, who are you?"

Ulfric hesitated, but only for a moment. He knew hiding was no longer an option. "I think you know, Nazarian," he said, showing himself in the pendant's crystal.

"So, we have abandoned titles. Fine. Then shall I call you Aldinhuus, the defeated and dishonored once-leader of the likewise defeated and dishonored Knights Corporealis."

"Call me whatever you want. It's not a conversation I want from you. Take me to Vaka Aster."

"Ah. That tells me one thing. Your… bond with our creator has been severed."

Ulfric caught his slip-up too late. If he didn't polish the dullness from his wits, he would give more away. The Ecclesium would see three moves ahead in this game, no matter what Ulfric tried to hide. He was at the mercy of a master politician, whose life was spent outsmarting and outmaneuvering everyone around him. Ulfric would probably lose at a game of wits. Therefore, he knew it would eventually come down to a game of force.

"Why remain quiet, Aldinhuus? We've never formally met, and I have to admit some intrigue at who you are, the things you've accomplished in life. Balavad already told me what you did, how you bound our maker in a cage of your own being. A man who could do something like that, a betrayal so antithetical to not only what the Dyrraks believe in but to what even he believed in and swore an oath to keep others from doing, either that is a man with incalculable dedication to an even *greater* belief or a simple rogue with no beliefs at all. As I said, I don't know you, but I don't believe you are the latter."

He knew he was being drawn out for the Ecclesium's amusement, but he couldn't seem to resist. "If I'm a betrayer of incalculable dedication to my beliefs, what does that make you?"

"I'm no different from you, Aldinhuus. I believe in devotion and dominion. The principles came to me from my maker, as they did to us all, and I will simply do as I'm made to do. Which Verity I serve is hardly of import, given that they are all One ultimately. It's principles that define us."

"You hold principles to be more valuable than life?"

The Ecclesium sighed as if bored. "Life is nothing but a process of biology if we don't make something more of it. Take the Knights, for example. You have all but unlimited life. It would mean nothing, indeed you would probably seek ways to end it sooner, if you did not have a reason to live it. You live to serve. You have created a doctrine, a dogma even, about your role in the Cosmos. Did you think you were the only ones?"

Ulfric said nothing for a few moments. The truth was, he could find no argument to oppose what the man was saying. In fact, on more than one occasion he'd taken another's life for the sake of Vaka Aster, though she'd never asked him to do it, and it had always been to ensure her vessel stayed safe. What the Ecclesium was arguing was that the

Dyrraks were simply taking a life, or rather many lives, at the behest of another Verity. Did the reasons really matter if it was being done because a Verity deemed it should be? Human principles belonged to humans alone. But Verities were the ones who made humans, and therefore, any principle a human could conceive of was Verity-bestowed as well. Or so the Ecclesium seemed to think.

He supposed it all came down to one thing: in the end, one could choose to either side with the Verities or side with people. And Ulfric had already made his choice.

"Enough with your rambling justifications, Nazarian. I made a mistake when I let Balavad twist my will, and I'm here to right it. Take me to Vaka Aster. I'm not going to ask again."

"I have never served another man, Aldinhuus, or the avatar of one. And I'm not going to begin now."

The battle was underway. To any outside observer, the stillness with which the Domine Ecclesium sat at his planning table would have been akin to observing a statue. No muscle twitched, no lash blinked. The only giveaway that the man had not turned to stone was the swish of blood in the veins that stood out, prominently, on his forehead. His pulse was rapid, though his eyes remained fixed ahead and his breathing slow.

But inside his mind, a battle was being waged, and Ulfric was not finding it easy to win.

You shall submit, Ecclesium. You can't think you'll best a man who's lived as long as I.

If you could take my mind, you already would have, Aldin—ahh!

Ulfric had blindsided the man with an all-out, furious assault. Like a drill, he'd imagined himself pointed and sharp and pushed himself into the Ecclesium's pain centers, doing his best to make the man's mind believe his body had been impaled by a sword, straight through the heart. And for a moment, it worked.

The Ecclesium clenched his fists hard, and Ulfric *felt* his hands, felt them as if they were his own. Leaping into the advantage, he willed himself into the man's forearms, biceps, shoulders, and pushed with all his might up from the table. The Ecclesium fought back, somehow retaining control of his legs, and bent his knees, trying to force his body back into the seat.

No—you... cannot... he grunted mentally.

Then Ulfric had an idea. Before them sat the Himmingazian Fenestros taken from Gusun's bag. If he could get the Ecclesium's hand on it, it was possible that the Verity spark that bolstered so much of Ulfric's physical being could still be accessed by his spirit, even through the medium of another man's hands. If he could touch that celestial stone, his will would be that much strengthened, and he would prevail.

He reached out with the Ecclesium's hand. It was like being in a dream. That feeling you had when you held one end of a rope, the other end spilling over the edge of a cliff with someone you loved hanging from it. You had to pull them up or they would fall to their death. You knew in your bones the strength was in you, but somehow, irrevocably, horribly, your dream muscles were failing you—you couldn't hold the rope. Then, with the feeling of triumph of overcoming a nightmare, with a final heave, Ulfric forced the man's arm another inch and felt the resistance begin to lessen. He was leaning forward now, reaching out, a finger about to brush the stone's surface.

A dagger stabbed through the reaching hand, spearing it to the wooden tabletop.

"Aahh!" both Ulfric and the Ecclesium cried.

But worse, his grip on the Ecclesium's mind came completely loose. The rope slipped, and Ulfric was forced back into a corner of the man's thoughts once more. The Ecclesium's self-inflicted pain gave him back his edge, pain bolstering power.

If Ulfric could have been panting in his current state, he would have. *I nearly had you, you bastirt.*

The Ecclesium swiped his lip across his shoulder to wipe away the sweat. *But you didn't. If you can use my pain against me, I can use it against you. Remember that.* With the slowness of a slime mold, the man rocked the dagger hilt back and forth, sucking air through his teeth in a painful hiss, then pulled it from the table. *I would whittle myself to nothing but bones if I had to, to keep you at bay. But I don't have to, Aldin-*

huus. You're nothing but dust in my thoughts. If I can't sweep you out, I know someone who can.

"Ecclesium, I heard a yell?" came a voice from the doorway.

Like a striking snake, Ulfric leveraged the distraction a fraction of a heartbeat before the Ecclesium realized he'd let him. The bloody fist snapped up the Fenestros in a death grip, and Ulfric shouted an incantation in Elder Veros that pulled the celestial stone's power through the Ecclesium's body in a shock wave. The Dyrrak's will was smashed into the corner of his mind and pinned there. Ulfric stretched himself in his new quarters like a man awakening from a deep sleep.

"Ecclesium?" The Dyrrak venerate had taken a step inside the chamber, his attention sharp.

Ulfric blinked his new eyes and pushed himself to his new feet. The movement was hardly fluid, more like a doddering elder, but he quickly mastered his borrowed limbs. He'd had practice by now, and the Ecclesium had no advantage that could best the Fenestros.

He turned to the venerate. "It's nothing, Venerate. I'm... I do not wish for any further disturbance, am I clear?"

"But... your hand."

"It's nothing but a test of my faith. Shall I test yours next?"

"I'll leave you be, Domine Ecclesium." The guard retreated without a second glance.

Ulfric's new form flushed hot from foot to cheek, the Ecclesium's rage, and perhaps more than a small bit of fear, coursing through him like fever. *What in the five realms do you plan to do, Aldinhuus? My body is no more powerful than your useless pendant against Balavad. You're nothing—*

Ulfric shut the voice out. Never had he so completely controlled any form like this but his own, and he was not going to waste time letting the betrayer plague him. He sent a summons to Urgo and Yggo, then left the chamber.

His Verity awaited him.

CHAPTER TWENTY-NINE

lfric could have kicked himself for not asking Gusun and the chancellor who their accomplices in Elezaran were before it was too late. He might have had better luck of accomplishing a discreet getaway with more aid. As it was, the bruhawks would easily be able to carry him as Vaka Aster's vessel, but they would be slower and more vulnerable guarding such a valuable body of cargo.

At least, he reflected as he raced up the stairs toward the Verity chamber at the peak of Citadel Suprima, *they'll only have the burden of one body.* He planned to shed the Domine Ecclesium's skin at the earliest opportunity. Despite his brief inhabitations of the Dyrrak Ravener at Udunum Island and, earlier, the Ravener urzidae in Arc Rheunos, Ulfric had not until now experienced what wearing the flesh of a real monster was like. He found it as loathsome as he found the man under normal circumstances.

And the Ecclesium fought like a monster. His will bashed against the barriers Ulfric erected in the man's mind to keep him at bay like relentless storm waves against a battered shore. Ulfric couldn't relinquish his focus on holding the man off for a second. Every step up the citadel's many stairs, every glance around a corner to see and prepare for whomever he might encounter, every reach to put his hand on a door handle, all were accomplished with the utmost struggle. He could only dedicate a fraction of his concentration to the mundane tasks, performing every movement interminably slowly and deliberately, the bulk of his mental focus taken up with keeping the Ecclesium under control.

Then an extraordinary turn of luck struck. It occurred to Ulfric to take stock of what weapons he had at his disposal. He'd grabbed a long leather coat from the back of the chair the Ecclesium had sat in and put it on before leaving the planning chamber. Its overlong sleeves helped to hide his wounded hand, which he'd wrapped in a cloth that had been lying on the table. Flowers of blood had spotted the outer layer of the linen, but it was not dripping. He'd sheathed the Ecclesium's dagger, but only as he walked through the citadel did he think to search the coat's inner pockets.

He knew the feel and shape of what the Ecclesium's uninjured hand found immediately, and the cry of rage echoing from the Ecclesium confirmed it. Ulfric stopped walking and darted into a nearby shadowed alcove before he pulled what he'd found free. A Fenestros. A Battgjaldic Fenestros, to be specific.

Could this luck possibly hold? he questioned. *With this, we now have three of the four Fenestrii we need to cage Balavad in the Knights' possession.* With the two Battgjaldic Fenestrii the Knights held, and this, all he needed was to find Eisa and retrieve the stone from her chest. Then they would be equipped to defeat Balavad once and for all.

He had a moment of hesitation then. He was at a crossroads. Alone in the citadel, he was more vulnerable with fewer resources to steal his body back. And he hadn't yet considered how Balavad would react upon realizing Vaka Aster was gone. It could prompt the usurper Verity to accelerate the war against Ivoryss, both in speed and intensity, though Balavad would lose the option to outright destroy Vinnr completely.

On the other hand, Ulfric was almost certain that with the power of the two Fenestrii he now possessed, along with the power of his most convincing disguise as the Ecclesium, if he found Eisa, he could best her and take the last Fenestros the Knights needed to cage Balavad.

Then they could regroup and attack Balavad's new vessel at the time of their choosing, with numbers, tactics, and strength their advantages.

But that would leave Vaka Aster, and Vinnr, vulnerable. And Balavad had never struck Ulfric as a creature who would be willing to let bygones be bygones, or one to fight fair. The brutal Verity might wipe Vinnr out in a short but final storm of wrath at losing his new pet, Knight Nazaria.

It had to be Vaka Aster first, Ulfric decided, and, placing the Fenestros back inside his pocket, he continued upward.

The citadel was all but abandoned, a skeleton crew left behind to see to essentials was all it contained. He wasn't sure he'd have made it to the Verity chamber otherwise. It was difficult enough to pass for the human he wore when they were his ally, but when his host was fighting as actively as the Ecclesium was, he doubted he'd be able to say more than a few words to anyone he encountered without arousing suspicion. But once he laid the Domine Ecclesium's hand on the Verity chamber's door, he began to feel a sense of triumph.

Still, he had to be cautious. He was in the land of his enemy, and though any Ravener would be helpless against his Fenestros-empowered self, the Battgjald Verity wouldn't.

The heavy iron door swung inward on nearly silent hinges. Ulfric stood before it and stared across the chamber at the gaudy raised throne he, as the vessel of Vaka Aster, had previously been expected to sit at.

At its base, a funerary table, much like Penitent Rock at the top of the outer citadel's rampart steps, stood. He lay upon it, or rather, the vessel lay there. He only gave it one quick glance before searching the rest of the large space. This doorway was the only way in or out, aside from the high, steepled windows in the northern and southern walls, a hundred stories above the streets of Elezaran. The chamber itself was empty of people other than his host, himself, and Vaka Aster. Quickly stepping inside, he pushed the door closed and laid the thick bar across it to lock it.

Slowly, reverently, and more than a bit nervously, he approached the table. On one side stood a plinth, atop which sat a metal pitcher and several squat, unassuming clay goblets. He glanced inside the pitcher and knew its contents instantly. The consecration elixir that turned those who consumed it into Balavad's playthings. The reason for its presence was obvious to Ulfric. Those who wished to swear their loyalty to Vaka Aster, or whatever Verity duress pressured them to choose, were prompted to drink a cup to seal their oath, and their fate.

His body was laid out, again, like a corpse prepared for its last viewing before being interred or sent to sail the eternal seas. The Dyrraks had adorned him in a robe made of some luxuriant white fur, a snowy mountain cat he thought. But that type of cat was only found in the mountains of Yor. How long had the Dyrraks had it? And how had they preserved it so remarkably, having last had dealings with Yor many hundreds of turns ago? Again, he lamented the rift between the kingdoms. Dyrrakium had so many secrets and skills that the realm as a whole would be better off sharing.

This held his focus for only the briefest moment, though, as he slid the Ecclesium's eyes to look upon his own face. It should have been familiar, unsurprising, humdrum even. He'd seen those deep lines, those heavy, gray-shot, wiry eyebrows, that long, straight nose ending in a sharp point, and that nine-pointed star on his cleft chin every time he'd looked in a mirror for the last seventeen hundred turns. Yet… it wasn't him, or if it was, it was merely a ghost of him.

His skin had faded to a colorless lead, and if he touched it, it looked like it would be as hard as iron. His eyes were open, startling him. Unlike the limpid flesh of his face and hands, which were crossed over his middle, his eyes burned with a kind of animus, the raging starlight of a furious galaxy spinning inside the orbs. The effect was mesmerizing, holding him frozen as he gazed at them.

Consequently, he did not hear the bar slide away from the door's catch, nor the iron hinges as it swung inward.

"I did not summon you, Domine Ecclesium," said a voice that cut Ulfric's borrowed ears like knives.

He spun, dreading having to look into that ghastly face. Balavad had taken the form of a Battgjaldic woman, but it was still the Verity unquestionably. She stood unnaturally tall, a full two heads taller than Ulfric, with long arms and a surprisingly fragile, thin neck. Her hair, parted into multiple ropes and bound in metal beads, hung nearly to her waist, the tendrils looking more like a cat-o-nine-tails than hair. And the eyes, wide and as black as the void between stars, shined with an unholy light as they beheld his face, perhaps even his spirit.

"Your Holiness," Ulfric said carefully, giving the charade his every effort. His host's body was nearly vibrating with Ulfric's effort to keep him at bay. "I came to bring you news of treachery." Ulfric was gambling with what information he could use to get himself out of this fix. He didn't wish to give away the chancellor's interests and jeopardize her hold over the Dyrrak fleet, but the news of Sveinungr would get to the Verity eventually, he knew, if it hadn't already.

Naturally, it had. There was no way to hide news from Balavad, who could look inside the minds of any who drank the consecration elixir. Yet the caveat to Balavad's acknowledgment that she did know surprised Ulfric. "The Fifth Phase Sveinungr's treachery is noted. No matter, though. The war fleet is hardly necessary to taking Ivoryss."

Hardly necessary? Ulfric was disturbed. If the fleet was so unimportant, why… ? That was when he noticed the Ecclesium had fallen silent in their shared mind at last. No, not completely. There was a brittle laugh reverberating in his skull.

Alarmed and off balance, Ulfric refocused on Balavad when the slide of the Verity's long robe brushed over the stone floor as she approached. Holding steady, he awaited her. When she came to a standstill before him, her cold, void-filled eyes gazed into his. And like her eyes, her breath against his face was cold when she spoke.

"But if you were you, Ecclesium, you would have known that."

It wasn't fear Ulfric felt exactly, nor even caution. He wondered if it was more like how a sparrow felt when it sensed the shadow of the hawk above it, a knowing that doom soared close, an acceptance of the futility in fighting nature that settled into its weightless bird bones and rapidly beating heart. In short, fate.

He gambled then, rejecting both futility and fate. "I do, of course, Your Holiness. I only bring the news to ensure your confidence in my loyalty." And though futility, it seemed, had become his constant companion, he gambled further, hoping to deflect the Verity's accusation regarding his identity: "And learn what new ways I might secure our prize of total dominion." The Ecclesium's mind was not totally open to Ulfric—the man was too canny for that—but Ulfric had gleaned enough, or perhaps he simply understood the man enough, to know his pernicious ends.

The brittle laugh that came from his nemesis whipped over him, gouging into his flesh like fishhooks. Even though his skin wasn't his own, the barbs raked his spirit nonetheless.

"A clever one. I should like to know to whom I'm speaking. Show yourself to me."

A black vapor, one he was already too familiar with, oozed from the Verity's own body. Oily, baleful, it encased him, eating at him, at the Ecclesium, like acid. The pain of it focused Ulfric's mind like few other things could have, and he gritted his teeth against a groan. The game was up, and the fool had lost.

Or had he?

With an effort that felt herculean, Ulfric slammed his hands into his pockets, gripping the Fenestrii of two realms in them like a man clutching a tree in a cyclone. He channeled words into the Fenestrii, much like he would have his klinkí stones, to create a protective barrier between himself and the Verity. A glow of muted luminance faded into a visible spectrum, not around him, but from his borrowed skin. He felt its warmth and a moment of relief. But only a moment.

The hand holding the onyx Fenestros of Battgjald suddenly blazed, lit in flames that licked up the arm and incinerated the sleeve into instant ash. Ulfric cried out and jerked his arm up, dropping the burning celestial stone. It was not his arm, not his pain, yet every singed hair and cell of it might as well have been. His concentration dissolved. He felt torn like paper, one part of him wanting to reach out and clasp the injured limb as one would any wound, the other part of him reaching out with the burning hand, reaching toward the...

You have lost, Aldinhuus, the Ecclesium croaked and yanked the nearby pitcher of elixir to his lips, gulping down the contents in convulsive swallows.

The next thing either of them knew, the fiery arm was doused, the oily miasma of Balavad withdrawn. They blinked, now both sharing the Ecclesium's form equally. Like the last time Ulfric had been tricked into drinking the contaminated elixir, it slid down their throat and into their stomach with the perfidious smoothness of deception. It had no taste, no temperature; it was the liquid of lies.

Once it settled inside him, the Ecclesium reeled, clenching his belly with clawed hands as if trying to rip it open and remove the poison now attacking him with saber-sharp slashes. Ulfric spared himself this time and retreated to an unfeeling corner of the man's mind where he could watch and hear his transformation, but not pity him. The Ecclesium chose his destiny the moment he betrayed his maker. And he had chosen it freely.

Ulfric had ridden inside a Ravener before and knew what to expect from the altered senses. The part he most cringed from was feeling the slip of Balavad worming her way into their shared skull. He was discovered, no way to escape it now, but he was not yet caught.

Using the Himmingaze Fenestros to project his call with all the energy left for him to muster, he shouted: *Yggo, Urgo, to the window of the citadel! I need you!*

He just had to get this no-longer-usable meatsack to the window, and the bruhawks could fly him and the memory keeper to freedom.

With a last gasp as himself, the Ecclesium fell to one knee. To Ulfric's horror, the Dyrrak clutched the memory keeper and ripped it from his neck so hard that several of the copper links in its chain broke. "Here... is the source... of his wysticism—Aldinhuus—" And he slammed the crystal-centered dragør edifice into the stone floors, cracking the crystal, destroying Ulfric's one portal of escape.

Balavad watched impassively. As the Domine Ecclesium's eyes blanched to the uniform flat slate of ancient, weathered stones, Balavad said, "And you have become a vessel yourself now, haven't you, Ecclesium? Not of a Verity, but of a mere man. Either way, it's a desire I think you never held. What power in being Vaka Aster's servant when there is so much to be had in ruling her realm? And now, a servant to Aldinhuus. What this could lead to makes me more than a little curious."

The Verity waved her hand, and in a fluid, unhesitating movement, the Ecclesium stood. Long-limbed, even more than his natural Dyrrak form, he stooped in a bow of subservience the man in life would never have taken. There he waited obediently for a command. He didn't have to wait long.

"Stallari"—Balavad looked penetratingly into the lifeless gray eyes— "it pleases me to meet you again. I do think it fitting what, or who, you've become." Without dropping her eyes, the Verity waved a hand suggestively toward the Ecclesium's sheathed dagger. "But as I no longer have need of you, I no longer have need of the Dyrrak, either."

Balavad gave another short wave, and the Ecclesium withdrew his dagger and brought it to his throat in a singular, swift motion, drawing it across the Phase-marked skin once, then again, then again, severing all but his spine. His blood, now black as pitch, gushed free in a torrent, and then his lifeless body hit the ground. The black blood pooled around the necklace Ulfric had once upon a time given as a token of his love to his only daughter, Isemay, who would never wear it again.

CHAPTER THIRTY

Bandits or bears Mylla could handle. A gimgree sloth, though they had claws that could slice a woman in half, wasn't something to worry about. Mylla would have smelled one of those before it could have gotten within fifty yards of her. And she doubted that Griggory, for all his peculiarities, would toy with her. So if he hadn't vanished for the sake of fun, she had to prepare herself for quite its opposite.

She slid even deeper into the shadows, moving as soundlessly as a bird on the wing. Her hand slipped into a carryall hanging by her side, finding a strange comfort at touching the Fenestros she'd brought back from Ærd. Something was out there, something that felt big. And given where they were located, she didn't have to stretch her imagination about what it might be.

What she knew of dragørs could be summed up in a page. Old as the realm, once the only sentient creatures in Vinnr, and nearly as powerful as Vaka Aster herself, they had retired to the wild corners of Vinnr ages ago, shunning humanity. The only people who regularly saw them in the common era were Ivoryss's northernmost people, the Magdastervians, who'd built their city right up to the Howling Weald's borders some thousands of turns ago—and had paid for the foolish decision more than once.

Through the Magdastervians' history, they'd managed to avoid being wiped out by the creatures not because of a truce or by paying tributes to the great beasts. There was nothing the dragørs wanted from people anyway. They'd only managed to keep their city erected by having weapons large enough to slow a dragør, though none could stop them, which were crewed by fighters willing to stay behind and sacrifice themselves to the dragørs' wrath long enough for the rest of the city's people to escape into the sea. Dragørs shunned the ocean.

Magdaster had been leveled at least twice before the inhabitants had learned to stop encroaching on the Weald and leave the dragørs' territory to the dragørs. As a result of existing in the shadows of the great beasts, and remaining alive at their whim, the Magdastervians Mylla had met always seemed to be a bit more keyed up and a bit more ready to solve problems with aggression than your typical Vinnric. Stave, shockingly, was perhaps the most reasonable of them, at least that she'd known, but she he couldn't blame them for their brashness.

And now here she was, in the Howling Weald, and potentially being stalked by a dragør herself, and without even an emberflare petard, much less cannon, at her disposal.

Mylla had put about two hundred yards between herself and the campfire, hoping its light and smoke would keep the dragør's attention off her, when she heard a noise so improbable that her mind was simply unable to interpret it—a man's laughter. It seemed to be coming from north of their campsite and from higher up. In a tree, or perhaps a knoll. *No,* she told herself. *You misheard. That must be a cry of fear... or pain.* She had no idea what to do, but it had to be Griggory, and she couldn't very well abandon him and run, could she?

Ever so slowly, unwilling to risk igniting even the dimmest of light through her Mentalios, she moved in a wide arc through the underbrush toward the direction the noise came from. As she'd guessed, the ground rose at a mild slant, and the half-moon light showed a mound or berm continuing up into darkness. To her own ears, she made no more sound than what was typical of a forest at night, only the occasional crackle of a leaf or brush of cloth against the flora, which could easily be the sound of a small animal or wisp of breeze.

She'd been slinking along for an untold number of minutes, though it felt like hours, hearing nothing more. Was she too late? Had Griggory been killed or perhaps taken to a dragør den as a late-night snack? Before she could despair, another sound came to her, much closer than the laugh or cry of fear from earlier. A heavy, echoing grunt, like the sound of big ocean waves crashing inside a cavern as deep as the earth.

No matter how big she'd imagined dragørs to be, that sound came from something five times bigger. Her heart beat so hard, just once, that it seemed it would explode in her chest. Then it froze for a few beats and finally started to gallop. She sank down to her knees, trying not to gasp in fear. She'd faced death dozens of times. But she'd never faced a dragør.

As she tried to get ahold of the panic, the breeze picked up, making the trees rustle in the forest's mild song, showering her with the woodsy scent of night-blooming vegetation. It was deceptively peaceful, and she wanted to simply wait here, letting the forest calm her and soothe her fears until morning, when Halla's light would show her all was well. Griggory had simply wandered off, and she'd find him racked out against a tree trunk, snoring.

Stave would tell her to stop being fatuous, that wishes are for romantics and poor planners. But how did one plan for coming face-to-face with a dragør? All she had were her wystic stones, her hallowed sword—which might be more useful than a regular sword, *if* it could slice through scales, but was that an *if* she wanted to count on?—and the Ærd Fenestros.

Finally catching her breath, she stared up the slope and realized she was close to the top of the knoll. There seemed to be a clearing, and she could see the darkened treetops on the other side brushing up against the sky. Stars ringed their crowns, reminding her of the last moments of the tessalope that had dissipated into nothing in the Ærden fortress. Despite the sky's sparkle, the hollow at ground level was still utterly black. If Griggory was there, or the dragør she expected, she couldn't see anything but inky shadow.

Steeling herself, she slunk forward a few more paces, stopped, waited, heard nothing, and repeated her process. Shortly, she was at the edge of the hollow, and any hope she'd had for better visibility once she reached it was quickly dashed. The trees were simply too tall to allow any moonlight to reach the ground. The moon had only risen a couple of hours ago and was still too low in the sky to crest them.

Crouched down, she reached for Star Spark's hilt, wanting to be prepared. The chape at the base of the blade sometimes stuck, so she twisted it just slightly to ensure it would draw smoothly.

The metallic clink it made seemed to fill the hollow. Mylla froze. A rustle came from ahead, then the dim blue light of Griggory's Mentalios flared, illuminating just enough of his face and chest to show her he was facing her, looking into the dark for what had made the noise. She stood up straight, breathing a sigh of relief at having found him, and in one piece.

Then, behind him, the Mentalios light glinted from two barrel-sized globes, golden and fiery red.

Not globes—*eyes!*

They swiftly rose from head height to far above Griggory. Mylla gave a cry as the titanic outline of the dragør became visible in the starlight. Her cry died weakly, her lungs simply giving out, the remainder of her air draining from them as if from a punctured water-skin. She breathed, "Behind you!" to warn Griggory, but it came out as a meek wheeze.

Griggory's lips moved as he said something, but in her terror, she couldn't hear much less understand his words. Fortunately, her arms hadn't given up the way her lungs had, and without thinking, she gripped the Ærd Fenestros within the carryall. With her other hand, she ripped Star Spark free of the scabbard and pointed it in his direction, but up, toward the now-towering figure of the dragør. She charged, ready to protect her companion from the monster. Or, more likely, to die.

She saw it clearly as the beast's jaws cracked open. Then, there was nothing but fire.

CHAPTER THIRTY-ONE

"That was foolish of you, Mylla. Pointing a sword at Heart of Purple Might like that. What did you think would happen?"

Mylla's eyes were still closed, but she'd been listening to the melodies of the forest for the last few moments, wondering if they were the sounds the Cosmos made when the dissipated remnants of your spiritual matter returned to it, leaving a lifeless body behind—if that. Apparently, the sounds included Griggory's voice, and when she realized how unlikely that was, her eyes peeled open.

He was kneeling beside her, holding Star Spark's hilt for balance. Its tip was planted in the dirt, and Mylla nearly cursed him in outrage at the sacrilege.

Now that her awareness was returning, she noted that her left hand felt unnaturally hot where it rested at her side. Woozily, she tilted her head and saw it lay gripping the Ærd Fenestros, which was glowing red and putting out intense warmth. Despite this, her hand was undamaged, and she realized she didn't want to let go of the orb. "I saw fire, Griggory," she mumbled. "I saw a dragør. How—"

"Yes, yes. Heart of Purple Might, as I said. He's a bit bigger than last time I saw him, but I'd know my old friend even if I were blind. Do you happen to have any honey?"

Unable to make sense of anything, beginning with the fact that both she and Griggory were alive, she merely asked, "Honey? Where would I get honey?"

"Yes, of course. My mistake. He just loves honey, you see. I've always brought him some in my past visits."

Sense was slowly coming back to her. They were still in the clearing atop the knoll, her back to a tree as she sat on her bum. The sky had changed, dawn light beginning to paint the treetops. "Griggory, what in Vaka Aster's mighty breath is going on? There was a dragør, it came at me—no, at *you*—and I know I didn't fend it off with Star Spark. You and I should have been cooked... did you say *your friend*?"

Griggory gave her a magnanimous, unreadable grin, stood up—leaving Star Spark planted in the ground like a metal sapling—and turned halfway. His hand rose and pointed toward the edge of the clearing. "Mylla Evernal, Knight Corporealis and newly ordained Warden Temporalis of Vinnr and Ærd respectively, please meet Heart of Purple Might, kit of Magnificence of Oceans Tempests."

Her eyes followed his arm slowly, as if they were even more reluctant about what they were about to witness than she. And there it was. The size of a two-story building, a mighty, toothy beast with shimmering silvery-purple scales that made bucklers look like dinner plates, four legs as wide as oak trunks, eyes that glowed even in the dawn light, and teeth like daggers—no, make that teeth like *swords*. These serrated meat-mashers became all she could focus on.

Mylla's head swam, and though she'd never passed out in her life, even when Eisa had once hit her in the temple so hard in a training scrap that she'd needed forty stitches to close the wound, she thought she would faint. Those *teeth*...

Through vision edged with ragged blackness, she saw Griggory face the creature. "Forgive her, Purple Might. She's new to your excellence. It can be, ah, overwhelming for the young."

Mylla wanted to snort at being called young. The unintended insult helped clear her head, though. "You kn-know this dragør?"

"We go back many, many, many turns, we do. Purple Might and his kindred have long been tolerant of my many, many, *many* questions and have for ages given their leave for me to wander the Weald at my leisure."

To Mylla's overtaxed mind came the memory of an overheard conversation between two Prelates of the Conservatum from dozens of turns past. They'd been perusing an old register of the Knights Corporealis members, one that had been maintained, as far as she knew, since the Order was founded.

"Dragør Tamer?" one had asked. "I'd love to know the story of how Knight Dondrin got that name."

Mylla remembered thinking at the time that the name must have been metaphorical, but now she voiced it aloud without a hint of doubt. "Dragør Tamer."

"Pah! No, no, no, no. That old nickname is as wrong as spoiled mead. Dragør *Friend*, if anything," Griggory fussed.

You are fortunate not to be cooked, speck, said a deep, frightening voice in Mylla's head. *Mortals seem to have grown more foolish since last I had any to-dos with one, waving a sword at me as if you could possibly do more than wind up in one oddly mixed slag heap together. I am most curious how a Fenestros of Ærd came into your possession, though.*

Mylla's hand flew to her temple and rubbed as if to ward off a headache. But the beast's eyes were staring straight at her, *into* her, red and yellow like the throat of a volcano. And she knew whose voice it was without question.

Y-you can speak through the Mentalios? She stopped, felt as if she was failing to adhere to some important formality, though she had no idea what kind of formality one used with a dragør, and added: *Master Heart.*

Could a dragør smile? She hoped that's what he was doing, because the way the edges of his mouth stretched back farther, exposing yet more glistening teeth, was no less terrifying whether the expression was mirth or doom.

Master Heart, a fine name. Griggory, why've you never called me that? The dragør again lowered its head, the movement, like everything about the creature, so massive it felt as if the ground groaned at accommodating it.

Griggory and Purple Might were quiet for a moment, staring eye to eye, and Mylla got the impression they were speaking. Griggory seemed capable of communicating with all manner of the worlds' oldest creatures without saying a word, and she found that despite how frustrating it was to be kept in the dark, she admired the old man's many abilities and experiences. He may have been unaccountably odd, but when one had lived as long as he had, and had seen firsthand how transient and circumstantial all behaviors and rules people lived by were, what expectations or manners did one really need to follow anymore?

As the two elders—for there was no denying she was among elders —spoke, she felt a moment of chagrin. She had thought she might faint at the sight of Purple Might's teeth, but now she realized she must have just awoken from a faint. She'd thought the dragør was going to cook her, and instead of fighting it, she simply fell over unconscious. What else could explain how she'd so badly misjudged the wall of flame she'd felt was about to scorch her? *It's a dragør, Mylla. I'm sure you're not the first to be overwhelmed at the sight of one. At least give yourself some credit; you faced Balavad, and he'd nearly had to kill you to get you to stay down.*

The self-pep-talk gave her time to grow... *comfortable* was not the word, rather *accepting* of the fact that she was in the presence of a creature whose very existence made the humans of Vinnr seem an afterthought.

Soon enough, the great urgency of their mission pushed her to put aside her awe and fear. With a clearing of the throat, she said, "Excuse me. My apologies for interrupting." They both finally acknowledged her. "My apologies also for drawing a weapon against you, Master Heart. I never would have if I'd known, well..." She waved a hand across the glade to encompass the situation, giving Griggory a slightly exasperated scowl for not informing her of such an important matter *before* she nearly fumbled herself into becoming a dragør's dinner. "Would I be correct in guessing Griggory has explained why we're here and what we're searching for?"

The dragør blinked at her slowly. *I've never seen a speck gather its wits so quickly before. Except you, of course, Griggory. I thought you said you forgot to mention me to her, as it is obvious from her memories she's forgotten me.*

"It slipped my mind, it's true," Griggory averred. "But Mylla has seen and done much that has whittled her shock into a tamed thing. Would I be right in saying that, Mylla?"

She could only nod dumbly. What did the dragør mean by her having forgotten him? A churning pit began to form in her stomach.

Ah, the tessalopes, of course, Purple Might said.

Griggory nodded as well. "Among other things." He turned a grin on her that she could have sworn nearly beamed with pride.

She cleared her throat. "I know, Master Heart, that the business of us, um, specks, must seem mundane and ordinary to you, but if Griggory hasn't already, I think I should explain why we've come into the Weald."

You seek the Ærden Scrylle, the dragør said in a tone that had Mylla almost wishing she'd kept her mouth shut. Almost. *I've been waiting for an Ærden Warden to come and claim it.*

"You have it?! But that would mean—" The pit widened, the churning increased. "How did you get it?"

Purple Might's eyes narrowed. *Impertinent little speck, aren't you? Should I be offended that one whose life I saved can't be bothered to remember me? I'm not convinced you're as enfeebled as you pretend, young Warden Knight. But I shall warn you, only once, that dragørs are not one for games.*

"Allow me, if you would, Purple Might," Griggory cut in. "Mylla, I'm afraid I have some, ah, not entirely comforting news." Sunlight dripped from the upper leaves of the glade's treetops, finding the golden flecks in Griggory's eyes, making what should have been a merry twinkle something less so. He stared at her without saying another word until Mylla had to prompt him.

"Yes?" she said, raising her eyebrows, knowing but unwilling to accept what Griggory was about to tell her, despite the dragør's veiled threat.

"My friend Heart of Purple Might, you see, ah—well, he..." A confused expression washed over his face, as if he'd forgotten what he was about to say.

"What is it, Griggory?" she pressed.

"Well, there it is then. I can't say. I really can't."

I killed your father, speck, Purple Might supplied.

All the heat that she'd been enjoying from the Ærd Fenestros suddenly vanished, leaving her numb despite still holding it in one fist. "Why?" she whispered.

The red-gold orbs of his eyes flared angrily, then calmed. *You are not a shredded meat between my talons right now because I can see you're truly addled, speck,* he said. *So I will explain. Those many turns ago, I was tracking uninvited rogues in the forest. But I came upon an unexpected scent —you as a youngling being carried by a man. It was clear that you were attempting to escape him, and the moment you did and had run off, I meted out the justice I thought was warranted. I have lunched on the odd speck here and there, but I draw the line at innocent children. As you fled, I followed you back to the byway, where, as you know, more ruffians had already committed another slaying. Your mother, Griggory tells me.*

"So you thought my father was a bandit who'd kidnapped me?"

To all appearances, that's what happened. The great beast stretched its neck, the tip of his snout extending so far it reached the tops of the trees. With what would have been a small shake on a creature that wasn't the size of a castle's barn, he settled back on his haunches once more. *My judgment may have been hasty, but I have kept the Ærd artifacts since then nonetheless.*

Her tongue felt as thick as a hunk of shark meat, and as rubbery. "Hasty? You burned Greven to ash just because he *might* have been a danger to me? It never occurred to you to simply ask?" She knew her impertinence had passed into the land of dangerous foolishness, but she simply couldn't believe she'd lost one of her parents to a mere misunderstanding.

Griggory moved to her and tried to put a sympathetic hand on her arm. She was having none of it. Shoving the Fenestros back into her carryall, she yanked Star Spark from the ground—eliciting a wince from the old Knight—slammed it back into its scabbard, and turned away.

"Knight Evernal, you need to understand—"

"I know!" she interrupted. "I know that *specks* aren't important enough to a mighty dragør to bother with a simple inquiry. I get it that we're just weak, useless, mortal meatbags to them. Just give me a moment to put my thoughts in order before I do something I'm not sure I'll regret."

Griggory spun her and yanked her by her forearms toward him so quickly and so hard that her neck snapped in painful whiplash. Upon blinking back the shock, she found herself nose to nose with the man. His greater height meant that she stood on the tips of her toes, but his strength was holding her up, not her own. So astounded, she merely gawped at him, her arms bent between them, his hands like manacles on her wrists.

His head tilted sideways, as if curious, and he said in an utterly neutral tone, "Purple Might and his kindred have chosen to assist us in the fight for the Cosmos, but if you keep up your petty childishness, *you* may not be around to participate. Your grief will have its time, but it isn't now. You swore an oath, like I did and like our friends did. So why don't we see what the Scrylle has to say before the day gets away from us, yes?"

Mylla merely stared at him in indecision. And just a little embarrassment. Her petulance and outrage may have been justified, but he was right. The world required so much more of her right now. Her personal grievances would have to wait their turn.

She gave one curt nod. Just as abruptly as he'd taken hold of her, he released her, and she dropped back to the ground. In her surprise, she'd tensed her whole body, and hitting the ground stiff-legged made her reel just a bit as if she had no more grace than a beetle.

Straightening, she set her clothing into order. Carefully keeping her eyes averted from Purple Might, in a voice she controlled so tightly that it gave away no hint of emotion, she said, "Fine. Let's see what it has to tell us then."

HEART OF PURPLE Might had indeed kept Fimm's artifacts close. After Mylla agreed to look inside, the dragør took one claw that was easily as thick at its root as Mylla's thigh, and carefully dug beneath on of his hind scales. The artifacts were wedged there and dropped to the grassy ground with two soft thuds.

Mylla didn't know how long she looked into the Scrylle—an hour, three?—before giving up. Now, she sat cross-legged in the daylit glade, numb and empty. In a distant way, she surprised herself at not raging inside, but even that feeling, like all feeling, seemed impossible now. No, not impossible. Pointless.

The Verity Fimm, like all Verities, didn't care about their fate. And if she did as Fimm had asked her back in Ærd, the only reward she and her fellow humans could expect was annihilation.

Griggory cleared his throat suggestively. "So, by your expression, it's clear you didn't see what you hoped to."

"No." She looked up to see him raise his heavy gray-shot eyebrows, asking without speaking what she *had* seen. She found she lacked the desire to tell him. She noticed, as well, that sometime while she'd been gazing into the Scrylle, Purple Might had departed. Unexpectedly, she felt disappointed. Fearful as the creature was, it was still a dragør, an ancient creation of Vaka Aster that dwarfed everything else she'd ever encountered in its magnificence.

Griggory still eyed her.

"Look for yourself, be my guest," she muttered.

"Oh, no thank you. I already know what it contains."

This caught her attention like nothing else could have. Her head shot up, her neck stiffened. "You already—well, why didn't you tell me!?"

"Mylla, I would if I could. Trust me. Knowing what I know is a burden I'd much sooner not carry if the choice were mine."

She became aware that her mouth was open, stuck in mid question. The fact was, she didn't know what to ask him. Finally, as if her tongue decided for her, she said, "Are you telling me you're under the same

constraints as the tessalopes? If you tell me what you know, you'll…
you'll be cursed into becoming a Fenestros or something too?"

He seemed amused by that, infuriatingly so. "Something, yes. Or I'll
simply be silenced in other what I assume would be unpleasant ways. I
don't know, really. I haven't tempted that fate."

She stared at him incredulously for another moment, then rose
from her seat, considered picking up the Scrylle and its inset Fenestros, decided she wanted no more to do with them for the moment,
and reached for her carryall.

"Well?" Griggory said. "Are you going back to Ærd, then? As Fimm
requested?"

The look she shot him was so filled with ire that it tainted the air
for a moment. But her ire wasn't directed at him. "No. No, I'm not. I've
had enough of the Verities. If we want to save Vinnr and the other
realms, we're going to have to do it ourselves. You *know* what the
Scrylle said: 'Fimm's last vessel will sing the Syzyckí Elementum and
bring the destruction of destruction, the rending and sewing, the end
of the five.'" She gripped Star Spark's hilt angrily. "Fimm told me the
truth. The Scrylle will show me how to stop Balavad. If I take the artifacts back to Fimm, it'll be the end of the five realms, and Balavad will
have nothing left to destroy. I don't know whether to be more amused
by the irony or contemptuous of it. The Knights and I may be as
powerless as insects next to Balavad's strength, but even the Verities
and their limitless cruelty aren't strong enough to kill my *hope*. If they
want to end the Cosmos, they'll have to do it on their own. I won't help
them, not anymore. Until then, I'm going to fight for my companions
and our worlds."

And that was that. She'd said it aloud, her oath and duty be damned.
If any Verity truly cared about such a thing, then let them strike her
down here and now for her faithlessness. She'd put her faith in them,
and in her oath, in the belief, however wrong it had been, that the pact
was two-sided; she and the Knights had protected the creators in
return for their protection. If anyone was to be accused of faithlessness, it was them. And she was done.

She said as much to Griggory, who merely looked at her with his inscrutable expression. If he was disappointed, it didn't show. Was he surprised? Unsurprised? If so, whichever it might have been was equally unreadable on his grizzled face. For the first time, Mylla noticed that his mark of Vaka Aster, the nine-pointed star on his chin, was faded to a light blue-green, so faint it could be mistaken for a smudge of dirt. Nothing, it seemed, lasted forever. Not even an oath.

When she was done speaking, instead of trying to talk her out of it, he merely said, "So what will you do?"

"I'm going to Magdaster to join the Knights." The deeper meaning of his use of "you" instead of "we" struck her then. "And you?"

She may not have been able to read any surprise on his face, but she was sure it was unmistakable on hers when he said, "I believe Heart of Purple Might and I will stay… behind. For a time." He eyed the Scrylle pointedly, still perched on the ground between them.

Guessing at his intent, she said, "Take it. Go to Ærd if that's what you want to do. But if you have any faith in our fight left, you won't. Regardless, I'm through with Fimm, with all of them."

His lips curled in a small smile. "Thank you, thank you. But don't you feel the artifacts might be useful to you?"

"You seem to know the future, Griggory. You tell me." She tried to disguise the rancor in her voice, which was slowly seeping back, but failed.

He merely blinked at her a couple of times, then bent to retrieve the artifacts. "At least keep the other Fenestros," he averred. "A celestial stone is a celestial stone, after all."

True enough. And so, this was where they parted. Though she'd known him only briefly, he was a Knight and in most ways the very heart of Vinnr's history. Realization that she would regret never seeing him again, if indeed this was the last time she would, struck her. "What do you want me to tell the others?" she asked, her voice softer.

"That I'll see them when the time is right, of course." He looked up at the sky, as if something caught his eye. When she followed his gaze, she saw nothing. "The time," he repeated.

"Until then, I guess."

"Yes." He dipped his chin in a farewell.

With that, she turned and paced toward the edge of the glade, intent on first retrieving the rest of her meager belongings at the campsite they'd set up the night before, then on returning to the byway and back to where she belonged. With the Knights.

CHAPTER THIRTY-TWO

In the Anzuru Desert, some hundred miles south of Elezaran, the capital city of Dyrrakium, a figure strode purposefully and with a haste that few people could manage for more than a few steps. The figure held itself erect, militantly so, and paced with missile-like certainty. Any who might have crossed the figure's path would immediately have chosen to step aside before being trampled, because there was no doubt whoever this was was on a mission and would never let something as insignificant as another person get in their way.

Her Stygian hair fell in a long braid down her back, now dusted liberally with red powder from the endless sands of Dyrrakium, so thick in many places that it stained both the braid and her clothing like blood. The glaive she carried in her hand flashed brutally beneath Halla, its edge so keen it seemed to slice the very air as she passed through. The woman stared straight ahead, neither blinking nor breathing, and even her eyes had a dried crust of red sand coating them.

Yet, she did not falter, did not feel. For the figure who once was called Eisa Nazaria, Nazarian Most High and Heir of the Sixth Line, was no longer the inhabitant of the body that bore her face. Or if she was, she was buried deeper inside than any ancient ruin had ever been buried in Dyrrakium's thousands of turns of history. She was simply a vessel, a tool, borne forward with unearthly power by Balavad's artifacts that, like Dyrrakium's ruins in its soil, lay buried deep in her chest.

Uneasy whispers traipsed through what could still be called, though loosely, her mind. Of Ulfric Aldinhuus, who had somehow slipped through Balavad's fingers, along with the Knight called Symvalline Lutair, and had even meddled in Arc Rheunos, a realm that had been destined to fall during the last Equifulcrum. Somehow Balavad's plans there had been discovered, thwarted, and ruined. Mithlí once again passed freely through the Great Cosmos, and Mithlí's freedom meant one thing, one unthinkable thing: only by keeping the other four Verities shackled and banished from their realms would the Syzyckí Elementum be avoided; if they were all free, Balavad's designs on Cosmos supremacy would come to nothing.

But they weren't all free. The dried and cracked lips on Eisa's face split in what might have once been a smile but was now a rictus filled with jagged teeth that would make children wail in terror. Vaka Aster, for one, was still trapped fast in the shell of Ulfric Aldinhuus's body.

Hours passed as the whispering continued, and Halla began to drop under the horizon. The glinting red sands became a virtual sea of blood, but the figure of Eisa was undaunted and unwavering in her progress. For blood was what she'd been sent to Anzuru for. Getting closer to the foothills leading to the high peaks and aeries of the southern mountains, Balavad's whispered thoughts did not stray from focus, focus on Aldinhuus.

Perhaps the Stallari of the Knights Corporealis's absence from his old body was a boon, an unforeseen advantage. It left Vaka Aster completely without a link to the outside. In every way, Aldinhuus's body was a prison, and without him there with Vaka Aster, the prison could not be altered, moved, or undone. The farther Aldinhuus was from Vaka Aster, the better, in fact. If not for the fact that the insufferable human had undone all of Balavad's ages of work in Arc Rheunos...

An enormous shadow darker than the darkening sky swept over

Eisa. Any normal person would have dropped to the red earth, cowering in fear. Only one thing in these far reaches of the Empire of Dyrrakium had a shadow like that, and it was not a thing that suffered encroachment by any wandering human.

But Eisa was not any wandering human. Her striding ceased and she looked up to search the sky for her visitor. Her prey.

There, a dragør, one of the fire-red species that lived in these southern reaches of Vinnr. It circled back overhead, having already made its assessment of her, and from this distance, Balavad could see through Eisa's eyes it was coming back, ready to make a meal or an example, or both, of the intruder. Deep in Eisa's mind, Balavad had a moment of what passed for smug triumph. The creature did not recognize what he was, not yet.

It began to dive, its speed increasing so fast that a normal human would already be squeezed in its great claws before that person could think to react. To Balavad, the descent was nearly languid, giving him plenty of time to observe through Eisa's eyes the creature as it came at him.

Two things occurred in a blink of an eye that were odd enough to momentarily unsettle Balavad. First, a voice, the voice of his host, Knight Nazaria, burbled from some sunken, tightly contained hollow space in her mind. *Flee, before it's too late!* Balavad had believed her spirit utterly quelled and chained inside a pit too deep to ever emerge from again, much less have the sensibilities to still grasp the world around her. To whom was she calling? The dragør, he realized when the next thing happened a moment later. It was subtle, a shift. Perhaps not in the diving dragør's features but in its aura or its thought. It hesitated, hearing the warning.

But the creature's descent had already brought it much too close to the Verity. Eisa's arms raised the glaive Fate Forger, a hallowed weapon, at the same moment the jet-black Fenestros in her chest began to incandesce. White fire arced through the air between the Fenestros and the shaft of the glaive like lightning, coalesced briefly in the heavy blade, then shot from the weapon into the dragør's chest. The creature blazed in a ball as bright as Halla for a moment and flapped its wings in an effort to stall its drop or escape that scything fire. To no avail. It thumped to the earth hard enough to raise a cloud of red sand, the light from Eisa's glaive making it glow like crimson stardust. White bands of fire spread over the creature, tightening like ropes until the dragør was immobilized. It raged and thrashed, but the more it fought, the tighter the fire bands grew around it. It bellowed and belched fire at its captor, but Eisa's form never moved. She merely stood inside the dragørfire as one might a light fog, untouched and unmoved.

After some time passed, the dragør stilled, catching its breath. It was wrapped like a spider's victim lying on its side, the bands of wystic fire holding it crackling. Balavad commanded Eisa toward the creature. It eyed her with a wrath that itself burned, but stayed in place. It was not a stupid creature; it knew when it was outmatched.

From a pocket, Eisa's free hand withdrew a small smoked-glass vial. The liquid inside appeared nearly purple through the darkened glass. She pulled the cork free and held the vial up, as if making a toast. Words slipped into the air, spoken in a tongue foreign to most Vinnrics, and to the dragør, their shapes blunt and hard. The vial's contents rose as vapor and began to pour like oil-smoke from the container, moving toward the dragør like a stalking snake. The dragør tried to squirm free of its bonds, unwilling to be touched by the wystic elixir. It drew in a deep breath, readying to once more attempt to inflame its captor. As the dragør inhaled, the smoky elixir, as if finding its target, arrowed into the dragør's nostrils. The beast's eyes shot open wide, it roared, and a moment later, went limp. With the slowness of congealing blood, the creature's eyes hardened and glazed into a featureless gray orb.

The figure of Eisa waited several moments, then, satisfied, she lowered her glaive and the wystic bands of white fire drew back toward the Fenestros in her chest and extinguished.

"You are now mine to command," she said. Any who'd known Eisa in her lifetime would have struggled to recognize the rough, reedy tone.

The dragør rose to a crouch and lowered its head until its jaw rested on the ground before her feet, its neck laid bare. If the Verity using Eisa had wanted, he would only have had to swing the glaive once to sever the dragør's head. But that was not his design. For now, he was done using Eisa to pace through the desert; instead, he'd ride.

He had more dragørs to catch.

CHAPTER THIRTY-THREE

In the early summer heat of Halla, Symvalline paced back and forth along the highest walkway of Magdaster's outer curtain wall. As she walked, she scanned the ocean spreading in the western distance. Soon she stopped in the same place she'd stopped several dozen times in the last three days, chewing her lower lip in concern and no small amount of anticipation.

"Why haven't they attacked?" she said, peering with rapt attention at the amassed fleet of nearly a thousand Dyrrakium ships anchored off the Magdastervian coastline.

Though she'd come to a halt beside Mallich Roibeard, he had no response. It was the same question they'd all shared since their enemy's fleet had arrived three sunrises prior. Arrived, and done nothing. They merely bobbed at anchor in the crescent-shaped bight cut into the shores at the farthest edge of Magdaster's great wall. No Dyrrak ambassadors came to sue for either peace or surrender. No warning shots were fired to signal their intent. No Dyrrak airborne attackers were launched to begin battle or even to scout the walls. They simply floated there, out of range of Magdaster's emberflare cannons, but not out of sight of those who watched from the walls. Symvalline's concerns were Mallich's too, and though he didn't pace, the same bottomless well of anxiety curdled in his gut.

"Why hasn't Ulfric returned?" she added. This time, she turned her gray eyes to him, their color different to Mallich's but similar in shape. His eyes were a leonine brown but, like hers, lay deeper in their sockets above wide, heavy cheekbones. They shared these traits with most other Yorish, as they did their measured calm, but even that was starting to crack.

"I suppose we shouldn't lose track of the one good that's come of this," he said, skirting the subject of Ulfric's whereabouts. "The longer they wait to attack, the more likelihood there is Bardgrim and his Glisternauts will get here in time."

The side of her mouth curled up. Whether in gladness or doubt, though, was hard to say. "You know the Himmingazian better than I, Mallich. Do you really think him capable of delivering on such an unlikely guarantee?"

Mallich released a snort, not of condescension but of assurance. "That other-worlder is nothing if not capable of truly astonishing surprises. Even if he can't deliver an air fleet and a selection of Himmingazians willing to fight for Vinnr, he may well bring on something we couldn't even guess at. I wouldn't write him off for anything."

Symvalline sighed. "I'd like to be glad of your certainty."

"Do."

With a nod, she said, "I know you don't know what's become of Ulfric any more than I do, but I'm trying to tell myself that the Dyrraks are as they are because of him. It's possible he's persuaded them not to fight, though I don't know how that could be. Or he's hamstrung them in some way. Whatever it is, I'm not sure how much longer I can take the waiting."

"Have you thought on what we should do if he doesn't return? We are in no position to take the battle to them."

Though she hated to hear the words "if he doesn't return" spoken about Ulfric, she didn't begrudge Mallich's saying them. They were Knights and had to be realistic if they were going to fulfill their duties. "No, I know. But even once the battle begins, *if* it does, we're of little use here at all. The Knights, I mean. Perhaps we should consider taking the interrealm well to Dyrrakium—with or without Ulfric. With Vaka Aster's Fenestrii and the incantation Ulfric taught us, any of us can cage Balavad. That is where the end of this war will be found. It may even save countless lives if we're able to achieve it before the Dyrraks launch their campaign against Magdaster."

"We only have two of Balavad's celestial stones, Sym. Even if we could enter Dyrrakium unseen, even if we could find and somehow surprise Balavad's vessel, we'd still need two more of his Fenestrii."

"Eisa has one…" She trailed off, knowing the subject of Eisa would touch a bare nerve. "And another, maybe both, of his remaining stones is sure to be there. It would just be a matter of stealth and secrecy and some luck to find them. We could prevail, but not if we continue to sit here waiting for doom to strike first." *Waiting for Ulfric to be lost to me forever,* her mind added disagreeably.

"I fear what would happen to Eisa if we were to remove the stone from her more than I fear the Dyrraks or Balavad himself," Mallich said simply, an uncommon husk to his voice.

Symvalline tilted her eyes toward him, sympathy drawing her to him, as any healer's would. But her sympathy went deeper than a healer's; it went the depth of a friend's.

Though neither had looked back, they'd both noted two sets of footsteps approaching from behind, and Stave's gruff voice broke in: "Any change?"

Safran stepped beside Symvalline on the right and Stave beside Mallich on the left, the new arrivals gazing over the battlements too.

"Nothing to note," Mallich said.

Sym, we heard your thoughts about attempting to infiltrate Dyrrakium covertly, Safran sent to them all. *While I echo your impatience and see the advantage in bringing the fight to Balavad, I wonder at the wisdom of it. Until we know what's become of Ulfric, any action we take could be putting him in jeopardy. And he advised we wait for him here.*

"I know, of course, I know." Symvalline sighed.

"Might be that he's the Stallari and likes to tell us what to do, and might be that he's got himself some smart wystical way to control people like puppets and such, but he's still your man, isn't he?" Stave gruffed. "And I know if your roles were reversed, Ulfric would dig through a mountain with his bare hands to get to you if he feared for your safety. Rook's balls, I'd tear this here wall down myself brick by brick if it came between me and Safran, and Roi would too… if he had a heartmatch, that is." Stave looked at Mallich's stony features and cocked a grizzled eyebrow. "Why is it you never found someone, then, Roi? You'd think in fifteen hundred turns you'd have had the time, you would."

Stave, perhaps that's enough, Sym sent him sharply, her eyes still on Mallich's features, which had hardened further. She caught Stave shooting her a confused glance and gave him a tiny shake of the head. She knew the truth and suspected Safran did as well, though it didn't surprise her that Stave had never intuited it, being less concerned with affairs of the heart. His belonged to Safran, and that was the extent of his bother about the subject.

Mallich *had* found someone he loved, ages ago. Eisa Nazaria. And though his love for her had and ever would be hopeless, he felt it no less strongly. Symvalline could not pity him, because she wasn't convinced his devotion to Eisa through so many turns wasn't at least some part of what had made him such a stalwart, loyal, and formidable Knight. But she had always wished there was some antidote to the pain he felt, something to ease his hopeless, unrequited yearning.

He had somehow managed his feelings all these turns, and she didn't feel it was her place to press him about them, now especially. Mallich was dedicated to his role as Knight Corporealis and would not appreciate being diverted from it through hers or anyone's unsought sympathy. He proved this the next moment.

"Look, there. Are you all seeing it?" He pointed toward the fleet's main ship. The *Gildr*, the Knights called it.

A thin trail of white smoke that barely marred the blue sky rose from the ship's deck, then without warning there came an explosion that rocked the calm day. The sudden blast and concurrent concussive force was loud enough to make Symvalline's ears pop. Bright red and yellow flames shot from the *Gildr* over the water, many of them whipping into nearby ships, and the water beneath the *Gildr* itself was churned into a froth. From somewhere deep in the center of the ship's hull, a ball of fire shot toward the sky and belched out dense black smoke. The char-colored cloud bled out and up, dark and thick enough that the Knights observing from their post couldn't see through it until it was dispersed by the sea breeze shortly afterward. After the initial blast, smaller secondary explosions rattled out for several more minutes until everything that could had combusted. The seaborne inferno raged, the fire spitting and sputtering in its fight against the ocean. Yet even as it lost its fight against the seawater, it emerged the true victor nonetheless, for the *Gildr* was utterly destroyed. The ship's broken hull sank so quickly that it was as if it had never been.

The Knights looked on speechlessly.

It was Safran who broke the stillness. *There, from the smoke. Is that a Dyrrak fighter?*

They had all nearly missed it, but it grew clearer quickly. Approaching with great haste was the Dyrrak version of the Dragør Wing Fighter ships of Ivoryss.

"It's just one ship," Stave said, puzzled. "They must be suicidal, coming at us like that."

Mallich strode to the nearest watchtower, calling to the sentries posted there, "Alert the rest of the Watch and Commander Nennus. A Dyrrak fighter approaches. Do not—I say again—*do not* open fire. It appears to be a messenger."

One of the sentries acknowledged Mallich's command and began chiming the alert horn as the other sped from her perch to the nearest stairway into the walled city.

"You think that's the case?" Symvalline asked as Mallich returned. Her heart galloped. Was this the opening salvo to the battle she'd hoped to avoid? Or, as her instinct told her, was the destruction of the Dyrrak warship the portent of something far direr than battle?

"We'll know soon enough."

They followed the fast-approaching fighter with their eyes. But they all realized at once it would not make it to the city wall. The craft had sustained some kind of damage, either before or during the blast, and was losing altitude rapidly.

Mallich turned and shouted toward the sentry still at his post. "Soldier, what's the fastest route down there?" The soldier seemed not to understand why the Knights would wish to run toward the enemy and dithered. "Now!" Mallich spat archly. His volume seemed not to have risen, but none on the wall missed his command. The Knight spoke little, but each word he uttered still carried the force of all those he held back.

The sentry didn't need to be told twice and outlined a route that took them to the closest of the wall's sally ports. The Dyrrak craft crashed through the heavy tree canopy outside the wall's southern expanse just as the Knights took to their heels toward it. Each of them knew that whatever was to happen next, the Dyrrak flying the fighter could give them enough information to potentially tip the hand in their favor. If they weren't dead by the time the Knights reached them, that was.

The stoic guards at the base of the wall were harder to persuade to let the Knights through, until Stave used the power of his klinkí stones to persuade them. The heavy iron bars on the single-wide, barely head-height door were thrown across it to bar any outside intruders before the Knights had barely stepped foot into the Weald outside. The acrid smell of smoke immediately drew them in the direction of the crashed fighter. None had high hopes they'd find the pilot still alive.

They underestimated the pilot.

She was obviously wounded, but all but Symvalline immediately recognized the woman hanging halfway through the broken cockpit covering. It was Chancellor Seldeg Aoggvír. And she was undoubtedly dying.

Mallich approached her first, stepping cautiously amid the smoking bits of ruined airship dotting the charred forest floor. The woman was twisted halfway around so that her back was positioned against the craft's hull, her eyes staring into the sky above. Blood poured from her shoulder and neck. Too much of it. But it was the unnatural arch of her back that spoke more blatantly of her imminent death.

"Chancellor," he said, stopping beside the craft. It had lost its landing struts, and the fighter's cockpit was barely a head higher than Mallich. He now stared straight into her slack face.

At his words, though, the Chancellor blinked. Her lips moved, but nothing issued from her broken body. She didn't stop trying though, and Symvalline, observing from a few feet away, felt a tug of deepest pity for the dying woman. Whether friend or foe, her death was going hard.

A slight convulsion shook the woman, sending a small gout of blood sputtering from her lips. This seemed, by some twisted marvel, to aid her voice. "... held them, held them off as long as I could, Knight Roibeard. But they are coming. The Raveners have taken control of... the... fle... ee—" A blood-choked gurgle ended her words, but the woman continued trying to speak. The taut muscles in her throat clenched over and over as she spat and coughed, trying to say something more. To warn them? That part was done. What else could she say?

There was only one more thing that Symvalline wanted to know, *had* to know, that this warrior could tell them. She paced forward to look into the woman's face. "Have you seen Ulfric Aldinhuus? Do you know what's become of him?"

Even as she choked, the woman's eyes rolled toward Symvalline. As a heavy breath left her, the words "... gone to Dyrrakium" sighed out with it. And those were her last.

CHAPTER THIRTY-FOUR

Jaemus pulled his head and torso from the *Glistering Horizon*'s engine housing and stood up straight, stretching his lower back and emitting a long, not-altogether-relieved groan. The work was done, the Glisternaut fleet—at least the sixty-eight ships they could assemble—ready to go to Vinnr. He'd tightened the last bolts on Cote's command ship himself, and though Jaemus was reasonably pleased with the work, he was nearly ecstatic it was over. Mystae or Knight or whatever he was, he was still just a warm body with tired muscles and a nerve center that was telling him there would be a hefty price to pay for all he'd just put them through.

The now-familiar pinpricking of claws running up his leg and torso told him Scintilla was back. "Gah! I wish you wouldn't do that," he proclaimed, uselessly, he'd learned. The flittercat, which had arrived with one or another of the loads of supplies the Magdastervians had delivered, had a mind of its own, and being nearly invisible and faster than a fleech rendered it in undeniable charge of its own fate. The fate it seemed to have decided to claim was to scare the Cosmos dust out of him at every unsuspecting opportunity. He couldn't very well shoo the cat away, not knowing whether that would result in his disembowelment or, given Scintilla's unfathomable proclivities, something worse.

Jaemus had concluded it was not just his imagination that the creature was slyly amused at his discomfort and impotent fear of it.

Under duress, he had learned there were three things the beast loved, which he was obliged to provide anytime he was ambushed by it: Himmingazian food (perhaps due to it being mostly derived from aquatic life); hardy scritches along its spine and rump, which Jaemus had found was the only thing that stilled the creature long enough for him to get a good look at it; and, oddest of all, his lifemate.

Case in point: "That's the last one?" Cote said, approaching from the ship's upper hatch. Immediately, Scintilla was gone, bounding in one leap to Cote's chest, where it latched on with its uncannily long, sharp claws. Cote, rather than reacting with the horror Jaemus originally had, smiled. Smiled! And reached into a pocket he'd begun stowing dried veeshock morsels in. Immediately, Scintilla began making a deep-in-the-throat rumbling sound that Jaemus had only lately learned was an expression of pleasure instead of the growl of imminent violence he'd originally assumed it to be. Cote began feeding the cat the veeshock, a look of contentment on his face different from any Jaemus had previously seen.

Presently, he muttered, "I can't believe you've befriended that stabby beast, despite all the warnings I've passed on from the Magdastervians."

Cote merely gave him an indulgent chuckle. "Has it occurred to you that they might have been, you know, having a little fun at your expense?"

"Do those talons look like fun?"

Choosing to ignore his misgivings—again—Cote brought the subject back to the fleet. "So we're done?"

They stood atop the *Glistering Horizon*'s hull, looking out over the assembled fleet that bobbed around Isle Stonering in the Never Sea's mild waves.

"The very last," Jaemus said and, to his surprise, beamed. It felt good, what they'd accomplished as a team of Glisternauts, and he was magnificently proud of them all.

Cote tossed a few veeshock crumbles aside, and Scintilla jumped free to finish its shameless gobbling of the morsels. Cote stepped up to Jaemus and grabbed him around the waist, pulling him in for a kiss. It landed on Jaemus's half-open mouth, which was in the process of groaning yet again, the strained and overworked muscles in his back reminding him how much torture he'd just put them through.

Jaemus reached back and pressed his hands against the sore spots, and Cote let him go, smiling in understanding. "I thought you were invincible now, being a hero," he quipped.

"Hero, sure. But apparently being invincible doesn't make me impervious to the rigors, I mean, *miseries* of hard work. I thought once I made glint engineer I could delegate this stuff out for good."

"And miss out on all the satisfaction of knowing your own hands are responsible for constructing the best of the best? That's not the Jae I know."

"It's true I like knowing the job is done and done well." He frowned theatrically. "But I've had toothaches that were more pleasant." Despite his grumbling, he was already feeling better, but that didn't mean he wasn't going to milk the moment for all the attention he could get.

Twenty-four Glister cycles had passed—about five Vinnric days, he calculated—and the Himmingazians were ready to go. Whether by some supernatural miracle or wystic phenomenon that not a man or woman in Himmingaze would have believed in a few cycles ago, or by sheer Himmingazian competence and grit, they had achieved the impossible. He would have to remind himself to take most of the credit for it sometime later.

Cote picked up one of the wrenches scattered nearby, giving the housing panel bolts a few last tugs. Jaemus merely stood and watched his lifemate for a moment, enjoying the stolen instant of time before things grew serious again. Cote's shoulders were broader than his, though he was just a smidge shorter than Jae. His darker hair contrasted with his light eyes, and he bore himself with such command that he was practically majestic. In truth, Jaemus had never known what Cote saw in him, but he'd never doubted the love and affection between them. Even when they argued, the verbal sparring was only the thinnest and least important layer of a relationship whose foundations seemed rooted in the very core of eternity.

Cote began gathering the tools and placing them in their case, the clanks and clinks pulling Jaemus from his musing. He regretted bringing focus back to the task at hand, though it had to be done. "It should be you, you know," he said seriously.

Cote stood and turned to look at him. "Me what?"

"This hero business. You're much better suited to it than I am. When this is all over, what do you think of the idea of asking the Creatress for a Mystae spark of your own?"

The fact that Cote didn't respond immediately assured Jaemus that he wasn't the first to have had the thought, and this both elated and terrified him. He'd already considered what life would be like if he never aged and Cote did. If he never died and Cote did. That was not what Jaemus wanted and never would be, and he'd had to ponder the possibility that it might not be his choice. Just like being ordained as a member of a warrior class, *twice*, had not been.

As his lifemate so often did, he sidestepped the subject. "Let's consider that more after this is done." His green eyes sparkled in the misty morning light, and Jae's breath, like it always did when Cote looked at him that way, caught briefly.

"Whatever you say, love."

"I think it's time for me to gather the crews," Cote said after a pause, and Jaemus nodded.

———

NOT LONG LATER, a total of fifteen Glisternauts were assembled on the bridge of the *Glistering Horizon*: four pilots, eight copilots, and three mechanics. Jaemus himself served both as copilot and "mechanic" (though the word was naturally a bit too simplistic for his true role) for the *Glistering Horizon*, the other copilot being Heleina Gibbaden, recently promoted from navigator. The painful memory of Heleina beaning him with a heavy piece of Dyrrakium crockery not so long ago easily replaced the ache in his back.

As he looked over the crew, Jaemus's lips curled up in a mischievous (and possibly slightly smug) grin. How surprised his fellow Knights and their Magdastervian allies would be when the Himmingaze armada arrived. He knew they'd had their unspoken doubts he could assemble and modify the ships in time to be of any use, but they'd openly questioned where he would get enough pilots who were willing to put everything on the line to help other-worlders that, until just recently, they'd never even known existed. Why should Himmingazians fight for Vinnr—even if the fight was in reality over the fate of the entire Cosmos? He'd merely reassured them it was as easily said as done, and with time as limited as it was, they'd chosen to drop the matter, either trusting him or giving in to his whims.

And that was where his secret advantage lay, the one that made his lips curl in unsuppressed joy.

As was proved by the assembled crew, he had no need to persuade that many Himmingazians to fight for Vinnr at all. He only needed those who now stood before him and Cote, because Jaemus's specially collected fleet of sixty-eight ships were to be, by and large, unoccupied. Among Jae's many contributions to the Glisternaut tool chest was the invention of remote pilotry. (And wouldn't Ulfric Aldinhuus positively bubble with envy if he knew this technology existed? Jaemus could hardly wait to bask in the stubborn old man's admiration.)

Hence, their sixty-eight ships only needed a crew of twelve, aided by the backup mechanics. The fleet would be divided into four squadrons, each commanded from a cosmocruiser, which would carry the pilots and copilots who flew them all from the cosmocruisers' bridges. The Himmingaze population itself would hardly know they were missing before they'd return.

He hoped.

Luckily, and as Jaemus had expected, of the thirteen assembled with him and Cote, ten came from the *Bounding Skate* and needed no persuasion at all to go to Vinnr's aid. They knew what was at stake. Most felt they'd already been part of the fight since the beginning and had no desire to abandon it now. Again, his heart filled with pride at being a member of such an inventive and, yes, noble people.

He was glad to see that Spark Engineer Saxton and Flight Leader Drustim had joined the crew as well. Saxton had needed no nudge at all to join the crew. Apparently, witnessing the appearance of a man from amid a beam of incandescent blue light and then witnessing that same man be aided—and not eaten—by a slangarook were all it took to spark an appetite for greater adventures in the young man, once he'd subdued his understandable terror. Jaemus instantly felt a kindred spirit with the spark engineer and his ambition. As it turned out, Saxton was equally convincing on his own in enticing Drustim onto the crew, and Jaemus had barely needed to say much at all to lock in their final member.

Cote took two deliberate steps forward, letting his eyes roam the crew now standing in complete silence. With one hand, he stroked the velvety fur of the flittercat, who clung to his chest and had nuzzled its head under his chin, emitting that ghastly deep-throated churr. The moment to join the fight was at hand, and Jaemus suspected everyone there, even the two who'd never seen the imposing and imperious (and frightening) Dyrraks up close, understood the gravity. Jaemus wasn't going to ruin the mood by suggesting that the miniature monster clinging to Cote somewhat diminished his commanding presence. And did it really, after all?

"Glisternauts," Cote began, "my fine and brave friends, you've all been briefed on what we're about to set out to do. When we still thought we were alone in the Cosmos, living in a world that seemed on the very verge of coming to an end, you all joined the Glisternauts. Not because you were hopeless that Himmingaze was doomed, but because you *had* hope, and you had belief, that a new world and a new home could be found. You joined the Glisternauts to seek out a better future and a new home for the people of Himmingaze.

"And now you know it has been found. All of us here, with two brave exceptions"—he nodded at Saxton and Drustim—"have seen that world, Vinnr, for ourselves. And though it may not be a world we will live in, through the courage, aid, and even sacrifice of some of those from Vinnr, we stand here today with our own home and our own future returned to us.

"Now, Glisternauts, it's our turn to help them. And once again, to help ourselves. That's the reason you are here! Because believe me, and you've seen it yourself, if we don't go to Vinnr's aid now and return their help, this brief renewal of Himmingaze, this brief glimpse of a future so bright that we have barely yet begun to imagine it, will be lost —irrevocably. The people of Vinnr are not strangers to us, just like the people of the other worlds we haven't yet seen are not, not truly. They *are* us, and we are them. We are all part of the same Great Cosmos, and we have all chosen to do whatever we can and whatever we must to ensure not just our own but everyone's future in it.

"Glisternauts, I am proud to stand among you and to fly with you. Proud and humbled. And when through our courage we help win this day, win this Cosmos, the rest of the worlds will be too."

He let these final words ring throughout the bridge until silence steeled back, then he smiled. "Are you ready, Glisternauts?"

The cheer that erupted from the other crew members, Jaemus included, nearly shook the bridge's walls. Come what may, the Glisternauts were ready to face the Dyrraks. He hoped he was too.

CHAPTER THIRTY-FIVE

Leaving Griggory behind, Mylla had every intention of following the byway directly to Magdaster after collecting her traveling goods from her and Griggory's campsite. Worry for her friends and guilt for leaving them so she could pursue her own ends gnawed at her, as well as, perhaps, a bit of guilt for neglecting the duty she'd sworn herself to so long ago.

Yet, steering directly to Magdaster wasn't what she did after all. An unplanned detour called to her, and her first undertaking upon leaving the cold campsite was to seek out the last place she'd seen her father, Greven.

She'd thought she had already put the past behind her now that her last questions about her true origins and the events that had made her an orphan had finally been answered. She should likewise have been feeling not glad but at least satisfied that her father had not died a coward, a traitor, and a deserter of her and her mother. Circumstances had forced him to flee first Ærd then the bandits on the Great Province Byway to save his only daughter, knowing Ayanna was already dead and there was nothing he could do for her. And those same circumstances had led to his death by dragør, the results of, Mylla couldn't deny, her own reaction to the trauma of her mother's death before her eyes. But she'd been a child, dammit, and she wouldn't beat herself up for acting as one. Heart of Purple Might had been trying to aid Mylla, misunderstanding her behavior, and as with herself, Mylla could not find fault with the dragør for that, even if she wanted to. Not that it would matter in the least if she did. A dragør was not an enemy any person, not even a Knight, could hope to challenge. At least not with any expectation of winning.

All the same, she was compelled to see Greven's final resting place, even though she knew there would be nothing left of him to find. Dragørfire left little behind that would last, and time would have erased any minute signs of the man that the dragørfire hadn't. She had to see it though, the desire a kind of pilgrimage that would at last free her from a lifelong sense that she was split between two identities and would never be unified in herself. Seeing her father's final resting place would let her put her past behind her once and for all and live only for the future she had yet only begun to fight for.

As she plodded through the forest, finding her way to the hollow where Greven had died by relying on her increasingly clearer memories, an unexpected and melancholic pining for Ulfric arose. The Stallari had in many ways become a father to her, and now that he was, to put it baldly, no longer strictly a man, and so far away at that, she missed him more than she'd ever imagined she would. She could have used his reassurance, or even his criticism, about the choices she was making. He'd always firmly but kindly helped her find her own path if she got out of her own way and listened to his wisdom. She feared what might have occurred in the days since she'd left her companions behind. Would she ever see him again, ever have another chance to seek his advice? If never before, she could certainly use some now. Had she done the right thing to forsake Fimm? The implications of her decision were too severe to bear thinking more about.

In their place, another unsettling thought reared up. Now that she remembered her own father, was it right for Ulfric's face to still be the one she wished to see in these troublesome times?

When she found Greven's resting place, it was by equal parts luck and memory. The shadows were different, the light hitting the forest at a different time of day from when she'd last been here. And, of course, the foliage had undergone hundreds of seasons of age. Yet, as she stepped into the little hollow, knowing it was the very one by a shelf of quartz-shot rock pushing up from the ground at the east end, all her doubts and gloom vanished. The hollow felt cooler than other parts of the forest, and the air inside was still, like a chapel. Instead of the ferns and moss-covered fallen branches that littered most of the Weald's floor, the earth here was covered with a short, bright green grass that looked soft and inviting enough to lie down on and close her eyes. Knowing that her father had died on that earth didn't ruin the impression. In some way, it made the area feel more inviting, as if Greven had transformed into this grass and was welcoming her into a fatherly embrace, long overdue.

From the edge of the hollow, she took in the space, feeling moistness close over her eyes. No tears fell, however. It was a peaceful patch of forest, and if a spirit could linger anywhere, she felt her father would not have minded lingering here.

The moment passed, and self-consciousness crept in presently. Did she expect to see him? Hear his voice in the wind? No, he was gone, her mother too. But she must carry on. She was needed elsewhere.

After speaking a brief mourner's prayer of peace, she was ready to leave the hollow behind. Before turning, however, she spotted a clump of dalla flowers sprouting in the hollow's only patch of sun. The blooms were small and early season. Thoughtfully, she stooped and plucked one, bringing the pale lavender-colored flower to her nose to sniff. Young as it was, it had barely a smell, but it was there, faint and light and gay. A scent she always associated with the joys of youth, just like the joy she'd felt as a child before Ærd had fallen to war and her life had been irrevocably altered. *Strange,* she thought now. *I don't remember having dallas in Ærd. That doesn't mean it didn't have them, though. I wonder if they're common in all the realms.*

"If you are out there somewhere, Papa and Mumma," she whispered, still holding the flower to her nose, "I hope I've lived a life worthy of the sacrifices you made for me."

With those words, she tenderly kissed the bud and knelt, laying it in the grass as gently as a mourner would lay the most fragile of bouquets on a grave. Rising, she turned and left the hollow, pacing purposefully through the Weald without looking back.

MYLLA DID NOT HEAD BACK to the byway, however. Halla was settling behind the western fringe of the forest not long after she left her father's resting place, and she abruptly decided she'd lingered on her own errands long enough. If she cut through the Weald toward Magdaster instead of following the Great Province road, she would save herself fifty miles or more of walking. The byway could be dangerous, as she'd learned so roughly as a child, and perhaps not at all strangely, she felt safer in the forest, despite its packs of wolves, bears, and of course dragørs.

She walked through the night and the entire next day, stopping only to drink from springs and gather the occasional early berries. She found herself feeling more vivacious than ever in her life, as if she needed neither food nor sleep at all. Realization struck her that having now been ordained by two Verities was what gave her so much greater stamina. So be it. It would come in handy in the near future, no doubt, as it was now by hastening her traverse of the woods.

She closed in on Magdaster on the second morning from the north, skirting the edge of the North Byway where the Weald thinned. Dawn light dusted the cobbles of the road with pink and pale yellow, the ambiance so inviting that she decided to take the road itself for the last few miles. By her estimate, she had perhaps fifteen to go, and at her pace, she'd be there before lunchtime. She'd probably be able to see the city's high, unbreachable wall long before that.

When the stone fortifications of Magdaster came into sight, however, it was not the sight she was expecting.

Dozens upon dozens, maybe some hundreds, of fighter ships not unlike the Knights' dragørfly scouts swarmed the skies over and around the city, firing emberspark cannons at the walls and city streets at will. It was a total attack, a full-blown battle launched upon Magdaster, and her friends.

The Knights were there and they needed her.

Mylla began to run, her legs moving at speeds none who didn't share the spark of a Verity could match. But it wasn't fast enough, she knew it deep within the cold recesses of her spirit. The bombardment was total, unstopping. And the Magdastervians had no air fleet of their own.

But—did they? As she sped onward, her booted heels clocking rapidly and surely against the hard cobblestones, her shock abated enough to realize she hadn't seen the full picture, not at first. There were more airships than just the Dyrraks', strange and unrecognizable. No, that wasn't quite true. Something about the gleam of the dark-gray metal that clad their hulls and the lines and shapes comprising their builds jogged thoughts of the brief glimpses she'd seen of the cosmocruiser captained by Bardgrim's companion in Himmingaze, just before Balavad's warship had swallowed them all. That wasn't possible though—Himmingazian ships couldn't be here, in Vinnr.

So she ran, not knowing nor caring what she could possibly bring to the fight at this point, not thinking about what one mere Knight could hope to achieve against such an onslaught. But she wouldn't quit until she found a way inside those walls. In the madness of the battle, one woman on foot would be practically invisible. If this fight were to be the end of Vinnr's freedom, she didn't want to see it fall alone.

She ran, not thinking about whether her friends would survive the battle. They would be concealed inside the safety of Magdaster's fortifications even if the walls themselves were overwhelmed by the sheer mass of Dyrrak fighters and their emberspark guns. As her breath grew labored and searing, she watched the fighting overhead, using it to help her estimate the distance that remained. Four miles, maybe three.

And she ran, not thinking about the huge black shadow soaring overhead and getting larger by the moment.

Until she realized what it was, and it became all she could think of.

Skidding to an abrupt stop, Mylla's head tilted and her eyes shot to the sky above her. A dragør swooped low enough for her to reach up and touch one of its deadly claws—if she'd been that bold, or stupid. Its descent was swift and utterly unbound by the natural laws of flight she thought she understood implicitly, and aside from the shadow it cast over the road, nothing, not a sound, not a scent, gave away its presence.

The beast's hind paws thumped to the road, sending a shiver through it, directly in front of her. Her first thought, or more accurately, her first *hope*, was that it was Griggory's "friend," if that was the right word, Heart of Purple Might.

This dragør's distinctive coloring told her immediately it was not. Upon this realization, all the blood rushed from her head, her heavy breathing and labored heartbeat so burdened by the sudden shock that she nearly keeled over.

This dragør was equally gargantuan, and equally terrifying. A beast of iridescent green and orange, handsomely accented with darker green and gray lines at its wing tips and along the crest of its forehead where its horns sprouted, it dropped to all four extremities just yards from her and spun with serpentine grace to face her. Frozen, her breath now entirely still, Mylla eyed the creature, knowing her only course of action was to wait for it to do whatever it planned to. There was no outrunning a dragør, and though she'd grasped Star Spark's hilt, her fear, as natural as the tides, did not abate.

The dragør lowered its head until Mylla stared down the bore of its great nostrils. It took a mighty sniff, and its smooth-scaled snout curled in the same expression as Purple Might's had, the one she hoped was a grin.

It drew back, keeping its luminescent titian eyes fixed on her, and its voice spoke in her head: *As Heart of Purple Might said, you are a staunch little speck. Most of your kind simply drop dead in fear when confronted by Vaka Aster's First Creations.*

She had to swallow several times before her voice cooperated. "You-you have spoken to Purple Might of me?"

HEART OF Purple Might, speck. Do not forget to whom and of whom you are speaking.

Its breath blasted over her, hot enough to make her skin feel tight. "My apologies, Master... ?"

You are speaking to Poppy's Noble Inferno, little Knight. But enough with the pleasantries. With satiny steps, the dragør moved beside her. It curled its great body around her in a semicircle and leveled one blazing eye on her. *Climb onto my back. It seems there's a battle to attend, and it would be a lie if I said the dragørkind weren't looking forward to it.*

CHAPTER THIRTY-SIX

"Drown me in fleech slime," Jaemus moaned. "That is… that is… it's the definition of impossible! We'll never be able to stand against that many."

The sight of dozens, *hundreds*, of Dyrrak attack ships, now amassed and assaulting the walled city of Magdaster—and the Glisternauts' imperative to somehow, some way stop them, was the definition in question. Standing at his station on the *Glistering Horizon*'s bridge, Jaemus tore his eyes from the chaos of war before them and looked to Cote. "Impossible!" he repeated, lacking further vocabulary in his fear.

His lifemate, unbelievably, was… smiling?

They'd jumped through the starpath from Himmingaze just under two hours prior and sped with as much haste as they could eke from their ships toward Magdaster. Jaemus watched the *Horizon*'s power readouts closely and enjoyed the briefest moment of triumph when his modifications proved to work. The Vinnric sun kept their power banks well charged, and he guessed the ships would be able to fly indefinitely thanks to his ingenuity and the fleet's skilled mechanics. But the moment's effervescing joy died instantly as soon as they got within sight of the city. The sky around it teemed with Dyrrak attackers, their weapons emitting an endless barrage of destruction at their target.

Fires burned in the besieged city, and their emberflare cannons returned fire nonstop. The Glisternaut ships had not yet been noticed, but even from their safety hovering low over the Howling Weald's canopy, the concussive wave of the Magdastervians' whale-sized cannons rumbled their hulls.

Cote had called the fleet to a standstill before engaging. The plan Jaemus had concocted, as optimistic as it was, had already failed. They'd had only half the time they needed to prepare for the assault, and thus had only achieved half their goal. Yes, the Himmingazian ships could fly perfectly well in Vinnr, but they had not been able to mount the Magdastervian weaponry aboard and train their crew on how to use them.

Yet despite the enemy bombardment ahead, Jaemus's immediate and most pressing concern was Cote's expression. "Why do you look so happy?!" he bleated.

"Why? Just look at those, those—I wouldn't even compliment them with the word 'ships,' Jae. Those little things the Dyrraks are flying are as fragile as reeds and as tiny as minnows. We'll sail through them like they're nothing but raindrops. They'll be crushed to junk, and we won't even need to turn on our reclaimers to reinforce our hulls."

Jaemus opened his mouth to rebut, but then thought better of it. The truth was that the Dyrrak attackers were miniscule compared to an average Glisternaut ship. He doubted a hundred of them combined had even half the mass of one of their cosmocruisers. And based on what he'd learned from studying Havelock Rekkr's ship, they didn't have lightning reclaimer fields, or something similar, to buttress their strength like Glisternaut ships did. The lightning reclaimers, all-encompassing energy fields built into all Himmingazian ships, were an early fleet invention. Not only did they harness the lightning that struck consistently from the Glister Cloud storms and channel their power to the ship engines, but they also protected the ships themselves from the blustery bombardment. It kept their ships in the sky in Himmingaze, and here in Vinnr, they would serve the same purpose, though against a different threat.

"So we can't shoot them, but we can easily knock them out of commission, that's what you're planning?"

But Cote was in command mode and already on the wave-speaker to the rest of the fleet. "New strategy, Glisternauts. Break into your squadrons, cosmocruisers at the fore, and make stacked pyramid walls. We want to come at them like a battering ram, knocking out as many in one attack as possible. They'll figure out quickly what we're doing, but that's fine. Our main mission is to get to the ocean vessels and find their resupply ships. Once those are sunk, we can start picking off the remaining, ehm, nuisances. All clear?"

The three other flight leaders aye-ayed, and Cote turned to Jaemus. "I need you on the celestial stone talking to the Knights. Let them know what we're doing and make sure they tell the local militia to keep their cannon fire directed away from us. It doesn't look like the Dyrrak ships' weapons have much punch, but I don't think the same is true of those, what did you call them?"

"Emberflare cannons."

Cote gave a single nod, then toggled the wave-speaker. "On me, Glisternauts."

And like that, Jaemus found himself a member of what he would have guessed was the most improbable and unconventional air force Vinnr would ever see. It wasn't until after the fight was over that he realized his assumption was much too limited in scope. A winged metal ship was just a winged metal ship, after all, essentially the same in any world no matter what shape or size. An invincible, winged, fire-breathing dragør, on the other hand, was Vinnr's own unique version of flying terror, one which he was about to discover.

On their initial approach of the Dyrrak fighters, Jaemus gritted his teeth hard enough to make his jaw muscles twinge and gripped his copilot controls. Vibrations throughout the *Horizon*'s hull rang from a barrage of at least a dozen emberspark guns and slowly dissipated.

"I was wrong! Reclaimers on full, everyone!" Cote was yelling into the wave-speaker. Turned out that despite the Dyrrak attackers' diminutive size, their weapons were truly a force to be reckoned with.

Not needing to be told twice, Jaemus had already toggled the reclaimer field for the *Glistering Horizon*. From his vantage through its forward viewscreens, he saw another cavalcade from the attackers as it was launched, clenched his seat armrests involuntarily in anticipation of the impact, then, moments later, relaxed completely with a lazy, pleased grin spreading across his face. The Dyrrak weapons had struck again—and failed to do more than make a sparkly light show for the Glisternaut crew to view.

"Full ahead," Cote said, his voice as calm as a distant star.

As the four Glisternaut squadrons accelerated, a mass of a hundred Dyrrak fighters bunched up some three thousand yards ahead, letting loose a full barrage. The Glisternauts closed in irrevocably, a tsunami of inevitable metal, gaining speed. They were close enough for Jaemus to see the slack Ravener faces of the attackers' pilots before the Dyrraks realized the Glisternaut ships were not only unaffected by their weapons but were also not going to turn, slow, or stop before—

With a great cracking heave, the *Horizon* impacted dozens of the relatively insignificant fighters. They exploded against the much more massive ship's viewscreens and hull in a festival of red and orange flames. The Glisternauts inside their ships were not even jiggled this time thanks to the impact dampeners that automatically came online when the reclaimers were activated. Even though the enemy ships had seemed to realize at the last minute that the Glisternauts had no intention of diverting from course and had begun to veer off, they'd been too late. In a single attack, Jaemus estimated that the Dyrrak airships had lost perhaps a hundred fighters.

Leaving, based on the swarm he could still see, some untold hundreds more.

To distract him from this bad news, he had the uncomfortable sensation of Scintilla climbing his spine like a fishhook intent on fighting back. "Off, get away! Go to your captain, creature of needles!" he cried, detaching the flittercat and holding it out toward Cote. The cat squirmed and, without warning, bit his thumb. Its talons had been piercing, but its teeth were pure knife blades. "Ah!"

His scream, or perhaps the taste of him, did it, and Scintilla launched from his outstretched arms to take residence on Cote's shoulders. Once stilled, it lowered its head and glared at Jaemus with eyes that glowed with grave-fire green, promising, he had no doubt, vengeance of the highest order.

"Easy, easy," Cote said to the beast steadily, his face and voice utterly languorous with unbroken concentration. He stroked Scintilla's neck a moment, then returned his hands to the platform of screens that controlled the rest of their squadron. "Form up again, Glister-nauts. We got lucky, but there's still so many of them that this is going to take some time. Drustim and Joburg, you get over the city and protect them. Drustim, you're unit leader. Mye, you and your crew come with us."

Flight Leaders Drustim and Joburg gave their affirmatives, and Flight Leader Mye said, "Where are we going, Captain?"

"The Dyrraks won't make the same mistake again. Now they know they're vulnerable, and they knew we know they're vulnerable, so they'll change their tactics and make themselves harder to hit. As long as they're able to recharge their weapons, the Magdastervians are going to take casualties. So we're going directly for their resupply ships before they can prepare something we can't fight."

"You—you mean like that?"

Jaemus had spotted it the moment he'd handed off the flittercat, a wall or mass of something airborne coming from south of the city. It reminded him in a distant part of his brain of the Glister Cloud, a roiling miasma curling across the horizon in a wide swathe, filled with tiny flickers of light. Only, instead of the kaleidoscopic gases and glittering asteroids composing the Glister Could, this miasma was the color of smoke, deep gray and thick as lava. Even as Cote had been giving orders, it had been getting closer, and now Jaemus saw that the mass *was* smoke, and the flickers appeared to be embers bursting from the source of the flying conflagration.

Jaemus pointed toward what was coming, and Cote followed his finger. The gray cloud began to thin as what was creating it broke from its tight formation.

Jaemus didn't need to ask what they were. They were so alike the slangarooks, but with huge leathery wings instead of waving gossamer fins, that for a moment he forgot to be afraid. The slangarooks were friends to the Creatress, his mind rationalized, so it stood to reason these Vinnric versions of the creatures had to be the allies of Vaka Aster. Allies that breathed fire and spit embers. Allies who, he could see even at this distance, had teeth and talons so large and hooked that he had no doubt they'd cut right through the hulls of the Glisternaut fleet.

But would Vaka Aster's allies have eyes the color of old stone, as blank and opaque as Balavad's Raveners?

He seized the Fenestros he'd placed between his thighs with one hand and channeled fervently to the Knights: *I think we may have some unexpected, er, issues.*

After what we just saw from down here, novice, your Glisternauts can handle it, Stave sent, his voice practically jovial.

Weeellll, maybe? But could you ask the Magdastervians to target their cannons a touch differently? These look a smidge hardier than the airships.

What it is, Jaemus? This time, Stave's voice was not jovial. In fact, if his voice could take shape, it might have been a hammer.

Dragørs. You know, just some flying, firebreathing harbingers of destruc-tion, he finally eked out. And as he did, a beast even larger than Hither shot like a meteor from the center of the cavalry toward the *Glistering Horizon.* Before a wave of fire washed over the viewscreen, Jaemus saw several others veering toward their chosen Glisternaut targets in the same way, every bit as deliberate and organized as his own fleet had been moments before when attacking the Dyrraks.

CHAPTER THIRTY-SEVEN

He, Cote, and Heleina braced themselves, counting on their lightning reclaimers to absorb or deflect the dragørfire as the Glisternaut fleet was bombarded by the world-melting inferno of a horde of red dragørs.

Jaemus finally had to admit he may have been a little too confident in his engineering abilities the moment the *Glistering Horizon* started its dive-bombing descent toward the middle of the Howling Weald, completely engulfed in a ball of fire.

"Balancers full throttle! Keep juicing the thrusters!" Cote, forehead clenched in painful concentration, yelled.

"Which ones?!" Jae and Heleina both cried.

"All of them!"

Scintilla seemed to find the raised voices—or perhaps the eyeball-melting fall—unenjoyable, and Jaemus just caught a glimpse from the corner of an eye of the creature flickering from Cote's shoulders to somewhere unknown. At that moment, he envied the "somewhere unknown" part of that sentiment. Anywhere would be better than the center of a fireball. Panicked, Jaemus gazed overhead, certain the hull must be burning away. It looked like it was still intact, but he didn't trust his eyes to tell him the truth, at least not about this.

Instead, he peered forward through the viewscreen, seeing nothing but a red haze. He had a duty, though—Cote was keeping them flying, and his role right now was to handle his share of their remote ships. Quickly, he discovered only one of his had suffered an attack, but the wave-speakers were exploding with alarms from the other crews whose squadrons had worse luck. As Jaemus took inventory, Cote expertly finessed the *Horizon*'s controls and, miraculously, the ship's dive evened out to a flatter horizontal plane. Jaemus had never felt happier to have his weight settle onto his bum.

"We're all right, we're in control," Cote said a moment later. "Good job, Glisternauts."

As unbelievable as it seemed, heat suffused the bridge, bringing it to a definitely un-Himmingaze-like temperature. Yet now that his fear of splatting into the ground had receded somewhat, Jaemus realized it was merely radiant—no fire had penetrated the ship. The hull was still there, and they were still flying. Sweat covered his face and oozed beneath his clothes.

Novice, novice! Stave sent. *What's going on? You still alive up there?*

Alive, and flying, though I can't believe it. As he spoke, the dregs of the dragørfire blew clear of the *Horizon*'s viewscreen, giving him a clear picture of the skies.

Yes, they were alive—for the moment. Their descent had not been straight down, and their long, sloping drop had taken them quite a ways from the heart of Magdaster and over the Weald. Luckily, they hadn't been pursued, and Cote steered the *Horizon* around sharply to return to the fight. What they saw was nothing short of doomsday.

The wormlike flying dragørs were everywhere, red as fire themselves, streaking through the air like comets. Glisternaut ships were ablaze all over the sky. Those that weren't falling were pursued by the relentless creatures. Using remote links from the cosmocruisers, their pilots zigzagged the ships in a volatile dance of inconsistent patterns, sometimes attempting to regain control, sometimes attempting to escape, and other times their movements appeared to be nothing but panicked madness.

The city below was no better. It looked as though the dragørs had split their factions—those engaging the Glisternauts, and those attempting, it appeared, to turn the city into ash. Already, new fires glinted through volcanoes of black, billowing smoke, far bigger and more potent than even those caused by the Dyrrak weapons.

"Captain Illago, what do we do?" Flight Leader Drustim cried. "The reclaimers barely stop the fire from melting our hulls. They won't take that kind of force for long."

For once, Cote suffered a moment of indecisiveness, but his uncharacteristic pause ended shortly. "Protect the city. Form your squads up in groups of five. Pursue from the rear, repeat, pursue from the rear. If you're chased, try to get these… these—" He shot a look to Jaemus.

"Dragørs?" he offered. "Vinnr's cousin to the slangarooks."

"Flying 'rooks," Cote said shortly, "and get them to—"

Before he could finish the command, the ship was hit violently by a blunt force that joggled it from its not-quite-steady course. Something in the engines screamed in protest, followed by an enraged, or terri-fied, animal yowl that definitely came from inside the ship.

Jaemus shot a glance at Cote. "Was that—"

"Scintilla!" Cote said, and for the first time since the fight began, his expression darkened with concern.

"We hear you, Captain Illago," Flight Leader Joburg responded. "Lead the 'rooks into each other."

"Acknowledged," Cote grunted, most of his mind focused on trying to keep the *Horizon* on a steady flight course.

Then another turbulent strike bumped the ship, tilting it to one side and giving everyone aboard whiplash. Jaemus stared into the retreating back of the dragør that had hit them and saw its lengthy passing tail—half as long as the *Horizon*—whip so hard into the viewscreen that it cracked.

"A few more hits like that," he said, his voice surprisingly casual, "and we'll nothing but bolts united in a common fall." *Casual because my ability to feel fear is as broken as this ship is about to be,* it occurred to him.

"I've never seen anything living that had so much sheer power," Cote mumbled, his hands and eyes in a frenzy of keeping them and their seventeen-strong squadron in the sky. "Find me a target, Jae and Heleina. We're going to show these worms what it feels like to get smacked."

Heleina, who had experience striking things with a blunt instrument, pointed out a likely victim first. "Toward the ocean, tall tower. See those three dragørs heading for it?"

"Got it," Cote acknowledged, and juiced their throttles. "Warn me if…"

His voice trailed away as they all witnessed the ugly but inevitable. Another cosmocruiser, the one piloted by Drustim and Jae's new friend Saxton, was set upon by seven dragørs at once. It was like watching a school of piranha go after a whale—except the piranha were a tenth of the whale's size, breathing fire and ripping it apart with talons. The horde dug their hooks into Drustim's outer hull and held tight, necks curved down to emit torrents of flame directly onto the ship. All seventeen of Drustim's squad were falling from the sky like soggy leaves, fighting to stay up, but without pilots of their own, the remote ships were at Drustim's whim.

Witnessing the calamity, Cote cringed but didn't hesitate. "Joburg, Mye, take control of Drustim's squads. Sweep them back toward the *Deep Sea Gem* and save her!" He tilted his chin at Jaemus. "Can you take one of their squads?"

"I'm on it."

He activated his remotes and suddenly had five more ships under his control. They were linked to his console and required little more than eye movement and attention to control, but there was no way around the devastation of losing Drustim, Saxton, and their third crew member Fex. As they all watched, the *Deep Sea Gem* cosmocruiser barreled into the ground of Vinnr; there was simply no way to stop it. And if the ship exploded, it was impossible to tell with how alight with dragørfire it already was.

The Dyrrak fighters had thinned, letting the dragørs wreak their havoc without interfering. And there was no reason not to, really. The dragørs were superior in every way, from strength and size to ferocity and sheer literal firepower. They were devastating the Glisternauts and

Magdastervians alike. But to Jaemus nothing could be more devastating than losing their friends and fellow Himmingazians.

"Jae, Jae." Cote's voice sounded a world away. "This fight's not over yet. Jae?"

He blinked and looked at his lifemate. Pain and grief pulled Cote's features into sharp angles and grooves. Jaemus knew his own face looked the same. "We can't fight those things. They're pure destruction."

"Ask the Knights. There must be some way stop them. The celestials stones, or the Scrylle—something."

He gave a brief nod and glanced toward Heleina. She had tears in her eyes, but her focus remained firm, unflinching. She caught his glance and scowled, despite the tears, her message seemingly: *We are Himmingazians, and we are tough. We'll get through this.*

Yes, we'll get through this, he thought. *We don't have a choice.*

CHAPTER THIRTY-EIGHT

No one could argue that Mylla's life experience was typical, and she would be the first to admit she probably had a little more tolerance for the extraordinary than the average person. But no one, not even the Stallari himself, could ever have been prepared for the singular thrill of riding a dragør.

When Poppy's Noble Inferno proposed—*commanded* was probably the more apropos term—that Mylla climb onto her back, Mylla had only done what would come naturally to anyone with an ingot of a survival instinct: she hesitated. It wasn't possible to vacillate when commanded by a dragør for long, however, given the alternative, and she'd timidly begun searching for the best way onto Noble Inferno's scaled and wholly unsuited-for-human-comfort back. In the end, she'd been persuaded by one pushy talon to clamber the beast's leg to her flank like a granite wall, finding the dinner-plate-sized scales rough and grippy like sandstone and surprisingly climbable.

The next challenge had been finding something to hold on to while in flight, as she suspected the ride would be both fast and rough. Her hands were hardly large enough to grasp the thick scales, and the beast obviously wore no harness. When Noble Inferno leaped skyward, Mylla grimly clung to her back—but only long enough to have reached deadly heights before tumbling indecorously off like a sack of wheat tossed from a wagon.

"Aaaahhh—!" she cried, then her spine struck something as hard as a tree—the tail she later realized—that knocked her scream silent. From there, she was free-falling like a stone, but only for a moment.

With uncanny gentleness, the huge taloned paw of the dragør's hind leg closed around her in midair, enveloping her like a cage.

You specks are quite a lot of trouble... Noble Inferno grumbled, and carried on without so much as a *whoopsie.*

Once she got her breath back and collected herself, Mylla took in her new situation. They were flying into battle, and she now dangled like a worm on a hook. True, the dragør's talons were harder than steel and her scales were impenetrable, but the spaces between those talons were still just spaces. Anything that slid between them would be stopped, but only because it struck the soft, easily perforated meat of Mylla's body. Likewise, all Noble Inferno had to do was flex or relax her claw, and Mylla would end up crunched to bloody bone meal.

Master Inferno, she sent upon deciding aggravating the dragør was the lesser of two evils. *I'll be no good down here, and you'll have one less talon to fight. Is there any way to fix me astride you?*

You think one less talon will hinder me, do you?

No... of course not. I just think I could be less burdensome to you if I were not... down here.

True, you are a burden. Very well.

The next moment, the hind leg did the unthinkable and released Mylla with a backward kick that arced her upward behind Noble Inferno and past her tail. Too breathless to scream, Mylla reached the apex of her arc, expecting to fall straight down, then blinked in disbelief as Noble Inferno spread her great wings like a sail and arrested her forward momentum to a near halt. Her back ended up just beneath Mylla, who fell not hundreds of feet to the forest floor, but only twoish.

Climb up and lash yourself to my horns, speck.

As her stomach settled uneasily, she did as told, using her belt and her shin-cover bindings to create a harness of sorts around her waist that affixed to both back-sweeping horns just behind Noble Inferno's forehead, which was marked with the nine-pointed star of Vaka Aster, Mylla now realized.

As she tightened the last knot, praying to the Great Cosmos that it would hold, Mylla finally had time to see what she'd been missing during the frenzy of not falling. Behind them, the forest canopy spread out for endless miles, a solid blanket of treetops all the way to Yor's Great Lochanian Forest, Lake Cuffdeach, and beyond to the eastern Almull Sea. And within that vast stretch of horizon, the canopy now erupted with the rising of more, more, and more dragørs. Her breath caught again at the sight, and some emotion she could scarcely recognize swept through her. Wonder, tinged with humility. She was indeed a speck among giants, a very small being in a Cosmos that contained a great many awesome ones.

And these particular awesome beings were on her side.

She looked ahead to Magdaster and realized they had reached the melee. The speeding mass of twenty Dyrrak attackers coming straight toward them in an ill-planned kamikaze run, emberflare cannons already firing, was a clear tip-off.

Noble Inferno grumbled, *Brace yourself*, and roared.

True to her namesake, an inferno streamed from the dragør with the force of a sunburst, drowning the first Dyrrak attackers twenty yards ahead. Mylla white-knuckled a horn with one hand and her klinkí stones with the other—as, to her horror, Noble Inferno flew through the fire she'd created toward her next target.

Mylla nearly screamed, but it would have done no good. The fire would simply melt her into oblivion in, she hoped, no more than a heartbeat, and there was simply nothing she could do to stop it.

"Warm" didn't quite describe the sensation she felt of Noble Inferno blasting through the fire and debris. But that was all—she was not dead, and when she dared open her eyes, she found them well past the danger.

What in Vaka Aster's eyes?! she cried, not believing what she was seeing.

What are you whinging about? Noble Inferno grunted.

Aloud, she said, "I should be dead. No human should have survived what you just flew through."

Foolish, foolish. You have been ordained by more than one Verity, speck. No dragørfire can touch you now.

The dragør's tone bordered on scornful, but Mylla didn't care. The elation blasting through her was enough to shield her against any contempt, no matter how great, because by the Verities, she had just survived being roasted by dragørfire! So ecstatic at the sheer wonder of her newfound advantage was she that she'd have fought Balavad hand-to-hand at the moment if the Verity had confronted her. She was more than invincible now—she was fireproof!

Water and lightning! cried a familiar voice. *Knight Evernal, did I just see you sitting on top of a dragør?*

Her surprise at hearing the Himmingazian had to compete with the many other anomalies claiming her attention, but she somehow brought her focus to him.

... Jaemus Bardgrim?

Yes! Oh Verities' smiles, tell me you can help us. We're getting destroyed up here.

Don't worry, Bardgrim. Get your ships out of the way as fast as you can and let the dragør flight handle the Dyrraks.

After a short consideration, she could understand the talkative 'Gazian's presence here. He seemed nearly as devoted to the Knights as she, and his courage was a fact none could argue with. The presence of the rest of the Himmingazians was a mystery, but now wasn't the time to solve it.

Only destroy the Dyrrak ships, not the foreigners! she called, using the Fenestros in her carryall to amplify her voice and hoping the rest of the horde of dragørs heard her too. *They're allies.*

None bothered to respond, and she could only hope for the best.

Around her, the skies teemed with dragørs. Their myriad colors and designs, all hues of a Vinnric rainbow, were remarkable, some colors she'd never even seen before. Their unusual nature made her wonder if the constant charm of the Fenestros was enhancing her sight.

Their beauty could not overshadow their ruthlessness, however. The chaos of battle was so thick that soon the sky was filled with nothing but fire, smoke, and flying shrapnel. Around her, the dragørs attacked like beasts from a Verity's prophecy of doom. Dragørfire, talons, and tails tore through the Dyrrak ships, ripping them to pieces or burning them to dripping meteors of metal that rained to the earth. Nothing could survive, and even the nimble attackers were not agile enough to escape a chasing dragør bent on decimation. Mylla held on to Noble Inferno's horn with all her formidable strength, being jigged and jogged and jerked in every direction as the creature navigated the battlefield. The only thing she, a thing of almost utter insignificance inside this maelstrom, could do was grit her teeth and bear witness. This was a Knight's fight no longer.

The next moment, she realized how right this was.

Turn away, Anzuru cousin! Noble Inferno growled, banking hard toward the city and making Mylla's neck crack from the sudden redirection. *You are descendants of Vaka Aster's First Creations, not an instrument of Battgjald's maker. I do not wish to fight you.*

Anzuru cousin? she thought. Then she finally realized something her hindbrain already knew. There were two kinds of dragørs in the sky: those of many hues from the Weald, and a swarm that was fully crimson, snout to wing tip to tail tip, their deep red like lava on the wing. And they were attacking the Weald flight.

A blast struck Noble Inferno nearly center in the belly, and she roared with an expanse of rage that nearly deafened Mylla. Though her ears rang, she had no trouble hearing the dragør's voice in her head: *Tell those Magdastervian specks to cease their fire, or we shall join the crimsons in their task.*

Yes, yes! Knights, do you hear me? she yelled through the aid of the Fenestros. *It's Mylla. I've returned from Ærd.*

Novice? Stave responded, filling Mylla with relief to hear a familiar and much-loved voice.

Yes, she said, instantly echoed by Bardgrim. *Yes?*

Nov—the old novice, Mylla, that really you?

It is. Stave, tell the Magdaster forces not to fire upon the Weald dragørs.

I'm riding one as we speak. They're with us, and we're here to help. The silence that followed was an expression of undiluted doubt. *Stave, did you hear?*

Which dragør are you riding? This was Roibeard.

She's the green and orange one. Master Inferno, she said, addressing her companion, *can you fly by the tower ahead to show them?*

Are you truly asking me to prove my identity to the mortals? Noble Inferno scoffed.

You have nothing to prove, Master Inferno. It's me who must be proven.

In what could only be described as a truculent veer, the dragør tilted them ninety degrees and buzzed one of the few towers along Magdaster's great wall that was still standing. As they rushed by, she saw the faces of several soldiers crewing an emberflare cannon below stricken with a disbelief that was made unfortunately comical by an equal measure of terror. But the mission was a success. Noble Inferno careened so close to their group that Mylla could have jumped into it, and she heard them yelling "Dragon rider!" before Noble Inferno flew back into the dragør–Dyrrak fray.

Nothing you do can surprise me anymore, Mylla, Roi said in his usual saturnine tone. *Can you and your new allies take care of these red dragørs? It seems they've been twisted by Balavad, and we have no defense against them.*

We will not, indeed we cannot, kill our own kind, speck, Noble Inferno broke in. *That is the province of you lesser species.*

Mylla was about to jump in and try to avert total disaster, but Roi beat her to it.

Am I speaking with Master Inferno? he sent.

Noble Inferno let out a roar of flame that demolished at least twenty nearby Dyrrak attackers, but still found time to insult the Knight. *A privilege that won't outlive today,* she said.

Nor should it, Master. We are humbled by your presence, and our grati-tude can never be fully expressed. We don't seek your aid for us but for Vaka Aster.

Which wouldn't be necessary if not for you. But... She gave a mollified sigh, or at least Mylla hoped it was mollified. *We came for Vaka Aster, as is our duty, one we do not shy from*—the jab wasn't nearly subtle enough for Mylla to pretend she missed it—*and shall see to it that our Creator's realm is protected.*

Four of the smaller crimson dragørs had homed in on Noble Inferno. Upon craning her neck around to look in all directions, Mylla could see them planning their attack, now mere moments away. *Noble Inferno?* she nudged.

Ssst-sst-sst, the dragør shushed. *I see them, speck. Grab ahold.*

The world's most unnecessary words, as Mylla's hands, now numb and bloodless, hadn't relaxed once since she'd lashed herself to Noble Inferno's horns. The Anzuru crimsons closed in, spewing flame at Noble Inferno. At the last moment, Mylla saw a black talon raking through the air toward her. She flattened herself to Noble Inferno's skull, and the talon missed her by a hair. Knowing how vulnerable she was had been one thing, but now she was not just vulnerable, but a target.

Noble Inferno fought back, lashing her tail through the air whip-strike fast and sending one of the attackers rolling away into a Dyrrak fighter. The fighter was destroyed, the dragør merely rerouted. The remaining three gathered again and shot toward them head on like the tines of a pitchfork. This time, Noble Inferno had some help, but not from another Weald dragør. A Himmingazian ship bigger than Asteryss Keep swooped through the air from above and angled into the oncoming beasts at high speed. They struck it like a bug striking the teeth of a grinning horseback rider at full gallop before they'd had a chance to stoke their flames. Two careened away, stunned and dropping toward the earth and out of sight. The third sank a talon into the ship's hull and held on. The ship continued into the din of battle too quickly for Mylla to see what happened next.

What are we going to do, Master Inferno? The crimsons seem as invulnerable as your own mighty selves.

The dragør contemplated this silently before speaking. *Our cousins are tainted with something unknown to us, but the changes it has wrought are quite clear. Perhaps... tell those flying the metal bubbles to lead the crimsons out to sea.*

It was her turn to pause. *But I thought dragørs avoided the water.*

Not water, our reflections. The sight of our own great might can be stunning, as you know, speck. If the crimsons are as mindless as they appear, they may not know better than to follow their prey. They'll be subdued, for a time, maybe long enough to for us to eliminate the Dyrraks.

Mylla wanted to ask "And then what?" but didn't. She relayed the directions to Bardgrim instead.

He sent: *So it's a divide-and-conquer kind of strategy. I think we can do that.*

Watch out for the ships in the water. They'll have weapons too. At that moment, she realized she'd seen many Glisternaut ships in the fray now, but she'd yet to see them fire their own weapons. Some memory she couldn't fully dredge up on the spot made her think they didn't have any.

Pfft, he scoffed. *Their so-called weapons are no more dangerous to the Glisternaut fleet than spit on an electrical fire.*

How are you fighting them?

It's an effective new method we recently invented. We're calling it "smash 'n' bash." Let's just lead these big red beasties where they'll harm nothing but the jellyfish.

She didn't know what he meant, but internally she applauded his panache. As uncertain as she'd been about remaining in the Knights when this all began, she was quite certain of her delight at having this Himmingazian among them, bombast and all.

And then it came to her. She knew exactly what the "then what" part of the plan to eradicate the crimson dragør threat would be. She just regretted having let Griggory take the Ærd Scrylle, as she should have known she would.

CHAPTER THIRTY-NINE

The *Glistering Horizon* and its remotely operated ships dodged dragørs and bashed into Dyrraks at as much speed and with as much force as their pilots could eke from them. Any innate hesitation to tussle or squeamishness at the violence around them, or that they were inflicting, had died in the Himmingazians along with Drustim and her crew. Their friends had sacrificed their lives, and as the Verities were their witness, the Dyrraks would too.

This is what it must feel like to be Vinnric, Jaemus thought. *This kind of fight-lust must pump through their hearts like blood. Not sure it suits me, but for now—*

He leaned his body and his will against his consoles and sent a swarm of ten Glisternaut ships piling into an equally sized group of Dyrrak fighters. The Dyrraks that weren't fast enough to avoid his barrage crumpled and dropped. Jaemus felt himself sneer and knew he wouldn't have recognized his own face in a mirror at that moment.

A dragør unlike any he'd seen so far passed by his viewscreen, inches from where he stood, and Jaemus nearly tumbled backward in surprise. Had he really just seen what his eyes were telling him he had? Because it looked as if Knight Evernal had just swooped from the sky like a myth, riding astride the head of a humongous dragør.

That alone was enough to make his breath catch. But then they flew straight into a mass of Dyrrak fighters, and her dragør emitted a scorching storm of dragørfire that lit the fighters up. The dragør and Mylla flew into the inferno, and he was sure he'd just witnessed another of his new friends die. Yet he was mistaken. Evernal and her stunningly large dragør erupted from the other side without even a smudge of ash or singe of hair. It was the most unbelievable of the mounting unbelievables he'd been witness to.

Water and lightning! he shouted through his Mentalios. *Knight Evernal, did I just see you sitting on top of a dragør?*

Jaemus Bardgrim?

Yes! Oh Verities' smiles, tell me you can help us. We're getting destroyed up here.

Don't worry, Bardgrim. Get your ships out of the way as fast as you can and let the dragør flight handle the Dyrraks.

As she spoke, he witnessed a dozen more Weald dragørs, evident by their different colors and larger size, engaged in single combat with the crimsons and the Dyrrak ships. He put what was happening together quickly. There were more dragørs in the world than these red southern variety, and somehow Knight Evernal was leading them. If Jaemus had thought the crimson dragørs were large, what he saw her flying upon made him feel meek and tiny indeed. The creature looked large enough to swallow the *Octopod* in a gulp. And there were dozens of these massive multihued dragørs. Jaemus was suddenly very grateful he was fighting for the side he was.

"Cote, back the fleet off and clear the sky for the colorful dragørs. You're probably not going to believe this, but they're on our side."

Cote shot him an unreadable look. And why would it be? They were part of something so terrible and so divergent from their old lives that there simply wasn't an expression in the Himmingazian experience to account for what his lifemate and the rest of them were feeling. Despite this, Cote lacked for nothing in adaptability.

Through the wave-speaker, he spoke immediately to the rest of the fleet: "Joburg, Mye, backup has arrived. The larger dragørs are allies. Draw your squadrons away from the fight and we'll join you over the city. Our role now is to protect the people of Vinnr trapped there."

They sent their acknowledgments, and Cote, Jaemus, and Heleina led their remaining squads toward the city wall, harried every yard of the way by the Dyrraks, though thankfully, the enemy dragørs seemed to have their hands, or claws, full with their Weald cousins.

The Dyrrak fighters came at them in an endless swarm. Jaemus and his fellow pilots did their best to keep the fighters from getting too far over the city proper. Even though their lightning reclaimers were remaining effective as both shields and battering rams, a falling Dyrrak fighter still created dangerous debris for those below. The dragør fights likewise veered over the walls a few times, but the Glisternauts avoided them. Dragørfire and dragør strikes had already proved the Glisternaut ships were no match and likewise unneeded.

Yet, as the battle waged on, his confidence developed cracks. The greater Weald dragørs were doing some damage to their slightly smaller crimson cousins, but the unnatural vitality of their Ravener transformation made them nearly unstoppable. And though he'd now watched dragørfire's power to melt even air to plasma, there was one thing it was less effective against: another dragør.

Jaemus was sure he wasn't the first to think of it, but if these creatures were invincible, how were they supposed to defeat them?

Cote and Jaemus piled through a small clump of Dyrrak ships—how many had their fleet destroyed by now?—and came out of the debris with Mylla and her enormous dragør just below them. They were in a confrontation with a reduced swarm of the crimsons, who were now charging full speed ahead at Noble Inferno.

"See that?" he yelled to Cote. Yelling, he noticed vacantly, had become his default mode, as the intense situation seemed to warrant equally intense reactions.

Instead of yelling back, or answering at all, Cote maintained his cooler head and plunged the *Glistering Horizon* downward, smashing into the charging crimsons. It was a direct hit, and though it shook the ship bow to stern, they sped ahead, still under control.

A screeching, pounding racket echoed through the ship's interior, coming from something outside. No one had to tell the Glisternauts they'd collected an unwelcome passenger, probably one of the dragørs they'd just smashed into, but the situation quickly righted itself. A Weald dragør swooped over their bow, and a moment later, the ship vibrated teeth-rattlingly. They were familiar by now with the sensation and its cause: the Weald dragør had unleashed an inferno, knocking the crimson from its perch and giving the *Horizon* a good shaking.

As the crew gripped their seats and controllers, waiting for the shaking to subside, Knight Evernal reached out to Jaemus. *Bardgrim, if you can, lead the dragørs out to sea. It's their weakness, and it might slow them long enough to give us the upper hand.*

So it's a divide-and-conquer kind of strategy. I think we can do that, he sent back, and told Cote the plan as he and Knight Evernal shared a few more words.

Acknowledging Jaemus, Cote directed the ship toward the sea. It was an arduous turn, as the ship was still shaking from the Weald dragør's blast. Fire had skimmed them several times by this point, but as long as the fire was indirect, the consequences hadn't been severe. Up to now, they'd just needed to hold on to something stable until it passed.

But it didn't pass. Far from it—the shaking worsened.

"Cote, C-Cote," he stammered through his juddering jaw. "What's happening?"

"I think we've lost our stabilizers."

Jaemus didn't have to ask what that meant. He'd designed almost every system aboard this ship, or improved on the old ones. He knew what happened when it couldn't stabilize as well as he knew his birthday. (If you counted by Himmingazian cycles. He had no idea how that would translate in Vinnric turns. And why in the worlds was he thinking about his birthday when they were moments from becoming a plummeting-out-of-control metal coffin?)

"Take over my remotes, Heleina, Jae!" Now Cote *was* yelling. "I've got to… keep us…" His face was a mask of concentration, sweat was dripping freely from his hairline, and he leaned forward in his seat, controls in hand.

The ship suddenly dropped a hundred feet straight down. Jaemus's stomach countered by rising so far into his throat he gagged. The straps holding him to his seat strained painfully, cutting into his shoulders and waist. Heleina gave a grunt and a curse that Jaemus found perfectly suited to the moment. Cote, quiet now, pulled back so hard on the main control stick that it appeared he was trying to wrench it from its moorings.

But they stopped falling. Instead, the tilted ninety degrees to the side, leaving all three crew members dangling from their seat straps.

"Over the ocean, Jae. Help me steer! If we're going down, we might survive it if we're over water."

Jaemus was speechless. *Might* survive? What kind of muddleheaded nonsense was this?

Beside him, Heleina yelled, "I *did not* fly across the stars and risk the Council of Nine Crests charging me with treason for a 'might survive'!" And she threw herself into operating the ship's navigation systems with the verve of a live-at-all-costs zealot. Which seemed like a much better attitude than Cote's silly "might die" to Jaemus, and he yanked himself closer to the controls, gripping the secondaries like a miser grips gold.

Fate threw them one bone, and that was their preset course toward the Verring Sea before they'd lost most of their controls. Through what he knew was more luck than skill, together they pulled the *Horizon* out of its vertical tilt enough to reach the water at an angle that allowed them to skate across it rather than cut straight in. The large Dyrrak sailing vessel that happened to be in their path served as the one thing that could slow their crash. Unfortunately for the Dyrraks, it was split into ragged halves in the process. Likewise, unfortunately for Jaemus and his crew, their impact with the ship finished the job of smashing their forward viewscreens.

Jaemus realized it would happen a second before it did, and yelled, "Get down!" Of course, he needn't have. His fellow Himmingazians may not have been born fighters, but they were still survivors. Already they'd found safety by ducking behind their consoles, leaving Jaemus the last dunce to react.

The viewscreen disintegrated as they scythed through the Dyrrak ship and burst from the other side, moving comparatively sluggishly. Their skim across the Verring Sea ended a hundred yards from the already half-sunk Dyrrak ship, and they began to do the same, sinking like lead as water filled the bridge.

For the Dyrraks, drowning was a real threat. For Jaemus and his crew, it wasn't even in the top ten of their concerns. Once Jaemus adjusted to the jarring calm of submersion enough to leave the safety behind the console, he released his seat harness, looked to his left to see Heleina doing the same, then looked to his right to see Cote—wasn't moving. His lifemate floated in his seat like kelp in placid water. Blood rose languidly from a gouge on his head.

No, no, no, Jaemus thought and pulled himself to Cote's seat. They'd been underwater for less than a minute, but he knew they couldn't stay there. Himmingazians could survive in water, but that was it. He needed to get Cote to dry land to assess his wounds and do what he could to treat them. And he *would* be treating them, because there was no way in the Great Cosmos he was going to entertain the idea that Cote was dead.

This was confirmed, to his great relief, upon his grasping of Cote's arms. The pulse in his wrists was strong and steady. He'd only been knocked out, nothing worse. Jaemus would have gleefully called it a day then and there, if not for the pesky war still being waged all around.

As he motioned to Heleina his intention to swim to the surface, something whooshed past him, something unseen but uneasily felt. At first he feared it was some ghastly unidentified Vinnric sea monster, then he remembered they weren't the only ones aboard the *Horizon.* The stowaway flittercat Scintilla was with them. He felt the sensation of the underwater current created by their passenger as it passed through the shattered viewscreen. The flittercat moved impressively fast, and Jaemus, one arm linked around Cote's back, followed.

Even before they broke the surface, he noted the vast amounts of debris from the murdered Dyrrak ship floating willy-nilly. This was a boon. They would have less chance of being spotted by survivors or crew of the other Dyrrak ships if they weren't the only things bobbing around.

Bardgrim, are you there? It was Knight Evernal.

Depends on what you mean by "there," he returned, too stunned and concerned for Cote to remember to be direct, as the Vinnrics seemed to prefer. Come to think of, as everyone he'd ever known did.

We saw your ship go down, Knight Evernal sent, *and we'll try to get to you as soon as we can. Just hold tight.*

He planned to hold tight—he didn't need to be told—to anything that would keep them afloat and alive. He and Heleina broke the surface, and he slowly spun around, taking in their situation.

It wasn't good. In their last moments of trying to control the *Horizon*'s descent, they'd lost track of the remotes. These had gone down en masse without anyone to pilot them. Naturally, Jaemus had built in autodetector systems for such an event, and they'd self-piloted to the nearest dry-ground landing site. It was good that they were spared—Himmingaze would want them back, after all—though it was less and less clear if there would be anyone left to take them back. All this meant, however, was that Jaemus, Cote, and Heleina were surrounded by hundreds of enemy ships with none of their own nearby to aid their escape.

And that was when things went from bad to worse.

As Jaemus dragged Cote to a nearby floating bit of a wreckage and took hold, a shadow of ominous portent passed overhead. He knew it was no Dyrrak attacker without even looking. The shadow slid by like a serpent, not like a ship. Steeling himself, he raised his head for a look.

A crimson flew in the near distance and was already turning back for another pass. It sensed them, he knew it. But hadn't Knight Evernal said they couldn't fly over water? More pressing, was it searching for them? Would it see them? 'Gazians might be waterproof, but by no stretch of the imagination were they fireproof.

The crimson slid low over the water as if it were swimming through the air, its flight jogging slightly left and right, as if searching. Jaemus, too terrified to speak, motioned for Heleina to dive. But she'd already done that on her own. He pushed away from the wreckage to pull himself and Cote down too—but something held him up.

Frantically, he thrashed around, trying to free himself. He was snagged on the wreckage, and a moment later he discovered by what: the strap of the map case he still kept the Himmingaze Fenestros and Scrylle in.

He yanked the strap hard with one hand, holding Cote tightly to him with the other. But the strap was tougher than Stave's kill-or-be-killed training regimen and wouldn't break. He attempted to dive, but that was as useless as if he'd attempted to fly. The chunk of wood he was attached to must have been a mast or a beam, and pulling against it to try and yank it underwater with them was like trying to pull the sky into the sea. He only managed to roll it over so that now he was stuck ninety percent submerged, with only his and Cote's heads breaking the surface. Was that enough to hide them?

Glancing sharply up, he saw the dragør closing in. The creature's long neck was bent downward, its nostrils flared as it sniffed the water's surface. And it was no longer zigzagging. It was coming directly toward him.

He couldn't escape, and if he released Cote to sink from sight, his lifemate could be lost in the turbulent, debris-strewn water. He might never find him. But if he didn't let him go, they would both be crispy dragør snacks in a moment.

Water and lightning, his mind yammered. *Water and lighting, andwaterandlightning,* and he closed his eyes, the last voluntary action he believed he would ever take.

As he drew his last breath, the sea around him and Cote rocked and frothed. The dragør, it must be the dragør. Despite his unwillingness, his eyelids shot open on their own, cruelly forcing him to witness their doom as his final foe attacked. But that wasn't what he saw.

To his stunned, uncomprehending eyes, it appeared that somehow he and Cote had been encased in a crystal prism. The light bent around them, distorting and magnifying the sky and what floated beyond. The trick of perception almost convinced him that he could reach out and touch the clouds above, which seemed only inches away.

Boggled, his mind wondered momentarily if this was what happened when you died. But at the same time, he wasn't so sure he was dying. Because, after all, the dragør had stopped its flight toward them and resumed a back-and-forth pattern, as if it had lost sight of its prey.

Needle-sharp nails sank into the back of his neck. Amazingly, the sensation didn't even startle him. He knew the feeling well enough by now. Scintilla was back, using Jaemus as his own personal flotation device.

The words of Commander Nennus flitted through his mind then: *Flittercats can bend light. If they want to be seen, they will be. If not...*

Jaemus turned his head to one side, chancing to hope he might catch sight of the cat, who it turned out, had just risen in rank from "nuisance" to "greatest and most wonderful being in the Great Cosmos." The strange perception of magnification intensified right in front of his eyes, and he knew that though he couldn't see Scintilla, the creature was right there.

"You just saved our hides, boy. I don't even care if you were doing it for Cote more than me. But I promise on my glint engineer honor that I'll get you so much veeshock for this that it'll be as high as a mountain, and you'll be able to sit at the very peak and reign over all the other flittercats."

From his shoulder came the deep, throaty rumble signaling the flittercat's pleasure.

"Me too, Scintilla. Me too."

CHAPTER FORTY

The crimsons could fly over water. It was inconceivable. Mylla didn't know much about dragør lore, few who lived in these times did, but Noble Inferno herself had said dragørs couldn't abide the sight of their own reflections. What had gone wrong? And by the Verities, how were they supposed to fight creatures who apparently had no weakness?

As she watched Jaemus's ship dive into the Verring Sea in the midst of hundreds of their enemies, her stomach bottomed out with it. The realization that not only had their one advantage turned out to be a fanciful, empty wish, but worse, that she was currently helpless to go to her companion's aid sucked her faltering spirits into a dense, bleak fugue.

Panic-struck, she sent: *Bardgrim, are you there?*

Depends on what you mean by "there," her fallen friend answered immediately. He sounded stunned, but he was alive, and that was enough to tentatively arrest her plunging hopes.

We saw your ship go down, and we'll try to get to you as soon as we can, she assured him. *Just hold tight.* To Noble Inferno, she asked, "What happened, why didn't the water stop the Anzuru dragørs?"

They no longer see in the way the rest of us do...

Noble Inferno sounded puzzled, and Mylla realized the reasons didn't matter. What did was saving her companion, if it was even possible. "Please," she said, "tell the Weald dragørs to keep the crimsons at bay and let no more out to sea. We must protect the Himmingazians too."

The other-worlders? They merely need to rejoin their leader, this Mystae Bardgrim, and go home.

Please, she pleaded. *This is a fight for more than Vaka Aster, and they have as much at stake as we do.*

The dragør huffed what Mylla *hoped* was assent, and that was the best she could hope for. But she didn't dwell on Noble Inferno's recalcitrance, especially not since what she was suggesting was what Mylla had in mind anyway.

If they couldn't beat the crimsons, then they would expel them from the fight.

She'd already realized that, and her allies had to find some way to even, or better, to improve, their odds. After all, it was one of the first lessons Ulfric had ever taught her at the Conservatum when she was still a recently parentless child. At first, she'd been frightened by his size and his stern glares, but that fear had quickly given way to affection when he came to collect her from her room one day, not for a class, but to play the game called dark stars. It was a game of throwing skills, where each contender had several white stones and half as many dark stones. The object was to collect everyone else's stones by being the best at throwing one's own into a small bucket held by a Prelate statue that rose from the grand fountain in the Conservatum's central courtyard. Everyone had to stand at the same distance, but if you chose to throw a dark stone, you were allowed to step closer. If you chose to throw two, you could stop closer still. If you missed, you lost your advantageous dark stones, as well as many white ones. If you made the shot, you collected everyone else's who had missed, thus gaining more dark stones and the opportunity to throw from an easier distance.

Collecting the most dark stones, Ulfric had taught her, was how you bettered your odds. "First and foremost, Mylla, remember that you can never count on luck or skill, but you can almost always count on the odds. Strengthening the odds in your favor, that's the real skill. Study your counterparts, learn how to improve your odds, and then you'll have the most advantages."

Upon discovering just how dangerous, not to mention numerous, their foe was, the deep recesses of her mind brought the old lesson to the fore, searching for a way to tilt the odds in Vinnr's favor. The Vinnric defenders couldn't get any more powerful or any more numerous—they had no air or water fleet to call on, Yor could never get to them in time, and the army in Asteryss was already on their last leg. The hundred or so Weald dragørs were by no stretch a negligible force, but their code against harming their own kind and the indefatigability of the Ravener dragørs meant the defenders' only remaining option was to be wilier than their foe. Through wile, Mylla had hit upon the way to diminish their enemies' number, and thereby, their strength.

Boxing up her fears for Bardgrim and shoving them to a corner of her mind temporarily, she reached out to the Knights. *Roibeard, are you there?*

For the moment, Mylla.

Who has the Vinnr Scrylle?

It's with us. Were you able to find Ærd's?

She heaved a sigh. Someday her impetuousness was going to be the death of her. *No. Well, yes, kind of—it's a long story. But I know what we must do if we're going to stop the Dyrraks and their pet dragørs.*

A heavy, displeased growl rumbled through Noble Inferno all the way up to where she sat between the creature's horns. *Call dragørkind "pets" once more, speck, and I may forget you are an ally.*

My deepest and most humble apologies, Master Inferno. She was finding that as her familiarity with the creature grew, her fear of her lessened. Or perhaps she'd simply run out of room for that particular terror. *Roi?* she went on, not even pausing long enough for Noble Inferno's response.

We're here, he said. *I think I can guess what you're planning.*

If it's to send them out of Vinnr altogether by starpath, you know me well.

Mylla, we do that and we'll only be putting the folk of other realms in danger. These creatures are controlled by a master who desires control of the whole Cosmos. We'd just be doing Balavad a favor by sending his Raveners and dragørs into an unprepared, hapless realm.

No, that's not entirely true, Roi. There's one realm that has nobody left for Balavad to harm. Ærd.

There was a brief pause, then: *Are you saying he's already taken Ærd over?*

In a sense. There's no life left there, save... Save the tessalopes, but how could she explain them to Roibeard and the rest of her companions, especially since she hardly understood what they were herself?

Save what?

Never mind. There's no one there. I think there was a war. It swept through the realm, and that's why I'm in Vinnr to begin with... but now isn't the time to go into that. We're coming to the walls. I need the Scrylle. I'll be able to move through the battle with Noble Inferno and open the starpaths to reduce their numbers quickly. She'd only just learned the trick to summoning the starpaths, but Eisa used one to exile Mylla to Himmingaze, so she knew it could be done. She just had to figure out how and hope that the fact that Vinnr depended on her would be all the boost she'd need. *It's the only option we have, Roi.*

Safran's voice came through the link. *Mylla, is Knight Dondrin with you?*

No, he came back with me from Ærd, but has since... gone. I honestly don't know to where. But he's not alone. He has a dragør of his own. He's... well, he's an odd one, and I don't have a clue what he's doing or why. I don't even know if we'll ever see him again.

Griggory couldn't stay in one place if his feet were staked to the floor, Roibeard said. *Do you see the northernmost tower, the one with both cannons still flanking it?*

The frenzying Dyrrak fighters, battering Glisternaut ships, and billowing clouds of smoke and fire made the atmosphere over Magdaster nearly impenetrable, but with so few watchtowers atop the wall still standing tall, Mylla quickly spotted the northern one. The Weald border north of the sprawling city had fared better, as most of the fighting was still occurring over the western and southern regions.

The Dyrrak fleet had arrived from the southern sea, but if the Himmingazians and Weald dragørs hadn't arrived when they had, the city's damage would have spread so much faster.

I see it. I'm on my way. And with one sweep of her enormous wings, Noble Inferno passed through fire and chaos and reached the tower.

Mylla looked down and saw her friends awaiting her on the wall. An oil-and-water mixture of joy and anxiety stabbed so sharply through her at the sight that she briefly thought she'd been impaled by a spear. Anticipating the landing, she began undoing the lashings holding her to Noble Inferno's horns. Noble Inferno lowered swiftly like a hawk about to pounce, reaching with her rear talons to grip the wall. Then, with the force of a hurricane, something slammed into the beast's flank.

Mylla screamed breathlessly as she found herself dangling by only her belt from the side of Noble Inferno's head. Worse than the sudden impact, her carryall, only secured by one loop, opened. From the corner of her eye, she saw the Ærd Fenestros within it fall into a cloud of smoke, glint like a shooting crimson star, then disappear below.

The crimson dragør that had sideswiped Noble Inferno and nearly sent Mylla falling now tumbled beside them. Noble Inferno let out a roar, even as she regained control and checked their descent, immersing their attacker in flames. Mylla reached out and grabbed hold of a horn, wrapping her arms and legs around it like a life raft. In all her life, never had she felt so exposed.

The crimson dragør burst through the flames, and that's when Mylla realized just how much worse things could get.

Knight Eisa Nazaria sat astride the crimson's neck, one hand holding a set of reins, the other gripped to the haft of her hallowed glaive Fate Forger. The double blades, one on each end, gleamed despite the metal having sometime recently been burnished from their old mirror-bright silver to onyx black. It gave the appearance that whatever poison now ran through the Knight's veins had likewise tainted her celestially consecrated weapon.

Everything about the sight of her one-time companion shook Mylla to her toes, from her ghastly paleness to her lifeless eyes to the celestial artifacts embedded and glowing with her chest. Only one word could describe the Dyrrak Knight, who had been a woman of unshakeable honor and devotion once. Now she was just a monster. A monster who rode a crimson dragør that had been made equally monstrous.

Eisa's smooth gray eyes fell on Mylla. Did they widen? Like the other Knights, she must have believed Mylla dead, so if the woman had any of her old self still lurking in the deep cracks of her mind, she would likely be surprised to see her old trainee.

Mylla had little time to consider this, as Noble Inferno and Eisa's crimson raged into each other, claws first. The beasts sank their talons into whatever they could grip on the other, bellowing and gnashing their teeth, locked in a midair battle. Their wings whipped cyclones of air that threatened to pull Mylla from the horn she held, but that was the least of her problems.

The crimson gave a thunderous growl and pushed away from Noble Inferno and dove. Noble Inferno, now reacting out of pure, unrelenting wrath, adjusted course to give chase, but she didn't need to. The crimson was simply getting enough distance to take a mighty breath, pumping the bellows that created dragørfire, spin to face its pursuer, and roar straight into the oncoming Noble Inferno.

The survivalist in Mylla, with no better options, didn't release her grip of Noble Inferno's horn, and she clung on with redoubled intensity. Maybe dragørfire couldn't hurt her, but being slammed by a dragør with enough velocity to turn a building into rubble still would.

CHAPTER FORTY-ONE

Having as a friend a creature that can render you invisible has my highest recommendation, thought Jaemus. *Especially when swimming through a sea full of people who'd sooner use you as target practice than throw you a rope.* He just hoped he'd never be in another situation like this to *have* to recommend it.

Nature likewise decided to lend a hand in the way of an incoming tide, pushing Jaemus, Cote, and Heleina to shore shortly after narrowly escaping the crimson dragør's detection. Immediately, Jaemus discovered another thing that was going right today, if anything could be said to be going right when a Cosmos full of celestial beings and their creations were at war. The Glisternaut ships being remote piloted from the *Glistering Horizon* were neatly lined up within walking distance. Unscathed and molested, they'd apparently been forgotten by the Dyrraks and dragørs once they'd settled to earth.

Jaemus had a choice now. Wait out the battle safely on the ground, doing what he could to keep Cote and Heleina safe. Or take the nearest Glisternaut ship and rejoin his companions who were still in the fight. He'd known his decision before the water had even dried from his face. He just wished he could say something to Cote before leaving him behind.

As if his lifemate could read his thoughts, even unconscious, Cote's eyes blinked, and he jerked a little in Jaemus's arms.

"Cote!" Jaemus crowed. "Thank the skies and sea."

Heleina moved closer, grinning. "Knew our commander was just having a moment to himself," she said, and the relief in her voice almost equaled Jaemus's own.

"What happened?" Cote mumbled blearily. "Have we won?"

Jaemus reached for his wrist to check his pulse: still strong and steady. "Not exactly. How are you?"

Cote reached for his head and gingerly ran his palm over the wounded side. "I'm glad my head is still attached, but it hurts enough I almost wish it weren't."

"How many fingers am I holding up?" Heleina asked, kneeling next to him with a hand raised.

"Four, and one thumb," Cote said, squinting.

"And where did we go for our first getaway after you made Glisternaut commander?" Jaemus, ever one to err on the side of caution—if anyone important were asking, that was—asked.

"We went to Vann because you wanted to collect some processor cores to modify. I *wanted* to go to somewhere else, but—"

"You're fine," Jaemus cut in. "I'm so glad." One of Cote's many qualities was to be ever so helpful in reminding Jaemus of specifics about things in their relationship that Jaemus preferred to stay a little more... vague. "Love, we've still got a rather fraught situation in front of us. Scintilla and Heleina can stay with you, but I'm afraid I should probably..." He drifted off, staring meaningfully toward the skies over the city.

Cote had sat up and followed his gaze, though he didn't need to. "Of course, Jae. But I'm not about to let you do this alone." As he spoke, he rose, but slowly. First he got to one knee, groaned as he pushed himself to standing, tried shaking Jaemus's helping hand from his arm, then wobbled alarmingly.

"Commander," Heleina said, beating Jaemus to the coming admonition. "I think you're likely to hurt yourself more than help anyone else in your state."

Cote went green, well, greener, in the face, a look that Jaemus knew was harbinger to a good spew. "Here, sit down," he said. "You're not going anywhere like that."

"Okay, okay." To his credit, Cote wasn't obstinate in the same burdensome way he occasionally accused Jaemus of being. "I think maybe I should."

As soon as he was bum-down in the sand once more, Scintilla, who'd returned to a visible state, curled up on his lap, rubbing his fur-covered face against Cote's chin. Absently, Cote reached into a pocket of his Glisternaut uniform and retrieved a mass of soggy veeshock. The flittercat rumbled and snagged the treat, undeterred in the slightest by its unappetizing state of near-mush. Cote's normal color came back once he'd settled, but he was clearly shaken.

"Come back for me when it's over, Jae. Heleina, Scintilla, and I will be waiting."

"Well…" Heleina said, her tone apologetic. "I'm not quite done here yet. I have it in mind to make these miscreants regret what they did to Saxton and Drustim and Fex."

Jae's eyes cut to her, surprised at but approving in an almost avuncular way of the fight in her voice. Cote merely nodded. "Show them the Himmingazians aren't that easy to stop, Glisternaut."

She smiled, then looked to Jaemus, who had to take a moment to find his words. When they came, they were direct: "You take one long-ranger and I'll take the other. We'll both be able to control the rest of the grounded ships from those."

With an "I'm on it," Heleina was off to claim her ship.

Cote reached up with one hand and grasped Jaemus's. "See you soon, Mystae."

"Try not to let that flittercat eat you while I'm gone. I hear they like innards." He gave Cote his bravest smile, hesitated, then scritched Scintilla briefly behind one ear before returning to battle.

CHAPTER FORTY-TWO

Noble Inferno and the crimson dragør ridden by Eisa slammed into each other with the force of continents clashing, their talons, wings, and roars churning the sky to chaos. The only thing that kept Mylla from being flung into oblivion was her celestially endowed strength that helping her hold Noble Inferno's horn with a literal death grip.

The crimson attacking them was no slouch and fought with the same bottomless desire to rend and gouge until the opponent succumbed. In the turmoil, Mylla caught glimpses of the creature and its rider Eisa, and found it not at all surprising that her former mentor commanded the largest of the red dragørkind she'd seen. Eisa's beast was still smaller than Noble Inferno, who outsized them all, but not by the same flea-to-bumblebee proportion, more bumblebee-to-dragørfly.

But mostly she just clenched her jaw and held her breath as the fight between the two dragørs took them on stomach-turning drops and heart-stopping upsurges through the air. Mylla's ears had been assaulted by so much close-range roaring that, in their own defense, they now rang so loudly she could hear nothing else.

Except one small but objectionable thing—in a moment of stolen silence as Noble Inferno detached from her foe and plunged, the sound of the last piece of leather cord holding Mylla to the horn snapped with a rueful *twang*. Now if she lost her grip, she was going to be flying on her own.

Noble Inferno's dive took them straight into a mass of Dyrrak fighters, and Mylla braced as tightly against the back of the horn as she could. The dragør seemed to sense her vulnerability and decimated the ships by fire instead of simply ramming them. Another nine Dyrrak craft were destroyed, falling into the city as bolides of sparking black smoke. If Mylla were not mistaken, it seemed there were fewer of the fighters now harrying Magdaster. But then she looked to the west and saw another wave of them, some hundreds on their way. The Vinnric defenders had barely made a dent against their enemy. This time her heart sank rather than stopped.

Noble Inferno kept moving. *Where are we going?* Mylla sent, hastening a look behind to see Eisa's dragør closing in.

There is only one way this can end, the dragør replied. *You must get that Scrylle, Knight Evernal.*

Then a new voice was channeling itself to Mylla. Not a dragør's, because she sensed it linking through her Mentalios instead of speaking directly to her mind. But the rasp of it was so foreign, so biting that she was at first unable to understand what she was hearing.

But then she remembered hearing that voice before. When looking into Balavad's Scrylle in Himmingaze.

Why do you run, Knight? the Verity asked. Mylla shot a look behind her and knew without another doubt the Verity spoke through Eisa, using the Knights' wystic Mentalios lens for his own foul ends. *Haven't you realized that you cannot fight forever?*

Maybe it was riding on a magnificent dragør that gave her courage, or maybe she had simply had enough of this malignant Verity, but she retorted with rancor equal to his in every measure, *Neither can you.*

If a sneer could strike out, it would feel like the burst of stinging pressure into the very center of Mylla's brain as Balavad responded, *We shall see.*

And then the crimson caught them, lunging onto Noble Inferno's back from behind and stabbing its talons into the softer flesh of Noble Inferno's wings. A rain of fire spread over Noble Inferno's broad back, encompassing Mylla, who—for reasons she didn't know—held her breath.

The bellow Noble Inferno gave could have cracked the sky. Her tail came whipping over her back, trying to dislodge the crimson, unsuccessfully. Mylla held on, stealing looks over her shoulder, with no idea what to do but wanting nothing more than to reach for Star Spark hanging at her waist. But if she relaxed one finger, she was doomed.

She had her klinkí stones, however, and what little good they would do. Mentally withdrawing them from her pocket, where she'd unconsciously stashed them, she shot them one by one into the crimson, hearing them *plink* uselessly against its armored hide. The beleaguered onslaught did have one effect though. It diverted the creature's focus from dodging Noble Inferno's thrashing tail and drew it to her.

Before the crimson's jaws could dart in and remove parts of Mylla, Noble Inferno showcased a new aerobatic maneuver. Ears, legs, and wings tucked against her body, her enormous aerodynamic bulk screamed like a missile straight ahead, a maneuver that enhanced their speed so much that Mylla's grip began to slip. Behind her, the crimson hunkered down against Noble Inferno's back, barely maintaining its own grasp.

Master Inferno, you must slow down. I'm slipping.

When I tell you, let go.

Let go?! I'll be smashed to a pulp.

At that moment, Noble Inferno turned in a barrel roll. Immediately, Mylla, now upside down, slipped from her perch and was left dangling by only her hands from the horn. She didn't even have time to scream before Noble Inferno growled, *NOW!*

If she'd had a choice in the matter, she might have hesitated, but her hands had already given up. Down she fell, the empty air streaming past her becoming the coolest thing she'd felt since her first immersion in dragørfire. With her eyes shut, she called on her klinkí stones to form a net around her but had little hope they'd protect her from such a high-velocity impact as hers was sure to be.

Her internal timing was spot on, and she hit the ground precisely when she expected to. Except—the earth's hardness had sometime in the recent past transformed from unforgivably solid to decidedly puffy, like a feather pillow. Her eyes shot open, and she found herself cocooned in a watery blue glow, the cerulean hearts of more than two dozen other klinkí stones pulsing like heartbeats within the envelope.

Her friends had caught her, and now they lowered her not to the ground but to the city wall by the north tower. She'd lost all sense of where she was in the sky as the dragørs battled, but Noble Inferno had brought her to the exact place she needed to be.

When her feet touched down and the Knights withdrew their wystic stones, Mylla practically fell into Safran's embrace.

"How did you know?!" Mylla nearly wept with relief.

Noble Inferno told us to prepare, Safran assured her, hugging her tightly.

"Though she was a bit scant on the details," Stave barked vexedly.

"It's not over," Roibeard, ever the pragmatist, stated. "The starpaths, we need to open them now. The city is almost lost."

He held out the Vinnr Scrylle, the Fenestros already joined to it, and Mylla reached for it, her confidence she could open the paths and send others to Ærd without being taken in herself suddenly waning. She'd never done this before, and as far as she knew, none of her companions had either. But they had to try.

As her hand closed on the cool star-forged scepter, it was abruptly winged aside. Something had struck it, something too fast for Mylla's regular eyes to see, but with her Knight's senses, she caught a glimpse of what looked like a klinkí stone strike it, but bloodred.

The Knights, all stunned, looked in the direction the projectile had come from, and beheld their former member.

"Eisa," Stave growled, his axes already drawn.

"No, she's not Eisa. She's Balavad now," Mylla said, not with fear or anger, but with profound numbness. Eisa had never been kind to her, but she had been a Knight, and Mylla's respect for and loyalty to those of her Order were unshakeable. Would nothing she valued be left uncorrupted?

The top of the stone wall was six yards wide and three hundred feet from the city floor. A narrow and treacherous place for hand-to-hand, or Knight-to-Knight, combat. Yet it seemed it would end here, by Balavad's reckoning. The Knights under other circumstances would have liked their odds of five to one, but these were not other circumstances.

"Bring it round, bring it round," one of the Magdastervian soldiers yelled behind Mylla. She heard it distantly, her mind too focused on the nemesis approaching from down the wall to pay much attention. Following this came the creaking of metal, something that sounded heavy. What were the Magdastervians doing?

She glanced sharply backward, having long since drawn Star Spark without a thought. The emberflare cannon, a monstrous contraption inside the bore of which Mylla could easily sleep, was being spun on its base, apparently to try to target the Ravener Knight.

"Get out of here! Run!" Roibeard yelled at the brave if hapless Magdastervians. "That will do us no good up here."

True enough. Even if they managed to aim it at Eisa, the fallen Knight would hardly stand in its trajectory and wait to be blown to smithereens. With the Magdastervians' city in ruins, they were now beyond desperate and frightened and had lost their reason.

Mylla saw their faces through slits in the weapon's shield plate, saw them hesitate, then saw them turn and run, following Roi's command. Even for men who'd lost their senses, there could be no doubt as Mylla had thought earlier—this was a Knights' battle.

It was Roibeard who stepped in front to engage their one-time companion. Mylla saw he held one of the Himmingaze Fenestrii, but his hand was lowered unthreateningly. "Eisa, if you're in there at all, fight. Fight Balavad like only you can."

The crowing sound that came from her throat was probably a laugh, but it was garbled by so much malignancy that it might as well have been airborne cancer. "Mallich Roibeard, oldest of the remaining Knights except the wandering one. Eisa Nazaria chose this." The hands that were once Eisa's held Fate Forger across her body in a combat-ready stance. At those words, she pulled the glaive into her chest, bumping it against the onyx Fenestros embedded there. "Why would she give it up for any of you?" The eyes, gray and dead but still somehow able to pierce like knives, stared at them, burning.

Roi turned his head half to the side, saying to them sotto voce, "Don't listen to Balavad's words, and don't harm her if you can help it."

"There's none of Eisa left to hurt, there isn't," Stave gruffed.

Mylla, surprising herself, interjected, "She is and ever was our companion. We have to help her if we can."

"She saved your life not long ago. Don't make me wish she hadn't," Roibeard warned in a voice Mylla had never heard from him before. It was as dark as storm clouds on the horizon, as threatening as a rumbling volcano, and even Stave Thorvíl hesitated at hearing it.

"Aye," he merely said.

"Come, Knights Corporealis," Balavad called through the fallen Knight. "Show me your worth and why my quin Vaka Aster chose you among so many other Vinnrics to assist her. I'm not convinced she chose well."

As the sky overhead blazed with fire and the city below did the same, Roibeard stepped forward. His own greatsword, Ruin Hammer, extended from his free fist, but he did not hold it high. Mylla wanted to warn him not to be so trusting, or so confident in Eisa's ability to subvert Balavad's will, but she knew she'd be wasting her words.

"Fight him, Eisa," Roibeard said. "We'll keep him busy."

And with a movement so swift he seemed to be made of smoke, Roi lunged at the fallen Knight, bringing his sword down hard enough to topple Eisa to her back. But he didn't strike to kill. He'd aimed his blow for the glaive's haft, where its impact would be easily absorbed.

The fallen Knight leaped to her feet instantly to face him, and he waited. It was the mistake Mylla had been afraid of. If she'd struck with her glaive, he'd have been ready, but the next moment, Roibeard was soaring through the air, propelled by a thin stream of what appeared to be white fire, over the heads of the watching Knights, and slammed bodily into the half-turned bore of the emberflare cannon. He bounced off and came to rest face-up on the wall.

Mylla barely understood what she'd seen, but the glow around

Eisa's abominable Battgjald Fenestros was stronger, and it had pulsed before Roi went flying. Like an invisible battering ram, the embedded artifact was a weapon they had no defense against.

"So much for the oldest," Balavad said through the fallen Knight. "Who's next?"

Symvalline ran to Roi. He was getting to his feet, but slowly, like an old man. *Alive, thank the—* Mylla's thought broke off when she realized she'd been about to thank the Verities. But at least Roibeard could still move. How many blows like that could a Knight withstand before they were broken beyond repair?

Safran sent, using the Mentalios link, *We cannot defeat power like that. We have to find a way to contain it.*

"Contain me? Do you mean like your Stallari did with my quin?" Balavad said.

Mylla's stomach curdled at the realization that Balavad now had access to their minds, having retained Eisa's own Mentalios. They'd even lost that small advantage.

"To do that, you'll need more of these." The fallen Knight reached inside a pouch hanging at her waist and withdrew the Ærd Fenestros that Mylla had dropped.

Eisa's dull eyes looked from the Fenestros to Mylla and tightened in studied concentration. "But with this here, that means you have been to Ærd. Come closer."

The fallen Knight whispered a word in Battgjaldic, and suddenly Mylla was being dragged toward her by an unseen force. The other Knights reached out to stop her. Stave got a grip on her baldric, but the next moment, he too was struck by the white fire. With a garbled curse that nearly rivaled Balavad's weapon in ferocity, he fell to his knees instead of being launched backward. Safran jumped to his side and gripped his arm to pull him away from the constant stream of thin flame coming from Eisa's Fenestros. It wrapped around her too, and she cried out voicelessly, her mouth a yawning *O* of pain.

"Stop!" Mylla yelled, feeling foolish and more impotent than when she'd been a child abducted by mother-murdering bandits.

Presently, the fallen Knight did, not so much heeding Mylla's plea as seeming to lose interest in those who were no more a threat to her than irritating insects. Mylla was forced toward her with a furious yank. Ready with Star Spark, she swung it and clashed against Eisa's glaive, then froze there, the two weapons seemingly welded. A hallowed, vessel-destroying weapon wielded by a Knight could fell giants, but against another of its kind, it was no different than any other. Mylla too felt as if she'd been melted fast to the spot. Not a muscle in her body could move, even her heart and lungs sluggish.

The fallen Knight gazed at her with dead eyes. "But you have been to Ærd and are a twice-ordained servant now. I see why the dragørs' fire could not touch you."

Mylla gazed back, and it was now equally apparent that Eisa's corrupted body was just as immune to the fire, for Mylla saw clearly the ordination marks of two Verities on Eisa's face: her old nine-pointed-star of Vaka Aster on her chin, and also the three chevrons of Balavad's order of protectors cascading down her forehead. There was one question answered, though it hardly mattered now.

"Not only am I twice ordained," she whispered, "I'm the last Ærden. You failed even there, Balavad."

She had no idea why she was taunting the monster, but if her day was to be marked by foolishness, why stop with the simple things like losing the Ærden artifacts?

With a twitch of the lips that would have been a smile had the fallen Knight been capable of mirth, she said, "How nice for you, Knight Evernal." Though Eisa's eyes didn't shift, she spoke this time over Mylla's shoulder. "Attack me again, Vaka Aster's creations, and I will tear this one's eyes from her head and use them to choke each of you slowly to death."

Mylla's body was angled enough that she could see from the corner of one eye that the Knights had regrouped, weapons raised, behind her. They'd been on the verge of charging. Her gratitude swelled considerably when they didn't.

Eisa's master spoke again. "And for me, now the time has come for me to finish what I began in Ærd."

The fallen Knight went silent abruptly, and the miasma that had once nearly sucked the life out of Mylla aboard Balavad's warship erupted like startled bats from a cave around Eisa's body. Mylla saw it pouring from the celestial stone in her chest, straight at Mylla, then straight *into* her. The immobility she was experiencing changed. Still she stood frozen in place, and a roiling, oozing sensation began to spread through her. A sick and aberrant feeling, it seemed to sink into her skin and wend around her veins, following their paths and coursing throughout her body rapidly.

She knew what came next. The pain, the nearly unendurable pain. So when it struck, she wasn't surprised. But this time, somehow, she *did* endure it.

A million knives all stabbed her at once—or that was what it had felt like before. Now, though, the pain was muted, prickling rather than piercing. She gritted her teeth against it instead of screaming herself voiceless, knowing without a thought that she was now stronger in all ways thanks to Fimm's spark, asked for or not.

"Is that... the best you... can do?" she taunted again. But this time, she had a reason.

Over the fallen Knight's shoulder, a lone Glisternaut ship dove from the sky. Its course was blatant and straight. In mere seconds, Balavad's stolen body would be smeared to paste along the top of wall. Mylla too, but she was prepared for that sacrifice. What else was this if not her duty? She knew Eisa, the old Eisa, would have agreed.

CHAPTER FORTY-THREE

The buzz of the diving Glisternaut ship's engines cut through the air like the thinnest of knife edges through a soft, ripe fruit. A mere heartbeat before it struck the fallen Knight—and Mylla—Eisa turned, and Mylla was suddenly free from the wystic bindings that held her. Seizing the opportunity, she snatched the Ærd Fenestros from the distracted Knight's hand and leaped aside before the ship could strike.

Yet, the foremost lesson Mylla was to learn in life over and over was that when it came to conflicts with Verities, nothing ever went right. This moment was no different when the expected impact never came. As the nose of the ship closed in, it was batted away from its target by Eisa's Fenestros-channeled force with no more pomp than a fly is swatted.

The ship's momentum carried it forward until it crunched to a dead stop against the wall's robust northern tower and hung there, embedded. Bent and distorted, Eisa blasted it for several seconds, ensuring it would never fly again, As the wreckage broke under the assault, Mylla scrambled back to the Knights. Her heart twanged for the surely dead pilot, whoever they were.

When the fallen Knight's interest wore out, she cut off the awesome power of Balavad's artifacts and eyed the Knights. They faced her, unflinching.

Eisa studied them, then her mouth cracked in a grin that would make birds drop dead from their branches. "Knights," Balavad said through Eisa's mouth, "this is the third time we've faced each other, and this will be the final time I make you this offer. Become my servants willingly, and be rewarded generously, and I will leave the rest of the Vinnrics as they are—piteous, lesser creations of Vaka Aster. My dominion is already complete, as you must see." The hand of the fallen Knight swept over the city side of the wall, pulling their attention to the destruction.

Magdaster was indeed a ruin. The fires and falling ship debris had leveled nearly everything that stood taller than a person. What citizens hadn't already died were all now trapped in whatever spaces they could find to escape the spreading destruction. Even if they could get to the sea, they'd know by now that there was no safety from the crimson dragørs there either. The city walls had withstood a great deal, but even they would eventually crumble under the Raveners' and dragørs' onslaught. And Balavad would surely continue this devastation if his demands weren't met. Then what would be left for them but a dark future as minions of a greedy, corrupted Verity among the blackened bricks of their shattered home?

What the Verity was telling them was the Knights could change that fate with one choice. It was a choice that made Mylla's blood turn to ash in her veins. No one spoke, all understanding the consequences of either choice in their bones.

"Ouch. The Council is not going to like what we've done to the fleet at all."

The voice came from behind them, so unexpected that even Eisa's focus was distracted. Jaemus Bardgrim joined them a second later, emerging from a gaping hole in the wrecked Glisternaut ship with, miraculously, only minor abrasions on his head and arms. He'd picked up a sword somewhere, though he held it almost like a garden hoe.

"Novice!" Stave blurted. "I thought you knew how to fly one of those things, I did."

Bardgrim gave him an unreadable look, but merely said, "So did I. Ahem." He jerked his chin to indicate Eisa. "Based on that bit of unexpected aerial skylarking, I take it we're not winning, are we?"

The distraction wasn't enough to last, and Roibeard's focus had returned to Eisa. "Your promise is false, Balavad. Even if you don't corrupt the rest of the Vinnrics with your poison, they will still be no more than slaves."

Mylla felt a sharp poke in her back and glanced beside her. Symvalline held the Vinnr Scrylle tucked within her sleeve. The Vinnr Fenestros was missing, knocked free when Eisa had struck it from Mylla's hand, and with a meaningful look at Mylla and a glance toward the Ærd Fenestros she still held, Symvalline pushed the Scrylle toward her.

At first Mylla wasn't sure what Symvalline wanted her to do, and with Balavad's access to their Mentalios link, she dared not ask. Then she had an idea—the starpath plan had been to send away the crimson dragørs, but why not start with Eisa? No, that would be pointless. Eisa's embedded artifacts made her as capable of returning as she seemed capable of all else. But one thing they knew was that she was only controlled by Balavad; she wasn't Balavad's vessel. A Verity could only take a vessel from their own creations. Which meant the fallen Knight's powers were, despite what they seemed, limited. And coming as they were from the Fenestros and Scrylle buried in her chest, then what better weapon against them than another set of the same artifacts?

Symvalline must have seen the spark of the idea in Mylla's eyes, and she stepped in front her abruptly, letting the Scrylle slide from her sleeve, and with the legerdemain of a practiced illusionist, she swapped the Scrylle for Mylla's sword and confronted Eisa. "You can attempt whatever you like, Verity—an attempt is all it will be. You've forgotten that we are just a few of those who stand against you. Stallari Aldinhuus endures, and Vinnr will never be lost and never surrender while Vaka Aster's cage can yet be unmade."

Bardgrim now stood beside Mylla, and as she discreetly attached the Fenestros, she nudged him with her elbow. He saw what she was doing, tucked his sword awkwardly beneath his arm, and pulled the Himmingazian artifacts from a pouch, already joined together. His movements were less polished and secretive, but the action was easy enough.

They looked to each other. *Ready?* she mouthed.

His expression morphed to puzzlement, and his lips parted as he prepared to ask the question whose answer should have been obvious, but Balavad made his puppet speak first.

"Stallari Aldinhuus should have been one of my own creations. But now he is dead. I crushed his spirit along with that pretty dragørfly bauble he bore. Odd jewelry for a man; it seemed more suited for a child. And now my quin's tomb is forever sealed."

Symvalline's legs seemed to been swept from beneath her, and she would have clattered to the ground if Roibeard hadn't caught her elbow.

For Mylla, the words were too surreal to believe. So she did as anyone would do when faced with such abominable lies; she ignored them. To the Knights, she cried: "Ready your klinkí stones! Attack now!"

They hesitated, but not much. The Knights were still warriors, and a warrior's true strength came from being able to fight amid profound suffering, even suffering as profound as losing a leader as loved as Ulfric had been.

The air swiftly filled with the Knights' cerulean wystic stones, even Roibeard's, who appeared to have lost all hope that Eisa could be spared. Channeling all the rage in her through the Scrylle scepter, Mylla used its power to direct the cavalcade of stones at the fallen Knight.

Balavad had already outwitted her again, however. Eisa's own wystic stones formed a shield before her, a mushroom-cap-shaped bulge of red that each of their own klinkí stones first struck with an audible *thunk*, then adhered to like iron to a magnet. The blue glow illuminating their centers began to slowly bleed out and join the red morass of Eisa's shield, turning it a muddy, bloody magenta.

This time Balavad struck back. The purple-red wall of stones reversed and flew back at them. They would have burned holes through them all if Mylla wasn't already running full speed at the monster. Snagging her sword from Symvalline, she charged, Scrylle and Fenestros raised like a torch, whispering an enchantment through the celestial stone to screen them all from the oncoming wall of death.

Amazingly, it worked. The klinkí stones struck nothing but stopped midair and clattered to the walkway. Mylla used the force field she'd created to keep running, and behind her, the others joined. The distance was short, only three dozen feet, and she finally caught a break. She saw the surprise on Eisa's face as Star Spark was driven at her. The reprieve was attenuated, though, by the fallen Knight parrying her sword thrust just before it went through her chest, making a terrible wound through Eisa's shoulder, but not a lethal one.

She'd driven the sword hilt deep into Eisa, and there Mylla stood, face-to-face, fist to shoulder with her. The monster in Eisa, unbelievably, smiled, showing Eisa's teeth, which had changed from pure ivory to translucent, like glass. And also like glass, they were now wicked shards, designed for ripping meat.

Stunned, Mylla released Star Spark and fell back a step, waiting for the rest of the Knights to follow her lead and plunge their own weapons into their enemy—yet, they didn't. She chanced a glance back and saw the klinkí stone wall she thought she had stopped now raised once more and spanning the walkway, hovering between her and her companions. Ominous spikes of blood-colored light rippled and pulsed over the surface facing the Knights, threatening clearly what would happen if they tried to step through.

"I shall have that," Mylla heard, and a moment later, her Scrylle-wielding arm was snapped in two just above her wrist as the fallen Knight broke it.

Mylla shrieked so loudly that her vocal cords seemed to tear, dropping to her knees as agonized tears sprang to her eyes. The broken arm flopped unnaturally, and the sight of it, more than the pain, made her vomit her stomach empty in one great gush.

"Foolish and troublesome but not for much longer," Balavad said.

On her knees, she cradled her broken arm and looked up to her one-time companion's desecrated form. In that moment, Mylla felt for the first time something too foreign and unique to her to recognize at first—she felt beaten. Through the wash of tears, she watched Eisa's arm raise the Scrylle like a hammer and knew it would be the instrument of her death. Behind her, the rest of the Knights were yelling and cursing, trying to get to her. But there was no chance. The twice-ordained, infested-by-a-malevolent-Verity, fallen Dyrrak Knight bearing not one but two celestial Scrylles was simply too powerful.

She closed her eyes, bowed her head, and waited.

But the blow didn't fall. For a split second, she wondered if something miraculous had saved her. Then, as if she'd fallen into the heart of a volcano, dragørfire exploded around her.

Mylla looked up through the inferno at her nemesis. The screen of red was too dense for Mylla to see more than the vague shape of Eisa, who stood as if frozen, the Scrylle still upraised, looking past her. Mylla fell back on her rear and pushed hard with her legs to scoot out of the fallen Knight's reach, never taking her eyes from where Eisa stood.

As if cut with a knife, the flames stopped and showed her something... indescribable.

The Ærden Fenestros Eisa held aloft was changing. From the fist-sized solid-matter orb, it evanesced into an insubstantial mist that flowed free of the Scrylle setting, still the muted reddish hues of the original celestial stone. Eisa's dull eyes were fixed on it, and she lowered the Scrylle, holding it away from her body as if it were a predator that could unexpectedly strike.

The mist began to grow, expanding and shifting in the wavering heat of the dissipating dragørfire, completely disjoining from the Scrylle. Eisa flung the Scrylle scepter blindly away, and Mylla heard it strike the stone of the wall, though she didn't turn to see where it landed.

The Fenestros, having become amorphous and unrecognizable as a celestial stone, expanded and swirled into a columnar shape enclosing Eisa. A shape Mylla recognized. It gradually coalesced into thicker and thicker horizontal tendrils that wound around each other, continually growing, continually rising. Several of its tendrils whipped around Eisa's legs, arms, and even her neck. The fallen Knight tried to fight them, but they merely tightened down, immobilizing her. The column spread out and over Eisa, embracing her within its shifting mist. Where her body made contact with it, tiny lights of all colors and hues erupted and blinked, then evaporated like sparks, and the column kept growing up, now piercing the smoky, fiery pall over the sky, and it grew down along the wall, like the roots of an old oak spilling over stones. Mylla, aghast and paralyzed with awe, could only watch as the Fenestros, for lack of a better word, *sprouted* once more, becoming the tessalope. And trapped within the time walker's "trunk" was the fallen Knight.

"Back away, Mylla, come here."

The voice belonged to Griggory, whom, she realized when she jerked her head around to look, had somehow appeared behind her. And not only him, but perched on the mighty bore of the emberflare cannon was Heart of Purple Might, his golden-ginger eyes blazing like the fire he'd just bathed her and Eisa in.

The klinkí stone wall had fallen, and the ancient Knight stood surrounded now by the others on the walkway. Their eyes, which would normally have been staring in surprise at the sudden appearance of their old companion and the enormous dragør, were instead fixed on the thing happening to the Fenestros. Their reactions were only natural, said an oddly detached voice in the back of Mylla's mind. It wasn't every day a titanic wystic creature from another realm appeared in front of you and, again for lack of a better word, *consumed* your enemy.

A hand, Griggory's, reached under her armpit and hauled her to her feet. As she held her injured arm, her teeth clenched against the cry of pain that wanted to escape, she heard Eisa roar in fury. When Mylla looked back, the translucence of the tessalope's trunk was growing darker and denser around Eisa, like sap solidifying into amber around an insect. The fallen Knight let loose another wrath-filled bellow, and with her jaws cracked wide, she suddenly froze there.

"What's happening, Griggory?" Mylla asked, followed by a desperate, "Can she get free?"

"Heart of Purple Might released the tessalope. You see, it's the dragørfire, it helps the Fenestros seeds to grow."

Like pinecones in a forest fire? Safran asked, struggling as they all were to find an analogy that would help them make sense of what he was saying.

Griggory shrugged, neither confirming nor disconfirming her idea, then went on as if it were unimportant. "Eisa—or what's left of her—is trapped in time right now. For her, a moment will be the same as an eternity. Such is the power of a tessalope. But for Balavad..." He let the words hang. None of them needed an explanation of a Verity's susceptibility to forces of the Cosmos. His sharp blue gaze, the same color as the hearts of their klinkí stones, took them each in, one by one. "The time walker won't keep her forever. Knights and friends, the *time* has come. We cannot win this war. Nothing can. Except—"

Before he could reveal the way to victory that they all but strained from their skin to hear, running bootsteps approached from the stairwell leading to the top of the wall. Purple Might's jaws cracked with menace, and a puff of flame burst free as he turned a languid head to see who was coming and whom he might have to crispen.

There was a faint squeal, then: "Great Verities' blargy eyes, call the beast off!" cried a gruff, older man's voice Mylla vaguely recognized.

Roibeard paced quickly past the base of the cannon. "Commander Nennus, is that you?"

"It is! And Brun and the Rekkrs. What is that..."

The commander was still speaking, but Mylla had stopped listening at *the Rekkrs*.

Havelock.

With Purple Might assured they were friends, the two commanders and two more men were ushered forward to join the group of Knights, and she watched them step around the cannon in single file. She remembered Nennus, commander of the Magdastervian forces, and knew Tannir Brun, commander of the Asteryssians, from their short but tense association. The third man was Henrick Rekkr, father of the man she'd loved, still loved, Lock. All of them were covered in soot, and some bore minor injuries, their blood mixing with the ash on their skin and clothes in a bitter paste.

Lock was last. When he came around the cannon's base, Mylla's breath caught. Their last words to each other had been cold, but her heart toward him had never been. She'd had to let him go, her duty and her fate at odds with his. His loyalty had never wavered, like hers had, and he had stayed in Ivoryss after Balavad's first attack when she had gone, believing still that her duty lay with Vaka Aster instead of Vinnr and the people in it, including those she loved. Then, she hadn't yet known what her future would bring, but she'd known she would forever regret losing him.

Their eyes found each other, and though time was against them, everything they wanted to say to each other, the love they still held, passed between them in that brief but eternal glance.

"—Syzyckí Elementum, you understand."

Griggory was explaining something to the group, something important, and Mylla tore her eyes from Havelock's to catch up.

"It's all up to you now, Mylla," the ancient Knight finished. "The fate of the Cosmos."

"Wha—" She cleared her throat. "What?"

"'Where the Five Flames have burned, Fimm's final vessel will sing the Elementum.' It's the agreement the Five made when they broke from the One. The Elementum will rejoin them."

She was trying hard to follow, and was comforted to see the rest appeared to be struggling as well. "You mean all five Verities will be one again at this Syzyckí Elementum?" she asked.

"Ulfric and I read of it in the Arc Rheunos Scrylle," Symvalline said. She paused, her eyes squeezing shut in a spirit-deep pain Mylla's broken arm could never hold a candle to, then continued. "We read, 'The final age of the Great Cosmos will turn on the Union of the Five, the Syzyckí Elementum. It will bring the destruction of destruction and the remaking of the unmaking.' Griggory, do you understand what it means?"

"Destruction of the destruction," Stave mumbled, looking as

pensive as was possible for a man who thought of subtlety as an insult. "That doesn't sound good, it doesn't."

"Hush, everyone. Griggory?" Roibeard said, drawing their attention back to the man who seemed to have some, and if fate were with them, *all* the answers.

Their hopes fell as soon as he spoke. "I'm not saying anything." He held a finger to his lips in a gesture of secrecy, staring directly at Mylla. "Remember? I can't tell you. I'm not *able* to tell you. But I've learned a few things in my turns about *implying*."

"Erm, excuse the interruption," Bardgrim interrupted, "but I'm—as unbelievable as it is—with Stave here. What exactly is the 'destruction of the destruction'?"

Havelock took a step toward the center of the group. "Does it really matter?" They all looked at him. "If this Syzyckí Elementum stops Balavad, then Vinnr will be saved."

Roibeard was shaking his head. "The five realms are the province of each Verity, created independently while they've been separated. If the Verities become one again, we don't know what will become of their realms." He looked to Griggory once more. "Do we?"

Griggory still had the social graces to look troubled. This, more than anything he could have said, told Mylla that he didn't know.

All that had happened in Ærd was rushing through her thoughts now. At Roibeard's questions, a lock against what she'd most feared the Verity of Ærd's words meant clicked opened. "Fimm told me to bring the Ærd Scrylle back, that it could stop Balavad if I did."

"Stop him how?" Stave asked.

She shook her head. "I wish I knew, and the creature serving as Fimm's vessel didn't say. I think Fimm was telling me that's how to stop him—by uniting the Five."

The creature serving as Fimm's vessel... Safran sent, looking at Mylla closely. *As Fimm's final vessel? Mylla, what you said to Eisa about being the last Ærden, is that true or is there another?*

"The final vessel is a time walker, another creature like that," she said, gesturing toward the tessalope encasing Eisa. "So that makes me the last *human* Ærden, I guess." Even as she said this, however, something in Safran's words, or perhaps in her implication, set her teeth on edge.

Thoughtful silence fell over the group. Roibeard finally broke it.

"These are our options. Continue this fight, which we will lose, and soon Magdaster and the rest of Vinnr will burn. That would leave any of us who manage to survive with the task of protecting the remaining celestial artifacts from Balavad, hoping to someday find his vessel and cage it. I don't need to tell any of you that even if we somehow win in that scenario, we will still have lost." His eyes found Symvalline's. "Some more than others."

"And in the meantime, Balavad will be free to wreak the same destruction on other realms," Symvalline said, and Mylla didn't need to read minds to know she was thinking of Isemay, safe in Arc Rheunos—for now.

"Or, we chance the Syzycki Elementum," Roi finished simply.

With a certainty stronger than any she'd ever felt, even the certainty she wanted to become a Knight, Mylla realized this was her task. As the last Ærden, it almost seemed her destiny. She straightened her shoulders and said simply, "I'll do it. I'll take the Scrylle to Fimm."

"Yes!" Griggory chirped enthusiastically, drawing inquisitive glances from all.

Roibeard put a supportive hand on her shoulder but remained hesitant. "Even then, we don't know what the outcome will be. It may stop Balavad, but it may end the world, all the worlds, at the same time. It's a risk that we have to weigh against continuing to fight. Some will die if we fight, but all may die if we don't."

Mylla caught Brun and Nennus looking at each other. Nennus gave a subtle shrug, and Brun tilted her chin in a sharp agreement, then spoke up. "This last thirty-night, we've seen everything we've spent our lives protecting burned and blasted away. You Knights have as great a stake in what happens next as we do, but your loss is different—not greater or lesser, just different. So, if this is a vote, the commoners of Vinnr vote for the Syzycki Elementum. We'd rather die as Vinnrics than become one of those monstrosities."

Roibeard nodded at the commanders, then turned to Bardgrim. "And you, Jaemus? You must decide for the Himmingazians."

"Me? Decide? For Himmingaze?" He dissembled, casting his glance left and right but avoiding eye contact with anyone. Finally, he gave up when Mylla caught his gaze. She was smiling, only a small smile but one that showed her understanding, and her shared reluctance to being the one all their people's hopes for a future fell on. "Er, well, you know all Himmingazians have a desire to visit the stars. Perhaps if—in the completely off chance, mind you—we're all instantly dissolved into Cosmos dust, it'll just be that much easier to get to them."

It was the closest he could come to agreement. Roi released Mylla's shoulder as Griggory held something out to her. She looked down. It was the Ærd Scrylle, its native Fenestros attached. She took them, then looked toward the tessalope imprisoning Eisa. Its internal lights of all colors dashed along the fibrous tendrils chaotically. Like in Ærd, there was a suggestion of a face along its trunk, looming high above them. The cavities of its eyes glowed with a hot luminance, and if it could be said to bear an expression, it was one of suffering. Inside its unusual body, a battle was being waged, and Balavad would win eventually. The question was, how much time did she have before he did?

She returned her attention to the pensive faces of her companions, then let her gaze stray skyward, seeking her other, albeit temporary, companion. "It's a long walk from the starpath gate to Fimm. I'm going to need a ride."

CHAPTER FORTY-FOUR

The cold winds of Ærd had grown even more biting in the days since she'd been here, but Mylla didn't have to suffer them for long. From her perch once more atop Noble Inferno's head, holding the dragør's horn with her one good hand, she tensed against the wind, not even bothering to create her klinkí stone bubble for warmth. They wouldn't be flying long, not with Noble Inferno's speed.

The uncanny once-living walls of Fimm's fortress rose before them just minutes after they came through the starpath well. The tessalope faces were gone this time, and Mylla wondered where the remaining ones were. Outside the wall, Noble Inferno lowered her head, and Mylla jumped to the hard-packed barren earth.

She stood before her companion. "Master Inferno, I have no idea what will happen to me, or any of us, when I go in there. Would you like me to open a starpath and return you to Vinnr before…" Before what? The end of all things? Before these unexplained Five Flames could scorch the Great Cosmos in a celestial conflagration until it fused like sand into glass?

It matters not, Knight Evernal. Here, there, when this day ends, what difference will it make?

The dragør spoke with a flat surety that confused Mylla. Like Grig-

351

gory, the dragørs had a knack for obfuscation. Perhaps that was where he'd come by it.

She shook her head at the frivolous contemplation. There were heavier matters to attend to now. "I thank you for your aid, whatever my thanks is worth to you," she said and bowed as she would have before the Arch Keeper once upon a time.

Surprising her, Noble Inferno said, *And I for yours.*

After a blink, she spun to the gap in the wall behind her and passed through.

Outside, the Ærd sun had long since set, but even if it had been fully ablaze, the darkness in the fortress was total. Mylla's wystic stones served their purpose as light once more, and she paced doggedly to Fimm's seat. As she neared the Verity, its eye-lights sparkled high overhead, too high for her to reach even if she'd stood on her toe tips, but they at least provided her with a point to navigate toward. It was utterly silent within the titanic hall, making her feel entombed. *It could well turn into my tomb,* she reflected.

Her arm ached, but less than it could have. Symvalline had used the Himmingaze and Ærd Fenestrii briefly to salve the sharpness of the pain, but they didn't have enough time for Mylla to be fully healed by the celestial stones. They all knew that whatever it was she had to do in Ærd would not require a sound body anyway. The time had arrived when this was a Knights' fight no longer. Now it all came down to the Verities.

Nothing moved, no sounds were heard, and though the walk felt interminable, soon Mylla came to stand before Fimm. The Verity in its giant tessalope form remained as motionless as all else in the hall.

Wasting no time, she pulled the Scrylle and Fenestros from her carryall and held them out to the Verity. When she spoke, her words were direct. She had no more time for reverence or appeasement. "I've done what you asked, Creator. Here it is. Now, as you promised, please stop Balavad. I speak for the creations of all Verities when I say we'd rather die than become the usurper's slaves."

The vessel had been so still that when it spoke, Mylla was almost startled. "What you ask requires something in return." Fimm's eye-lights blazed.

"What?"

"You, Warden Evernal."

This wasn't something that she felt good about hearing, exactly, but then, she felt little anymore. If anything, she was simply weary and ready for it all to be over. "I already told you I am prepared to die."

Without a hint of warning, on either side of her the two last tessalopes flared into sight. Where it had been pitch black a moment ago, their lights danced along the tendrils of their impossibly tall, trunk-like bodies, flickering and sparking. Both time walkers were staring down at her, if they did really see from their eye-lights, when she glanced at them.

Fimm continued, taking no note of the time walkers. "The Syzycki Elementum does not require your sacrifice, Warden. It requires my last vessel."

This statement elicited a stronger reaction, one she chose not to examine immediately. "... But I thought... isn't the tessalope—aren't you occupying the last vessel already?"

The answer came next. "The vessel must be where the Five Flames have burned. It is your choice to make, Warden. Become the last vessel and sing the Syzycki Elementum."

So it was true. As the last Ærden, this was her ultimate fate, as much as she wished it weren't. It seemed so unlikely that she, a simple, relatively fragile being would be chosen as a vessel, especially in light of the creature now serving in the role: a time walker, massive, powerful, wystic beyond anything Mylla had encountered besides the Verities themselves. What could she possibly offer in this service that a time walker couldn't? But what was worse—she shuddered—she was going to burn? Was that what was needed?

With her arm and the Scrylle still extended, she fell to one knee and bowed her head. "If there is any other way, Fimm, my creator, I beg you..."

"There is not." Mylla's blood chilled. "The Five Flames have already burned in you. Only you, in our eternities, have been touched by all the fractured Five. Only you can sing the Syzyckí Elementum."

With sudden, inestimable relief, she understood, and the moments in her life the Verity must be referring to poured through her mind. *Touched* by all of them. That was it! When she'd been a child dying in Arc Rheunos, Mithlí had healed her. In Vinnr, Vaka Aster had ordained her. In Balavad's warship, he'd infused her with his celestial venom, and in Himmingaze when the Knights had joined together to undo the banishment spell, Lífs must have in some way touched them all. Then, finally, on her trip to Ærd, she'd again been ordained, a second time, by her own maker. How extraordinary Mylla's life had been with all its myriad encounters, and she had no trouble believing that among the realms, she was the only living person who'd experienced the presence, even the intervention, of all five celestial creators.

The relief that this meant she wasn't about to be set afire, that she had already gone through that trial, only lasted a moment. Then reality crashed back in. If she were to be Fimm's final vessel and, therefore, the catalyst of the Syzyckí Elementum, she may be about to discover that there are worse things than burning.

She thought of Lock's words, whispered in her ear as he'd embraced her before she and Noble Inferno took the starpath from Vinnr. *If we come through this, Mylla, I won't ever leave you again. And if we don't, then we'll be together in the Great Cosmos for eternity. Just know— you're not alone, no matter what.*

But she was alone, alone and afraid. And this fate, or destiny, or curse—whatever it was—made her so. The emptiness she felt now, she wouldn't wish on anyone. Lock, her friends, the people of all the realms, they deserved a future where this emptiness and this fear would never happen to any of them again. And it was a gift only she could give.

"I shall do as required," she said and raised her head to stare into Fimm's eye-lights.

The wystic creature, impossibly, rose from the throne of wood and briar. Around where it had seemed attached to the wall it sat against, the thicket of growth cracked and groaned as its branches, large and small, broke apart. The tessalope had grown into the fortress, and Mylla thought perhaps it *was* the fortress, and its exertion to stand after who knew how many hundreds, perhaps thousands, of turns seemed as if it could bring the whole structure crashing down. The thought flitted through her mind and was gone, however. She didn't fear the collapse of this great building, not when the Verity had more important plans for her.

At full height the tessalope stood twice as large as the other two tessalopes with them. It bent forward at some joint high over Mylla's head, and a bevy of vine-like ropes reached out. She expected them to take the Scrylle with its Fenestros still attached, but oddly, it merely plucked the celestial stone from its mount. Mylla craned her head to look up at the monolith, and her eyes were snared by its gleaming eye-lights. They were like Ulfric's eyes had become when Vaka Aster was part of him. There were galaxies in there.

The next moment, she felt more than saw those lights flare, showering her in a blaze of wonder, then closing over her like, well, like the tomb she'd thought this place might become. A furious wind buffeted her from the inside, and then she did burn. A spirit-deep heat infused her from outside in and inside out in one massive surge, as everything around her grew so bright that sight failed her. She closed her eyes until it passed or she died.

Death, of course, was not her fate, at least not yet. When the buffeting heat subsided, her eyes opened to take in the fortress about her through an entirely new kind of sight. She rose to her feet, slowly, breathless at what she saw. When she'd been flying on Noble Inferno and thought she was being protected by the enchantment amplified by the Ærd Scrylle, colors had been different, stronger. Now she saw colors and lights that no human language had words for. And in the surrounding miasma, even movement and sound appeared to her in a way she could only describe as "vision" yet was anything but.

The interior of the fortress, still standing despite losing its tessalope foundation, was no longer dark to her. The feeling of it was unlimited, boundaryless, the lack of what people would call light only a different luminance to her different eyes. Still on either side of her stood the two tessalopes. And before her, the Fenestros Fimm had taken morphed into its true form, as she now understood the Fenestrii to be. Like the celestial stone in Magdaster, it dissolved to mist before her eyes, then reshaped into a matterless column of radiant tendrils. Now there were four time walkers standing with her. Fimm's last vessel was once again an agent of its own being, and none looked even vaguely treeish any longer, with no more wandering flickers of illumination along their shapes and pools of gleaming lights for eyes. They were now ethereal, rising and spreading in every direction as waves of tinted air. In each, one thick, unbroken beam of light radiated strongly along their core. These rays of solid luminance seemed to Mylla's eyes to be trapped within the amorphous, wavery beings, but at the same time, they seemed the only thing keeping the time walkers from dispersing completely into formless, invisible energy.

Energy. Of course, she realized. *That's all time is, all they are. Just energy waiting to travel the Cosmos again. Will they be freed by the Syzycki Elementum?* If so, it seemed that at least one good thing would come of the event. Despite their fearsome appearance, Mylla had felt deep in her bones that they were incomplete beings, trapped in an unnatural state.

These marvels held her focus for only a handful of breaths, though it felt much longer. The press of time wouldn't allow her to dwell on them. She already knew what had happened, what was happening. Her senses were no longer only hers; she was merely the lens through which Fimm the Verity now experienced the world. To Fimm, what Mylla perceived was muted. To Mylla, it was wonderous beyond anything she'd ever imagined.

She knew the celestial being could hear her thoughts, but she chose to speak aloud anyway. "What do I do now, Creator?"

No answer came, but for the moment this didn't concern her. Her focus was taken by the strangest sensation flowing through her limbs. Her arm moved, but she wasn't moving it. Fimm controlled it, just like she imagined Balavad had controlled his puppets. Her first instinct was to fight. Then... she gave in. She'd chosen this, to let herself become not a person but a vessel. The Verity had taken over.

Her arm reached over her shoulder and drew Star Spark from its sheath. Mylla observed it happening, nothing more than a spectator. The sword crossed over her front and pointed to the ground, and Fimm swung her other arm to strike the Scrylle sharply against the blade.

The celestial scepter rang loudly upon impact. Its sonorous frequency was pure, like sound made crystal, and the Scrylle vibrated in her hand like a tuning fork, up her arm and through her body. Around her, the wavering tessalopes responded and circled her in a columnar shimmer. Her body lifted—by the time walker or by some celestial force, she didn't know—as she rose toward the fortress's ceiling. Instead of diminishing, the depth and volume of the Scrylle's humming increased, taking over the interior of the fortress, turning the space into an ocean of melodious sonance.

As her body continued upward, she was struck by the thought, and slight fear, that this ocean of sound would deafen her, or worse, its vibration seemed potent enough that it could shake her to pieces like shattered crystal.

Now sing, Mylla Evernal, Fimm commanded her.

She didn't ask what she was supposed to sing. She merely parted her lips, heaved in a great gulp of air, and voiced the same note the Scrylle played.

A second later, all her fears were forgotten when the hum of the vibrating Scrylle crescendoed, and like the shattered crystal she'd imagined, the fortress burst to billions of fragments. In what was undoubtedly the greatest explosion ever seen, splinters of a forest's worth of trees and brush flew in every direction, accelerating over Ærd's landscape for miles and miles, propelled by speeds too great for the eye to perceive. Nothing touched her, however, and still her body ascended into the sky, higher and higher. The tessalopes, which were now amorphous waves of distortion, rose with her. Their undulating light tendrils branched and spread in every direction, higher and higher into the sky and in every direction until they were lost to sight.

What came from her was nothing human lungs were capable of, and that was appropriate. Shards of the splintered fortress hadn't touched her because Mylla knew herself to be human no longer. Her body, like the tessalopes, was breaking apart, transforming from matter to energy, mass to power. The Great Cosmos was nothing but dust, and she was returning to it in the same form she and everything had begun as. The tessalope waves and she were all expanding, resonating to the same frequency she sang, spinning into the void of the Cosmos, growing into eternity. This was the song to unify the Verities into the One, the song of the Syzyckí Elementum. It would make them whole, even as she dissolved.

And still she sang.

CHAPTER FORTY-FIVE

Shortly after Mylla traveled to Ærd, the time walker trapping Eisa in Magdaster burst apart from the middle like an overfilled waterskin. The tessalope had been solidifying slowly, its outer surface turning a layered gray-brown bark-like substance, and when it exploded, the Knights were showered with shards that pierced and poked their skin as easily as wood splinters would. They'd been watching the thing closely, preparing for what came next should Mylla not return, or return too late.

Eisa, or rather the Verity mastering her, stepped free of the now-misshapen tessalope with a gaping hole in its center. The wystic being was emitting sounds like leaves in wind that none, save Griggory, could identify or understand. The creature reached out with a viny tendril and wrapped it around Eisa, but the tendril blew apart in shreds as easily as its trunk had.

"Where is the Ærden?" the fallen Knight asked.

"If you want to get to her, you'll have to go through us," Roibeard said gravely.

"As you wish," she said and instantly targeted him with white fire through her hallowed glaive.

This time, the Knights were ready, each of them prepared to fight to the death. They'd accepted that either hers or theirs was the only way this could end. Roibeard pressed the Vinnric Scrylle to the hilt of his greatsword and gripped them tightly, then swung at the fire, whispering a protective enchantment. This time he managed to deflect it.

Let me do the honors, they heard as Heart of Purple Might leaped toward the fallen Knight from his perch atop the emberflare cannon's bore.

Before the dragør's mighty talon could skewer her, Eisa gave a guttural shout in Elder Veros, and five Anzuru crimsons shot from the smoke-covered melee above and pummeled into Purple Might like fire-breathing battering rams. The mass of dragørs fell to the city, tumbling and ripping at each other as they smashed into a courtyard below. The wall beneath the Knights' feet shook at the impact, and every warrior atop it knew the Weald dragørs, too harried and busy with the crimsons, would not be able to help them with this fight.

Eisa raised a hand and thrust it forward, sending her nine bloodred klinkí stones into the company of Knights and soldiers. Safran, having taken up the Himmingazian Scrylle, used its power to send her own wystic stones to meet the onslaught. The force of the stones clashing into each other shattered them all like so much friable clay, leaving Safran with only the Scrylle and a hallowed dagger for defense. Stave immediately moved up behind her. Their bond made them synchronous. She would be the shield, he the blade.

Symvalline and Roibeard moved together in similar fashion, Roi passing her the Scrylle while he leveraged the greater length of his sword. They charged Eisa as one, while behind them, the Vinnric fighters Brun, Nennus, and Havelock Rekkr and his father brought up their rear. Eisa's glaive came down and shot fire. This time, the spear of light bypassed the Knights. Behind them, they heard cries of pain but couldn't turn to look. Roibeard saw his opening as Eisa's glaive was lowered and swung Ruin Hammer in a heavy arc toward her weapon arm, as Symvalline aimed a borrowed shortsword in a crossbody overhand chop.

The Knights' attack was caught up short when their weapons struck a shield of black vapor that materialized before Eisa. The considerable strength behind Ruin Hammer's swing sank it deep into the substance as it took on the consistency of wax. The blade barely penetrated before slowing and stopping. Roibeard tried to retrieve it, but the pliant yet glutinous ichor held on. Similarly, Sym's shortsword remained fixed. Behind the ichor, they heard the distorted voice of Eisa laughing.

Symvalline abandoned her sword and reached over and put a hand on Ruin Hammer's hilt, aiding Roi to wrench it free. It didn't move. Safran stepped up and touched the Fenestros affixed to the Himmingaze Scrylle into the murk, chanting words to weaken the barrier. Before their eyes, it bubbled like boiling oil but held—for a moment. Then, with ghastly slowness, it began to soften and melt, but instead of giving the Knights hope, it only made them wonder what new unimagined weapon would come next. Stave stood to one side with his weapons ready to attack, but they'd lost track of Jaemus and Griggory.

As the substance lost its form, the Knights regained their weapons and Roi said, "When it's clear, I'll go first. If she's fighting me, she can't strike you. Aim for the artifacts in her chest, try to separate them from her somehow. And Knights, don't hesitate to do what you have to."

Symvalline knew what pain saying those words must have caused him, and wondered if he was offering himself as the bait because he wouldn't be able to bear Eisa's death. She could have told him that he would, somehow. After all, she was still drawing breath, and her own beloved was dead. But she didn't tell him, mostly because she had her doubts any of it would matter moments from now. It was becoming unavoidably clear that they were bested in this fight.

The waxy shield thinned and pooled at their feet, and they saw Eisa bringing her glaive down to aim its caustic light. Roi put one foot back in a warrior stance, Stave the same. Sym retook the Vinnr Scrylle from Roi, and she and Safran chanted through the celestial artifacts, pulling their power into their own weapons. All of them could feel Eisa's own power, a celestially enhanced nimbus burning around her like the core of a star on the cusp of going nova.

Then Jaemus's voice came roaring from behind them and inside their Mentalios links at the same time: "Neither of us has ever fired one of these things before, and I don't know how good my aim is, so I suggest everyone get down!"

They did it, all but Eisa, who glanced over their prone bodies with eyes that widened in shock. The emberflare cannon thundered deafeningly, sending a red and orange cascade of plasma streaming directly into Eisa's chest.

For the thump of several heartbeats, the world was silent. As the Knights' hearing recovered from the acoustic assault, ringing replaced the silence. Symvalline was first on her feet, reaching down to assist Roibeard. Safran and Stave used each other to pull themselves up, and together they turned to see what had become of their enemy.

The emberflare at this proximity would have vaporized a human being, but Eisa was more than human and her body had been flung backward a hundred yards into the shambling ruins of the next tower down the wall. The hole in the tessalope had widened where she and the emberflare had shot through, but the wystic creature still stood. Griggory and Jaemus rejoined them, the Himmingazian wearing a complicated look of both stunned surprise and fiendish elation. Congratulations would have to wait, however, and as a unit they turned and sped over the wall in pursuit of Eisa, her fate unknown.

They found her lying amid the shattered blocks of stone from the crumbled tower. Her glaive was gone, but her skin was unmarked, and from the way her body draped limply over the wreckage, it was clear more than a few of her bones had been shattered. Roibeard picked his way speedily toward her and dropped to his knees.

"Careful, Roi!" Stave shouted, but it was pointless.

Symvalline stood beside the rest of the Knights, weapons raised and ready to attack if needed, as Eisa's eyes opened. They'd changed. Their lifeless dull gray sheen was still present, but it had receded to what would have been the whites of her eyes. Her irises, so dark the pupils barely stood out, had returned, and they came to rest on Roibeard's face.

"… Roi…" she whispered through lips smashed and bleeding, and the voice was once more Eisa's own.

"Fight it, Eisa. You can beat him."

"He's... he's left... for now."

"We have the Vinnr Scrylle, we'll help you." He turned his head sharply and yelled to Symvalline, "Bring it to me, now!"

The ringing in Symvalline's ears was worsening instead of lessening, but she ignored it. It was the battle and the fear and sadness that they were about to lose a dear companion that was making it worse. So much raw emotion always meddled with perception. She began to scramble over the broken stones and saw Eisa's hand reach for Roi's.

"... can't," Eisa murmured, "can't save me. Take it." She pulled Roibeard's hand to her chest and laid it against the gleaming black Fenestros above her breasts. "Give me... freedom."

"If I remove it, you could die," Roi said, and the moisture falling from his cheeks was not battle sweat.

"It's my... choice."

Symvalline, followed by Griggory, reached them, and they knelt awkwardly in the rubble.

The Dyrrak Knight's eyes fell on her. "Symvalline. Tell Ulfric I'm sorry for giving up... on you... for losing my faith."

"I..." Symvalline couldn't speak then, her chest locked against the sob that wanted to break free. The ringing grew louder, enough so that she didn't hear the scraping of Stave's and Safran's boots as they joined them. She only realized they were there when she heard Stave's gruff voice.

"You never let me win a fight, Eisa," he said. "And that made me better than I ever could have been without your teaching. My gratitude to you will outlive us all."

"You couldn't... have beat me if I'd blinded myself and... tied my hands behind my back."

The words were spoken like old Eisa, the Eisa before the Cataclysm, wryly amused and teasing. Symvalline could see Stave struggling to smile at her, to show he could take a good ribbing, and somehow he managed it.

Eisa, through broken lips, grinned back for a moment, then she grimaced and her eyes sought Roibeard's. "Do it," she said. "… need it to end."

With a nod, but without speaking or looking at Symvalline, Roi reached for the Vinnr Scrylle and Fenestros, and she passed it to him. With his other hand still on Eisa's chest, he began to speak under his breath, using the power of Vaka Aster's artifacts to draw Balavad's from her. But before the deed was done, he stopped, cleared his throat, then looked to Sym.

With an expression of such profound pain that she could barely meet his eyes, he said simply, "I can't," and held out the Scrylle.

Safran had moved to Roi's other side. Handing the Himmingazian Scrylle and Fenestros to Jaemus, she looked into Eisa's eyes, using the Mentalios to say something to only her, and gently pushed Roi's hand aside. Instead of letting Sym take them, she retrieved the Vinnr artifacts and resumed what Roi could not. With a measured slowness that couldn't have been anything but agonizing, Balavad's Scrylle and celestial stone withdrew from Eisa's chest into Safran's hand, leaving an open slot in the breastplate armor that had been form-fitted around them. Eisa's eyes rolled back to show only that dull grayness before the Scrylle and celestial stone were completely free.

Then it was over. Eisa was dead. Through some Cosmic kindness, the abused flesh the artifacts had withdrawn from knitted together before she drew her last breath, and the toxic elixir that had changed her into a gangly, pale Ravener lost its potency. When Roibeard reached out to close her eyelids, the whites of her eyes, along with the rest of her, had returned to normal.

They all sat around her body in a vigil for some unknown time. Jaemus was the first to stir, saying, "I'm so sorry to interrupt, but does anyone else hear that?"

Symvalline was jolted from her grief, realizing he was right. The ringing had reached a pitch that she could no longer tell herself was just in her ears.

As she opened her mouth to comment, the wall began to vibrate subtly beneath them. Smaller pebbles from the crushed tower bounced atop larger stones, dislodging and rolling to and fro. The Knights rose, not quite steadily. Roi sheathed Ruin Hammer and bent to lift Eisa's body. "We need to get off the wall," he said huskily.

As they searched for a way to access the tower's stairwell, the vibrating, along with the humming grew continually.

"What is... what in the wo—" Jaemus began, and Symvalline looked to see him holding the Himmingaze artifacts at arm's length, staring at them with eyes as round as the moon.

The white and gold Fenestros of Himmingaze had turned into a mist and was swirling around him like a golden cloud, growing in size at a rapid clip. As she looked, Roibeard and Stave pulled the second and third Himmingazian stones from their clothing, given to them days ago in case of need, and Jaemus scrambled to get the final one from his pocket. Each of the celestial stones transformed into mist as they were retrieved, and the Knights released them into the air. Instead of falling, they simply hovered, growing less and less corporeal.

Sym glanced at Safran to see the two Fenestrii she held in the Scrylles doing the same. Beyond Safran, the time walker that had held Eisa for a short time had resumed growing and lost the solidity it had started to acquire. It was now, like the other Fenestrii, a miasma of every color and hue, swirling in great tendrils toward the sky like tree branches of unalloyed light. As she watched, they broke through the blanket of smoke hanging over the city, instantly clearing it, and streamed up to the heavens and beyond her sight. And the sonance resonating all around them, now a thundering pure wave of sound, was so loud it seemed to be shaking the whole city—and still it continued to build.

She'd have cried to the Knights, "Run!" but knew it would do no good. This was the Syzycki Elementum, and they were all now at its mercy.

CHAPTER FORTY-SIX

It was the same in every corner of the Great Cosmos. A sonorous, melodic resonance, blanketing every form, every creature, rushing in to fill every space down to a pinhole and tinier, a disembodied power that left nothing untouched by its harmony. The scattered Fenestrii in each of the realms erupted at the melody of the Syzycki Elementúm, and the tessalopes were free at long last to disperse once more into their true essence: time. Bound to a material form no longer, their reach, too, encompassed all things, even eternity, and their threads connected the infinitude once more together.

In Arc Rheunos, Isemay and Salukis woke in their rooms in Everlight Hall, instantly alert to the crescendoing sound. Dressing quickly, fearing the worst, they met each other in the hallway, then rushed hand in hand to the Verity's chamber—and saw something they couldn't understand.

The colorless woman sat on an ornate wooden chair, motionless. When they pushed the door open, her eyes fell on them, colorless as well, making her appearance ghostlike. But this wasn't what addled their perception. The five Fenestrii of the realm had transmogrified into great luminescent columns, and the Verity herself shone like a star. The fortress around them began to shake, and Isemay and Salukis grabbed each other in an embrace, the only safety they could feel.

"Mithlí!" Isemay cried, not daring to approach the woman. "What's happening?"

Arc Rheunosians began to gather in the hallway behind them, crying out in fear and concern. The voice that came from the Verity was an octave lower than the boundless, sourceless sound filling the air, though in the same pure tone, when she answered. "The remaking of the unmaking, Archon."

She said nothing more for so long that Isemay was about to beg for something more, some greater detail that would explain it. Then Mithlí said the last thing the Verity would ever say to her creations. "You have nothing to fear."

The illumination of the room exploded, forcing all in Everlight Hall to squeeze their eyes shut and throw their arms across their faces.

But, as Mithlí had promised, Isemay was not afraid.

IN HIMMINGAZE, much the same occurred. Vreyja Bardgrim and her friends, who'd never lost their belief in the Creatress, were gathered at the Verity's shrine on Isle Stonering. They'd been holding a vigil until Jaemus and the Glisternauts returned. Her son and Jaemus's father, Jovus, had joined them, having finally come around to accepting what Vreyja had been hinting at all those anni-cycles. Yes, Verities were real. Yes, the realm of Himmingaze had once had a cadre of great warriors and scholars called Mystae, who'd been tasked with serving their Verity the Creatress, but had failed abysmally and nearly doomed the realm to nonexistence. And yes, her grandling and his son Jaemus Bardgrim, with the aid of friends from far-off realms of the Great Cosmos, had saved them all.

It wasn't Vreyja, however, who'd finally convinced him, along with the Council of Nine Crests and the rest of the population of Himmingaze, of all these miraculous things. She didn't even have to try in the end. A slangarook named, of all oddities, Hither, and the entire slangarook shoal had converged on Vann and the many floating cities around the realm and spoken to all the Himmingazians in a manner that none could understand but all finally came to believe was real. The creatures of the Never Sea spoke directly into their thoughts and reminded them of the many wonders they'd for so long denied. Every Himmingazian, young and old, heard the shoal's voices, and none would ever doubt again what they learned.

When the melodious sonance erupted, growing louder by the second, most were frightened. Vreyja and her ilk on Isle Stonering, however, were sanguine. Acceptance that the realms were in good hands, those of her grandling, her old and dear friend Griggory, and their companions, buoyed her spirits, and her intrinsic peace spread easily among them all.

Hither was not among them when the Creatress heeded the call of the Syzycki Elementum, so no one but the other slangarooks saw the great water dragør erupt into a prism of many colors, which danced off into the Cosmos, leaving Hither as the creature had once been: a powerful, enduring predator, oldest of the Himmingazians, and like the slangarooks' cousins in Vinnr, the first and favorite creations of their Verity.

———

GENTLENESS WAS APPARENTLY NOT the Verity's main consideration when choosing to return Mylla to corporeality, and her body coalesced violently, each and every ingot of her flesh, blood, and bones regaining shape all at once. Chills swept through her as she blinked her eyes, noting in shutter flashes that she was under a sky that was both familiar and foreign, lying on her back on the hard earth. She felt like herself, she realized. Completely normal once more. Nothing at all, in fact, like a Verity, or its vessel, or even particularly like a well-adjusted person.

Looking into the vast sky overhead, its millions upon millions of glowing stars reminding her just how unremarkable she was, she let herself stay in place and simply be. Just taking it in. This life, long though it was, would continue, and she could finally rest knowing it would continue without the corrupted threat of Balavad. The Verity was no more, or at least, no more what he was. They were reunited as one, and there was no need for them to fight over dominion of any realm, for they were all now one realm.

She hoped, at least.

She sat up and took in her surroundings. Star Spark and the Scrylle lay at her side. Chilly wind rushed over a cliff face that was no more than a few paces from where she lay. She gathered the sword and celestial artifact and walked to the edge. Over two hundred feet below, the stars glinted off waves crashing brutally into the cliff wall. A fall from this spot would have been the death of anyone, even possibly a Knight, and she counted herself lucky for having been reanimated far enough from the lip to avoid that fate.

Still, she thought, spinning the Scrylle contemplatively in her hand, that didn't change the fact that she was the only living person in an empty world, and now she had no Fenestros to open a starpath, and no Verity to request help from.

"Well, isn't this a fine ending," she said aloud. "I guess Stave was right: no good apple goes unbitten."

What are you grumbling about, speck?

She turned sharply to see Poppy's Noble Inferno pacing toward her from the gloom on her four stout legs. Mylla had completely forgotten the dragør was there.

"It's good to see you weren't harmed when the fortress was destroyed, Master Inferno. I have some bad news, though." She waggled the Scrylle. "We have no way to get home."

The great beast's titian eyes flared, then her mouth curled in that oddly smile-like way. *You think the starpaths require a Fenestros to travel. Your kind are too... young to have learned other ways. My kind are not so limited. Come, up on my back once more. And hold on tightly. The ride will be chaotic for someone as fragile as you.*

She hesitated, wondering how it could be any bumpier than it usually was, but knew better than to ask for an explanation. If she waited too long, Noble Inferno would probably leave without her.

With Star Spark sheathed and the Scrylle tucked into her carryall, Mylla made the now-familiar climb to her new "friend's" neck, wrapped her arms tightly around one horn, and said, "Ready when you are."

Noble Inferno blew a great jet of fire into the empty air. At first, Mylla thought nothing of it. Just another dragør inferno like the many that had filled the skies over Magdaster. But the fire didn't dissipate or die out like it should have. Instead, it began to swirl, looping itself in a great, fiery ring before them. Distantly, Mylla heard in the back of her mind Noble Inferno saying something, but the words were foreign and lost to her. And frankly, she was too entranced by whatever wysticism was turning the dragørfire into a vortex to bother to pay attention. And tired, so very tired.

Then Mylla heard Noble Inferno command *Tightly now*, and they shot into the center of the fiery ring as if from an emberflare cannon.

CHAPTER FORTY-SEVEN

Ulfric awoke staring at a strange ceiling. This was the least of disorienting sensations, however. It wasn't so much the ceiling that was odd; it was the perfectly ordinary sight of it. No glimmers, no waving lines of color, nothing to suggest his weirded eyes, so altered by being made Vaka Aster's vessel, had ever been different. Along with that unexpected development, the weight of his prone body, settled on something hard and flat, was unmistakable, all two hundred and ten pounds of him. The air was hot and still around him, and from outside came loud voices, yelling. From this height, he couldn't tell if their cries were alarm, rejoicing, or something else. But at the moment, this didn't matter to him. He felt, well, he felt *himself.*

He drew a great, heaving breath, the first he'd really drawn into his own lungs, not the lungs he shared with his maker, in ages. The air filled his chest like a drowning man's first full breath upon feeling earth once more beneath his feet.

I'm me! I'm myself again. How can it—no! Don't ask the question. Take a moment to revel in this, Ulfric. It may not last, and it is so much better than being a rat.

He raised his head cautiously, looking down the length of his body to confirm it was real. And speaking of rats, his eyes locked with the beady black orbs of his last host. The creature sat on his chest, staring at him with a level of curiosity that spoke of much deeper intelligence than a human had ever given a rodent credit for before. But then, Ulfric wasn't surprised about that. He had just, after all, shared this tiny creature's mind and body.

The moment came back to him: the Ecclesium's unmasked intention to trap Ulfric in his own body by smashing the memory keeper, Ulfric's horror but quick utterance of the incantation to transfer his spirit into whatever living thing was near. And then this small, utterly unprepared rat, which had been innocuously nosing around the chamber's corners, was suddenly sharing its mind with a foreigner. Through its eyes, Ulfric watched Balavad force the Domine Ecclesium to sever his own throat, then watched the Verity grind the memory keeper he'd made Isemay to bits beneath a booted heel.

The rat, understandably, had started to panic, and Ulfric had been forced to immediately switch his focus to mastering the beast. He couldn't let it react, let it show itself, or Balavad would have known Ulfric was still "free," in a sense. The rodent's mind was intelligent, but still merely a rodent's, and Ulfric had been able to overtake it easily and quickly. And like a rodent, they'd skulked deeper into the shadows, waiting for Balavad to be gone.

The rat's pink nose twitched at Ulfric's glance.

"Thank you, little one," he offered. "You saved me."

The creature's nostrils flared, a look that seemed to say *As if you gave me a choice!* Then it jumped from Ulfric's chest and scurried back to its comfortable hidden home.

He sat up, swung his legs to the ground, and stood, if a bit shakily. He should have been more cautious, should have been practicing furtiveness and been on alert for danger. But, strangely, he felt no fear. What had happened? Why was he so unconcerned for his own safety? He'd watched the Domine's life spurting from his cut throat, then seen Balavad's vessel loom over Vaka Aster like a vulture. The Verity had stood there for quite some time, as motionless as a statue. Ulfric had feared then, believing his enemy to be contemplating destroying Vaka Aster's vessel at last. Vengeance for Battgjald's annihilation, while

Ulfric was more helpless than ever. He'd only been able to watch and wait for the final stroke of doom to befall his realm.

What then? He closed his eyes, trying to remember, to dredge the events up as if from a deep swamp. The rat had been a fortuitous host at a hopeless moment, but somehow sharing its body, or more to the point, its mind, had muddled Ulfric's. There'd been a strange sound, hadn't there? A noise that he'd first thought was just ringing in his ears, but it hadn't faded. And the Fenestrii—something had happened. They'd... exploded? No, it hadn't been that, not exactly. They'd—the only thing his thoughts could come up with was that they'd somehow sprouted, like saplings from the forest floor, but in tendrils of light rather than wood.

He shook his head, the puzzle too difficult to solve at the moment. Upon looking around, he found not one but two bodies lay in the room with him. The Domine Ecclesium's corpse, lying in a thickened pool of blood, wasn't a surprise, although the blood's color having turned back to its natural dark crimson rather than black was. It was the other corpse that shocked him.

Balavad's vessel lay near the doorway, limp and prone, eyes staring at the ceiling. Ulfric approached it cautiously, waiting for a trick. Though tricks like this seemed far outside Balavad's character, such as it was. The Battgjaldic woman's body didn't twitch or groan when he toed it, and Ulfric could do nothing but stare in wonder. This woman, though still much taller than an average Vinnric, was profoundly different from the last time his eyes had beheld her. Her skin had lost the deathly pallor of a Ravener, and her back had lost the hunch that seemed to be a symptom of Balavad's infernal consecration. Even her eyes were more like those of any of the humans Ulfric had encountered in other realms. Though she had dark crescent-shaped pupils, the irises were a serene copper shade, a bit like Mallich Roibeard's. Most noteworthy of all, she looked at peace.

Surprising himself, he realized he pitied the woman, even felt a hint of grief at her state. Had she ever had a choice of what would become of her? Had Battgjald once thrived before Balavad had become so bent on dominion? Could the people of their realm have been their allies if not for their misguided creator? The saddest of all was that they would never know. Battgjald wasn't merely out of reach—it was no more.

As he stared down at her lifeless body, he thought, *Balavad has not simply abandoned this woman as his vessel, she has even been released from his service completely. The elixir that made her monstrous is gone, the same way it was removed from the fighters in Arc Rheunos, and the Vinnrics Vaka Aster rescued from Balavad's warship before that.*

His next thought jolted him like thunder. *If Balavad has relinquished his vessel...*

Then where was Balavad now?

The shouts and cries from outside the citadel had moved inside, and he could hear them coming up the stairs to the tower. Quickly, Ulfric barred the door. If Balavad had left his vessel, there was every chance that the rest of the Dyrraks were once more their unsullied selves. He was beginning to suspect he knew what happened, and if it were true, nothing he might experience in another hundred lifetimes could amaze him more.

The Syzycki Elementum, he thought. But regardless, if by some miracle beyond reckoning had occurred and the thing he'd known only to be described as "the destruction of destruction" had happened, that didn't mean he had a believable explanation for why the leader of Dyrrakium, Domine Ecclesium Starkas Nazaria, lay nearly headless and utterly exsanguinated almost at his feet. After what the Dyrraks had so lately been through, they would be difficult to reason with. And Ulfric was certain he'd lost the glamor that had made them all revere him as Vaka Aster's living simulacrum. If his vision had returned to normal, it was certain the appearance of his eyes had too.

As he halfheartedly swept the room for the celestial stones, believing in his heart that they had dispersed into the ether upon their transformation, he heard a rustling at one of the arched windows. Turning, he smiled broadly.

"Urgo, Yggo, there are no words in any of the five realms to tell you how happy I am to see you."

The bruhawks churred affectionately, dipping their heads up and down in excitement. He stepped to the window and stroked the back of Urgo's neck, lamenting the loss of the memory keeper to help him communicate better with his old friend. Despite this, it seemed they knew him, recognized him once more as himself, not as what he'd been —a shell for their creator. And at that, Ulfric realized his guess was right.

I am me, and only me. The cage was unmade, not by anything I did but by what the Syzycki Elementum did. They are the One again, unified and complete. And so, the Great Cosmos is as well. The One Verity has no more need of an earthly vessel to be bound to the realms. We are all part of one realm now, joined together in a new age.

He chuckled, realizing that despite the enormous joy of he felt that his worst fear, the ending of the realms, hadn't come to pass, he had so many questions now that he doubted he'd ever learn all their answers. Not in another thousand turns anyway. Were the other realms truly as unharmed as Vinnr? What would the One Verity do now? And, most personally pressing, what would become of the Knights?

He'd no more than had the thought when he was addressed by a voice. One that was familiar, for he'd lived with it in his own mind for weeks, but one that was also many. The voice spoke in dozens, hundreds of tones, as if composed of countless speakers at once. It was Vaka Aster, and it was much, much more. It was the voice of the One.

She asked him a simple question. He knew how Symvalline would respond, and was certain he knew how Isemay would too. The rest of them would make up their own minds, but he didn't hesitate a single heartbeat before giving his answer. Then he turned to the bruhawks.

"You've already done so much during this exploit, friends. How do you feel about one last journey? It's time to rejoin the rest of the Knights, and we have a very long way to go."

CHAPTER FORTY-EIGHT

Hallumbrum had come and gone, and dawn was no more than an hour or two away. Symvalline sat with her legs dangling over the edge of Magdaster's great wall, fatigued beyond any measure she'd ever felt before. Knights could go for days, even weeks, without sleep or food. But Symvalline couldn't, for she was no longer a Knight.

The Syzycki Elementum—they all knew now what it had been. The crescendo of the rising harmonic that had shaken Magdaster's walls, the very earth itself, exploded throughout the realm just after the Knights had reached the wall's base. It had seemed as if the entire Cosmos had suddenly burst open. The Knights had clutched each other as the note reached its peak, fearing the worst. And then... all was calm. A peaceful hum had followed, rapidly diminishing like the ripples over a lake touched by a light breeze. Like the soft brush of air in the wake of a dragørfly's wings.

None of them had needed to ask what had happened. Mylla's quest had been a success. The Syzycki Elementum was complete. If they'd needed further convincing, the sight of the hundreds of remaining Dyrrak attack craft in the air abandoning the battle en masse and returning to their ships would have done it. More than that, however, was the immediate and unusual transformation of the crimson dragørs of Anzuru. As the last note of the Elementum died away to a soft hush, Symvalline looked to the sky to see the dozens of crimsons shifting from grossly elongated flying worms back to a form much more like their Howling Weald cousins, compact and stout like equines, but smaller. The fighting overhead ceased, and both species of dragør had settled all along the walls to lick their wounds, perched on the ancient structure like gargoyles.

With no one left in the air to engage with, the remaining Himmingazian ships landed outside the wall in a compact formation. The handful who had controlled them all emerged, each of them bruised, overwhelmed, and stunned, but in one piece. She'd learned later they'd lost three of their own, and they'd been buried like heroes with all the Magdastervians who'd died as well.

From the ground, the Knights watched the dragørs, fascinated, knowing they must have been speaking to each other but unable to penetrate their conversation, even with their Mentalios lenses. The Magdastervians, choosing wisdom over combat, retreated to whatever shelter they could find while the dragørs communed. Before long, the crimsons launched in one grand flight and angled their great bodies south, returning home to Dyrrakium. That more than anything else assured all present that the battle was finally and truly over.

Even though the battle, like all battles, lasted a finite amount of time, the aftermath invariably went on for much longer. As the proverbial dust and the actual smoke-and-ember-infused air settled, Jaemus had gone to see to his home-worlders, while the Knights immediately rushed back into the city to provide any aid they could. At least half the interior buildings suffered total destruction, as had the watchtowers lining the wall. The wall itself, however, had sustained negligible damage. The Magdastervians had constructed it in desperation and determination to withstand any attack a thousand turns ago, and it had done the job admirably. The one other group of battle instruments with minimal damage were the emberflare cannons themselves. Constructed from Magdaster's best steel, the best steel in the whole of the realm, they would probably be around long after even the Knights had dissipated to dust.

Symvalline had dived into her role as healer without a second thought, doing what came naturally to her. Though she of course desired to help those in need, she worked herself ragged mostly out of a need to stay busy and keep her mind off the death of her heartmatch.

Yet shortly after the Knights had begun to help, they'd been caught up at the same moment by a sound like the song of the Elementum, the chime of a thousand voices, all coalesced into a singular note, resonating in their minds. They'd had no reason to make a guess at what or who it was; there was only one entity it could be.

Knights Corporealis, Mystae, Wardens Temporalis, and Archons—you have served your maker well. Our gift is now yours to do with as you will. Those of you who wish to retain your spark of ordination and serve your realms everlasting may. Those who wish to return to your common selves may as well. The choice is yours.

Theirs. The choice to remain invincible and immortal, but given to a new purpose, not to aid their Verity but to aid their peoples. Or, the choice to be as they'd once been, mortal and ordinary, and thus able to relish life, short though it was, with the exquisite gratitude that came from knowing it was only temporary. Giving up possible eternity, something that in Symvalline's experience dulled into colorlessless in its repetition, for the simple but brief joys, which would shine all the more because of their fleetingness.

Symvalline had chosen in an instant. Her life had been more meaningful to her as a healer, a mother, and a partner to Ulfric than it had as a Knight, and she preferred to keep those experiences sharp and beautiful in her memories, rather than losing them to the inevitable deterioration of infinite time.

The others, Mallich, Safran, Stave, and to no one's surprise, Griggory, had chosen differently, but Symvalline felt nothing but happiness for them. Though, in Mallich's case, she wondered if he'd chosen to remain a Knight out of lack of hope for a better life, a life without Eisa, more than because of a fealty to such long-ingrained duty. Perhaps she would ask him someday. As for Knight, or Mystae, Bardgrim, she hadn't learned yet what his choice was.

Now she sat alone on the wall, feeling the weight of time and the weariness of humanity more heavily than ever. The city had quieted in night's embrace, regaining its strength for the days and thirty-nights ahead of healing and rebuilding. She should sleep too, she knew, but pushed against the need. Sleep was a threshold, and somehow, once she crossed it, she would be letting go of the last of what had made her a Knight. She was almost ready, but not quite yet.

As she stared into the sky, she wondered what had become of Mylla after she'd met with Fimm in Ærd. Was she still alive out there, with no way to return home? After granting the Knights their choice with regard to remaining as such, the One Verity had gone silent. No questions they sent were answered, no reassurances were given. They knew only that the realms were, as the Verity itself was, unified into one cosmic fabric. Would the Verity be present in their lives? Would they be able to call to it in times of need or uncertainty? They had no way of knowing, but given the silence they were left with after the last words, and a deeper sense of aloneness that Symvalline had never felt before, she doubted it.

And that, she felt, was for the better.

She'd feared she would never see Isemay again, with the Fenestrii being transformed and leaving no way to open the starpaths. Upon her voicing this worry, Griggory assured her she had no need to be troubled; he'd speak to Heart of Purple Might on her behalf. Though pressed, he didn't elaborate on what he meant, but she hadn't felt a need to require a definitive answer right away. She trusted Griggory implicitly, and if he said she'd be able to see Isemay, she believed him.

In a few days, after she'd regained her strength, she'd seek clarity on his meaning. But for the moment, she was content to watch the peaceful night sky, imagining Ulfric was up there now among the stars, smiling down at her. And she smiled back, if sadly.

A gleam of moving silver against the black ceiling of night caught her eye, and behind it another. They moved like the tail of a shooting star, but seemed much closer than any celestial body. Symvalline stood up, watching the streaking lights approach. They were not dragørfly ships, nor were they dragørs themselves, but she'd known creatures who shined this way for hundreds of turns. Two bruhawks were drawing near.

Without thinking, she chanted the words through her Mentalios link to Urgo and Yggo—but she'd lost her spark. Her Mentalios was now nothing but a lovely pendant and reminder of the man who'd made them. All she could do was wait until they were close enough to call to.

The two hawks descended to land before her, having seen her easily with their preternatural eyesight. As overjoyed at seeing the two Knight companions as she was, who they had with them rendered her completely speechless.

Urgo dropped Ulfric to his feet before landing beside him on the wall. Yggo released Mylla next to Ulfric and alighted as well. Symvalline stood there, silent as the still air, tears falling freely from her eyes.

No one spoke for several breaths until Symvalline finally said to Ulfric, "Balavad claimed you were dead." The two of them collapsed into each other's arms before he could respond, both weeping openly in joyful, relieved sobs.

<hr />

MYLLA SMILED AT THEM, a bit wistfully, and stepped aside. She and Poppy's Noble Inferno had emerged from the starpath well moments before Ulfric, Urgo, and Yggo had come through the interrealm well from Dyrrakium. The reunion between her and Ulfric had been equally jubilant, but short, as they were both anxious to get to Magdaster and learn what had become of their companions as quickly as possible. Noble Inferno had left them in the care of the bruhawks, who were more than capable of making the flight in a short time, seeming to have reached her limit with humans. Mylla had felt honored, even a little touched, to even receive a final *Farewell, Knight Evernal. For one so small and fragile, you have achieved greater things than should have been expected of you.*

Thank you, Master Inferno, she'd said. *I will be forever in your debt.*

As if you could ever have anything I would want, the dragør responded and then was off in the sky with a great gust of wind.

Despite the creature's dismissive words, she still smiled. At least she'd risen from the rank of speck to Knight in the dragør's view. Because, like the others, she'd made her choice.

Now, watching Ulfric and Symvalline bask in their happiness at being reunited, she knew it was the right choice. Though she'd loved Lock, and always would, she realized when the One had spoken to her that she would not be able to return to an ordinary life. Whatever ordinary was. Not a moment of her life after her brief, tragedy-filled childhood had ever been normal. And after being impacted, even shaped in a way, by the spark of the Five sundered Verities, she wouldn't even know how to fit into a commoner's life. Her purpose, her calling was to be of service to the common peoples of the Cosmos, but not one of them. And to her surprise, she found she welcomed the duty.

Symvalline stepped back from Ulfric, still holding his hand. With her other, she reached for Mylla's and smiled at her radiantly. "We should go tell the others you're both here. I expect that if there's anything that will shock Stave or the Himmingazian into silence for once, this will be it."

Ulfric laughed. "Not even death could make Bardgrim be quiet."

CHAPTER FORTY-NINE

Jaemus unleashed a string of curses of such profligate elegance that he was in danger of producing expansive, if obscene, poetry. Some of the words he borrowed shamelessly from Stave, some from Himm, and others he invented on the spot as was his nature as an engineer. If he were as skilled at engineering as he wished, however, the result of his exhortations would have been the proper fitting of the metal shielding he was currently attaching to one of the crashed Glisternaut ships. To his further disgust, it merely led to wasted hot air and a cramp in his shoulder from trying to force the metal plate in place.

"A mouth like that is almost enough to make me blush, novice," said Stave, who'd arrived in the makeshift shipyard unnoticed.

Jaemus swiped his brow, not caring that he was likely adding more grease and grime to his already grimy face. He'd been hard at work for over three weeks in the yards and had long since given up trying to maintain a presentable appearance. "Well, I may not have achieved much mastery with your teachings on the finer points of stabbing things, pun intended, but I'd say any partnership that ends with at least one of the party greatly expanding their vocabulary isn't a wasted one." After a thoughtful moment, he added, "And I guess you don't really need to call me 'novice' anymore."

"No, I guess you're right, I don't. I'm sorry you decided not to take your oath and stay in the Knights with us, though. And I have to say, more than a little surprised." Stave spoke distractedly as he walked around the small ship, examining its undercarriage with a critical eye.

"It was an… interesting opportunity, but I had to pass it up. I think I've performed enough heroics to last lifetimes already. I don't really need to live those lifetimes to fully appreciate it."

Stave nodded. "Fair enough. You being a Knight was a little like trying to fit an ax into a sword's sheath."

"An ax?" he said, cocking a skeptical eyebrow. "Me?"

"Ah, I take your *point*, I do. More like a what you're doing there, trying to force that plate into a slot that's just not the right size for it. Take it off and give it over. I'll take it back to the forges and work it into the right shape for you."

Jaemus had spent the last hour trying to get that particular piece fitted to the hull and was loath to once more have to remove the hundred or so screws he'd already threaded. But Stave was right. No matter how loud and inventive Jaemus was with his complaints, the plate wasn't going to join correctly.

Putting his aggravation aside, he reflected on the plusses. The Magdastervians had gratefully offered to help him and the other Himmingazians repair their badly damaged fleet, and not just repair but outfit them with their own specialized steel. And while they'd first assumed they would only get the ships back to Himmingaze if a dragør graciously agreed to create a starpath for them, Jaemus had been taking the opportunity to modify them into something that wouldn't just fly from place to place in one realm. No, between the fighting, the escaping, the saving of a couple of worlds, and so on, he'd had enough exposure to the Cosmos to formulate the final steps he needed to build a ship capable of star travel, and not by the starpaths. No, he was more than done with all things Verities. And from what the Knights seemed to think, the Verities were done with them as well. Besides, starpath travel was much too easy, if you were on good terms with a dragør. He relished seeing the rest of the Cosmos through good old Himmingazian, and Jaemus Bardgrim, ingenuity.

"Drink?" Stave said, and held out a flask of something ripe and dubious smelling.

"Is that the ghastly stuff I nearly choked to death on last time you offered it?"

"The same—Brun's own mix of hops and rye with a special fermented twist of my own. But it's easier going the second time, I promise, I do."

Shrugging, as he was due for a break anyway, Jaemus took the flask and swallowed an only partially cautious gulp. It burned like the last time going down, but Stave hadn't lied. At least this time the burning subsided to a dull glow before Jaemus grew worried that he was going to be fuming it from his throat like a dragør.

"... good stuff," he choked out, and passed the container back. "Would you care to grab a wrench and help me remove this panel?"

Stave, looking suspiciously disappointed at Jaemus's quick recovery, concurred. "Don't mind if I do."

They passed the next hour amiably as Stave filled him in on some late developments. The Knights who remained so—Safran, Stave, Roibeard, Mylla, and Griggory—had returned that morning from burying Eisa atop Mount Omina, entombed within the former sanctuary of Vaka Aster, a great honor. Roibeard had chosen to bury her there rather than returning her to Dyrrakium, reasoning it was what Eisa would have wanted. Despite her flaws, her faith in and loyalty to their Verity had never wavered. When Jaemus had learned she was to be interred there, he'd wondered if Stave would object, given his and Eisa's many proverbial crossed swords. But he'd been surprised, maybe all of them had been, when Stave had merely said, "She was never evil, only human. Like the rest of us."

Jaemus hadn't known her well and had stayed behind. The Knights, even in all their great strength, still grieved like anyone else, and he felt it better to give them the space and privacy to do that. After all, her real family had been the Knights Corporealis in the end.

"Did Symvalline and Ulfric come back for the service?" he asked.

"No, but they'd already said their goodbyes before leaving, they had." Stave looked into the middle distance. It was late in the evening, and though Jaemus had been working by the light of illuminate orbs, the night's darkness swallowed anything beyond the ship's immediate vicinity. After a moment, Stave blinked and added, "If my guess is right, they won't be coming back at all. They're in Arc Rheunos with their daughter now, and I expect that's where they'll stay until the end."

He nodded, thinking it fitting. And what was more, whatever their end, he knew it would be a long time coming. A curious thing had come to light since the Verities had unified, and unified the Cosmos in the bargain. Before the Syzyckí Elementum, the Himmingazians who'd been brought to Vinnr had nearly died from some innate incompatibility between worlds, and Jaemus had learned the same ailment had nearly taken Ulfric and Symvalline's daughter in Arc Rheunos as well. Yet, the Himmingazians, and Jaemus himself, had not left Vinnr at all in the three weeks since the Elementum, and they were each as hale and hearty as when they'd arrived. Another boon, he decided before overthinking or second-guessing it, that would make their star travel to the foreign realms of Arc Rheunos and Ærd easier. Not to mention whatever unknown worlds that might be lying in between and beyond.

He had one more question for Stave. "I'm assuming you all put the option to Griggory, taking on the role of Stallari now that Ulfric has left the Order."

"Oh, we did all right." He let the statement linger, apparently enjoying watching Jaemus's anticipation.

"And?"

"And he didn't even bother to say no. The old wanderer just hopped on his dragør and flitted off like a sparrow that's heard the seed was better somewhere else. Didn't even wave goodbye."

"I suppose no one was surprised…"

"Not a one. It's probably better this way, it is. Roi was practically born for the job, and he'll be a fine leader for however long he likes."

"I'm glad to hear it. He's definitely the most level-headed of Vinnrics."

"What are you saying about me, Glunt?" His voice was combative, but the smile he wore took all the challenge out of it.

Jaemus returned the smile, and then took a big risk, one he knew he'd never have taken if he hadn't been through all that had happened since Ulfric had first fallen through the Creatress's shrine's ceiling and nearly into his lap. He gave Stave a hearty and affable slap on the back. Stave took it in the spirit it was meant and returned the gesture, nearly knocking Jaemus from his feet.

"There," the stout Knight said a moment later as he pulled the panel from the hull, "we've got it off. I'll carry it up to my workshop. Come by tomorrow morning and it should be all ready for you, it should."

"See you later then," Jaemus said, or whispered through half-filled lungs rather, as he was still recovering from the "friendly" wallop.

It was late, and Cote would be waiting for him with a late dinner. Yet, he lingered. Climbing atop the Glisternaut ship hull, he lay down and stretched out and put his hands behind his head, looking into a vast star-filled sky full of places and potential he'd never before been able to do more than imagine were out there. Since he'd been a child, Jaemus had wanted to wander the stars, see everything in the Cosmos for himself. The limits of the Glister Cloud had firmly held him back before, as had the limits of celestial beings, who in the end, one had to admit, were somewhat less ineffable and faultless than one would expect. Now that all the Verities' petty disagreements had been settled, and Jaemus was free from the troublesome expectations of Knighthood that he'd never wanted, the only limits in the wide and mysterious Cosmos were those he created for himself. And as self-indulgent and confident, some might say *cocky*, as Himmingaze's greatest glint engineer was, Jaemus certainly wasn't about to do that.

AFTERWORD

To my treasured reader, I'm deeply grateful for your readership your presence in my wordy world. If my book has touched your heart with magic or transported you to another realm, would you consider sharing your thoughts through a review on your favorite retailer? Your voice carries immense value and can guide fellow readers to a tale that resonates with them too. Together, we can build a community of kindred spirits, connected through the power of storytelling. Thank you for your kindness and support.

Don't forget to join my newsletter at www.tammysalyer.com/news letter to stay up to date on new releases and receive a free collection of stories. Cheers!

THE FIVE REALMS

REALM OF ÆRD; THE ÆRDENS

Verity
Fimm

Characters
Ayanna (Mylla's mother)
Greven (Mylla's father)

Locations
Kaldrwoot

REALM OF ARC RHEUNOS; THE ARC RHEUNOSIANS

Verity
Mithlí the Everlight

Characters
Agatha Pahzi (Minothian)
Akeeva Raamuzi (Archon, false Verity)
Alvar (Deespora's heartmatch)
Arudara (Salukis's mother)
Ballio (little Zhallah boy child)
Browan (Salukis's father)
Bunefer (Zhallah)
Cylli (Zhallah girl; Kalisk's grandchild)
Deespora Raamuzi (Archon, leader of Zhallahs)
Drevor (Salukis's uncle)
Duripi (mother of Cylli and Onni)
Dwoon (Mura's younger brother)
Eleni (thirteen-year-old girl)
Erli Detzu (paramour of Mura's)
Gostav (Minothian guard)
Hertha, Mistress (Minothian attendant and child watcher)
Inder (Viddzu's son, Minothian)
Kalisk (female elder Zhallah rebel and council member)
Lysis (Mura's mother)
Mura (friend of Isemay's)
Neeka (little Zhallah girl child)
Onni (Zhallah boy; Kalisk's grandchild)
Phaemee (Salukis's aunt)
Pitaja, Master (tutor for children in Everlight Hall)
Poolan (Zhallah elder)
Rusa (thirteen-year-old Zhalla girl)
Salukis Engzu (Zhallah)
Toranzu, Kaneas (Minothian guard transformed into a Deathless)
Tulla (Agatha's daughter)
Viddzu, Kaneas (Minoth guard transformed into a Deathless)
Widin (elderly barrow tender)

Locations
Aktoktos Gate

Churss forest
Cordu Valley
Maerria
Minoth Valley Gate
North Tyrns
Pass of Thossos
Skaphia Caves
South Tyrns
Thallorn River
Tyrn Mountains
Valley of Minothia
West Tyrns

REALM OF BATTGJALD; THE BATTGJALDICS

Verity
Balavad; Holiness Prime

Characters
Corvus Rhafn (Flesh Caster)

REALM OF HIMMINGAZE; THE HIMMINGAZIANS

Verity
Lífs the Creatress

Characters
Cote Illago (commander of the Glisternauts)
Drustim, Flight Leader (captain of the *Deep Sea Gem*)
Fex, Ensign

Heleina Gibbaden (Glisternaut navigator)
Jaemus Bardgrim (Glint Engineer, Glisternaut)
Joburg, Flight Leader
Jovus (father of Jaemus)
Mye, Flight Leader
Sandar, Spark Engineer
Bannus, Ensign
Saxton, Ensign
Trabazan, Ensign
Vreyja Bardgrim (grandsirene of Jaemus)
Yanna, Spark Engineer

Locations
Bludghadda
Dry Quarter
Isle Stonering
Never Sea
Vann

REALM OF VINNR; THE VINNRICS

Verity
Vaka Aster the Vigil Star

Characters
Allanach (Yorish Knight before the Cataclysm)
Beatte, Arch Keeper of the Kingdom of Ivoryss
Brun, Tannir (commander of Dragør Marines)
Cympher, Chamberlain
Connaugh, Arch Keeper of Yor previously
Eisa Nazaria (Knight, Nazarian Most High, Heir of the Sixth Line)
Egsíl, Third Phase Venerate

Elinora Rekkr (Havelock's mother)

Fergus, Arch Keeper of Yor currently

Furthsom (Ivoryssian Marine)

Gara Aoggvír, Third Phase Venerate (Seldeg's niece)

Gusun Sveinungr, Fifth Phase Venerate

Griggory Dondrin (Knight, Yorish)

Gudmund Øster (Dastrart Age smith of Winter's Bite and Star Spark)

Gwinifeve Dye (Yorish Knight from Griggory's time)

Havelock Rekkr (commoner of Ivoryss, Dragør Wing Marine)

Havelock's five sisters, Lizet, Edytha, Emoni, Gelle, Hilla

Heart of Purple Might (dragør, sire is Magnificence of Oceans Tempests)

Henrick Rekkr (Havelock's father)

Irrick (acolyte of the Resplendolent Conservatum, hazel eyes)

Isemay Aldinhuus-Lutair (daughter of Symvalline and Ulfric)

Jarmand, Keeper's Guard Leader

Jimp Owers (Dragør Wing Marine)

Kòrmak, Venerate

Lillias Grannd

Magnificence of Oceans Tempests (dragør)

Mallich "Roi" Roibeard (Knight)

Mylla Evernal (Knight)

Nennus (commander of Magdastervian forces)

Ozlaus, First Phase Venerate

Peke of Magdaster, Knight

Poppy's Noble Inferno (dragør)

Safran Glór (Knight)

Seldeg Aoggvír, Chancellor of the Dyrrak Phalanx (Heir of the Third Line)

Serl (Stave's grandfather)

Sœrnec, Ambassador (Lœdyrrak before the Cataclysm)

Starkas Nazaria (Domine Ecclesium of Dyrrakium)

Stave Thorvíl (Knight, originally from Magdaster in the Kingdom of Ivoryss)

Sveinkí Edizriis, Fourth Phase Venerate

Sveinungr, Fifth Phase Venerate
Symvalline "Sym" Lutair (Knight)
Tannir Brun (Commander of Dragør Marines of Asteryss)
Ulfric Aldinhuus, Stallari (Knight)
Urgo (bruhawk)
Yggo (bruhawk)

Locations
Ivoryss; the Ivoryssians (kingdom)
Aster Keep (Asteryss)
Asteryss City; Asteryss for short (capital city of Ivoryss)
Dryft and Tarmvred (highest peaks to the north of Morn Mountains)
Gethbrond (coastal city)
Great Province Byway (runs between Yor and Ivoryss, south of the
Howling Weald)
Howling Weald
Kolga (Ivoryssian city surrounded by lakes with salt-rich lagoons)
Magdaster (northernmost city)
Morn Mountain Range
Mount Omina (Morn Mountains)
North Byway (only road through the Weald from Magdaster, links to
Great Province Byway down south)
Udunum Island
Verring Sea
Vigil Tower (Asteryss)
Wilt Mountain (Morns, where the bruhawk aeries were hidden)

Yor; the Yorish (kingdom)
Almull Sea
Great Lochanian Forest (meets Howling Weald somewhere on the
other side of the Morn Mountains)
Lake Cuffdeach
Umborough (Yor capital)

Dyrrakium, the Dyrraks (empire/kingdom; formerly Lœdyrrak)

Anzuru Desert
Citadel Suprima (Elezaran)
Elezaran (capital of Dyrrakium)
Penitence Rock (dais at the Citadel Suprima)

DYRRAKIUM CULTURE
Five Phases of Citizenship: body purification, mind purification, releasing attachments, overcoming weakness, devotion (faith and loyalty)

Six Aspects of Devotion: faith, strength, wisdom, duty, loyalty, dominion

GLOSSARY

anni-cycle (similar to a year in Himmingaze)

archaneology (lore within a Scrylle)

Archon (Arc Rheunos equivalent of Knight Corporealis)

Aster Games (annual sporting competition in Ivoryss)

barrow tender (gravesperson)

Battle of the Byways (Yor and Magdaster skirmish around 650 turns ago)

bizzle (Arc Rheunosian hive insect)

Bounding Skate (Glisternaut ship)

bruhawk (Vinnric, extremely large hawk related to dragørs)

Cæcra ad resrs, boromcad bea dord. Kucik kea kesrs, emsu kæ lækra (Cycle of light, balanced by dark, focus my sight, into my heart)

Cataclysm, the (event that left Dyrrakium exiled from other Vinnric kingdoms; when Lœdyrrak became Dyrrakium)

cave snouz (Arc Rheunosian mammal)

chelbiefin shark (Vinnric creature)

chookter (slang for commoner in Vinnr)

chuffee (drink of Himmingaze)

Churss Circle; Circle, the (gathering site for council in Maerria)

Conquestum Ecclesium (fight ceremony in Dyrrakium to choose next Domine Ecclesium)

constrained (Himmingazian word for "arrested")

cosmoscruiser (such as the *Bounding Skate*)

Council's Crest (Glisternaut ship)

cycle; Glister cycle (Himmingazian measure of time, close to a day in length)

dalla flower (Vinnric lavender-colored flower)

daystar (sun, Halla in Vinnr)

dead rolls (the dead of Arc Rhuenos)

deca-cycle (similar to a decade in Himmingaze)

Deep Sea Gem (Glisternaut ship)

Distalfulcrum (moon alignment in Arc Rheunos)

Domine Ecclesium (a title for leader of Dyrrakium)

dragør (Vinnric creature)

Elder Veros, aka Vertasian in Himmingaze, aka Varitika in Arc Rheunos, aka First Tongue in Ærd (language of the Verities as it's known in Vinnr)

Equifulcrum (moon alignment in Arc Rheunos)

Everlight Hall (Minothian stronghold in Arc Rheunos)

Feast of Five Seasons celebration (Ivoryss)

Feast of Future's Hope for the Equifulcrum (Arc Rheunos)

Fenestros; Fenestrii (*pl.*) (celestial stones)

First Tongue (Ærden term for Elder Veros)

fleech (Himmingazian flying water creature)

Flesh Caster (Balavad's warrior-priests, equivalent of Knights Corporealis)

flint glass (Vinnric type of glass made from a chemical reaction and can be sparked like flint)

flittercat (Vinnric mammal)

gimgree swamp sloth (Vinnric mammal)

Glister Bright and Glister Dim (light and dark parts of the Glister cycle)

Glister Cloud (celestial threat to Himmingaze)

Glistering Horizon (Glisternaut ship)

govel (Arc Rheunosian plant with red berries)

gramsire (Himmingazian grandfather)

gramsirene (Himmingazian grandmother)

grandling (Himmingazian grandchild)

Gusting Hall (main hall in Magdaster)

half-ager (teen in Vinnr)

Halla (the sun in Vinnr)

Hallumbrum (midnight in Vinnr)

heartmatch (Vinnric term for intimate partner)

High Halls (noon in Vinnr)

honeybread (Vinnric food)

icewine (Vinnric beverage)

interrealm well (portals to travel between locations in Vinnr)

Kahros the Seeker; Seeker, the (blue moon, smallest in Arc Rheunos)

klinkí stone (wystic stones used by Knights Corporealis)

kórb fruit (Vinnric fruit)

lifemate (Himmingazian term for intimate partner)

lind tree (Vinnric tree with copper berries)

Maiztos the Life Giver; Giver, the (red moon, middle-sized, Arc Rheunos)

memory keeper (dragør-shaped pendant made by Ulfric)

Mentalios lens (pendants used by Knights Corporealis to communicate by thought)

mindhold (mental control)

moved into the shadows (Arc Rheunosian colloquialism for dying)

muddlemind (Himmingazian term for crazy, lunatic)

Mystae (Himmingaze's equivalent of Knight Corporealis)

nightcap (Arc Rheunosian mushroom that's slightly sweet)

Octopod (Jaemus's ship)

oilfire (Vinnric term)

oldwood forests (Vinnric term)

Order of the Knight/s Corporealis; Knights, the; Order, the

phanx (insect of Vinnr)

plague-bringer (Arc Rheunosian term)

Primator (Balavad's ship)

puurite stone (Vinnric term)

Raveners of the Tooth; Raveners (Balavad's soldiers)

realm-jumper (universal term for anyone who travels between realms)

Reaper's Breath (Himmingazian plant used in funerals)

Resplendolent Conservatum; Conservatum, the (academy in Vinnr)

Resplendolent Prelates (the highest order of Conservatum scholars)

Scrylle (star-metal scepter imbued with celestial power)

shelksies (Himmingazian wrist-borne weapons)

shullet (Himmingazian ammo for a shelksie)

sight-link (how Safran sees through bruhawk's eyes)

silvflan (Vinnric mammal)

slag, slag it (Vinnric curse)

slaghammer (Vinnric curse)

slangarook (Himmingazian large dragørlike sea creature)

Song of Figments and Fables (Vinnric song)

songbox (Vinnric music box)

starpath well (portals between realms)

syke liquor (Dyrrak fermented drink)

Syzyckí Elementum (unification of the realms and their Verities)

tessalock (Ærdan device that shows the time in all realms)

tessalope; time walker (Ærden wystic creature)

thirty-night (Vinnric month)

timepath (universal term for how time connects the realms)

trogghopping (Vinnric oath of exasperation)

urzidae (Arc Rheunosian horse-size bear-like beast)

Varitika (Arc Rheunosian term for Elder Veros)

veeshock (Himmingazian animal/food)

Vigil Tower (stronghold of Knights Corporealis in Vinnr)

Vigilance (Knights' ship)

War of Rivening (the war that broke Vinnr's old kingdom into three)

Warden Temporalis (Ærden equivalent of Knight Corporealis)

Wing (Dragør Wing Marine)

wystic, wysticism (magic)

yorvic (Dyrrak large lizardlike creature)
Znopho the White Watcher; Watcher, the (white moon, largest in Arc Rheunos)

ABOUT THE AUTHOR

Tammy is an inveterate verbarian, who spends her days surrounded by the written word, both hers and others'. As an ex-paratrooper with the 82nd Airborne Division, her stories are often as gritty as a grunt's pile of three-week-old field gear. Her military science fiction Spectras Arise series debuted to acclaim in 2012, and her epic fantasy adventure series The Shackled Verities was launched in 2020. She's currently five books deep in a Weird West series called Otherworld Outlaws, featuring half-fae sawbones, a necromancer gnome, and a hoodoo cowgirl galavanting into mischief in the Old West.

When not hunched like a Morlock over her writing desk, Tammy runs and bikes silly miles with her super-cool weirdo partner in the Pacific Northwest playground and spends an inappropriate amount of time watching Henry Rollins videos on YouTube. Contrary to whatever ideas her last name might conjure, she's never really been much of a Slayer fan.

Fantasy, space opera, satire, and snark fans will feel right at home with Tammy. Learn more about her and her books by visiting www.tammysalyer.com. She hopes you enjoy reading her works and welcomes your reviews.